CHILDREN OF POWER

CHILDREN

Susan Richards Shreve

OF POWER

MACMILLAN PUBLISHING CO., INC.

NEW YORK

Macmillan Publishing Co., Inc.
866 Third Avenue, New York, N.Y. 10022
Collier Macmillan Canada, Ltd.

Library of Congress Cataloging in Publication Data
Shreve, Susan Richards.
　Children of power.
　I. Title.
PZ4.S5602Ch　[PS3569.H74]　　813'.5'4　　78-26828
ISBN 0-02-610510-1

First Printing 1979

Printed in the United States of America

For our children
Porter, Elizabeth, Caleb and Kate
and
Jeffrey Richards, my brother, who shared my childhood

I am grateful to the Jenny McKean Moore Fund for Writers and George Washington University, which gave me the time to write this book in 1977 and 1978. To George Mason University for release time from teaching. And to Yaddo for hours of freedom to finish.

FRIDAY, DECEMBER 17
1954

Sam Taylor bought the house on Highland Place in 1947 when he first moved to Washington from Wisconsin. It was a Victorian clapboard farmhouse, painted white, with turrets and stained glass windows, built by Senator Percy from Rhode Island the same year that ground was broken for the cathedral, half a mile up the road. Senator Percy had died there although he had intended to return to Rhode Island in his retirement, and the house went to a Supreme Court justice who was robbed and beaten one September afternoon on his own front steps. An actress whose name did not survive except on the deed lived there with her companion in the thirties and sold the house to one of Roosevelt's people, a Jew, who was the first Jew to buy a house on Highland Place. He was an intellectual man with an accent, the neighbors said. His family was German. Shortly after the end of the war, he died unexpectedly, and his widow sold the house to Sam Taylor.

On one of the rough cement walls in the basement of the house, there was a child's painting of a former occupant, a florid-faced man with black hair and the enormous furry body of a brown four-legged creature, perhaps a buffalo: "My Father as a Greek God by his son Ollie," he had written in black paint.

When the Taylors bought the house, they repainted and changed the wallpaper throughout, but no one got around to painting over the picture in the basement. In fact, Natty Taylor had, in fourth grade, painted another picture on the opposite wall of herself in a white robe with hair to her ankles: "Brunnhilde Taylor. Queen," she had written.

Natty Taylor left the house on Highland Place before dinner. She didn't even practice the cello for her first solo recital on Christmas Eve at the cathedral. Joe McCarthy was coming to spend the evening again.

"For dinner?" Natty had asked.

"Yes," Sam said.

"You'd have a common criminal spend the night in the guest room," Ellen Taylor muttered.

"I might, Ellen," Sam said, "if no one else was sleeping there."

So Natty left. She wasn't angry at her father as Ellen was, who'd closed the bedroom door and climbed defeated into bed. But she wasn't going to eat dinner with Joe McCarthy either.

"I'm meeting Filip DeAngelis," she told her father. "There's a party at Dick Carr's in Georgetown."

"Filip will bring you home?"

"If his mother will let him," Natty said. "Did you see the story she wrote about you and Joe McCarthy in the *News* today?"

"I don't read stories like that if I can help it," he said. He had been a newspaperman long enough to be selective even about himself. "I don't read the obituaries, either."

"Rosa said some terrible things about how you and Joe McCarthy had known each other as children."

"We did."

"She said you were good friends."

Natty put on her coat.

"We're not good friends," Sam Taylor said. "But Rosa's right. We knew each other as children."

He opened the door for her.

"I'm sorry, Natty," he said. "It's not always pleasant to grow up in this city."

"It's all right." She pulled up her hood against the snow.

The night was snow-damp, thick with soft crystals which melted on her cheeks and circled the street lights with hazy moons. Natty headed straight down Highland Place, walking in the street because the antique mossy bricks of Cleveland Park were slippery even in dry weather. She could feel her father behind her standing on the edge of their open porch without a coat, watching her move in and out of the shadows from the street lights.

"Do you have boots?" he urged her back.

"Yup," she called brightly without turning.

"Take a streetcar to Georgetown," he added.

"I will."

"And walk on the main streets."

At Reno Road she heard him call, "Natty," and then again, but she didn't turn around. There was plenty of traffic on Reno, and she could easily pretend not to have heard him at all.

Natty had not known her father at all until the summer after fifth grade. Washington had been particularly hot that summer, and Ellen Taylor had gone back to Wisconsin in June, leaving Natty with her father until Congress recessed.

"You can be his escort," Ellen told her absently, "and pretend you're grown up."

Every day she had looked at herself in the mirror on the bathroom door. Her breasts were small and perfectly formed as ant hills. They seemed impermanent. Sometimes she wished they would go away. Her hips had not yet begun to spread.

"You're going to be pretty," her father said one evening at dinner. She looked like a gypsy, with eyes so black you couldn't

5

see the pupils. It did not seem possible that she would be pretty, but it pleased her that he thought so.

She got up early while her mother was away and made his breakfast, changing the menu every day to please him; she saw him off to work at the front door.

Once that summer Edward R. Murrow came to town for a visit with old friends, and Sam Taylor gave a party for him. Her father bought Natty a new dress with tucks in the bodice and a purple skirt which didn't fit, although he had not noticed.

She stood in the living room next to Ed Murrow, pretending she was forty like her mother and lovely as the Renaissance madonna above the mantel. Occasionally the war correspondent gripped her shoulders, as though he had something important to tell her. He was a tall man with a long wise face that seemed just short of pain, although he was not dying then. She pretended she was his wife.

Late in the evening when most of the guests had gone, Ed Murrow sat down in a wing chair by the fireplace and put up his feet.

"Your father is one of the only honest men I know," Ed Murrow said. "The odd thing is I don't know him," he went on. "No one does."

"I guess," Natty said, not knowing what else to say, not knowing her father either except as a father. She knew he had a reputation for excellence—and that at home he was sometimes witty, sometimes darkly sullen—and that the mood he had at certain moments was unrelated to events. For all the seeming order of his daily life, the constant measuring and lining up of things, he was a tempestuous man who could throw his family off balance with a glance. And he collected drunks, ones he knew from newspaper work or ones he didn't know at all. He brought them home to stay for the night, sometimes for days and weeks.

"He has a secret," Ed Murrow said. "Sometime he may tell you because you are his daughter."

Later that evening after Ed Murrow had left, Natty and her father sat together at the kitchen table and talked about the evening's guests.

"I would have liked Ed Murrow's job in London," Sam Taylor said, suddenly melancholy. "I turned it down."

"How come?" Natty asked, arranging herself at the table to appear grown up.

"I simply did." He poured a drink, careful to measure an ounce. "The job I should have turned down is the one I have."

Since 1947 Sam Taylor had been chairman of the Federal Communications Commission. He had come from a newspaper in Wisconsin, where he was editor, to take the job, recommended to Truman by Senator Joe McCarthy amongst others.

After midnight he came into her room, turned on the light.

"Your mother is a lovely woman, Nat," he said, "but there're things she doesn't understand."

"I guess." Natty shifted, unaccustomed to this closeness.

"Sometimes there's a chemistry between people in which they understand each other without words," he said. "I believe I have that with you."

She wanted to tell him she didn't understand either—didn't even want to have to understand things about her father when she had her daily life and troubles at school and with her friends. It was the first time she knew absolutely that she had a responsibility to him.

That night she couldn't sleep.

Natty heard the familiar rattle of Will Barnes' pickup truck behind her on Newark Street. He stopped and called out.

"Are you going to Dick Carr's?"

"I was just going up toward Wisconsin Avenue," he said when she had climbed inside. It wasn't true. Since he'd let his sister, Eliza, off at Dick Carr's he had been cruising these blocks hoping for a glimpse of Natty.

The truck smelled of the barn where Will spent most of his

time. It smelled of manure from the bottom of his cowboy boots. Natty rolled the window down and it snowed in her lap.

Will Barnes had entered Sidwell Friends in fourth grade with Natty, who had just moved to Washington from Wisconsin. It was his first time off the farm except for state occasions honoring his father or some other holdover from the Roosevelt years. He hadn't gone to school at all.

Nell Barnes had looked at schools around the farm and in town and found that none was satisfactory for her children. So Will and his twin sister, Eliza, were taught at home by Nell, who also invited the cook's illegitimate daughter and the son of a local vegetable merchant who couldn't attend ordinary school because he'd been injured in a hunting accident. Will was not pleased to enter Sidwell Friends when Nell finally decided that a real school was necessary. But the fourth grade was delighted to have this strange and silent farm boy with his long hair and cowboy shirts and warm Southern speech full of expletives learned from the cook's illegitimate daughter.

On the third day at school the fourth-grade boys took Will Barnes behind the old shed at Friends where they smoked cigarettes and shared dirty pictures. They tied him up. There was a large metal trash can behind the shed, which they filled with Will Barnes, capping the top, tying it around with rope and pulling it up a tree with a homemade pulley.

Natty watched the end of this exercise from the playground, where she was hanging by one knee on the high bars, and saw a trash can rising from the ground. She turned right side up, jumped off the high bars and went off down the hill. Just as she got to the bottom, J. Paul, terror of the middle school, beat it around the side of the shed.

When she got to the shed no one was there. Only the trash can lying on its side with the lid still on. She took off the lid and peered inside.

Will Barnes crouched at the bottom.

His lip was bloody and he was crying.

"I'm gonna tell on them," Natty said.

"Don't."

"I saw them pull you up the tree," she said. "They can't get away with that."

"Fuckers," Will said. Natty had never heard anyone say that word before. "If you tell on them, they'll do it to me worse next time."

That afternoon after Nell Barnes had picked Will up early for an appointment, Miss Fletcher told the fourth grade they must be nice to Will Barnes. He was different; he had never been to school and didn't know any better. Everyone nodded seriously and agreed that they would help Will Barnes as best they could.

"Fuckers," Natty whispered to J. Paul in the locker room after school.

"I'll tell," he said.

"Tell," she challenged.

She knew he wouldn't dare.

"Is Fil DeAngelis coming to Carr's party?" Will asked.

"I'm meeting him there," Natty replied. "He has basketball practice."

"During Christmas vacation?"

"There's some kind of practice all the time."

It was not common for Fil DeAngelis to be invited to a party at Dick Carr's. They went to different schools and opposed each other on athletic teams, although Dick Carr was no competition for the dark Italian boy, who had, it was predicted, a national future in football or baseball—whichever he preferred. They were not good friends.

The light at Wisconsin Avenue was red, and Will glanced quickly at Natty, at the straight nose and full lips shadowed in the street light. Sometimes he put himself to sleep at night dreaming of making love to her in the hay he'd stacked behind the barn, leaving a stack unsheathed just for the ghost of her. Will Barnes did not connect except in dreams. In dreams he died for things, and probably would one day in fact. Natty knew that

9

people were afraid of Will. He had no sense of limitations and would do anything.

But in Will's dream of making love to Natty, just before he fell asleep, his own naked body, long and narrow at the hips, would turn into the thick dark body of Filip DeAngelis. He didn't mind Fil DeAngelis. In fact, he liked him. There was something simple and noble about the other boy which Will Barnes understood because he'd grown up in open spaces without another person in sight for miles except his own family. There was something unbelievable, too—as though Filip DeAngelis had fallen out of a Roman legend where gods fulfilled in innocent ways man's simple concept of them.

"Did you see the *News* tonight?" Natty asked.

"You mean the piece about your father?"

"And McCarthy."

"Bullshit."

"Yeah." She leaned back against the seat of Will's truck and shut her eyes. "He's coming for dinner again."

"McCarthy?"

She nodded.

"No big deal."

"I guess." She rolled up her window. The damp snow had filled her lap. "Except that Filip's mother writes about it all the time."

When Will Barnes' father had been Secretary of Commerce under Roosevelt, he had fallen in love with one of his young assistants, a boyish girl, strong-minded as he, and fathered Will and Eliza—already then he was over sixty and married to a woman who'd been crazy, put away in California years before. But he divorced that woman and married Nell and lived until the year of Will and Eliza's twelfth birthday. Before he died he'd had for years a national reputation for fierce determination and honesty and a sharp tongue. So Will Barnes understood growing up with your father in the paper every night.

"Don't read the *News*," he said. He pulled over on R Street in Georgetown just two blocks from Dick Carr's house.

"Do you know about this party?" he asked.

"Not much," Natty said. "Dick told me yesterday that his parents were in Oklahoma. He always has a party when his parents are away."

"An open party?"

"Sometimes."

"Well, this one's closed. Did he tell you that?"

"He said he was inviting people. Not just everyone," she said. "He did invite Fil."

"Something's going on there tonight," Will said. "I had this funny feeling when I dropped Eliza off a while ago."

Dick Carr did not always include Natty in his parties, which were frequent and well known. She was pleased to be asked. He was not well liked at Sidwell Friends, with a reputation as a bully, but he had a kind of power. He was an enormously tall boy, nearly six-eight and otherwise undistinguished. He had grown up on an Oklahoma ranch—the third son of a father who had been an oilman and was now a Senator.

"Mean," Sam Taylor had once said of Paul Carr. "He's the meanest man in Washington." And people were wary of Dick Carr, whose genetic traces of bad seed were likely germinating beneath the pale surface of adolescence. His favor was important.

Natty had known him from the beginning of her years at Friends School.

"Gimp," he'd shouted at her on the playground when she first arrived in November 1947 from Wisconsin, after the accident which had damaged her leg. Once he had tripped her when she was in the middle during a dodge-ball game.

Later in the fourth-grade year Natty had kicked him in the shins when he cheated at jacks. No one hit Dick Carr; he was too big to hit. Thereafter he treated her with new respect. If he called her "gimp," which he was fond of doing, he called her that behind her back.

For Natty's part, as she grew up, she wanted the favor of Dick Carr's group, which became the central group in high school, the clearest expression at Friends School of the spirit of the times.

11

They were fun-loving and irreverent. They took risks and counted the cost worth the gain in popularity.

They respected Natty because she was different and could not assume a common demeanor, but they often excluded her in ways that made her susceptible to the odd magic of their place in the minds of people around them.

"It's not that I want to be in the middle," she said to Fil about Dick Carr's group. "I just want to be untouchable."

Filip didn't understand.

"Or else famous like you," she said. "Which is the same thing."

As it was, Natty balanced peripherally—sufficiently herself to be apart, yet desiring their recognition to affirm that sense of self still liquid at seventeen.

Alexander Epps was walking along R Street, and when he saw Will's truck opposite, he balanced the top of a tin garbage can on his head. Will and Natty watched the top fall three times before they pulled over and offered him a ride. Alexander was often drunk.

"Going to Carr's?" Will Barnes called out.

"I believe so," Alexander answered in soft Tennessee, "and traveling alone."

He climbed in beside Natty and put the top of the garbage can across their legs.

Alexander Epps was the son of a novelist who was the most outrageous man that Natty knew.

The first time Natty had met John Epps was at a party in Georgetown last summer. He had taken a handful of her breast right there in a room full of people.

"Foam rubber," he'd guffawed. "Alexander," he drawled, "come take a look."

So Natty and her friends forgave Alexander certain absurdities like wearing three-piece French suits and waving his hair and kissing ninth-grade girls with his tongue flopping across their gums. For such a father one would have to be a saint.

Alexander kissed Natty now.

"This is a special privilege," he said, helping her out of the car.

Natty shrugged. One couldn't count on Alexander to make any sense at all.

"Hey," the front door of Carr's flew open. "Natalia." Dick Carr swooped her into the front hall of his house as if he'd been waiting just beyond the door for her to come.

Inside the light snow on her hair melted instantly; her face was wet.

"S'Natty," Dick Carr shouted, pressing his face against her hair. "S'Natty," he called again, louder over the dance music, and this time the foot shuffle stopped abruptly. Someone turned the record player down.

"Natty?" a voice downstairs.

"Yeah," Dick Carr shouted back. "And Epps and Will Barnes."

Al Cox slid down the banister in a paper birthday hat.

"Natty . . . beautiful Natty," he sang and swung her around in the hallway. "Come on," Al said, taking her arm. "There's booze." He handed her a cup. "Fish house punch."

"What's that?" she asked.

"Lethal," Al said and laughed. He pressed the punch cup to her lips and made her taste it. It was sweet on her tongue and burned her throat.

In the recreation room Alexander Epps was standing on the piano in his stocking feet twirling the lid of the garbage can. No one noticed. Will Barnes had not come downstairs.

"Do you know where Filip is?" Natty asked Al Cox.

"Not here yet."

"He said he'd be here at seven-thirty."

"Well, love, he broke his promise."

The recreation room was dark. Couples wound around each other like pretzels on the dance floor. Natty could barely make out a couple on the couch.

Someone turned the music up.

"Dance?" Al Cox took her in his arms. "Natty . . . beautiful Natty, you're the only only girl that I adore."

He tightened his grip around her and slipped his hand down the back of her skirt while they were dancing. It moved swiftly against her bare flesh. She grabbed his hand.

"Jeez, Al," she said and he laughed out loud.

"I hear McCarthy's got a home away from home at your house," Al said.

Natty shrugged.

"I read in tonight's paper that there's pressure on your father to resign the FCC," Al said. "Implication by association, or some such crap."

"He won't," Natty said.

"That's good," Al said. "He shouldn't." He broke from Natty. "It's hot down here. Want a Coke?"

The Coke was spiked. Already light-headed, Natty set it down behind the lamp on a side table.

Paulette Estinet came up and spoke to Al in French. "Excuse me," she said. "Al and I can only speak to each other in French."

Al put his birthday hat on Paulette's head and pressed her onto the dance floor, leading with his hips.

Paulette had been at Sidwell Friends School only two years— her father had been premier of the third French Republic and the new government sent him to Washington, which the Estinets found dreadful beyond conversation—all except Paulette, who knew immediately what to do and was elected cheerleader in her second month at Friends, singing cheers in an accent thin and fine as French pastry. Even the long blond perfect Wilson High School cheerleaders were practicing cheers with French accents.

Natty sensed that the people by the piano were talking about her. She was certain of it, although the piano was across the room and she couldn't hear them. She couldn't even make out who it was, except Anne Lowry, who kept tossing her head in Natty's direction.

"So where's DeAngelis?" Dick Carr asked, pulling Natty down with him on the chair.

"I don't know," she shrugged, at once pleased and cautious to be sitting on Dick Carr's lap. "Basketball, I guess."

"What do you see in him, anyway?" Dick asked. "His nose is too big."

She laughed. "I like big noses."

"Reflected glory," he said. "That's what you see."

"What do you mean?" she asked, sensing in Dick Carr a gentle shift to a less pleasant temper.

"He's a hero. A famous jock." He turned her toward him on his knee. "And you're his sweetie."

"I don't think that's what I see in him," she said.

She had considered her motives. Certainly she felt a sense of protection with Fil DeAngelis. He was well known and people thought better of Natty for their association. It fulfilled childhood fairy stories with happy endings. When Natty was small, she was given a collection of opera librettos adapted for children and she spent hours rewriting the tragic finales. Sometimes with Filip, she believed she could arrange a happy ending with the same ease of reordering the visions of Puccini or of Verdi.

"He's sweet," she said.

"Sweet," Dick Carr laughed. "No jock is sweet, Nat. It goes against the grain."

"As a person he's sweet," she said. "Honestly."

Occasionally a sports reporter said that of Fil DeAngelis. Not that he was sweet, but noncombative. A natural athlete without the fierceness necessary to winning at all costs. One reporter said he was too gentle to be professional.

"Let's call the boy to see why he isn't here," Dick said. He grabbed Natty around the waist and playfully kissed her neck. "I can be sweet, too," he said.

"Sure," Natty said and followed him up the stairs to the library, where the phone was. He followed her into the library and shut the door.

Mrs. DeAngelis said that Filip wasn't there just now, that he'd come home from basketball practice and then had gone to a friend's house, but no, she was quite certain that he'd not gone to Georgetown to meet Natty or he would have told her.

"He's not coming?" Dick asked.

"I guess not," she said.

"If he doesn't come, I'll take you home in a while, Nat," he rumbled after her, and she knew suddenly that he'd had too much to drink. Just as she started to open the library door, he kissed her, flipped his tongue into her mouth before she could shake her head away.

Filip DeAngelis crept up the back stairs of the narrow row house on 39th Street. But Rosa heard him anyway.

"Filip," she called. "Is that you?" He didn't answer, but he knew she'd be up instantly.

On the bed in the front room his younger brother, Johnny, rolled back and forth, muttering quietly, his knees pulled up under his chin.

"Hi, Johnny," Filip called automatically, and Johnny didn't answer. Never did. A section of his brain had been destroyed at birth by a wartime doctor careless in his use of forceps.

"The fates," Rosa DeAngelis thought with vengeance, and still she went to Mass every day.

"What are you doing home so late?" Rosa asked, coming into Filip's room without knocking.

"I was at basketball practice."

"Until seven-thirty?" She sat down on the bed, opened the school binder he'd thrown there and leafed through the papers.

"Mother," Filip complained.

"You weren't with Natty Taylor, were you?"

"I would have told you."

"No, you wouldn't have," she said. "You and Angela tell the truth when it suits you. I called Angela at Radcliffe tonight and she's not there. At the library with a friend, her roommate says. Always with a friend. You know who it is?"

"A boy."

"That's right. And she's spending the night with him."

"Not Angela."

"Not Angela, ha!" Rosa laughed bitterly. "Of course Angela. And tomorrow she'll call me. Mama, she'll say. I hear you called last night while I was at the library. Some library, I'll say. I'm telling you the truth, she'll say. Then don't believe me, she'll say and hang up. A dollar fifty for that stupid conversation."

Rosa's own mother had expected the absolute worst of Rosa when she was growing up. In defense against her daughter's promised disgrace, she told Rosa black stories of men's intentions and disloyalties and abuse, picturing a wanton and single Rosa without even virtue to sustain her.

"I don't," she'd say to her mother. "Honestly, Mama, I wouldn't," Rosa maintained, and it was true.

"Agh," her mother said, disbelieving. "Tell the priest in confession. Just tell him."

And now Rosa could hear her mother's dark voice, songlike and accusing, in her own.

She opened the notebook to the history section. "Tell me, Filip, were you with Natty Taylor or not?"

"Not," Filip replied. "I want to change, Mother."

"What's this seventy-five in a history test?"

"What do you think it is?"

"How do you plan to go to college next year with seventy-fives on history tests?"

"Listen, Mom. I'm going into the bathroom, if you don't mind, so I can change my clothes, and we'll talk about it later." He took his clothes into the bathroom and locked the door.

Rosa DeAngelis looked in the mirror over his dresser. She was forty this year and still beautiful, though her eyes had frayed thick and heavy with gray pouches under the eyes, as southern Italian eyes become growing older, but worse now since Antonio had died. She still dressed to be beautiful even when she stayed home all day with Johnny. She knew Antonio would expect her to maintain herself. Sometimes she'd pretend that he was coming home that night and dress to greet him just to have someone to dress up for. But she knew she was pretending. She was a sharp, realistic woman who knew it made good sense to take care of herself. That was all.

"You'll marry again," Filip had told her.

"Not me," she'd said. "I loved your father," she said, "but you know he had a mistress in Tuscany he saw every summer he went to visit his parents. I know. I found a letter once and he thought I had forgotten how to read Italian." She'd clapped her hands above her head like dancing. "My mother believed men are no good. Even you, Filip. Someday you'll be no good, though you are sweet now." But later that day Rosa had made a point of coming in his room when he was talking on the phone to Natty.

"Remember what I said to you about men today, Filippo?" she said.

"Yeah," he nodded, holding his hand over the receiver.

"Your father was better than all of them put together. Loyal," she said softly. That woman in Tuscany"—she went over and shook him on the bed, the hot anger she had had since Antonio's death indisputable—"she was nothing. Antonio DeAngelis was loyal to me and to this country. Don't you forget that."

Antonio DeAngelis had died at the bus stop on Calvert Street in April 1953, waiting to go downtown to testify before the Permanent Subcommittee on Investigations, chaired by Senator Joe McCarthy. He was thirty-nine years old.

There was an older woman with him also waiting for the bus. When Rosa, summoned by Mrs. Lloyd next door, who had been out walking her dog, had rushed down 39th Street in her robe, the woman was holding Antonio's head in her lap.

He was dead before the ambulance arrived.

Rosa didn't scream. "So composed," Mrs. Lloyd told Mrs. Peters two houses down the street. "You never would have known it was Rosa." She had sat down on the pavement in her flowered robe and held his hand. But he was dead already and didn't know the difference.

"He's young enough to be my own son," the older woman who had been with Antonio told Rosa while they waited for the ambulance to come.

"We were standing at the stop," the woman said. "He had just walked up and didn't say a thing to me." She shook her head. "He seemed preoccupied and then he touched my arm. 'Madam,' he said, and he looked terrible. That's all he said. 'Madam.' So polite, like he didn't want to bother me. And then he fell over."

The doctor told Rosa he'd had a heart attack.

"He was under great pressure," Rosa said. "It was a mistake," she'd continued. "Antonio was the wrong man. McCarthy found the wrong man." But she'd said her rosary in the hospital chapel before she went home to tell the children. Kneeling in the empty chapel she was so angry she forgot the words to the Apostle's Creed.

Once years before, right after the war, Antonio's parents had come from Tuscany to see what a mark their firstborn son had made for himself in America. He had left Italy in 1931 when he was seventeen, had come to America in the heat of the Depression. Come not to New York, to the countless Italian communities scattered in the hill country of the Northeast, but to Washington, where he had met Secretary of Interior Ickes at a coffee shop, and the Secretary had found him a White House job as Roosevelt's driver. At the outbreak of the war he had signed up. He had a willingness to work harder and longer than anybody else, to do anything—the jobs that other people wouldn't do. And he was smart. He remembered things. At the end of the war he was in England on a special assignment with Eisenhower. He went to Normandy, and Truman decorated him for bravery in the invasion. When his parents came from Tuscany in 1949, Antonio DeAngelis held a top position at the Federal Trade Commission, and people talked about him. They said he was as smart as anyone they knew, with a mind like mercury, and that he had a genius for being in the right place at the right time. Which had been true up until that afternoon on the North Pier in New York City waiting for the passengers from Italy to disembark. Someone picked his pocket while he was standing on the pier. He didn't even think about it at the time.

"Such a bother," he said to Rosa later. "Not the money," though there'd been fifty dollars, "but all the identification and papers with phone numbers and whatnot."

"You ought to keep your hand on your pocket when you're in a crowd," Rosa had gently chided.

"Rosa, I am always in crowds. How can I keep my hand in my pocket all the time?"

And that had been that.

He had done the things people do when wallets disappear—ordered new identification, filled another wallet with phone numbers on slips of paper and forgotten the whole matter. Until 1953 when he had received a hand-delivered letter from the Permanent Subcommittee on Investigations requiring that he make a loyalty testimony on his behalf. Antonio DeAngelis was on the Communist rolls.

"We will lose everything," he said to Rosa one night before the testimony.

"That's not so," Rosa had insisted. "These things don't happen here."

"They happen here." He rolled his wine glass back and forth between his fingers.

"So how does Joe McCarthy find you a Communist?"

Silent, he tapped his fingers on his lips.

"How? Tell me."

"You are such a woman, Rosa," he said. "You never shut up." He sighed, resigned. "You remember that wallet taken in New York when I went to pick up my parents on the ship?"

"Of course I remember." She shook her head. "He took fifty dollars."

"He took my name," Antonio said. "Antonio DeAngelis."

"So?"

"So he is a Communist, Rosa. He takes my name. Antonio DeAngelis, party member."

"You know that?"

"I can guess it."

"You are not sure."

"I see no other possibility." He spilled out the rest of his wine in the sink. "Bad wine. Will you please stop buying bad wine for supper? We can afford better."

He went over to her, ran his fingers through her thick black hair and kissed her forehead.

"What do you tell the committee?" she asked.

"I tell the committee the truth. I am Antonio DeAngelis from

Tuscany, now an American citizen, who has served the United States government in war and now serves it in peace."

Rosa was silent.

"What do you think I tell them, Rosa? I am Antonio De-Angelis, Communist. I am a spy for the Communist Party in the FTC and pass on valuable information to the Russians," he said impatiently but without anger. "You should drink more bad wine to unmuddle your brain."

"They will not believe you," she said sadly.

"If I tell them I am a Communist?"

"If you tell them the truth."

He made a cheese sandwich, cut it in half and gave the other half to the dog, who chomped it in a single bite.

"You are right," he said. "They may well not believe me."

And they had not. There was no chance from the beginning.

"We have a responsibility to your father," Rosa said when Filip came out of the bathroom.

"We?"

"We," she said absolutely. "His children and me," she said. "To clear his name."

Rosa had noticed that Filip did not talk about his father since Antonio died. Not about his living or about his death. And now he moved away from her, into the closet, rattling things on the shelves as if in warning to her.

"He wouldn't be dead if it weren't for the shame of the circumstances," she said. "I believe it is possible to die of a broken heart."

"He died of a heart attack," Filip said.

"It's the same thing," she replied.

"You have been unreasonable about things since he died, Mother," Fil said. "It drives me crazy."

"That's true," she said; she pulled the barrette out of her hair so it fell around her face like a girl's. "His dying has made me unreasonable."

Since Antonio's death, Rosa had an excessive fear of disasters. She wished her children small again so she could watch them in sandboxes. She had by nature a Latin imagination which could conceive dangers in innocent places, and now with the whole responsibility for her family she expected the worst.

When Filip was small she was afraid of many things—that he would, for example, run into the street after a ball—so she explained to him in careful detail what would happen if he did to make an impression.

Later she heard him explaining fearlessly to the little boy next door about the car, the split body, the blood and splintered bones —just as she had told him to ensure his safety.

"Filip," she had said. "Don't you understand the danger of cars?"

"When I can drive," he said very sweetly, "I want a blue convertible."

Now she wanted to pull him out of the closet and explain to him about dangers like automobiles and Joe McCarthy, who had killed his father. If he was not cautious, if he didn't believe in dangers, then he was susceptible to the worst of her imaginings.

"The coach from Dartmouth called," she said. "He wants to have lunch with you."

Filip came out of the closet and shut the door.

"Okay," he said.

"Would you like to go to Dartmouth?"

He shrugged.

"I'd rather you went to Harvard so you can watch over Angela."

"If Harvard offers me a scholarship."

"You can't play football in college," she said. "Just the other day I read about this boy—"

"I could fall off the streetcar tonight and be killed by a car. Think of it, Mother. Perhaps we should build a bomb shelter in the alley."

"Filip," she said softly.

"I'm going now," he said. "I'll be back by one." He stood in the door, waiting for his mother to leave his room.

"Be home earlier, please."

"So you can sleep."

She got up, straightened the bed, picked up Filip's clothes from the floor.

"Where are you going?"

"To meet Natty," he said evenly, expecting her response.

"I don't want you to." She stood next to him in the archway of the door. Her dark eyes were wet. "We've been through this."

"It has nothing to do with Natty."

"Joe McCarthy is her father's friend."

"Her father was one of the first people in Washington to speak out against McCarthy."

"He's forgotten what he said."

"He's known McCarthy all of his life," Filip said, trying to be patient with his mother, knowing her loss but wanting to be free of its restrictions.

"McCarthy killed your father."

"Listen, Mother," Filip said, turning away from her, unequal to the level of her feelings, to the same possibility for feeling in himself.

"As long as Joe McCarthy is living with the Taylors I don't want you to see Natty," she said. "It's a matter of principle. And love."

He turned and went down the stairs three at a time.

"I'm leaving. I'll be back by one."

"Twelve."

"Twelve-thirty."

"Twelve or you're not leaving this house."

"Okay. Shortly after twelve."

"Where're you going?"

But he shut the front door without answering.

Rosa went in the room where Johnny rolled back and forth on his back, oblivious to her. She picked up the telephone and asked the operator for Angela's room at Radcliffe.

"Person to person," she said.

"Angela's at the library," the voice at the other end said.

"Give me the number."

"I don't have it. I'll give her your message."

"There's no message," Rosa said.

When she called the library at Harvard the woman at the

23

other end said they couldn't page Angela unless it was an emergency. Rosa put down the receiver. She sat down at the end of Johnny's bed.

"I think I'll jump off the Calvert Street Bridge," she said to him. Johnny didn't respond.

Senator Joe McCarthy sat in the lavender wing chair, his arms hanging lifeless along the sides, his head drooping slightly against his chest. His face, relaxed now, fell in folds and pouches like a spent balloon.

Ed Marlowe, who worked in Sam's office, watched him from the Taylors' kitchen table. He had been watching him for some time, through two cups of coffee Sam Taylor had given him. At first the figure in the living room had seemed to be a black bear.

"It would appear," Ed Marlowe said to Sam, who had just picked him up at the Tavern where he was on the crucial upward swing of a semiannual binge, "that you have a black bear sitting in a wing chair in your living room." By the second cup of coffee the shimmering space between the kitchen and the living room had cleared, the black bear had lost his hair and assumed the empty shape of Senator Joe McCarthy. Half-asleep.

"So," Ed said to Sam, "Joe McCarthy's moved in."

"He's here for dinner."

"A special treat."

Ed Marlowe watched McCarthy after Sam had gone upstairs to speak to Ellen, and in the time that Sam was gone McCarthy never moved.

Ed Marlowe was Sam's assistant at the FCC. It was not a designated job. What it meant, in fact, was that a part of Sam's salary went to the support of Ed Marlowe and his wife and their child, because lately Ed could not hold a regular job. They had met when they were both reporters in Wisconsin, and for years Ed Marlowe continued to get and lose good jobs. When he had lost too many, he moved to Washington to be near Sam, and Sam hired him in effect to do a job that wasn't necessary. Ed knew it.

"It's a nonjob," he told his wife, Judith. "It's the same whether I'm there or not."

"I don't know how Sam puts up with you," returned Judith.

"He likes losers, Judith."

"A man is known by the company he keeps," Sam's chaste Catholic mother would tell him time and time again. And if she was angry she would add for good measure, "You're going to grow up to be just like your father," long after Sam had grown up.

And perhaps it was his father in him—a comic drunk, John Taylor, who had died when Sam was ten and never held a decent job but one, and that undertaker for the county. But he'd lost the undertaker's job shortly before he died when the casket holding the body of Sara Granger dropped off the back of the wagon while John Taylor was racing his horse too fast across the Wisconsin valley. Sam Taylor had loved his father in spite of the fact that his mother said John Taylor was "no-account" on the hour as though there were confirmation in repetition—that his gloomy older brother said John Taylor doomed the family from the start—that all the neighbors laughed at him behind his back —that Sam's sister started drinking herself when she was thirteen years old, straight bootleg, raw as witchhazel. But Sam's memories of John Taylor were of a warm, intelligent man so full of stories he could make the darkness sing.

"A boy would go to hell for loving such a man, you know," his mother told him. If that was true, it was certain that his mother wasn't going to hell at all.

"You won't like my friends," Sam had warned Ellen when he married her. And she had not.

"We could go anywhere," she'd said in a rare outburst of temper. "We could have the President for dinner and instead we have Ed Marlowe sitting across the table."

And now Joe McCarthy in defeat.

Joe McCarthy was a square and burly man, unkempt, his eyes circled by black patches as if he'd been in a street fight—now startled as a child's eyes might be, now set and full of anger. But not a man to be afraid of. Somehow the body was too abused to have the power for destruction. He looked terrible.

Once Ellen Taylor had taken her childhood friend from Racine to the Capitol just as the Senate recessed for lunch. Senator Joe McCarthy had passed them, waved at Ellen, and the friend, Marie, had screamed like a catbird. Right in the Senate chamber as though she'd been attacked.

"Marie," Ellen had whispered, mortified. "Hush."

"That's Joe McCarthy," she had said.

"So?"

"It's like seeing the devil in your own bedroom."

"Oh, Marie." Ellen shook her head.

But such was the power of Joe McCarthy at the time, even a year ago, when the lives of people were strung together by the madness which bore his name.

Joe McCarthy had come to Sam's because his wife was in Wisconsin with the child they'd adopted and Sam had said whenever—the house was open.

Sam Taylor turned the knob of Ellen's door. It was locked.

"Ellen?" he called quietly. He heard her slap across the bare floor in cloth slippers, heard the lock turn.

The first time Sam had seen Ellen Steward was the summer he was twelve. He was driving his father's old wagon he'd used to carry bodies to the cemetery down Apple Street, and Ellen Steward was standing on her grandparents' slat porch.

She had on a white dress that came below her knees; the sun was coming up behind the house, and she stood, still as china, in a circle of light.

Sam got down off the wagon and went up the walkway just below the steps where the younger child was standing.

"You the Steward girl?" he asked.

"Yes, sir, I am," she replied.

"You come from Virginia to live with your grandparents after your parents died, I hear."

"Yes, sir, I did." Her voice, not Southern, was still softer than the hard Midwestern Sam had known.

Later Sam thought she must have been frightened of him to have been so formal.

"That's a terrible thing to lose your parents being so young and all."

"Yes, sir."

In spite of himself he said, "You're awful pretty."

Then he raced his father's wagon down Apple so fast that Mr. Kroager stopped him at the corner of Main and paddled him right there in broad daylight in front of Kroager's Market with Mrs. Baumer waiting to have her apples weighed.

Ellen Taylor was the only child of her generation, raised by her grandparents, who lived forever after her parents had died, by aunts and uncles who had never married and loved her as though she were their own and saw in her their future. Ellen Taylor was at fifty still a child—a lovely child with the fresh fawn skin and wide-set eyes of a much younger woman—and with a child's unreasonable instinct for survival.

When Sam had knocked she was sitting on her bed in a loose gown, her feet curled under her, reading an English romance.

Ellen had married Sam Taylor late, after Bill Wentworth, the high school football star and center at Wisconsin whom she'd married in the first place when she was eighteen. Sam had known her most of her life and would have gladly married her. Ellen was curious about Sam Taylor but didn't have the courage to love a man whom the Batty Club which met at Dawson's Drug ridiculed behind his back for his differences from other children growing up in Manawa.

So she married Bill Wentworth, who ran his father's shoe store at the corner of Apple and Drake. They had two sons, who were the spitting image of Bill Wentworth, everybody said, and Sam heard about her from time to time. He never failed to quicken when he saw her on the street.

———

Sam had left Manawa, had gone to Milwaukee as a journalist and then an editor in Madison. He won the Pulitzer Prize when he was thirty and had offers from other papers around the country, but he remained in Madison.

He was never interested in marrying anyone as he had at one time been interested in Ellen Steward.

One winter she came to Madison and called him. He hadn't seen her for five years and was astonished to find her at thirty exactly as he had remembered her. His hair was thin and gray over the ears. His knees cracked. Sometimes he worried that he would never father a child. She had come to Madison for a trip. Later he was certain she had planned the whole visit just as it happened. She was bored in Manawa, she said. Bill Wentworth sold shoes and played pool at the fire station on Friday nights. He had grown fat.

The first night they were together Ellen asked Sam Taylor to sleep with her. That was a startling move for a Midwestern woman in 1936, but Ellen had about her a sense of fair play that could allow her to pursue the football center when she was eighteen and leave him for Sam Taylor on the rise when Bill Wentworth had gone to lard. Which is what she did.

"You'd be plain crazy to marry Sam," Sam's mother had told Ellen. "He can be mean as a snake one minute and soft the next, like one of those lizards you pick up at the traveling circus which change color on your frock." But Ellen married him and had learned on mornings of his temper to crawl under the covers and pretend to sleep.

Lately, since Joe McCarthy, Ellen Taylor had gone to bed. It had happened once before shortly after Natty's birth when Sam was a war correspondent in Europe. She had panicked unreasonably in an elevator in Madison and had to be taken home in a taxi cab. The next morning she was afraid to go out of the house.

"It's peculiar," she had told her grandmother, who came to care for her. "I just feel as if something will happen to me outside."

"Like what?" her grandmother asked, perplexed.

"Just something."

She had waking dreams of disintegrating and would not let herself fall asleep. Some nights her mother's head as Ellen remembered it when she was a child floated dismembered from her body, surreal, above Ellen's pillow.

By the end of the week she was staying in her room. Finally her grandmother hired a nursemaid for Natty and Ellen went to bed. Some nights she was afraid to step out of bed to go to the bathroom and had to call her grandmother to take her.

"I have the most peculiar feeling," she would say, "that something's under the bed."

She never told Sam what happened, and by the time he came home from Europe she was well.

Lately, unaccountably, the old fears had come back, and she had spent more time in bed than out of it. Some days she read two romances before supper.

Sam Taylor went over now and sat beside her.

"I had a strange call," he said. "A boy called a minute ago and said, 'If you've got Joe McCarthy staying in your house, you obviously don't give a shit about your daughter.'"

"Is that all?"

"He hung up."

"Odd." She put her open book face down on her stomach. "Though it's probably nothing. Children do odd things all the time."

"Do you know Dick Carr's number?"

Ellen got up, thumbed through the papers on her desk.

"What are you going to do?" she asked. "I'm sure she's fine."

"I'm just going to check."

He dialed the number. He could hear music in the background.

"H'lo."

"Is Natty Taylor there?"

"Yes. Dancing."

"Fine," he fumbled. "If she needs a ride home, tell her to call her father."

29

"D'you want to talk to her?"

"That's okay. Just tell her I called to check if she'd gotten to the party."

He put the phone down.

"The call was a prank, Sam."

"You're probably right."

"You make too much of Natty. She's nearly grown and very sensible."

Ellen had never made much of Natty. Already her two older sons, who were uncomplicated boys, never sicker than with the chicken pox, had drained her. She had not wanted another child, had agreed only because Sam had persisted in the flush of their romance and then agreed reluctantly.

"Because it matters to you," she'd said truthfully.

And it did. Natty was a miracle to Sam Taylor, who didn't believe in miracles at all, and he had watched her grow with an unreasonable doubt that anything he loved so much could last.

"It's unnatural to love a child so much," Ellen had said. "It puts a weight on her."

"I'm sure you're right," he had agreed, "but I can't seem to help it."

And always the nagging senseless fear that he'd wake up one morning and she'd be gone. Not necessarily dead. But gone as though she'd never been.

"Is Joe McCarthy here?" Ellen asked.

"Yes."

"You asked him?"

"Jean is out of town," he said. "I told him to stop by. You won't be down?"

"I wish you wouldn't ask him," she said. "No, I won't be down. I'm too tired." She had been tired for months. Before the summer Sam had moved into the guest room by the library and listened to her wandering through the house half the night, unable to sleep.

He went downstairs and heard her lock the door after he had left.

Ed Marlowe was drinking at the kitchen sink when Sam came down.

"I picked you up at the Tavern so you could work tomorrow."

"You caught me in the middle of a decent binge," Ed said, "and brought me back here to meet the devil."

"If that's the devil, then we've nothing to fear."

Sam took two beers out of the refrigerator.

"Are you going to join us in the living room?"

"What do you talk about? The old days in the party?"

"The old days when he beat the shit out of me behind Kroager's Market and used the blood from my nose to write his girl friend's name on the wall."

The older man sat down, rolled a shot glass between his palms.

"I think he's dying," Ed Marlowe said. "Look at him in the eyes. We've been behaving as though he were immortal," he said. "And everybody dies."

Joe McCarthy read the evening paper in a bad light. Sam handed him a beer.

"You saw the paper tonight?" McCarthy asked, tossing the folded paper down beside him. "There's a short piece by that stupid woman at the *News* about my spending time here."

"I heard about it," Sam replied. "My daughter is in love with that woman's son."

"The *News* is bloodthirsty."

"Bored. It's a quiet time."

"Bloodthirsty," McCarthy blurted.

Joe McCarthy had suggested Sam Taylor to President Truman for chairman of the Federal Communications Commission in 1947. He suggested him because Sam had a reputation for being competent and wise. Though they had known each other as children they'd seldom seen each other since the war, when Sam had been a special correspondent in Europe. There were no political reasons. Sam Taylor voted, and that was as political and partial as he had ever been until he came to Washington.

In Sam's early years at the FCC they saw each other occasionally, but after the terror in Washington, around the country, they did not see each other at all.

Even as a child growing up Sam Taylor had sensed something in Joe McCarthy that did not settle with a reasonable mind.

After the Senate's censuring of McCarthy, after the country's simpleminded worship of the man turned like a sea change to anger, Joe McCarthy came one night to the Taylors' house on Highland Place. He had been drinking.

After that night he came many others, sometimes alone, often with his wife—empty as the issue he had roared after, almost as if he'd been on strings. Surely the circumstances had been more dangerous than the ravage of one man; they had, after all, depended on the docile acquiescence of the whole country.

Or else the issue had never mattered to him in any deeply personal way. He liked the process and the possibility for winning.

Sam looked at Joe McCarthy, sitting in the bad light. He was bile green.

"You look terrible, Joe," he said softly, not unkindly.

"I feel terrible."

Filip DeAngelis was the most brilliant high school running back in Washington. "In the country," the *Post* had said when it was announced that he'd made first-string high school All American. When he was fourteen the Cincinnati Reds had reportedly offered him $50,000 to sign, and according to the *Sports Illustrated* he had matched the American record for broad jump in an off-the-record practice jump for the IAC, so he was expected to train for the 1956 Olympics after his freshman year. Fil DeAngelis had been born at the right time for his collection of genes.

So when he boarded the streetcar at Calvert and Wisconsin most of the people sitting in the rows along the windows recognized his face. It was in the paper nearly every Saturday morning all year long except in the summer. It was a recognizable face—as black as any white man you could find, heavy-boned with a long sharp Roman nose. It was an arresting face even in a football helmet.

"You the DeAngelis kid?" the older man already in the seat said to Filip when he sat down.

"Yes."

"I seen you play."

"Thank you." He said thank you often. That and "I'm grateful."

"Grateful," Rosa would say, reading the morning papers. "What have you got to be grateful for? You work hard. You earn what you get. Next time they interview you in the paper don't you be grateful."

"What do you want me to say, Mama? 'Sure I'm good, Mr. Povich. The best around. I got it coming to me.'"

"And stop saying you want to be a schoolteacher when you grow up. If you go to college four years and end up being nothing more than a schoolteacher, I'll jump off the Calvert Street Bridge."

"I take my son to see you," the older man next to Filip was saying. "Now, he's a scrawny kid. He's never gonna be a football player, but I think maybe we go watch the games he'll have a good time." He pulled the bell. "You seem like a nice kid," he said. "Quieter than the rest of them. I read about you wanting to be a schoolteacher and carrying the cross in church."

"Thank you," Filip said awkwardly.

"I bet you have girl friends by the dozens," the man said, making his way down the aisle. "Football players have girl friends by the dozen." He winked.

But Filip DeAngelis didn't have girl friends by the dozens. He had Natty Taylor. She was a young Rosa—better than Rosa because she was not his mother, but reasonable and wise. She kept him from harm.

"Stay away from the girls, Filip," Rosa had said. "If you didn't play football, they wouldn't give you the time of day."

"You think I don't know it?"

"You could have your head turned," Rosa said, her hands on her hips. "Men aren't so very smart," she said. "Not even you, Filippo."

"If you don't stop looking after Filip as if he's breakable, something might really happen to him," Antonio had said to her. "You can't go everywhere with him."

"I'm worried about girls," she said. "He's innocent about girls."

"And when he was ten you worried about bicycles and before that streets and before that illnesses," he'd said. "Filip is getting along very well in spite of it."

But Rosa was not convinced. Filip had no sense of danger.

Filip had known Natty for a year. Friends had introduced them on a blind date, and that night, coming home in Tommy Larson's car, Filip had kissed her as he'd seen it done in the Saturday-afternoon specials at the Calvert Theatre; Tommy Larson, looking in the rear-view mirror, had to concentrate to keep from laughing out loud. It was the first time Filip had kissed a girl, although every girl around would have gladly lain with him in the back seat of Tommy Larson's car.

"We've gotta find a girl for the Angel," which is what they called him behind his back, and it was clear the Angel was too shy to find a girl for himself.

Everyone around knew Natty Taylor. Washington was a small town in 1953. Besides, Natty had a different way of doing things. Before she was ten she had a weekly newspaper, full of moral axioms and absolute truths, which she did up herself and sold around the neighborhood. And when the absolute truth of social justice failed her and the family she'd adopted in South East and provided with Christmas two years running bought a TV before the Taylors even thought to, Natty turned to giving miracle plays on the front lawn with all the non-English-speaking diplomatic children playing moral parts.

She played the cello and got good grades in school at a time when that combination was considered suspect—indicative of a girl without the promises of her sex.

On Saturday she went to St. Elizabeth's to visit Ezra Pound with Sean Wright, who had been paralyzed from nerves when he was eight. Now he wore all black and pasted his hair to his head and spoke in whispers. Natty went with Sean because he didn't like to go alone. Like Sam Taylor harboring drunks, she was generous with herself, particularly with outcasts, understanding her possibilities for being one of them.

And on Sundays for many years Natty took Alfie Brown next door, who had Down's syndrome, to the Greek Orthodox service at the cathedral because he loved to watch the enormous bearded priest shadowed behind the screen, moving like a god in darkness.

She was also a cheerleader. Only the best, the most acceptable, the most representative were selected to be cheerleaders. Natty was none of these. Dressed in maroon and white and saddle shoes and puffs of crepe-paper balls in hand, they'd fly up and down the football field, leaping and jumping and cartwheeling before the crowd gathered for this celebration of the perfect human form. It was a spectacle of the grace and the contained violence of the players, the splash of color and energy in the form of those girls selected to represent their time and cheer the players on.

It was a time of conventional beauty, almost pagan in its rites of selection. Only the perfect girl children retained.

"I don't know how Natty Taylor made the squad," the captain of the cheerleaders whispered to her best friend as Natty passed by the football field.

"She's good. I mean she's energetic."

"Yes," the captain agreed. "But . . ."

"Boys seem to like her."

"What about her leg?"

"You're right," the other girl agreed. "I don't know how she made the squad either."

Natty had one ordinary leg and one withered below the knee, which she operated like a pivotal stick. She walked with a pronounced limp.

"But you gotta admit," the friend said to the captain, "it's extraordinary that she did make it."

It was altogether possible that in a whole country of multi-colored bleating squads like this one at Friends School pacing the sidelines of competition, Natty Taylor was the only girl with mismatched legs.

At five years old Natty had piled her Christmas sled into a tree at her uncle's farm in Manawa and her leg was nearly severed at the knee. Her uncle got her to the hospital and the doctors put her back together as best they could, but her leg never properly developed.

Sam Taylor had sat in the rocker at his brother's house for days looking at the ice-bed course which Natty had driven.

"She'll never marry with half a leg," he thought to himself.

He intruded on Natty's sense of privacy with his concerns.

"I am fine," she'd insist, sensing his fears for her. "I can do anything."

"But you must be careful," he'd say.

Somehow his worry for her safety made her take risks she might not otherwise have taken, as if to force her freedom from him. She was determined to be normal in a time when normalcy of every kind was desirable above all else.

Besides, it was a game with Natty. She wielded her crutches like a general, and when Rusty Slover called her gimp in first grade she knotted her fist and boxed him in the nose, and it bled so hard his father had to come from downtown to pick him up.

Things happen to a child when a body's spoiled at an early age. She need not be so cautious because the damage is done, just as a valuable table irreparably scratched is something different than it was before. To know then that man is vulnerable and destructible—something that many do not know for years until something has failed them, their legs, their brains, their friends, their knowledge of themselves—can give a sense of freedom to be reckless akin to winter birds' struggle for food in frozen ground. There is freedom from expectation too. You don't expect much from a girl with half a leg, and anything she does is astonishing. In Rome or ancient Greece she would have been discarded from the start. There is no struggle with quite the sense of flying as that from the bottom.

Natty Taylor was tenacious. That was the clearest thing people knew about her.

And Filip DeAngelis was not. He had never had any reason to be tenacious. Things fell upon him before he had a chance to think of them. He was graced from birth as if the gods had selected him for all the bounty just to show that they could be generous. He had a way about him, too, a kind of innocence, perhaps sustained into manhood because he hadn't had to struggle, which made people want to do things for him. Natty, who had not been innocent since she was five years old, wanted to do things for him, too.

A familiar girl sat down in the seat next to Filip where the older man had been.

"Are you Fil DeAngelis?"

"Yes."

"I'm Blanche." She smiled. "Y'know?"

Filip knew. Blanche the Virgin she was called. She made love to everyone around, and when she left Woodrow Wilson High in tenth grade it was generally assumed she had left to have a baby and not to recover from tuberculosis as her mother had said. There was a story that she had made love to fourteen boys one night on the beach at Ocean City—just rolled from blanket to blanket. Each new boy would turn his back on the girl he was with, make love to Blanche and then roll her over to the next blanket—or so the story went. She had a soft prettiness which would not last.

"You going to meet Natty Taylor tonight?"

Filip shrugged. He was headed in the direction of Dick Carr's with Rosa raging in his head; he didn't know if he'd get off the streetcar at Wisconsin and R where Dick Carr lived or not. Which was how he made decisions, in keeping with a boy to whom things came before he even wished them there.

He was afraid of Rosa. Not that she'd jump off the Calvert

Street Bridge as she promised him she would if he disobeyed her, but that something unspeakable would happen to her and he would be responsible. Filip believed in demons; anyone in such good favor with the gods would have to.

"I don't know," he said to Blanche. "Maybe I'll meet her later." It was nine o'clock and he was late already. He would call Natty tomorrow, he thought to himself. Tomorrow they would talk about Joe McCarthy and settle this thing once and for all before Rosa drove him crazy.

The streetcar rumbled past R and no one pulled the bell to get off.

"I'm going to meet a friend at Maxie's," Blanche said. "They have good music there if you want to come."

Fil pulled the bell.

"You getting off here?"

Fil nodded.

"To meet Natty."

"Nope," he said.

He got off on Wisconsin Avenue and M. Blanche waved to him out the back window as the green car rattled down M.

Clark's was on the corner. They had a juke box. He could stay until midnight and take the streetcar home after Rosa was in bed and Johnny had stopped rolling back and forth in the front room.

Clark's was nearly empty except for two bartenders, who recognized him. He ordered a Coke and played records for a quarter.

"You Fil DeAngelis?" the bartender asked when he brought him his Coke.

"Yes."

"You playing basketball this season?"

"Yes, sir."

"I see you made All American."

"Yeah," Filip said. "Thank you."

"Don't thank me," the bartender laughed. "Thank yourself."

If he stayed an hour and walked down R Street or finished his Coke and walked down R Street now, he might meet Natty coming out of Dick Carr's. Or he could just go to Carr's and meet her by accident. What could the demons do to Rosa if he only met Natty by accident?

He had just started his Coke when the door to Clark's swung open with a rush of cold air on his back and Blanche slid into the booth across from him.

"Will," Natty whispered, dancing with him. "Dick Carr must be drunk. He kissed me upstairs."

"Shit. What a special treat."

They danced over to an empty corner. "Do you still have a funny feeling about this party?"

"I do. But I don't know why." He did know that Carter Harold had asked his sister to a party at the Carrs' and Nell had made him come to watch out for Eliza, since she didn't trust Carter Harold, with good reason, but she didn't trust Eliza either. When Will had arrived at Carr's with Eliza he knew something was up. First off, only a few people from Friends had come, and those who had sat in the recreation room fell quiet as he walked in with his sister.

"Hi, Will," they said.

"How're you doing?" they asked.

"We're having a sort of meeting, but we'll be finished soon."

"The party'll start then."

What was odd was not the meeting they were having—Will was accustomed to selection and exclusion—but their good manners. As the night went on he knew something was happening which he wasn't in on—and poor lost Eliza, flat on her back with Carter Harold, was probably not in on it either.

"It's late," Natty said. "I promised my father I'd be back early."

"What about Filip?"

"He's not coming."

"I'll take you home," he said. "Wait here. I'll go get the car."

"Okay."

"Watch Eliza while I'm gone," he said. "And I'll meet you out front in about ten minutes."

Carter Harold took Natty in his arms to dance.

"You having a good time?"

"Sure," she replied.

Carter Harold lived in a house on Foxhall Road with multi-colored mirrored bathrooms and toilets that played music when they flushed and elevators and a glass dance floor over lights and velvet walls. No one knew anything about Mr. Harold, but Natasha, his wife, a Rumanian "princess" of peasant descent, neither beautiful nor wise but clever, had in a few short months become a rival to Perle Mesta as the Washington hostess. Like his mother, Carter Harold was a striking and ruthless boy. But predictable. He made no pretense of decency.

"Where's Filip?" Carter asked.

"He didn't come."

"Problems at home, I hear."

She shrugged.

"You have a ride home?"

"I thought you were here with Eliza." Natty looked over at Eliza, who was lying flat on the couch, her eyes open, looking at the ceiling.

"Out of it." Carter crossed his eyes. "Fish house punch."

"Will Barnes is taking me home in a second," she said. "You'd better watch out for Eliza till he gets back. She could be sick. She looks awful."

"Yes, she does."

A new record dropped.

"Circle," Paulette sang, taking Al's hand and Carter's away from Natty's waist. "Let's do a circle dance."

"Circle, everyone."

"C'mon, Nat."

Natty took Dick's hand and Al's on the other side.

"Come on, Eliza." Al tried to drag her off the couch. "Circle dance." She groaned and turned away.

The circle formed. Like automated tops they moved up and down, in and out, staccato rhythm to the music, rolling their hips like putty, swishing their long skirts.

"Anne." Al swung Anne Lowry into the center of the circle

and she went around from partner to partner, swinging in under one arm and out to the next partner.

"Natty," they called as Anne fell back into place. "You're next." And Natty, in the familiar circle dance, started around the ring.

Halfway around she was conscious of a kind of violation, nearly imperceptible. An accidental hand on her breast, below her waist, on her stomach as she went from partner to partner. Now certainly that was Peter von Trotten's hand which glanced her breast as she passed under his arm and on around the circle.

"You're terrifically subtle," she said to Peter. Carter Harold pulled her next to him and kissed her ear. The lights went out before she got away.

"Carter," she said. "I thought you were growing up."

"It wasn't me."

"That's surely you." She took his hand away from her waist, but he had her tight. Her skirt ripped at the waist seam halfway around.

"Jeez." She pulled away. "Now I've nothing on."

"Just as I'd hoped," he laughed and plunged his hand down the back of her ripped skirt. She wrestled away from him, biting his shoulder half in play, and holding her skirt around her, found her way to the stairs by the light in the hall.

Dick Carr stumbled into the hall as she was leaving.

"What's the matter?"

"Nothing," she said. "Except I seem to have lost my clothes and I've got to go home."

"How come? It's early."

"It's after one." She let go of her skirt so that it fell in folds halfway down her slip. "My father will be pleased."

"Yeah," he said, smiling slowly. "You look like it's been a knockout party."

Will Barnes was on the front step waiting for Natty.

"Nat." He pulled up his collar against the cold. "Did you see this?"

The lights on the front porch of the Senator from Oklahoma's house were hot yellow against the early-winter blackness beyond, lighting the boxwood wreath made of fine china, the antique sleigh bell above the knocker, the gray velvet cat whose forearms were stretched and nailed in a T, spread beneath the china wreath.

The cat was dead.

There was a tag tied with a string to the cat's back leg—a Christmas angel tag cut out of blue construction paper with writing on it.

Natty took the tag and read it.

"Samuel Taylor. Chairman of the FCC 1947–1954."

SATURDAY, DECEMBER 18
1954

"Christ," Will Barnes said, angling his car on the snow-slicked streets into the slowly moving night traffic on Wisconsin Avenue.

Natty sat next to the door in the front seat, pinioned there, her face flat against the cold window as if in pressing she could pass through the pane. Once, just lately, her father had told her she ought to have been the daughter of the fat shoeman from Manawa and she was meant to say "Absolutely no"—the complications of being the daughter of a man courting disaster in Washington were worth a hundredfold life with the fat shoeman from Manawa and her stepbrothers. Or perhaps she wasn't meant to say no at all. Perhaps she would have been better off with the shoeman and Sam Taylor had meant just that. Surely she would have been free of counting too much as she counted with her own father. But she'd said no to Sam Taylor, said she preferred a man who'd sold his soul in Washington to a shoe salesman in Wisconsin, and he had laughed. But later, unaccountably angry, he had told her, "Simple people are worth the hounds of heaven." He was a difficult man.

"Christ," Will Barnes repeated in the same tone.

Natty turned from the window, looked at the side of Will

Barnes' face, traced in charcoal under the street lights, looking for all the world like the dead cat on Dick Carr's front door—like the man in the car next to them and his wife, like the policeman on the corner of Calvert Street, a dead cat in uniform with a pistol at his side.

"Do you think someone crucified the cat himself?" she asked.

"Chr—ist," Will said. "I hadn't thought of that."

"Or maybe found him dead in the streets."

"No one would crucify a cat," Will said.

"It was a joke," Natty said, thinking of Alexander Epps and his peculiar humor. "I'm sure of it."

"Possibly."

"Alexander probably found the cat and put him on the door."

"Why Alexander?"

"It's like him to do something like that," Natty said. "He's crazy."

Natty couldn't get the cat out of her head. He hung, snow-brushed and stiff, on the edge of her vision. If she turned her head he moved to the other side, dangling, nearly believable, a Christmas ornament.

"For a joke it's not very funny," Will said and took her hand as he parked outside her house on Highland Place. The lights were off in her father's study, in her mother's room, in the kitchen, only a blue light in the living room for her mother, who never slept at night, to see by when she paced the house, blue lights in the halls and bathrooms. "Promises of heaven," Ellen Taylor would laugh as though it were some private joke she had that Natty didn't understand.

"What do you think that sign on the cat's leg meant?" Natty asked.

"Prophetic." Will shrugged.

"My father won't resign," she said. "He doesn't quit."

"I don't know, Nat. I don't understand kids and never did."

Natty knew about the possibilities for cruelty in children and so did Will.

"Remember in fourth grade with the trash can?" she asked him now.

"Fuckers," he said. "I remember," and they both laughed. "Now we're older and reasonable."

She recalled a story from when she had first moved to Washington. Slate Cromwell lived next door. He was sixteen then and smoked cigarettes by the tree in front of the Taylors' house, stubbing them out on the trunk. He had an English bike and spent his time, even at sixteen, riding down the street on the back wheel.

"You're from a hick town," he'd said to Natty once. "I can tell by your accent."

"I bet your father's a Democrat," he said another time.

Once he offered her a cigarette, and later he swerved his bike and ran over her toes while she was sitting on the bottom step in front of the house. It was not an accident. "Cut it out or I'll tell," she said.

"I didn't do anything."

That time she told her father.

"Just stay away from him," Sam Taylor said.

Finally he ran her down on the sidewalk of Highland Place in plain midsummer daylight.

Natty was walking to the Cleveland Park Pool and she heard Slate behind her riding in the street, heard his fine English bike whisper just abreast, and then a sudden turn and Slate had run into her and knocked her down!

Sam Taylor said he didn't want to see Slate around Natty again. He said it to Slate and his mother and called the Eighth Precinct about the incident as well. After that Natty didn't see Slate Cromwell often but she avoided older children for months, expecting the worst of them.

Around that time she made up her mind to be well known or in the center of things. Or both. She worked harder than anyone else in school and won prizes. She practiced hours on her cello without persuasion. By the time she was thirteen she'd played in several concerts in Washington and had been written up in the *Post*. In spite of differences she did what was expected of a girl of her time. And so the cheerleading. She intended to cover every front as protection against people like Slate Cromwell.

Will Barnes pulled her over next to him and kissed her long and hard and she let him kiss her in spite of the heavy smell of the farm, the weathered crack of his closed lips, the absence of desire which she could not name. He was a boy she had known and cared for but could not love. He did not touch her anywhere.

"I have to go in," she said. "It's nearly two."

Filip DeAngelis rang the front doorbell of Dick Carr's house and nobody answered.

"But I can hear them," Blanche said, standing down two steps from him, her collar upturned against the damp snow.

She had followed him from the bar down 30th Street to Dick Carr's.

"Afraid to be out alone," she'd said.

"S'okay," he'd replied. He didn't know what else to say—"Get lost"—"Go home." Already he was late—late for Rosa, which he'd never been before, for Natty, whom he'd promised, and tomorrow there was a basketball game with Sidwell Friends. Rosa would rage at him all night.

There was a clank behind the door and Dick Carr was there, tipping forward like a dancer, flanked by others Filip didn't know.

"A pleasure," Dick Carr said, "the all-metropolitan, all-star, all-gorgeous heart throb of the multitudes—Filip DeAngelis."

"Is Natty here?" Filip asked, ignoring Dick Carr's call to war.

"No." It was someone else pressing into the doorway next to Dick. "She went a while ago. She only stayed five minutes and then she left with some guy."

"Who?" Filip asked.

"D'you know?" the one boy asked.

"I don't remember," Dick Carr replied. "But off she went into the star-studded moonlight. Come in, DeAngelis. There's not a single hero at this party but me."

"I can't," Filip said. "I was supposed to be home an hour ago."

"What about your date?"

"She's not my date. Do you know Blanche?"

"Do I know Blanche?" The other boy whooped and took Blanche by the hand, pulled her in the door, and by the time Filip had reached the sidewalk Blanche had her coat off and was following the boy downstairs.

It was not like Natty to go off with someone else. He would call her first off before the game tomorrow morning.

Will Barnes parked his car around the corner from Dick Carr's house, turned off the lights and leaned his head against the back of the seat. Later he would pick up Eliza, poor drunken Liza, lost as any child could be. He'd lead her to the car like a wooden mannequin, lifeless except for the steady churn of too much whiskey in her stomach. She'd been a beautiful little girl. People used to catch their breath when they saw her as though she'd momentarily stepped from a picture book and would retreat to paper once again. And the face of Eliza as a child turned to that of Natty Taylor now. He closed his eyes and held that face against him as it just had been.

He loved her. He would go to the ends of the earth for her. He would fight armies for her, destroy anyone who tried to hurt her, anyone who was unkind to her or jealous or spiteful or spoke behind her back or wished her ill, or her father ill or her mother or even Filip DeAngelis, whom he could love almost without envy because Natty loved him. He felt a fierceness overtake him, complete as desire but more exact. A kind of single-minded purpose like the winning of an athletic competition—but it had to do with love. He would die for her.

Natty had a reputation for toughness. She did not talk about her private life. Almost no one had seen her cry.

When Will and Natty were younger, people talked about them in the same breath. They were similar in the distance that they kept from other people, in their combativeness. Will suspected that they were similarly vulnerable to simple hurts, but

49

he was not sure of this until their sophomore year in high school when she was elected cheerleader.

Will had wondered at the time why a reasonable girl like Natty Taylor would subject herself to the risks of visible imperfections by trying out for cheerleading. But she had, and he'd watched her day after day practicing in public next to other girls who were slim-hipped with long legs perfectly shaped as if by the hands of a sculptor. Some days he could not bear to watch her.

On the day of the announcement of the next year's squad he was sitting behind her in the Friends School lunchroom when her name was called out. Two seats away Dick Carr whispered to the boy beside him, "Sympathy vote," loud enough for Will to hear him clearly.

Later Will found her studying behind the science building. She had been crying.

"Were you there?" she asked.

"Yeah," he replied. "Congratulations."

"Big deal," she said. "Was it Dick Carr I heard make the remark?"

"What remark?" he lied, not wanting common knowledge between them. "I didn't hear one."

"Probably nothing," she said.

He didn't mention her crying, but he dated his protection of Natty from that day. She had given him a sense of purpose.

Joe McCarthy looked like Halloween in the blue light on the end table. The muscles in his face contracted in a slow dance, his pupils seemed to show through porcelain lids, stare at Natty like cat's eyes in the dark, though he was sleeping. Natty wished specifically that he were dead and did not even fear immediate disaster for such a wish. She made no effort to be quiet on the wooden stairs.

From her father's study, with the light off, she called Filip, angry at him for not meeting her at Dick Carr's, for Joe McCarthy sleeping in his devil's mask, for the dead cat hanging on the Carrs' front door—unreasonably angry at him for everything. It was nearly two-fifteen by the luminescent clock on the bookcase, and Rosa, who Natty had been certain would be sleeping, answered the telephone with a bark.

"Angela," she said. "Where are you?"

"Hello." It was Filip on the other line.

"Hello," Natty said, too angry for good sense.

"Filip?" Rosa said. "So you're home two hours late. Do you hear Angela?"

"It's not Angela, Mother," Filip said. "I've been home for hours."

"No," she snapped. "Minutes. I was in your room fifteen minutes ago and it was empty as jail. I thought you were dead."

"Of course. I nearly died five times tonight," he said. "The phone's for me, Mother. It's not Angela."

"It's Natty Taylor," Natty said. "I'm sorry to call so late."

"Could you get off, Mother?"

There was a snap on the telephone line and Rosa stood in the hall with her robe wrapped around her, her hand on the receiver but the receiver down.

"She's hung up," Filip said.

"Where were you?" Natty asked.

"I came," Filip said. "I was late and you'd left."

"Of course I left. You said you'd be there at nine o'clock. I left at twelve and you still weren't there."

Rosa lifted the telephone gently, turned the speaking end of the receiver away from her mouth so they couldn't hear her breathe.

"I was late," Filip was saying. "I had basketball."

"Until eleven? Fat chance."

"Did you hear something?"

"Like what?"

"Like Rosa picking up the phone a minute ago."

"No," Natty said.

"I went to Dick Carr's. They said you'd gone off ages ago with some boy."

"With Will Barnes. Big deal."

"They didn't say that. They implied it was, you know, some-one."

"Well, it wasn't someone," Natty said. "Did you see the cat?"
"What cat?"

"The dead cat hanging on Dick Carr's front door."

"A dead cat?"

"Yes," and she told him about the sign tied to the dead cat's front leg.

"Jesus, Nat," he said.

"Are you sure you were there?" Natty asked. "I can't imagine they took the cat down after I left."

"The cat wasn't there," Filip said. "Shh." He listened. "Just a sec." Quietly he crept out of his room, down the stairs, and just midway he caught Rosa putting down the receiver.

"Goddammit, Mother," he shouted, waking Johnny in the front bedroom. "What do you want? Stay in my room at night so you can see I sleep all right, come to school with me and to my doctor's appointments and the locker room? You drive me crazy."

"Filip," Rosa said, sheepish, but he had run back upstairs.

"Rosa was listening."

"I'm sorry I didn't have a chance to say that Joe McCarthy's sleeping in our living room," Natty said. "She would have liked that."

"Listen, Natty."

"Don't listen Natty me. I had a creepy night and you tell me you're out practicing basketball until eleven o'clock and I'm sup-posed to believe you."

"Listen, Natty—"

Natty slammed down the phone.

If they'd taken down the cat after she'd left with Will Barnes, what had they done with it? Tossed it in the trash by the side of the house or in the pink-ribboned wastebasket in the lavatory? What did you do with a dead cat decorated for Christmas? Or maybe Filip hadn't been to Carr's at all and the cat was still hanging on the door where she had seen it. Maybe Filip was afraid to tell her the truth, knowing she'd be angry, as Rosa was angry all the time since Mr. DeAngelis died—angry like a

ed his cousin in Appleton, his mother in Manawa
ime to time, his sister, who had inherited his father's
k. He had a deep fear of money that came of a sense
ce in being poor as though its jangle in his pocket
about unspeakable disasters. Somehow, through all
nd ruffle of his early life, that ethic substantial to
ves and misfortunes which says the only virtue is in
dged immovable in Sam Taylor's brain.

careful man, knowing his own capacity for excess,
at any instinct he had for order was part of the
rrounding his father's death and lost to him. He sel-
was cautious crossing streets and expected the worst
in the car in front of him, the Ambassador from
e Germans and his fellows at the FCC, but reason-
it vindictiveness. In spite of cautions he was not
e honestly believed in a worldly sense the native
possible—that anything necessary and within human
be done and that he could do it. In this, for all the
perament, he was flamboyant and had a reputation
that intrigued people who knew only his external

or's room was organized for contemplation, but, un-
not for making love. It had no smell except just now,
on the end of her father's bed, the comfortable and
pipe tobacco.

told him about the dead cat.

if your good friends see me as a cat," he said,
ghtfully at himself in the mirror above his bed. "My
ong," he said, "though my eyes would do. A weasel
ter."

asels aren't so easily found on streets in George-

you're right." He sat back down, fiddled with his
expect these friends of yours are prophesying nat-

ey mean you're supposed to quit your job."

mother animal cornered with her brood, sitting on her young.
She couldn't be accountable for Rosa's anger or for Joe Mc-
Carthy either.

Filip lay on his back in his clothes with the light off, the empty
receiver across his chest and beeping. He wanted to call her
back, but didn't.

"Filip," Rosa asked. "May I come in?"

"I've been expecting you," he said, exhausted.

She turned the knob.

"Hell, if I locked the door at four places, you'd come in. Slide
through the wood panel and examine my pillow for nosebleeds."

"You're going to be too tired for the game tomorrow."

"So why don't you stay here and talk the rest of the night just
in case I stupidly slumber off."

"I'm sorry, Filip." She sat down on his bed in the darkness.

"For which thing?"

"For bothering you," she said. "For listening on the phone."

Filip was silent.

"Always since I was small, things have been just right. There
have been bad things, but never so much I've thought, my God.
And since your father died I cannot help it. Wide awake, even at
my office when I'm working, I see Angela sleeping with the boy
from Harvard whose father owns Macy's department store and
you kidnapped by the coach from Dartmouth, run over on Wisconsin Avenue. I cannot help it. I have electric wires in my
brain."

"It's okay." He wanted to touch her arm, to say something
which would compensate in a small way for her sense of loss, so
his father's absence did not require his filling that place. As yet
he could not even think about his father as dead.

"I drive you crazy."

"Mother . . ."

"It's too bad," she said, getting out his pajamas, turning down
his bed, "for your mother to drive you crazy."

She gave him her hand. "Here, Filip, you can't sleep in your
clothes. It's not decent."

"I'll change."

"Will you?"

"You better sit here and make sure. Okay, Mom? It'll be a nice ending to a first-rate evening to have you here." He got up, heavy with tiredness, and changed out of his turtleneck and sweater, out of his trousers and heavy shoes, throwing them one by one on his chair while she watched him in the dark. He climbed into bed.

"Well," she said and bent over him, tucking him in, "goodnight then. Sleep well. Pleasant dreams."

"Jesus," he muttered, half amused.

"Don't swear." Rosa kissed him as she used to do when he was small.

In the last moment of consciousness Filip saw the game tomorrow afternoon, the crowd in the gymnasium beyond capacity, stacked like navy beans along the bleachers, screaming into the final minutes, and he heard his own name above the pulse beat in his ears—the final second fouled by a Sidwell player, the score 66 to 65 in favor of Sidwell. And at the foul line, overtime, concentrating on the magic backboard, he makes the first shot tying the game. The crowd explodes, shouting "DeAngelis!" with revolutionary fervor, and falls silent for the final shot. Hush. Hush. Natty in his mind's eye, standing to the right of him in maroon and white cheering, a mock traitor for the other side— his dead father, Antonio, on the bleacher, front row, just far enough away that he can't see his son's legs tremble. And *swish*, the shot is through the basket. Raised above the crowd heroically he grips the heads and shoulders of his fellow players.

"It was the team's win," he later says to the writer from the *Post*. And that evening on WTOP he says again, "I just did what I was there to do. It could have been anyone."

His father always intervened in the last moments before sleeping, and this night as others he shut out the visual memory of Antonio DeAngelis, unable to sleep with it.

When Sam Taylor had shared the front bedroom with Ellen there was about the pale lavender room with tiebacks and Victorian lady prints a warm sense of romance and abandon, the

sweet musk smell of Ellen books piled on the table spil inside out on the chaise. A after dark.

And now Sam Taylor ha where he sat this moment r His robe was on, his socks The room had a careful loo from pockets organized in c his bureau, his bed turned day's work.

"Why do you always hav would ask. "It's almost as t die."

"I am," he'd say mischiev

It was the room of a cel things and no interest in Minnesota summers with h clothes. He listened to cla books out of the library bought. He paid cash for never owned a television, l Then, crazily, he bought E bacher's on Connecticut A quins and silk lace robes a tiny woman looked like a ca

It was the manner of a life that he was passing th tion to himself. Before he w respected men in larger to work, and so he'd saved his Kroager's and bought all d were days when there wa bought a pint with the ma father at all. So the money spent frivolously on Ellen ran the garage on 21st and

He suppor and, from love of drir of provider could brin the waste American hard work

He was knowing t darkness s dom drank of the ma Ecuador, t ably, with reserved. H faith in the limits coul care of ten for boldnes reserve.

Sam Tay like Ellen's as Natty sa rich smell o

Natty ha

"I wonde looking tho nose is too would be be

"Dead w town."

"Possibly pipe. "So y ural death?

"Maybe t

"Ask these friends, Nat. I'll need to know."

"Do you think it was a joke?"

"I don't know," he said. "For the price I pay Sidwell Friends School they ought to be able to drum up more original talent than these clowns."

"Are you worried?"

"I think it's stupid, Natty." He had not, nor would he, mention the telephone call he had received that evening.

"Have you ever thought to tell Senator McCarthy not to come around? You know, call him on the telephone if he's lonely and stuff."

"No," he said. "It hadn't crossed my mind."

"Well," Natty said, getting up, "it looks pretty awful for the cat world if my good friends are collecting cats that look like you."

"Weasels," he said.

"Goodnight," she said and kissed the top of her father's head.

"Goodnight, Nat."

Later he came in after she had gone to bed and locked her window—something he used to do when Natty was small out of a sudden nighttime fear that she'd be snatched away. He had trained himself to have a rational mind, but he believed in demons.

Sam Taylor took off his slippers and his socks at the side of the bed, climbed under the quilt and turned off the light. Darkness settled and with it, uninvited, his own cat memory long since put out of mind.

He was seven or eight, spending the summer in Grand Chute with his grandparents, and Joe McCarthy was over behind his grandmother's barn with Hothouse Schneider and PDQ, Sam's older brother by a year. They'd found a tabby cat with all her kittens in the barn behind a lot of boards the Schneiders were using to fix up the back porch.

57

"A whore cat," Hothouse whooped. "Ain't no one's." He hoisted his new BB rifle. "I think I'll shoot it."

"You daren't," PDQ said.

"It's plain chicken, Hothouse, to shoot at a domestic cat like that," Sam said.

"Oh, goody good." Hothouse put down his rifle. "Why do you always drag your saintly brother along, PDQ?"

"Lemme git a look," Joe McCarthy said. "G'wan. Get outa the way." He pushed in between the boards, reached his hand into where the kittens were suckling, grabbed up a kitten and whirled it around and around by the tail. "This runt's got a tail like a dried-up worm."

"Let 'im go," Hothouse shouted. And they all whooped except Sam, who ran hellbent from the garage and home just as Joe McCarthy let the kitten go.

Later PDQ burst into the room he shared with Sam.

"Y'gonna rat?" he asked.

"Did he kill it?" Sam asked.

"What d'ya think?"

"I think you guys are chickens is what I think."

"She was nothing but a whore cat."

But Sam's anger with his older brother was immense. He beat him up for the first time ever until PDQ's nose was streaming red down his face like paint. He shouted "I quit" four times before Sam climbed off his brother and sat down on his bed.

"I'm gonna tell Mama on you behavin' like that," PDQ said.

"G'wan, do it."

"I'm gonna tell Papa when he gets home."

"See if I care," Sam said. "You can rat to the priest and the mayor and the whole shittin' city if you wanna."

And later that night PDQ said it was all Joe McCarthy's fault and Hothouse's. It hadn't been his idea at all.

"How come you done it then?" Sam asked.

"I done nothing. Just watched."

"Oh, shit," Sam said and went to sleep.

_____

Sam Taylor had no faith in natural man, no faith in those children from Sidwell Friends at all. With any children. Just sure knowledge that they could do anything.

Joe McCarthy was dreaming and laughed out loud. It was a party and the army was there dressed like the Union soldiers he used to play with at his uncle's, in blue with square-billed caps and walking on their heads without hands as though their skulls had invisible feet attached and could move about without difficulty. David Schine was there, looking like the rest of them, and Cohn, his head immense, the size of a slick black giant pumpkin, his body minuscule and withered so he rolled around the room on his head like a ball, rolled over to McCarthy and whispered in his ear, that same old whisper he'd been hearing for months shoot through his eardrum on air waves, but this time in another language.

"What did you say?" McCarthy asked.

Cohn's head rolled back and whispered once again, but McCarthy couldn't hear him still.

Joseph Welch flew through the front window in a jester suit, swooped into the crowd of soldiers upside down, and everybody laughed.

"Hey, Joe, y'ole weasel," McCarthy called out, but Welch flew right over his head without acknowledging.

"Jesus Christ," McCarthy said. "What's going on here?"

Stu Symington came in with Jean McCarthy dressed in an evening dress. There was no music but they fox-trotted around the room, in and out of the Union soldiers still on their heads. And Margaret Chase Smith in red with red feathers dancing with Eugene McCarthy, kicking up her legs like a chorus dancer.

"Jean," McCarthy called. She seemed not to hear him, danced right by him so close her dress touched his hand. She smiled benevolently at him and then rested her chin on Senator Symington's shoulder.

"Jean, what's going on?"

Someone who looked for all the world like Eisenhower in a

barmaid's dress passed champagne, and McCarthy took two, one for each hand, and drank them both down in a gulp.

People were crowded around now, looking at him without recognition.

"Did you hear about the story of the Jewish rabbi and the priest," he said.

There was no response.

"Well, there was this Jew, a regular Polack type, and he went to see his rabbi because he'd been messing around."

The crowd moved off without hearing the rest of the story. No one there he recognized but Phillip Jessup at the piano. A new and unfamiliar crowd moved in close on him as in a film memory.

"Did you hear the story of the Jewish rabbi and the priest," he began again.

"Jesus Christ," he shouted. "What's going on?"

Jean was dancing now with Harry Truman on a bicycle.

"Jean . . . goddammit . . ."

Roy Cohn rolled over once again and whispered in his ear.

"Whaddya say?" McCarthy asked.

He whispered again—this time louder, for the air seemed thicker, harder but no more distinct. And then again like bellows in his ear.

"I'm dead?" McCarthy said. For all the world that's what it sounded like Cohn had said.

"You said I'm dead?"

But Cohn shrugged his tiny shoulders. He could not hear.

"Well, I'm not dead," McCarthy said. "I'm every bit as alive as ever."

He got up, pulled the chair he had been sitting on over to the center of the room, through the Union soldiers on their heads, knocking some of them over with the chair legs.

"Quit the piano, Jessup," he called out, climbing on the chair.

Jessup looked over at him but their eyes did not engage.

"Have you heard the story," he began at the top of his voice.

Someone moved his chair and danced by. Everyone was dancing now, the Union soldiers and Joseph Welch on wings and Phillip Jessup with Margaret Truman.

"Well, there was this Jewish rabbi," he began again.

Ellen Taylor, sitting on the opposite chair, woke Joe McCarthy.

In the blue light, in her long robe, she looked like an angel, and he told her so.

She had come downstairs at three, unable to sleep predictably but waiting as she always did until the tiny silver minute hand touched the twelve of three o'clock. And then, quietly, in soft slippers, not to wake the sleeping house or even the dog sleeping by Sam Taylor's bed, she came downstairs. In the living room Joe McCarthy slept, his head thrown back against the wing chair. His face, supple as putty, moved back and forth, and he spoke out loud.

"You must have been dreaming," Ellen said.

"I was," he said, nearly awake now.

"I can't have you sleep in the living-room chair," she said. "We have a guest room, didn't Sam tell you? And the library has a day bed."

She got up to lead the way, not bothering to turn on regular lights, following the blue shadows along the carpet. Obediently he followed her. His head ached and he wanted a drink, but he walked behind her without requests.

"Here." She turned down the spread of the day bed. "It's made up," she said, "and there's a bathroom right next door."

Just as she was shutting the door to the library she said, "Do you remember the bathroom at Sam's mother's? It's in the kitchen and has a shower curtain around it. You and PDQ caught me in there one day and I nearly died of embarrassment."

It was the first acknowledgment that she had made in years of knowing Joe McCarthy when he was young.

"I remember," he said, and stretched out on the bed in his shoes. Just before he fell into a second, dreamless sleep he could hear her slippers on the linoleum of the kitchen floor like drumsticks muffled in lambswool.

She was shining the wine glasses in the drainer, holding them up against the light to be certain the water was gone. She rearranged the cookbooks in the bookshelf over the stove in alphabetical order and folded the dishtowels in perfect squares, so the corners matched exactly. At night she was precise about things, as though the order of activity would bring on sleep. She made a ceremony of drinking. Tonight she went into the cabinet and selected a silver liqueur glass with a snake's stem. It had belonged to someone in the family, as had most of the things in her cabinets. Her family was dead; she had inherited everything. Across the way Hank Saunders couldn't sleep. She saw him in the bathroom from her kitchen window nearly every night and wondered if he saw her as well.

She would have brandy and Benedictine in the silver cup, sit in the living room in the large soft chair which had been her grandmother's and watch the night leave outside the bay window, waiting for a dull settlement and even sleep. She would be someone she was not, drinking from her snake cup, looking like an angel in the blue light; climb outside her own skin and make stories about herself.

The *Ladies' Home Journal* she had been reading before dinner was on the kitchen counter opened to the feature article, "The Death of a Mother at an Early Age," with the weeping child's head and woman's body illustrating irretrievable loss. It said that when a mother dies before a child is ten the child suffers from a sense of loss throughout its life. Once recently, because her good friend Mary Beth had insisted, Ellen had gone to a psychiatrist at Georgetown University Hospital; for years she had been afraid of dying. That's why insomnia, she had decided. Sleep was too similar to dying to risk it. The psychiatrist had said it was not a fear of death she had, but a desire to die, and she had left his office permanently. But on the other hand, the article in the *Journal* made sense to her, as articles in women's magazines usually did. She did feel lonely and isolated and afraid of dying, as the article in the *Journal* said she should, since her own mother had died when Ellen was six, and now she couldn't even remember her mother past all those years, except as a tone of voice and occasionally a hint of memory in her own reflection.

The face she had seen on Joe McCarthy sleeping was out of Grimm—the stories her mother used to read to her when she was very small, with pictures of giants and giant trolls and dwarves and hairlipped rubbery frogs, stories of terrible misfortunes without resolve read in her mother's quiet voice, sitting with her on the carved wood bed in which Ellen slept alone now that Sam Taylor had moved into his own room. She had believed in those stories in a way she now believed in the romantic novels which were stacked beside her bed, beside her chaise, her own world more boldly peopled than Washington, D.C., could match. For all her common intelligence, which was as much protection from her differences as it was suggestive of the nature of a woman's mind, Ellen Taylor had extraordinary instincts for romance.

When the world outside the bay window was silver, she went upstairs, and just as the street lights on Highland Place and around the city were thrown off, she fell asleep.

The Syndicate had its first meeting on the morning of December 18 at Dick Carr's house after the party. Everyone selected as a member was in attendance except Alexander Epps, who was sleeping beneath the library table. They had, in fact, spent the night in the Carrs' recreation room, so there could be no excuses. The meeting was held in earnest. There were no jokes.

It had initially been Carter Harold's idea—his and incidentally Dick Carr's, who wasn't clever enough for ideas but jealous by instinct. And it had nothing at all to do with Sam Taylor or Joe McCarthy. Only Natty and Filip DeAngelis, who was despised and courted by his peers, as are the men whose talents match the spirit of the moment. The Syndicate had started quite by accident in the lunchroom at Sidwell Friends the Monday after the Friends–St. Albans game when Filip De Angelis had run three consecutive touchdowns, each time around Dick Carr's left end. That was in November, although the members were not contracted until mid-December. At first it was only between Dick Carr and Carter Harold and kept a secret.

"You had trouble with DeAngelis, I see," Carter Harold had said.

"Yeah," Dick Carr had agreed, still belittled by Saturday's game, with waking dreams of trouncing on DeAngelis' face, leaving him pockmarked with cleats, of heaving him head first into the goalpost without his helmet. As a child Dick Carr used to sit on smaller boys, beat them up behind the teacher's back, and children were afraid of him because he was so large. Especially girls. He would do anything to girls and lie about it.

"The thing that gets me is Natty Taylor," Dick Carr was saying. "How she can be a cheerleader for Friends when the guy that feels her up on Saturday night is some kind of folk hero for the other team."

Carter Harold was sympathetic.

In early November, Dick Carr asked Natty to the Harvest Dance and she turned him down.

"Going steady with DeAngelis?" he asked.

"No," she said truthfully. "I'm going to New York for the weekend with my mother."

"I bet," he said.

"You shouldn't bother with Natty Taylor," Carter Harold had told him. "Can you imagine kissing anyone with a nose the size of Fil DeAngelis'?"

But Dick Carr's anger was complete. He thought of doing the things to Natty Taylor that drunk men did to women in his father's barroom jokes.

In December there was a feature article in the second section of the *Post* about Joe McCarthy telling what had happened to him since the Senate's condemnation in late summer—how everyone who used to claim kinship to the man had turned coat and paid him no more mind than the empty shells of summer locusts—that Sam Taylor, chairman of the FCC, his childhood friend and former enemy, was the only man McCarthy could count on in defeat—that he and Jean McCarthy were at the

Taylors' on Highland Place once or twice a week for quiet dinners.

"Can you imagine?" Carter Harold said to Dick Carr after French. "The guy's a regular criminal and Natty Taylor's father entertains him like royalty. A liberal Quaker school like Friends supporting that kind of parent body—Jesus."

So the Syndicate as a group started that afternoon in December, though in fact its energy owed nothing to the man called McCarthy, who named the time's disease, but simply to a fierce jealousy of a seventeen-year-old football star whose talents would dissipate with age and count for nothing in the next generation.

For two weeks Carter and Dick Carr met in the senior shack after trigonometry and planned the Syndicate. Dick Carr named the club. He liked clubs. He had wanted to be in a fraternity at Wilson High but they'd turned him down because he went to private school. He wanted to belong to something with a name and purpose that gained a certain strength excluding other people. He liked that in football—the uniforms, the comradeship, the process of selection, of identity through collective association. Carter Harold was not interested in groups, but in the kinds of moves it took to win and in winning at any cost. They were perfectly matched and chose the members of the Syndicate carefully. It was easy to do. Sidwell was a small school, and they had all known each other for years. The members either had to have a deeply personal vendetta against Joe McCarthy or else be interested in strategy like Carter Harold, who could no more believe in the evil of a man like Joe McCarthy than he could in the good of any man.

Carter Harold had the list of seven members in front of him on the library table. He was the eighth member, but his name was by his own intention omitted from the list in case at some future time the list should become generally available.

1. Dick Carr: 2036 N Street, N.W.   DE-5710

He was the president of the Syndicate, by Carter Harold's selection.

2. Anne Lowry: 341 Kirke Street   OL-1310
                   Chevy Chase, Maryland

She had been selected by Carter because she was moralistic, without humor or a sense of proportion. She would feel religious zeal in carrying out the plans of the Syndicate and like her father, who represented Mississippi in the Senate and owned half the state without remorse, she'd rationalize any action as befitting the cause.

3. Alexander Epps: 1806 Sheridan Circle   FE-1234

He would do anything.

4. Choo Choo: 5418 Lowell Street, N.W.   EM-6543

Choo Choo was a natural choice. Even Dick Carr knew that. She had lived with her mother for the past two years, rarely visiting her father, a blacklisted Hollywood producer whose career had been cut short two years before when he was investigated by the House Committee on Un-American Activities.

"Only trouble with Choo Choo is that she's crazy," Dick Carr had said. "She goes to Dr. Baer twice a week for being nuts and my brother tells me she's about as crazy as a girl can get."

"But she doesn't have many friends," Carter had insisted. "She'd like to belong to a club."

5. Al Cox: 3021 32nd Street   FE-8301

Al Cox had been at loose ends for months. Two years out of Friends, twice out of Harvard, once for dropping his trousers at a donut shop, once for flunking, he had never been able to outgrow or grow into the role of an ex-President's grandson and so he was a messenger for his father's law firm and hung on street corners at night waiting for something to happen and went to drinking parties with younger people, hoping to be recognized. He was intemperate and wanted to be someone, which is why Carter Harold suggested him for the Syndicate.

6. Sukey Moorehead: 801 First Street, S.E.   OS-5083

Sukey Moorehead read medieval plays and saints' stories. Nothing in her daily life was equal to her need to be overwhelmed.

Her father, who followed the example of the early Christian

martyrs exactly, was a minister out of his time and had taken over a white parish in segregated Washington in the late '40s and brought in Negroes, served hot lunches to the indigent with white parishioners' money and modernized the liturgy, believing that the church had a role to play in change. When Sidwell Friends had turned down Ralph Bunche's children because they were colored, Moorehead took Sukey out of Friends and put her in a South East public school where the whites were working-class and unsympathetic to a girl who read saints' stories. She was lonely for her old friends and glad to be asked to join a group of them with purposes.

7. Paulette Estinet: 1970 Arizona Avenue   FE-5768

Paulette, like Carter, was interested in the process of things.

In early December, the group selected as members of the Syndicate were informed by Carter Harold and allowed the choice to decline membership. Carter told them, one by one, that the issue was Sam Taylor and Joe McCarthy—that Natty ought to be withdrawn from Friends School on principle.

Everyone asked agreed to join. Their decision, for the most part, had nothing to do with Joe McCarthy. They were simply glad to be asked to belong.

"I don't understand what it has to do with Natty Taylor," Sukey said at the meeting after Dick Carr's party. "Joe McCarthy and all."

"It's not Natty's fault, certainly," Carter Harold intervened. "She's a pernicious symbol of the whole mess. She's her father's daughter and has inherited his responsibilities for these things."

"Guilt by association," Dick Carr said triumphantly.

"I still don't understand what Natty has to do with Joe McCarthy."

"It's quite simple," Carter Harold said. "The only decisive way we can impress Sam Taylor is through his daughter."

"If she's forced to leave Friends School . . ." Dick Carr began.

"I never understood how she was elected cheerleader anyway," Anne Lowry said.

"Especially since she goes with Fil DeAngelis."

"Well, that's the point," Dick Carr began.

"She's not all she's cracked up to be," Al Cox said. "I used to date her."

"I expect she's leading Fil DeAngelis on because he's well known."

"There're things like that," Sukey said. "I've heard before. Like she's always doing these peculiar things."

"I know what you mean," Al said. "She's not really in the group."

"She goes with Sean Wright to see Ezra Pound on Sundays."

"That's sick. Who's Sean Wright?"

"A creep who goes to Montgomery Blair," Dick Carr said. "Someone says he sees a psychiatrist."

"And Ezra Pound?"

"A Fascist."

"Jesus."

"A real honest-to-God, Mussolini-type Fascist."

"He writes poetry, too."

"Yeah, and he's in St. Elizabeth's for being a Fascist and crazy besides."

"So you see, there's more than meets the eye," Dick Carr said.

Sukey Moorehead was visibly upset.

"You think she's really terrible?" she asked, confused. "She was popular when I was at Friends. She used to be, y'know, well liked and everything."

Carter Harold shrugged. "Things change," he said.

"You think she's terrible," Sukey insisted, needing a devil, willing to go after a devil.

"Not exactly," Carter said carefully.

"It's creepy," Choo Choo said, shaking her head. "It's really creepy about people and what they're like."

"We'll play it day by day," Carter Harold said, returning to the business at hand. "We'll meet at Carr's at ten every morning during vacation and make appropriate arrangements for the day."

"Like what's the ultimate plan?" Al Cox asked.

"For Natty to leave Friends," Dick Carr said. "On principle."

"Not necessarily," Carter interrupted. "We'll see what comes of things."

It seemed perfectly reasonable for Paulette and Anne Lowry to tell Natty at cheerleading practice that afternoon about Blanche the Virgin coming to Carr's house the night before with Fil DeAngelis. A kindness, in fact, the way Carter Harold brought it up.

Alexander Epps was awake and sober underneath the library table, but he didn't let on.

The morning before his father, in a sea of drink, had found his mother drinking bloody Marys in the pantry before breakfast and, raging at her for pulling him down with alcohol, had thrown her out the kitchen door into a light damp snow and locked the door. She had crouched in the corner of the porch until Alexander let her back in after his father had left.

At noon, skipping school, his mother sleeping on the library couch, Alexander had watched his father on a talk show about his new book, talking about Ernest Hemingway and what a coward he was and Mailer and how he'd done one book and downhill ever since, and O'Hara and John Knowles, nothing both of them—all men he knew and drank with and ate with in their own homes. Turning off the television, dressing finally, he had walked through Georgetown to a small bar on 31st Street, pressed his false ID on the sympathetic bartender and drunk all afternoon, until, no longer simply loose, his head so dizzy it seemed to roll behind him like a ball, passing objects that were unidentifiable as fact, he'd sauntered down to Dick Carr's, where there was going to be a meeting to mess up Natty Taylor's present life. And on the way Natty Taylor, with her old friend Will, had stopped to pick him up.

He had liked Natty Taylor since fourth grade. Since he could remember she had held out to him a promise that chaos was not implicit in life. He listened now to the group above him talking and talking like his father on television that morning and wept silently into his folded arms.

When Sam Taylor woke from a black sleep it was ten minutes before nine and the alarm had failed to ring. Initially he couldn't remember why it was supposed to ring on Saturday and lay in bed, his arms folded under his head, watching a cardinal in the tree outside his window—splendid in the early-morning sun, its feathers full of air, pillows against the cold, its beak pressed into its breast.

His father would have been seventy-eight this Christmas eve, and Sam wondered what he would have looked like at seventy-eight. At forty, the year when he had died, his black hair was over the collar and thick as beaver's hair, his eyes were black like Natty's eyes, without a center except in daylight, and his cheeks were sunken like china cups. He had looked to Sam then as old as a man could look and be alive, and Sam had known to look at him that he would die.

Lately he had been thinking about John Taylor. Thinking he would have liked him to know Natty now at seventeen with that mystery which she had that reminded him of something in his father. He would have liked his father to hear her play the cello.

He made scenes for them. His father forty, looking seventy-eight, sitting on the front porch of the house on Highland Place, drinking as he always had, but not oblivious—Natty flung across the porch in her jeans and heavy sweater, watching her grandfather, who held on his long thin finger a cardinal, puffed up in cold, its beak invisible.

Sam got up with the smell of coffee in the kitchen. Natty in the kitchen, Ellen still asleep, sleeping until noon, insulated by daylight.

Looking at himself in the mirror, he noticed the way his eyes sagged, the way his hair had gone white on the edges, the way he called his father to mind unspecifically. There were times the year that Sam was forty that he had expected unaccountably to die, to stop breathing at 18th and M streets on his way home. He was not a man given to superstition, but it is an odd triumph to outlive your father. Now he wanted to think well of him.

As he inspected the thick black pepper on his chin he remembered why the alarm had been set for seven-thirty and threw open his dresser drawer, tossing his socks about the room as if it were a game, his shirts thrown out on the floor, on the bed, until he found the only white shirt that seemed appropriate to wear to meet the President—his room a growing jungle of shirts and socks and undershorts. Finally, in frustration, he turned his sock drawer upside down and threw it empty against the closet door.

He was expected at the White House at ten o'clock.

There was an accident on Massachusetts Avenue, and traffic was tied up for blocks. Twice and uncharacteristically Sam Taylor pressed on the round horn and held it down until the cars around him beeped back in disapproval. And when he finally reached the parkway and turned off he drove at such a speed that he forgot to yield to the oncoming traffic from the zoo.

As he climbed out of the car on Pennsylvania Avenue across from the White House he realized that he was wearing mismatched socks.

"Mother," Natty called to Ellen Taylor, who had gotten up just before noon and put on a robe. "Did you see Daddy's room?"

Ellen stopped in the hall in front of Sam Taylor's room and shook her head.

"I've never known him not to make his bed," Natty said.

"Sometimes," Ellen Taylor began, but she didn't want to think —she wanted to have breakfast before Joe McCarthy got up. "Oh, well."

Natty went into her father's room after her mother had gone downstairs. She took the drawer out of the closet and filled it up with socks she rolled again, folded the shirts on the floor and on the bed, the undershorts, and put them back, made the bed for him, pulling tight the sheets as he liked, fluffing the pillow.

Outside the window a lone cardinal stretched, his wings extended, brushed like red paint against the snow—and he flew downward to the shelter with wild birdseed on the ledge outside the kitchen window.

Something in the day for all its brightness was making Natty immeasurably sad.

Still in her robe, Rosa bathed Johnny and dressed him for the day, all the time talking to him between silences, waiting for responses which would not come.

Filip, dressing in his own room for the game that afternoon, relaxed when Rosa took Johnny downstairs to the kitchen for breakfast. He didn't want to hear that crazy talk—Rosa talking, talking, talking and waiting, for God's sake, as though Johnny might one day blurt out, "That's all very interesting, Mother, but I simply wouldn't take that point of view." Talking as though it might make Johnny normal, just the constant sense of it day after day, year after year. Someday he would have to go to an institution. Everyone had told Rosa he would have to go, and before Antonio died she had made a decision to put him in a place outside Baltimore, a regular school-type place where he'd learn things, and then Antonio . . . and now the talking worse than it had ever been before, so it looked as though Johnny and Rosa would grow old together in the row house on 39th Street.

Rosa knew all that. Johnny would go to Baltimore in June. She's promised herself. The summer with Angela home if she wasn't pregnant by the Macy's department store son and Filip and no Johnny to accommodate her second self. She'd known all along that someday she would have to settle into her own house with no one to provide for, to alleviate that sense of absence but herself.

Johnny was someone to her that no one had understood. Not Antonio, who, in spite of himself, disliked imperfection and was grateful for Filip. Not Angela, who saw Johnny as weakness in Rosa. Even Filip, who allowed Rosa certain licenses without intrusion, saw his mother's doom in Johnny.

Once Antonio had seen Rosa and Johnny alone and berated her afterward.

"Rosa," he'd said. "Can't you see you're deceiving yourself?"

"He has more brain than you think," Rosa had insisted.

"You have more sense than you show," Antonio had replied.

Rosa did not bring it up again. But for years, in their hours together, Rosa had talked to Johnny about everything, about her most private thoughts, her fears for herself, her love for Antonio and constant anger at him, her sense of doubt. She would sit with Johnny, rubbing his arm, running her fingers through his hair, meeting his eyes straight on, following them with her own when they wandered, talking to him as though he were not simply a regular boy and her son, but as though he were a priest like the priest in Nesquehonong whom she used to tell, when she was young, what she did to herself with her hands.

Sometimes Johnny's head would roll back against the chair, his eyes vacant, staring at the ceiling or half closed, leaving only the whites between the lids. But sometimes he would connect, the black center would seem to warm and brighten with something Rosa honestly believed was understanding. Rosa had never quite felt like a mother with the others. She was a mother to Johnny. In dark childhood dreams her own mama would have called heresy, dreams of hell, Rosa thought of herself as the Mother of Christ.

"Tomorrow I am going to Wisconsin," Rosa was telling Johnny, feeding him his eggs. "Grand Chute and Manawa, where Joe McCarthy, who killed your father, comes from, and his accomplice, that man Sam Taylor I told you about the other day."

Johnny, always bright when he was eating, followed his mother's eyes.

"Elsa will take care of you and Filip," Rosa said. Elsa came every day to care for Johnny while Rosa worked, and had since Johnny was small. "And I'll only be gone two or three days. There's a story in Manawa about Sam Taylor—I want to talk to his mother and sister and people who knew him. I want to find out what kind of man it is who enjoys the company of criminals."

She helped Johnny from the chair and took him to the room downstairs which she'd fixed up for him, full of bright pictures and toys and plants in the window. He could sit for hours on the floor with blocks—sometimes able to pile one on top of the other, occasionally throwing them in frustration or falling into a long abstraction bent over the blocks.

"I am doing a story on Sam Taylor," she said, setting Johnny on the floor. "I don't know what it's going to be about. I don't even know what it is I want to find out." She kissed Johnny on the head and automatically, uncontrolled, his arms flew around her legs and locked. She had to disengage herself.

The *News* was hoping Rosa could find a relationship between Sam Taylor and Joe McCarthy which was interesting, possibly even damaging, about a public servant who in his private life took in Joe McCarthy.

Rosa wanted to find fault with Samuel Taylor when she went to Wisconsin—blameable moments out of his past. It was not simply because of Antonio's death and Joe McCarthy. In a way she didn't altogether understand, it had to do with Natty Taylor.

She made breakfast for Filip, sat down at the table with him.

"Listen, Mom," he said, apologetic but annoyed. "I know you like to talk to Johnny, but would you cut it out on the mornings when I've got a game? It makes me nervous to hear you."

"How can a little talking make you nervous?" she asked. "You can hear the trolley car from your bedroom window."

"I know, Mom," Filip said, "but the trolley cars just aren't the same."

The gymnasium was too hot and smelled of the sweet and sour sweat from the bodies of young boys, sounded with the steady thud of rubber on the varnished court, the hand slaps on the backs of one another, the explosion of the crowd like punctuation between silences. The score was tied late into the fourth quarter, tied again and again from the beginning, Friends leading once by two baskets and then St. Albans by one—the crowd in coats sweating as the boys were sweating, leaping from the bleachers point to point as if this game was final.

Natty stood in front of the Friends bench, her back to the team—young boys bent over, bare and sloping shoulders without flesh, watching their teammates play by play as Natty watched Filip. "Filip DeAngelis" rang through the crowd above the names of Friends or St. Albans as though he were a special halftime show.

Natty slid back and forth behind the narrow line defining the court, waving balls of maroon and white crepe paper, thinking of Filip, of whispering to him in a corner at a party that night, of lying with him in the back seat of her father's car.

From time to time, Filip thought he heard her voice, and once he glanced at her before a foul shot. Though his mind was on the team, on winning, on his body, as much at union with his body as it could reasonably be, although he was a part of a spectacle that needed the team and the game and the crowd for its expression, he was also like the bright preening cock, strutting outside the henhouse. The game was sexual, and the winning had to do with more than points—had to do with the unity of the crowd for him or against, with its pitch and high passion, with the girls along the sidelines, the cheerleaders turning their hips and thighs in fast time, arching their backs, their arms over their heads, spreading their legs.

The cheerleaders didn't talk about the game. They named their cheers, doing four or five a quarter in periods of time out, leaped in the air with each basket as though they were themselves the ball, and talked when they could in the silences about the players or about each other.

"You left early last night," Paulette said to Natty.

"I was tired," Natty said.

"Filip came."

"Yes," she said, adjusting her skirt, not looking at Paulette, who stood beside her at the edge of the court, sensing Anne Lowry move over next to her but not looking at Anne either, following the ball down the court, stopping with it, the shot, hand over the shoulder of the player who shot the ball. Foul called.

"Filip told me," she said.

"Oh," Paulette said. "You saw him? He came around near midnight with Blanche."

Natty slid away from Paulette, down the court across from the player from Friends shooting. He missed the first, arranged his feet again, spit on his hands, leaned over, bouncing the ball close to the ground, and then stood up. Natty watched him carefully. The second shot went through the basket without touching the rim.

"Who's Blanche?" Natty asked when the game had started again from the center.

"What's Blanche's last name?" Paulette asked Anne.

"I don't know. She's got blond hair . . ."

"And breasts the size of muskmelons."

"She goes to Wilson."

"I'm sure you've seen her, Nat."

Filip had the ball, a diagonal of the court free; he moved down, graceful, unassailed, and the ball slid through the basket magically. St. Albans was ahead by six points and the clock over the opposition's basket ticked off the final seconds in the last quarter.

Across the court on the St. Albans side, above the blue-and-white banner that stretched over the front-row-bleacher STA, above the second string, Natty saw Blanche with her long blond hair and breasts the size of muskmelons hidden under a square camel's-hair coat, and as she focused on the girl, the people on either side of her vanished, and though the distance was too great to see her face, Blanche grew until she was the only clear figure on the opposition's bench.

Another basket. Again Filip.

The Friends cheerleaders turned to face their spectators. F-R-I-E-N-D-S.

The seconds clicked off the final minute with one more basket and St. Albans had won by eight points.

Natty followed Paulette Estinet out of the gymnasium.

"What was Filip doing with Blanche?" she asked. "Did he bring her to the party or something?"

"I just don't know," Paulette said, her accent particularly French. "He came with her. I was there when he arrived."

"Well, thanks," Natty said.

Usually she waited for Filip. Usually they stood together on the floor after a game while people congratulated him and interviewed him for the paper the next day and girls squealed at him like piglets and young boys punched him gently in the buttocks in lieu of conversation. She liked to be there. She had never told him, preferring to pretend that the game was incidental, that she liked him for himself, unlike the others. And of course she did. But she liked to stand with him after a game in the midst of a crowd, although she disapproved of herself for liking it so much. She had never told him he was good. Other people did that.

"I'm sure it was nothing," Paulette said.

When Natty looked back through the gymnasium door, Filip was standing in the middle of the court, in the middle of a group of people. She could not see Blanche.

"You waiting for Filip?" Anne Lowry asked.

"Nope," Natty said, following Anne through the crowd.

"You're going to the dance, aren't you?"

"I can't," Natty said.

Outside it was dark and raining now, a steady rain melting the snow from the night before, and Natty walked home.

The young man on the left with his hand on Filip's arm was from *Sports Illustrated* and was doing an article on high school athletics for the April issue. He'd just come in from Minneapolis. He said he was impressed, shouted it in Filip's ear. Shirley Povich, the writer from the *Post*, tapped Filip on the shoulder, gave him thumbs up, said he'd see him that night. His son was giving a victory party.

A young red-haired boy thrust a program in Filip's hand and he signed it automatically.

"I've got a collection," the boy said. "You 'n' Phil Rizzuto."

Rosa passed through the crowd without waving, always good about games, never interfering unless he was injured. He could not see Natty.

"They want you to do a spot on WTOP with Larry Luce from Wilson at five," his coach, Al Burro, shouted above the heads of the crowd. "I'll pick you up after you shower." Al was always shouting. "Get into the locker room. The gym's getting cold."

Fil moved on to the locker room, the man from *Sports Illustrated* still on his arm.

The French cheerleader was at the entrance. He didn't know her name.

"Have you seen Natty Taylor?" he asked.

Paulette shrugged. "I think I saw her leave," she said.

"Leave?"

"I think so."

Going down the steps to the locker room he told the man from *Sports Illustrated* that he was going to be a teacher when he finished school (Rosa in his head: "Why did I bother to send you to school to be a teacher"), that he might play professional ball but probably not ("I couldn't stand to follow you around from place to place and sit in the stands with all the wives"—Natty talking), that it wasn't a one-man game, of course, that he was lucky and grateful for his talent.

Fil DeAngelis was not an ordinary athlete, and sportswriters liked to follow him. He was a gentle, quiet boy without pretensions. Occasionally a writer would say that in a situation that demanded aggression Fil DeAngelis might hold back.

Fil didn't say he was confused, that ever since it had all started with the sportswriters and the coaches and the college offers and the scouts from the pro teams, football and baseball, the scouts from the 1956 Olympic Broad Jump Team, sometime when he was around thirteen and confused enough just for being thirteen, he had lost all track of himself and felt reasonably familiar in his old bones only when he was playing athletics. Or with Natty.

The man from *Sports Illustrated* watched him dress. He was sitting on the bench when Filip came out of the shower and was still there when Filip left to go with Al Burro to WTOP.

Walking down Highland Place in the dark, giant steps, swinging his shoulders to music played out in his head, Fil DeAngelis felt enormous, leaped up in midblock, rushing forward without a ball in hand, and touched the highest branch that he could reach.

The lights were on all over Natty's house and on her porch, as though they'd thrown a main switch in anticipation of his coming.

He took the front steps three at a time. Through the slender pane of windows on either side of the front door he could see Senator Joseph McCarthy in the study. He was reading.

Natty answered the door before he had a chance to ring.

"Hello," he said.

She was in blue jeans and a flannel shirt. She did not invite him in.

"Hello," she said.

"Well," he said. "Are you ready?" Though it was obvious she was not. "We're going to Maury Povich's."

"I can't come," she said. She didn't mention Blanche or the night before.

"You can't?" his voice broke.

"Nope."

"How come?" he asked. "It was all planned."

"I just can't," she said. "Something's come up."

"Nat," Fil said quickly before she shut the door. "Are you mad or something?"

"Nope."

"Is it because I'm late?" he said. "I went to WTOP for a news spot live. Did you hear it?"

"No," she said. "I didn't hear it." She started to close the door. "I'd ask you in, Filip, but I can't."

SUNDAY, DECEMBER 19
1954

Someone else brought Blanche the Virgin to the Poviches' party. When Filip saw her standing by the stereo, he knew that he should leave, and didn't because Rosa would be waiting up for him with all her talk of Senator Joe McCarthy, because Natty Taylor had let him down.

"Just try to get the two of-them alone," Carter Harold had told Paulette Estinet. He liked Paulette. She was smart and did not need explanations. In fantasies Carter Harold was in Europe in the '40s planning strategy for either side—sometimes for the Nazis because the strategy itself was interesting, sometimes for the opposition's underground because of the high risk. It was a game that interested him, and that was what he liked about Paulette, although he sensed immediately that she needed to be associated with the winning side. Lately when he daydreamed of himself in Europe in the '40s, Paulette Estinet was with him.

"The study's the best place," Paulette told Carter later. "No one's there."

Filip was by nature innocent of subterfuge and easy to make arrangements for. He had never had reason to doubt. When he was small, Rosa was careful about his friends. She only read him funny stories or those with happy endings. When he was old enough to go to school he was larger than anyone and gifted. No one would have dared.

There was a quality of grace about him that touched people and made them better in his presence. People loved him; people on the street, strangers even who did not generally smile at passersby, would stop and talk to him.

Nothing bad had happened to Filip except Antonio's death, and that he'd put out of mind. There was no reason for him not to believe in natural goodness. He knew it in himself, uncontended, and simply believed he would find it in everyone he liked.

So, from the beginning, he did not believe the stories he had heard about Blanche the Virgin.

When she lay in the study, stretching and curling like a long-haired Persian cat, he thought she was very pretty and soft. He wanted to kiss her but he did not, in part because he could not figure a way to kiss her easily, in part because of his loyalty to Natty. Later he dreamed about her.

In the study they talked about the game, about Dick Carr and the Friends School coach. Blanche said that Dick Carr would play better if he kept training. As it was, he drank too much.

They left the study when Blanche heard a record and wanted to dance. People in the recreation room looked up when they came out together, confirming their expectations.

"Did you make out with Fil DeAngelis?" Paulette asked Blanche later as they were leaving.

"Yeah," she whispered.

"Do you think they did?" Carter asked Paulette later.

"*Quelle différence!*" Paulette said, laughing. "She has a reputation to uphold." But when Carter Harold kissed her neck in the car on the way home, Paulette pulled away, arranged herself against the door.

"We're business partners, Carter," she said. *"C'est tout."*

Joe McCarthy made his first telephone call at five a.m. to Roy Cohn, who had planned to sleep in that Sunday morning.

"Roy," he boomed.

"What time is it?" the other man asked.

"Morning." Joe McCarthy said.

"It's dark."

"It's a dark morning," he said. "What do you know about this woman Rosa DeAngelis?"

"Nothing. I don't know anything about her at all."

"Well, she's gone to Grand Chute to drum up information for an article in the *News*."

"Listen, Joe, it's early. I was out late."

"What kind of information do you think she'll find?"

"God knows."

Natty Taylor was sitting in the kitchen in the dark when Joe McCarthy came in.

"What for Chrissake are you doing up at this time of day?"

"Sitting," she said. She couldn't sleep for thinking of Fil DeAngelis. She thought about his not meeting her at Dick Carr's and wondered if he had lied to her. She had trusted him absolutely, although she knew that he was careless in the way of someone who does not understand people because he hasn't been hurt by them. He was at the same time incapable of protective defenses, because he hadn't needed them.

Now she had memories of lying with him on the couch in the back room, of hours together walking through the cathedral grounds, of kissing in the Bishop's Garden, of Blanche the Virgin.

"Your family doesn't sleep much," he said. "Last night your mother was ghosting through the house at three a.m."

Natty shrugged. " She likes to sleep in the daytime instead."

McCarthy picked up the kitchen telephone and dialed.

"Long distance," he said, "to Appleton, Wisconsin." And he gave the number. "Personal to Jean McCarthy."

Natty got up, turned on the fire under the teapot, burrowed her head in her arms when she sat back down.

"What do you mean she's not there? She said she'd be there." He slammed the phone down.

"She's at the lake with the baby," he said to Natty. "She said she was going to be at my cousin's and then they went to the lake for the weekend."

The teapot shook on the burner, rattling against the metal, singing high-pitched.

"Would you turn that thing off?" McCarthy said.

"Do you want tea or something?" Natty asked, getting up.

But Joe McCarthy was on the telephone.

"I'd like to speak to Bob," he said. "It's Joe McCarthy." He pulled a chair up, sat down in it, put his legs against the wall. "Yeah, I know. There's a clock right in front of me in Samuel Taylor's kitchen and I can read it fine. I wouldn't have called if it weren't important, for God's sake."

He turned to Natty. "Bob Larson's sick. Do you know him?"

Natty shook her head.

"He's a Republican Senator from Ohio. Always sick. Emphysema, I think." He rolled his eyes in disgust. "God, I'm sick, too," he said, "and I get up in the morning every goddam day of my life." Joe McCarthy had his hand over the receiver. "Do you know Rosa DeAngelis?" he asked.

"I know her son."

"Your father told me. I hope he's nicer than his mother. She hasn't got an innocent bone in her body."

"Filip makes up for that," Natty said.

It was Filip's innocence that had attracted Natty in the first place—a kind of noble affirmation that man is by nature good, which she didn't believe, but had a sense of urgency about, a desire to believe. He seemed to be free of complications and could love her absolutely as she wanted to be loved, although she couldn't return that kind of undemanding love. Occasionally she thought it was ignorance that marked him, which seemed, unlike innocence, indefensible. And then she'd tell him that people were not what they seemed to be. She wanted to believe in Filip's innocence, but she wanted him to know the things that she knew. More than once she had told him the story about J. B. Hyer.

J. B. Hyer was the toughest boy in Cleveland Park. Once he'd beaten up a boy two times his size, sent him home crying with a bloody nose. Another time, he'd taken Alfie Brown, who had Down's syndrome, and rubbed his face in mud because he talked so queer no regular person could understand him.

"He's no more queer than a bully," Natty had shouted at him when she learned of the incident two days later.

"So," he'd said, taking Natty by the arm, leading her down the vacant driveway by the Cleveland Park Club.

"Such a smart-ass girl," he'd said. He was thirteen or fourteen then, not tall but thick as the trunk of a tree. Natty was ten and too thin. He had pulled her down on the ground with him, held her easily with one arm and with the other hand unzipped his fly, pulling out his penis from between the slits of his jockey shorts.

"Suck," he said.

"I won't," she said, terrified.

"Someone queer-looking as you are is not gonna get a bunch of chances like this."

"Big deal," she'd said, but scared, knowing she'd probably have to because he was so strong and unpredictable and could ask more of her than that. That she could do, she had thought logically, that she could do and it wouldn't kill her.

"Suck," he said again. She hesitated.

"Go on," he said with fierce insistence.

And she did. The penis, which was not as large as she had imagined it would be, stood up at a tilt.

"Keep on," he said.

"I can't," she whispered. "I feel sick."

"Stupid girl," and he rubbed it himself until he gave a little

87

cry. Then he stood up, zipped up his pants and walked away. She didn't look at any of it—not at his penis when she sucked it or at what J. B. Hyer did to himself afterward.

"Who'd wanta screw a one-legged girl?" he said in disgust as he walked away. And then he called back, "If you tell, I'll kill you."

If Natty Taylor had been a survivor without imagination, she would have wanted to deny Filip DeAngelis his innocence, wanted to destroy it because it made mockery of the truth of things, wanted to destroy him for having some hope she could never have. As it was, every time she told Filip that story he cried and held her and she pretended that he could survive J. B. Hyer hands down.

"Senator Bob Larson's not well," McCarthy said, slamming down the phone. He sat down beside Natty, put his feet up on the table and leaned toward her confidentially, his eyes bright as candles. "I suppose you don't know about Senator Larson."

She shook her head.

"It is absolutely documented," he began, "that he accepted twenty-five thousand dollars during the election in exchange for favors. And I know," he said in a voice familiar to Natty, "for a fact that half of that or more went to his secretary, Amelia, in exchange for favors of another kind." His eyes caught fire. "And it's my conviction that she's been planted in that office by the party." The old demagogue McCarthy filled the empty shell, familiar to Natty only through television. "This country would burn its Robert Larsons if the tide could turn and the people could keep us from rotting inside out like we're doing now." He closed in on her as though what he was saying was of import to them both. "You know that."

She shook her head.

"You're young," he said.

"Not so young."

He leaned back in his chair, closed his eyes and rubbed them vigorously.

"You know," he said, "I've never thought that money was

important except to spend. Not like your father, who spends it all on worn-out folks like that jackass from Madison last night." He hesitated, studied Natty's fingers stretched out on the kitchen table. "Nice," he said finally. "You have nice hands. Farm women in Wisconsin have hands like pigs' feet."

She drew her hands up automatically and wanted to go upstairs. If Joe McCarthy had sensibilities, she didn't want to offend them; not out of any generosity, but an odd fear of retribution.

"So," he said, "I've been making investments. Your father should, too, but he won't. He has no confidence in the future."

"I guess," she said, moving away from Joe McCarthy's gaze.

"I'll have a ranch someplace with Jean and a small country law practice. We'll live decently." He looked up and down at Natty. "You're too thin," he said. "I lost forty-one pounds in a week once. You don't drink beer?" he asked.

She shook her head.

"I thought you probably didn't."

It was as though Joe McCarthy's memory consisted of small unrelated boxes with doors which opened for a second, spilling out the contents, and closed before the box was empty. He made no sense.

She went up the back stairs when McCarthy called Frank McTigue in Racine. She heard him ask Frank to have Jean McCarthy call him that afternoon. It was an emergency.

Filip knew that Rosa would be up when he came home but was surprised to find her dressed and her hair done, looking younger and more lovely than he had seen her since Antonio died. She was working at the desk in the living room and did not look up when he came in.

"Hello," he said, walking through the living room, passing the back of her chair as he went into the kitchen. She didn't reply.

"So," he thought to himself. "A new tactic." He made himself a chicken sandwich with four slices of bread stacked one on top of the other, sat down at the kitchen table to eat it. "Rosa silent," he thought. "It won't last."

He had fallen asleep at the Poviches' waiting for Stanley Ellis to take him home, since Rosa wouldn't let him get a driver's license for fear of accidents. And Stanley Ellis wanted to stay until dawn, hoping Blanche the Virgin would change her mind about him as the night progressed. It wasn't likely that Rosa'd believe that. She only believed the truth if it was bad.

"I didn't see Natty Taylor," Filip called out.

He heard Rosa get up, shuffle papers, walk across the room.

"She wouldn't go out with me because of the business with McCarthy," he said. "The fact that you're going to Wisconsin today to mess around in her father's personal life."

He finished his sandwich and stayed in the kitchen, staring at the wall across from him. In the living room, he heard Rosa back at the desk shuffling papers.

He wondered what Natty was doing now and thought of her in bed, of her small dark body against the white sheets—and naked. Of her eyes closed, her hair in slender strands across her face. He thought of Natty sick, nearly dying, of caring for her beside a white-sheeted bed, giving her hot soup in a cup, holding her neck with his large capable hands. In his reasonable mind he knew that Natty sick would lock her door against him— that his dreams of saving her would have to be dreams of another woman. He wrote her mental letters—"My darling, I will love you forever—every moment of my life is richer because of you, every day is brighter"—letters that he'd never write.

"You don't love anyone forever except your parents," she'd say, "and that is different."

"Did you hear what I said about McCarthy?" he asked finally, going in the room, standing next to the desk. "Do you know what you're doing to my life?"

"It's six o'clock in the morning, Filippo," she said quietly. "I was up all night." When she looked up, her eyes were wet.

He sat down on the couch, threw his head back. "Jesus," he said. "You're full of new tricks, Mother."

"I cannot be a mother with a son who goes out all night and doesn't let me know where he is."

"I told you I'd be home late. I had to wait for Stanley Ellis. You've got to trust me."

"You should have called."

"I fell asleep."

"It's a terrible feeling." She shook her head. "You're my son and I haven't got you any more." She rested her face in her palms. "I don't know what to do."

"Have you considered the Calvert Street Bridge?"

The Calvert Street Bridge was an old family story. It was the most popular suicide bridge in Washington, and once when Filip was small, Rosa had rushed out of the house after an argument with Antonio with the announcement that she was going to jump off it.

"Will she?" Filip asked, wide-eyed.

"Of course not," Antonio replied. "Your mother is afraid of bridges."

"Why did she say so then?"

"Occasionally your mother is full of hot air," Antonio said, "and wants to remind us of her importance."

"You usually think of jumping from there," Filip said. "I'm just reminding you."

When she looked at him across the small room her eyes were blacker than he remembered them, different, like a child's eyes, and suddenly Filip was sorry and knew that he'd said the wrong thing. That his mother, whom he always counted on to be in absolute control of everything, in spite of her own crazy tongue, had lost something, and he knew without understanding and wanting it to be so that it was Filip she had lost.

"I'm sorry, Mother," he said across the small space.

"There's nothing to be done for it," she said without anger.

It occurred to Carter Harold that Natty had been inadvertently responsible for the fight after the Poviches' party in which his brother had his nose broken by Dart Whittaker of St. Albans School. Inadvertently because Natty didn't know Dart Whittaker and had not in all probability seen Joseph Harold since fourth grade. But the fight was over the Friends–St. Albans game and whether Fil DeAngelis had been fouled in the third quarter by Dick Carr.

"The fact that she goes out with Filip DeAngelis makes us look bad," Dick Carr had said, toweling down in the locker room after his shower. "Like we're not worth her time."

Carter Harold acknowledged that was so and suggested their masculinity was in question by such a betrayal.

"Right," Dick Carr had agreed, thinking about the foul in the third quarter, about beating Fil DeAngelis to mashed plums. "You're absolutely right."

So on Sunday morning Carter Harold called Dick Carr at home and invited him to spend the day at the Harolds' farm in Middleburg.

"I think it would be a good idea to ask Natty Taylor, too," he said.

"Absolutely," Dick Carr agreed.

"Possibly if she understands the kind of tension she's creating at Friends School by spending all of her time with Fil DeAngelis . . . We'll have a sort of meeting."

"Then you're going to ask the whole Syndicate?"

"Why not?"

Carter said they could bring beer and lunch, go horseback riding, though maybe Natty wouldn't be able to join them with her leg.

"She'll try," Dick Carr said. "She tries everything."

"You're probably right," Carter agreed.

Natty was delighted when Carter Harold called. She said she'd ask and call him back.

"Where were you last night at Poviches'?" Carter asked. "I thought you'd be there."

"I couldn't go," she said. She wanted to ask about Filip, if he'd been there, but she didn't, and Carter didn't say.

"Where's your father?" Joe McCarthy asked when Natty came back downstairs.

"Asleep," Natty said.

"At ten?"

She looked up at the clock. "I guess."

"I thought your father was always up at dawn."

"Usually," she said.

Joe McCarthy made another call before she had a chance to telephone Carter Harold, and while he was talking, Sam Taylor came downstairs in his robe.

"You're not dressed," Natty said, surprised. Her father was always dressed for doing things even early in the day. "Is something the matter?"

"Either flu," he said, going to the refrigerator, looking at the contents on the shelves and shutting the door without making a selection, "or else I had too much to drink." He sat down next to Natty.

"I didn't think you ever drank too much."

"Occasionally," he said. "Where's your mother?"

"Sleeping."

"And he's been on the phone all morning?" He nodded toward McCarthy's back.

"Since five. I was here then and he came in and started making calls."

"Wonderful." Sam Taylor rolled his eyes as he tilted his chair against the pantry door.

"Do you want me to get your breakfast?"

He shook his head.

"Juice?"

"No."

"Coffee?"

"No, Natty," he said in mild irritation. "Nothing."

"He is full of accusations this morning," Natty said, indicating McCarthy, who had just left the room. "All about secretaries planted in offices by the Communists."

"He doesn't believe in the threat of the Communist Party any more than I do," he said, opening the morning paper to the editorial page. "He doesn't believe in anything."

"Then why has he made such a fuss about Communism?"

"A lot of reasons, I suppose," he said. "He found an empty

space and filled it. He was the accidental center of a play for power in the government, and we allowed it to happen. We had no more convictions than he does and were moved like reeds in a steady wind." He closed the paper. "It's a dangerous state of mind."

There'd been in Manawa at the time that Sam was growing up an old German cynic called Herr Schmidt by everyone around and ridiculed to his face for his bohemian ways, his tendency to drink. He was John Taylor's drinking companion for years. The story was he'd left his German village and come to America to seek his fortune, leaving his wife and children with the promise that he'd send for them. He'd bought a farm between Grand Chute and Manawa and done very well the first year, too well, and the other farmers around, who'd been there longer, were angry at Herr Schmidt with his strange ways and rich-yielding cows. At the county fair the second spring of Herr Schmidt's farming life in Wisconsin, Amos Tuttle was persuaded by his father to poison Herr Schmidt's cows, lined up in yokes among the dairy cows for the Oshgow County Fair. And the cows produced a poison milk that made the judges temporarily ill and very angry, believing as they had been told by the other farmers around, instigated by Amos Tuttle's father, that the strange Herr Schmidt had given his cows bad feed as a European joke on the judges. Within the year, he'd lost his farm and cows because the people wouldn't buy Herr Schmidt's milk. He had given up bringing his family to America, and word was his wife had taken another husband. He began to spend all his time at the alehouse at the end of town, later with John Taylor when he grew up.

It was a story that his father told Sam Taylor again and again when he was a boy—just the story, never with a reason given for the telling, until the spring he died and no doubt knew he was dying, because he grew philosophical in the last months.

"He ought to have lived the way he talked of living," Sam Taylor's mother used to say of those philosophical meanderings.

But what he told Sam about Herr Schmidt was that all along

he'd known about Amos Tuttle and the poison feed—for Amos Tuttle had told the boys in grammar school that he was put up by his father to do it one spring morning smoking rolled tobacco behind the schoolhouse. So John had known and everybody else and let it go—let Herr Schmidt's cows give poison milk and ruin him.

"You see," John Taylor told his son, "I just let it happen same as if I'd been in the business of poisoning feed myself. So I've always felt an obligation to drink with the poor old Kraut since I've been grown. What good it would do the both of us."

"Do you believe in stuff like that?" Sam had asked. "The devil and all those things that Mother holds to?" He was astonished at this man who had lived his life without regard for order or intrinsic value or any sense of absolute at all.

"Hell, no," he'd said. "Not the devil, at least, except as he runs free in me. But you have to believe in something. In believing, I suppose. It's what brought Herr Schmidt to America to raise his cows—and what we lost in letting them be poisoned."

Sam Taylor looked at Natty lying with her head hidden in her arms and thought to tell her about John Taylor. But no. He wondered if the land had lost its promises. Would she simply smile at him doubtfully and guess he was getting old and sentimental?

When the telephone rang it was Carter Harold again for Natty.

"Join us, please," he asked. "The weather's good. It'll be great fun."

"Terrific," she said, "but I have to be back early."

"No problem," he said. "Did you ask Filip?"

"No," she said.

"I meant to ask him last night at the party," Carter Harold said carefully.

Natty hesitated but didn't give herself away. If he'd been there, if Blanche the Virgin had been there with him, she could imagine with her eyes open worse than they would have done. And she didn't want Carter Harold to know anything.

"Will Barnes can probably bring me," she said.

"Sure," Carter said after a moment. "That'll be okay."

She knew absolutely Will Barnes would bring her, and she was right. He said he'd pick her up at noon. When he hung up the telephone in the long hallway of the Barnes pre-Revolutionary farmhouse he could not believe that Natty Taylor had called him unprovoked and asked him to do something.

"Who was that?" Nell Barnes asked Will when he had hung up.

"Natty," he said, sitting back down at the kitchen table with her, where they'd sat most mornings of his life planning the work to be done and the day ahead. "She asked me to take her to Carter Harold's farm for the afternoon."

Nell raised her eyebrows but didn't comment.

"He's not asking Eliza. Don't worry."

"I'm not worried," she said, pouring her coffee. "If he asked, she wouldn't be allowed to go."

Eliza had been confined to her room since Will had brought her home drunk early Saturday morning. Melvina, who'd been with Secretary Barnes and his mad wife twenty years and twenty with Nell—eight after the Secretary had died—brought Eliza meals on trays three times a day.

"Have you talked to her yet?" Will asked.

"Not yet."

"How long are you going to make her stay in her room?"

"Forever," Nell said and they both laughed, but without humor, since the loss of Eliza, or what had been the child Eliza, was an immeasurable loss to them both. Sometimes, irrationally, Nell thought that if she shut her in her room indefinitely, Eliza's unconditional wildness could be spent in the four protected corners of her yellow-flowered bedroom and Eliza could emerge unspoiled. As it was, there was no memory of the child Eliza at all in the present girl, who threw herself at people without qualification as though she wanted them to swallow her up and be done with it.

Nell Barnes depended on Will for everything, and he had not let her down.

"I thought Natty spent a lot of time with that athlete written up in the *Post* so much," Nell said, careful to be offhand.

"She does," he said.

"I just wondered."

"Wondered what?" Will snapped, suddenly irritated. "She does spend time with him and today she asked me. Big deal."

"That's nice," Nell said, getting up, carrying her cup to the sink. "I like Natty Taylor very much."

Nell liked Natty Taylor too much. Sometimes she imagined that Natty was Eliza. Inevitably she called to mind the fierce independence of a young Nell Barnes and could have been her own daughter. One had a sense Natty would survive without bitterness, as people do who have imagination and can count on it when nothing else is available. In 1946, the year that Will and Eliza's father had died, when Nell was only thirty-four years old, she'd had a heart attack and was told to give up the enormous farm and move in town, which she did not do. She was a reasonable woman and it didn't make sense to live as if she were already dead—only as if she were going to die. And so she rode horses and ran the farm, made steady although limited income from it and had by forty-two, which she now was, survived, with only minor inconvenience, two more mild heart attacks. It would be folly, however, to presume a long life, and so there was in the way Nell lived, the work she did, a certain insistence that every night she go to bed with her bills paid and drawers organized and Will, at least, ready to assume responsibility. Which he could do for the farm and cattle and Eliza and Melvina, but she questioned that he could assume the responsibility for himself.

And so she had a fantasy of Natty Taylor in the wings, like a well-trained understudy who knew her lines and gestures and could assume the role without a hitch.

Nell worried about Will all the time, although she admired him for a certain courage and strong will, a sense of fair play which was, however, threatened by a singlemindedness that made him sometimes fierce and petty, unable to rebound.

He folded up the paper, put it on the radiator by the door.

"Can I take the truck?"

"Take my car, Will."

"The truck is fine."

"Are you going now?"

"Yeah," he said. "I'll be back by ten tonight."

"You're not going to shower?" she asked. "You've been work-ing in the barn."

"So?"

"So you smell of manure."

"What a goddam shame."

"Will," she said softly.

"The smell of a little manure is not going to kill Natty Taylor, now is it, Mom?" And he walked out the door.

She watched him walk up the long hill, jaunty as a cowboy in his long tight jeans, his high boots, windup shoulders swinging side to side—pretending for all the world that he was winning his battles, and she wanted to run out and grab him and bring him back home to his people and tell Natty Taylor he couldn't take her anywhere until she gave up the athlete written up in the *Post*. That was the way she was thinking as the blue truck bumped down the driveway of Twin Oaks farm and turned right to Washington.

When Will was small, other children would torment him to see him rage—farm children, the butcher's son, children far less clever than he. But they learned early that if, for a moment, Will's innate sense of justice was violated he would explode like hard cider cracking a glass bottle, spraying the room with black apples.

Once Tommy Aikens down the road had taken Eliza's red wagon from the front porch, hauled it down the back path to his own porch and parked it there.

"I saw Tommy Aikens take my wagon," Eliza had told Will.

And off he had marched without a word to Nell in spite of Eliza calling after him.

"Tell Mama," she'd called, but he was halfway down the path by then. "Tommy'll beat you to butter if you cross him."

"Butter hell," he'd muttered to himself.

Tommy Aikens and his older fatter brother, Charlie, were sit-ting on the porch playing marbles when Will came down, pointed to the red wagon and said, "It's Liza's. You stole it and I'm taking it back."

"It's mine," Tommy said. "My own papa bought it for me for my birthday."

"Is not!" Will shouted.

"Look at the baby getting all afire," said fat Charlie, who was not brave but talked too much.

"Shut up," Will said.

"You take it and I'll tell Papa."

"G'wan and do it," Will said and in his anger tore the wagon handle from the wagon and fell over on the ground.

"Look at the baby now, Charlie," Tommy Aikens laughed.

And by the time Nell came down, summoned by an angry call from Mrs. Aikens, who muttered, "Such a lot of fuss on one borrowed wagon from a rich boy I never seen," Will had a cut across his brow that took fourteen stitches and eyes as black and puffed as winter plums.

Ellen Taylor was sitting on the chaise in a flowered challis robe reading with the winter sun behind her when Filip came in. She didn't hear him knock. She looked up and he was standing in the middle of her bedroom, still in his coat and boots. Automatically she pulled a cover over her legs and held her robe together at the breast, although it was buttoned to the neck.

"Filip," she fluttered. "I didn't hear you."

"He," Filip nodded in the direction of the first floor, "told me to come up. That you were here."

"Who? Sam?" she asked.

"Senator McCarthy," he said. "He said it would be perfectly all right."

"Of course," she said quietly. "It's just fine. Take off your coat."

Awkwardly Filip took off his coat, lay it across the unmade bed.

"My boots," he said looking at the tracks he'd made when he came in, flushing.

"No bother," she said warmly. "Sit down."

He did sit down at the end of the bed.

"Well, how are you, Filip?" she asked. "Natty said you did well yesterday—that it was a very good game indeed."

"She did?" he asked, surprised. It was Natty he had come to see Ellen Taylor about. When he'd called the Taylors' house at noon to speak with her, Joe McCarthy answered and said she'd gone off to some farm with some cowboy. Will Barnes, he presumed. Rosa had left early for Wisconsin, and Elsa was there to mind Johnny until after supper, so he'd thought of coming to Ellen Taylor to speak with her.

He had liked Ellen Taylor from the start. She was gentler and quieter than Natty, she listened to him as though the things he had to say were the most important things she'd heard said for weeks. She took him seriously, which Rosa with all her Mediterranean fire could not do. He always felt melancholy around her but pleasantly so. He thought she was beautiful.

"Natty's not here now," Ellen Taylor was saying. "She's gone to Carter Harold's farm."

"Senator McCarthy told me."

She looked askance. "Senator McCarthy seems to have the household in tow this morning."

"She went with Will Barnes."

"Yes." She leaned forward, folded the book across her lap. "You haven't had an argument, have you?"

"I don't know."

"You don't know?" She laughed quietly. "Surely, Filip, you know when Natty's cross."

"Well, she's cross," he said. "I just don't know why."

"She's been pensive lately. That I've noticed," Ellen said. "And that's not like her."

"When I came to pick her up last night," Fil said, "she wouldn't come. She didn't seem exactly angry."

"That's not like her either," Ellen said. "Natty's always pleased to have a fight."

"I was wondering," Filip began hesitantly, "if it has to do with my mother and McCarthy."

"With your mother?"

"With the articles she's doing."

"I saw the one on Sam and Joe in Friday's paper."

"I'm sorry."

"It's Sam's fault," she said with surprising bitterness. "He has McCarthy here. It's bound to cause trouble."

"Mother's gone off to Wisconsin this morning for two days to interview people in Manawa and Grand Chute about your husband and Joe McCarthy."

"I didn't know," she said, rolling the corner jacket of her book in tiny balls. "This is all so foolish."

"Anyway, I thought Natty might be angry at that," he said. "You heard about the party at Dick Carr's."

"Sam told me about a dead cat," she said. "Children are barbaric. I have no understanding of them whatever."

Ellen Taylor was jubilant when her daughter met the tailback from St. Albans School. It was the very best that she could hope for Natalia Taylor—that she'd marry the mirror of her time, that he'd be kind and uncomplicated and famous. She'd go to college, of course—someplace close to Filip—and they wouldn't marry until June, after their senior year, and then there would be a wedding in the Great Choir of the cathedral with Purcell on the organ and choirboys and sylphlike girls in picture hats and ribbons and organdy dresses quietly trailing on the marble floor over the Cross of Peace—and Natalia in a European lace mantilla like a dark Spanish princess. There'd be Senators and Congressmen in good standing with the Administration. Maybe the President. She and Sam had gone to Drucie Snyder's wedding in the Great Choir. There'd been candles all along the choir, and Ellen had quickened in anticipation as Drucie Snyder walked down to the main altar although she didn't even know the girl.

She had married Sam Taylor in the office of the justice of the peace in a yellow dress she'd made herself.

She had not told Natty any of this. Natty would say, "Oh, Mother, stop dreaming of things for me that you wanted for yourself."

"But Natty," Ellen would interrupt, "I only want what's best for you."

"I'll elope with someone when I'm thirty or so," she'd say, "and it won't be Filip."

"But what about children?" Ellen would ask as though this were a serious and definite conversation.

"I'll have some after thirty-five," she'd say absolutely. "I read in a magazine that it makes menopause a cinch if you have your babies late," she said. "Or maybe I'll just have dogs."

"You didn't see Mr. Taylor when you came in," Ellen asked Filip.

"Just Senator McCarthy."   .

She got up, wrapped her robe around her.

"I'll be right back," she said. If Sam Taylor's ill-bred, drunken cohorts were going to interfere with Natty's romance with this sweet-voiced football hero, then they could go—Joe McCarthy and Ed Marlowe, the simple-minded fool—and Sam himself. She was angry as she almost never was, her face bright-red with blood as though she were as drunk as they. They had interfered with her dreams.

"Sam," she called, walking through the downstairs hall into the study. "Sam."

Joe McCarthy was on the telephone. He cupped his hand across the receiver and motioned her to wait.

"Just a moment, Alex," he said. "No, no, I want to finish this conversation. I mean right now. Okay . . . okay." He replaced the receiver.

"The bastard," he said.

"Have you seen Samuel?"

"He's gone out to lunch," McCarthy said. "He thought you were sleeping."

"I was reading," she said. "I'm sure he knew that."

"Well." McCarthy shrugged. "He said you were sleeping and asked me to give you this note."

The note said he had gone to the Metropolitan Club for lunch with Ed Marlowe and would be back by five, darling—and that was that. She tore it up.

McCarthy was dialing the phone again. She started to speak to him, but thought better of it.

"Hello, Andrea," he said. "Is your husband there? It's Joe." He slammed his hand against the desk. "No, no, no," he said into the receiver. "Joe McCarthy."

She would leave Sam Taylor, she thought to herself, going up the steps. Pack her small gray suitcase and go to the Mayflower. Take a large room—a suite—and order flowers from Blackmere's and fruit, her meals on trays.

"Can you stay for lunch, Filip?" she asked. "Please. I'd love to have you." She did not want to sound desperate and laughed a tinkling laugh that was intended to sound like a girl's.

"I have to go," he said. "To basketball practice."

"You and Natty will be fine," she said.

"I guess," he replied without conviction.

"Come back, Filip."

"Okay," he said, putting on his coat. "You won't tell Natty I was here."

"Of course not," she said and as he left she called after him, "You will come back, won't you?"

"I'll really try," he said.

When he had left, Ellen Taylor picked up her book and couldn't concentrate on Lucinda's ardent love affair with Antoine de Mer. She thought of her own sons in Manawa and how they'd inherit the shoe store on Apple and Drake and marry fat German farm women. Sometimes she could kill Sam Taylor.

Sam sat with Ed Marlowe and another journalist from the New York *Times* at the Men's Grill in the Metropolitan Club. He had already had too much to drink and they had not ordered lunch.

Ed and the other journalist, a ritualized man from Princeton, were talking about another club in New York where the New York *Times* man went on Sundays and who else went there and how much vodka they put in bloody Marys and what sorts of conversations you might overhear.

There was a fourth man, a young man in his thirties who had come with the man from the *Times*—and sat now next to Sam running his fingers noiselessly over the highball glass. They didn't talk, but Sam had memorized the way the young man looked, his full lips and slender nose, the faint flush to his cheeks, the way his eyes darted in and out of focus like an animal's, the small hands, narrow with long fingers, inadequate for labor. A musty odor about the man, too, not like the showered and cologned men sitting in pressed pants at the other tables, but reminiscent of someone Sam had known well. Sam ordered another drink when the waiter came around, although he never drank at noon. He was unaccountably nervous and presumed it had something to do with the young man sitting next to him.

"Sam," Ed was saying and banged him on the arm.

Sam looked over.

"Where are you, old man?" Ed asked. "The waiter's asked for your order twice."

"Sorry." Sam burrowed in the menu. "Fish," he said. "Trout almondine."

"The wine list, monsieur?"

"Absolutely not," Sam said, and then he tempered. "None for me."

He imagined that the journalist from Princeton had made his assumptions. He had decided Sam Taylor was a farm boy from Wisconsin without presumptions and an incisive but uncultured mind which in future generations would be refined to intellect, but was simply sharp-edged now and capable of action. Although he knew the journalist from Princeton didn't have the imagination for such assumptions, Sam could not help himself. After these years in Washington, a certain kind of Easterner made him conscious of the smell of dairy farms on the bottom of his shoes.

"You've been staring at me," the other man said, conscious that he'd made Sam uncomfortable. "Do I remind you of someone?"

"You do," Sam said, "and I can't remember who."

The man laughed. "I have a common face. My mother's always told me so."

"Quite to the contrary," Sam said. "You have an uncommon face." And then the man laughed very hard, as though to have an uncommon face was as jolly a thing as he could think to have—and Sam laughed with him. He didn't know why.

When Sam Taylor was appointed chairman of the Federal Communications Commission he was among the most respected journalists in the United States. He had risen from cub reporter to editor of the Madison *Sun* in a short time because he was excellent at what he did and worked harder than other people. And he was honest. His editorials were syndicated throughout the country, and he'd had offers to go everywhere, but something in him was afraid to leave Wisconsin. Not afraid that he would fail at what he did in larger places, but afraid that he would succeed and what that would mean. He won the Pulitzer Prize for journalism uncovering a management exploitation of farm labor in Wisconsin, and the attic on Highland Place was full of medals and citations and articles about him. He had a reputation for wit.

But for all his wit, he was often a dark and melancholy man, as seekers after truth are apt to be. People did not know him. Even those who had known him all his life would say one thing about Sam Taylor and then another, just the opposite, and know that both things were true. He gave enormously to other people —to those who needed his gifts of self, never to those who had enough already—but what he gave was given on his own terms. He had relinquished nothing of himself to another human being. Except perhaps to Natty.

No one would have imagined that he was lonely. One expected him capable of having anything he wished to have or do or find or be. He expressed possibilities, and he knew that. He knew that people admired him and imitated him. He knew, too, how little all that meant. In quiet but pervasive ways he often felt a sense of great loss as though he'd died the day before and hadn't come to terms with the stillness of his own body. Then he'd have a longing to fill his kitchen to capacity with gentle drunk men who could not do without him.

He asked the young man next to him to come back for supper on Highland Place. And was embarrassed when the young man refused.

"That's very kind," the man said.

"Never mind," Sam insisted, quick to show recovery. "I often have people on Sundays." Which was true, but he wanted to be certain the young man did not feel chosen.

"We're going back to New York on the late train."

"That's quite all right," Sam said. "Another time."

He got up to go to the men's room and was more drunk than he had expected. The floor rose to meet him and the tables around the room were repeated on the patterned rug.

He raised his hand in greeting to two men whose names he didn't know.

Once inside the men's room he collapsed on the leather chair just inside the door. He wondered if there was a way to lock the door and be alone, but he was too tired to get up.

Later he decided that something in the gestures or the musty odor of that young man from New York reminded him of his father.

"This mare's easy," Carter Harold said, saddling a chestnut horse for Natty.

"It's all right," Natty said. He helped her on.

"Just pull on her lightly and she'll stop on a dime." He held his hands around Natty's and showed her how with a turn of his wrist. "We won't take off."

"I'm really fine," Natty insisted, exhilarated by this moment, by the chance she knew she was taking riding with this group who knew how to ride when she had been told by her family and doctors—"Never," they'd said, "you could not possibly ride without falling."

Even now, just sitting on the brown mare, she felt off balance.

But some sense of danger compelled her, as one is drawn to the edge of high places with an involuntary need to jump, courting death to understand the nature of destruction. To overcome it.

Will rode up alongside her. "Can you grip with your knees?" he asked quietly.

"One knee."

"Well, you'll need two."

"One's all I have."

"I don't like this a bit."

"Listen, Will, I've ridden before," she said. Once at a county fair in Wisconsin. Once on her cousin's farm in Appleton with her uncle holding her in front of him. She gripped with her one strong knee.

"This is stupid," Will whispered.

"Shut up," she said, angry now at the attention, certain she would ride this easy mare.

Anne Lowry was there, legitimate in jodhpurs and boots, a regular hunt jacket and hard hat and leather gloves. And Alexander Epps, sober without charm. The horse that Dick Carr rode was diminished by the length of its rider, who sat slouched from the waist up, still from the waist down, his legs stopping halfway between the ground and the belly of the animal, swinging back and forth like field-hockey sticks.

"He'll fall off before I will," Natty said to Will Barnes. But Will was not amused.

"So," Carter Harold said. "We're off."

"What about the others?"

"Paulette's not coming and Al's sick. I asked Peter."

"He's studying," Anne said.

"So we're all here."

"We'll go up over that hill and through the woods beyond the barn."

Carter rode up the hill between Will and Natty. He asked about her father and her plans for college and her general feelings about Friends School and Fil DeAngelis with diplomatic restraint. He told them about the farm and land use in Loudon County and about the horses. He spoke kindly of Eliza Barnes and said he was concerned about her drinking. He said she was beautiful.

When he cantered ahead to catch Dick Carr, Natty looked at Will for affirmation.

"I like him a lot," she said.

"He's full of shit is what I think," Will said.

"I thought he was really nice."

"If you like rodents, he's a dream."

"Will," Natty said. "You drive me crazy."

"I thought you were smarter than that," Will said. "I always took you for liking the right people."

"Why'd you come, anyway?" Natty asked.

"Why did you come?"

"I wanted to," she said.

In the woods Natty had a sense of confidence, following close on Will's horse, the last in line—the woods closed in around her, snapping its branches across her shoulders, across the flanks of the horse, and it was warmer there than in the open field, nearly comfortable. She began to like riding, the sound of the horse against the wet leaves and the smell of it. The snow was still on the branches sheltered in density from the sun. She began to think that she was good—and to imagine the brown mare jumping across the creeks, over the open fields, to feel it beneath her, under control. She was Royal and forgot the other riders in front of her. Even Will.

Will held his horse back. "Come on," he motioned. She walked her horse up beside him. "We're going out of the woods now," he said, "and they'll want to run for the barn, so hold her in." He pulled on the reins to show how tight they should be. "Give with her mouth," he said, "but don't let go."

She didn't tell him that she knew that already. That she was in control.

The horses came out of the woods one by one and gathered in a bunch.

"There's this hill," Carter said, pointing to the rising field in front of them, "and we can run our horses up, but it peaks with a drop on the other side and the barn's at the bottom, so hold them up there or they'll run for the barn."

Natty rode up ahead with Carter.

"Lean into her going up the hill," he said. "It'll be slow, so you should be all right."

"I know," she said.

"You've ridden?"

"Yes," she said. "Anyway, it feels okay."

"We'll go slow," he said. "Walk if you'd feel better."

Anne Lowry held her horse back until the others had gone off to have the field alone. So she saw Natty fall.

She saw Natty first looking awkward, but sitting her mare, leaning forward on the mare's neck—and wondered at Natty Taylor, why she had to cheerlead and ride horses with that stick leg of hers as if she were trying to prove herself, show up the rest of them for being less than she because they had two perfectly good legs. Her father had always told her to do with what you've got.

When Dick Carr cantered up, going at speed like the Oklahoma cowboy he'd been raised on his father's farm to be, it looked from where Anne was like he cut Natty off and her mare, surprised, reared back and that was how it happened. It even looked as if Dick Carr had been intentional, since a boy raised with horses all his life would know how not to ride straight across the path of a moving horse like that. But Dick claimed he hadn't seen her, that the path was clear when he started at the bottom so Natty must have turned into his path, and Anne Lowry said he was right. She had seen the whole thing. Will Barnes, who disagreed, had not seen what happened since his back was to them both. Natty couldn't account for anything.

Adelaide Taylor was thin as rice paper and crackled when she walked. In the light from the kitchen window she gave a feeling of transparency which was deceptive.

"I been sick years," she said to Rosa, who sat at her kitchen table drinking coffee black as tar. "The cancer," she said. "Fifty years ago I had it first, and lately they took everything." She made cups around her breasts. "These and now my daughter buys me rubber ones in the five-and-dime over at Appleton." She poured herself another cup of coffee, cut up fruit bread and pressed it on Rosa. "I never eat myself," she said. "Ulcers." She put out homemade preserves. "Then a few years back they took my innards." She pressed her gut. "A little here, a little there until there's hardly nothing left of me. But my heart's good." She got up and put some cookies on a plate. "Or bad. Sam would say it's bad." She passed the plate to Rosa. "Eat one. They're not stale. I made them for the church social Tuesday last."

Rosa took one, which had in fact grown hard.

"So," Adelaide Taylor said. "You've come about Sam, have you?"

"I'm doing a story about Sam and Joe McCarthy," Rosa said.

"Joe McCarthy, eh. Well, he's a wonderful man. He's a saint is what he is, and my neighbor down the road says you've done him in down South and the Communists are going to be multiplying like fruit flies. There won't be hardly any land we can call our own, so my neighbor says. They'll be a war and the Russians will take over, but I'll be dead and buried by then."

"Tell me about Sam," Rosa asked. "What kind of child was he when he was small?"

"I have my tombstone already, you know. Next to John's, though I warrant I won't see him there. He and I'll be sent to different places."

"You didn't like John Taylor?"

"I liked him when we were young all right. He cut a figure around town and all the girls were jealous of me catching him. You can ask Daisy Martin down the road. She's still living, you know."

"But you didn't like him later on," Rosa persisted.

"He was a drunk. He was fired for drinking from a laboring job at the factory in Appleton when he was twenty-eight. He had some idea that jobs were beneath him. He was fit for better things, to be a general or President. Nothing sensible." She got up, moved around the room, fussing, rearranging plants, African violets in the window, philodendrons, milk glasses filled with Swedish ivy, figurines on shelves, GOD BLESS OUR HOUSE in brown plastic, a picture of Christ in a gold filigree frame and on the walls, farm prints, artificial oils, dark with age. The kitchen smelled of pine oil. On the sparkling porcelain sink were rubber gloves and Ajax, ammonia, Isodol, liquid soap—a germ-free kitchen, and Rosa could imagine Adelaide Taylor getting up at dawn, cleaning her kitchen to perfection every morning as though a single cup of soup, a piece of toast and coffee the color of earth had sullied it the day before. She was a busy woman and even now spoke to Rosa from the sink, from the small desk full of Hallmark birthday cards with roses, from the broom closet.

"You know one time when he was forty, the year he died, and he had taken up burying the dead—bringing them here to our barn and draining the fluids into the ground . . . it stank for months. Well, Essie Waters died and he carried that dead woman up to the house right here into the kitchen to show me she had two nipples on one of her breasts. Now you can't raise children around a man like that who's more of a child himself than his own."

She sat down. In the gold light from the light-afternoon sun she looked as if the spiderwebs of wrinkles on her cheeks had been drawn there by an artist years before—so perfect were they, so delicately drawn on the surface of the skin, without gullies. "So, it's Sammy you want to know about. Sammy I call him. His father called him Samuel from the Bible—like the Bible ever meant a thing to him except for scorning. You know Sammy well?"

"I don't know him at all," Rosa said. "My son knows his daughter."

"Natalia," the woman said. "She has a crippled leg."

"I didn't know. I've never seen her."

"Even Daisy Martin—the one down the road still living—admitted my legs were good. That I had the finest ankles around. She said it's how I got John Taylor in the first place—him being from an educated family and me worse than the McCarthys. But Daisy said I'd lift my skirts for John Taylor when he came into the dry-goods store in Appleton where I worked. And that did it. He had to see what else there was above the ankles." She reached over, pinched Rosa's arm. "You know what I mean?" she asked. "Well, I should have kept my skirts down and waited around for someone else."

Adelaide Taylor went over to the corner of the room and pulled back a curtain. "There's the toilet, should you be needing it," she said. "Right here in the kitchen so's we could use the same pipes. My brother built this house cheap as possible."

"What was Sam like when he was small?"

"We don't get along. You know that."

"I didn't know."

"I had four. There's a son, the best I had, a marvelous son, handsome as a German prince, who worked so hard it broke my heart and then at twenty, just before he was going to marry, he died. Up and died without a warning. Of germs, the doctor said." She threw her arms open. "Well, you see my kitchen. There's not a germ could live for long in a kitchen like this." She took out some milk and eggs and sugar, measured them in a crockery bowl.

"Cookies," she said, "for the church social, Tuesday."

Rosa guessed that Adelaide Taylor regularly made cookies for the church social and never took them, never went herself.

"And there's Ravilla, who drinks herself, but don't write a thing like that down. It's one thing for a man to be drinking, but another thing entirely for a woman." She whipped the eggs and milk and sugar together, her wire arms whirling. "And it's all John Taylor's doing. And then a sweet son called Paul for my father, and Sam, who was the youngest. We don't get along, you know. If I died tomorrow, he'd come to Manawa for the funeral to weep at his father's grave who's been dead for forty years and died drinking. He'd greet the mourners at the house dry-eyed for me." She narrowed her eyes at Rosa. "What did you say your name was?"

"Rosa."

"Well, Rosa," she said. "If I had it to do again, I'd raise chickens. Egg-laying hens is what I'd raise and leave it at that."

"Why did Sam love his father so much?" Rosa asked, anxious to be done with Adelaide Taylor by dark.

"You're asking the wrong person that," she said. "One thing is John Taylor was Sam's job. I had to do man's work every day to keep us in food and shelter, and Daniel did the cows and kept the grass down, and Ravilla cleaned the house and put up in the summer, and Paul cut the wood and kept the place in shape. Those were the important jobs had to be done and no one around to do them. And then there was John Taylor, mostly drunk, who could fall down and break his neck or burn the house down with his pipe. And I gave that job to Sammy, who was the youngest. From five years old, he'd watch after his father, cover him up if he fell over, sit with him. Do you perm your hair?"

"What?" Rosa asked, looking up from her notes. "Do I what?"

"Perm your hair. I do myself three times a year and dye it as well. Can you tell?"

Rosa said she couldn't tell, that it looked natural, and what else about Sam Taylor and his father.

"Just that. I couldn't stand the man, smelling of liquor and smoke, sitting in the living-room chair like a rag doll, laughing and carrying on like it was some kind of carnival we was living. The Reverend Malcolm at the Lutheran church told me when John died I'd been patient long enough and it was right my trials should be over. But they weren't, you know." She sifted flour with baking powder and salt. "I got the cancer that next month and was back to work in three weeks and that before sick leave so I couldn't be dawdling, mooning about myself."

"So Sam loved his father."

"My brother told me someone had to love John—that God gives every man someone to love him, which, if you ask me, is malarky. Now Reverend Malcolm didn't tell me anything like that. But my brother has the hardening of the arteries, you know." She rolled the dough out on the counter top, cut the cookies in stars. "You should stay for supper."

"I can't," Rosa said, "but thank you."

"I never make supper unless I have a guest. Mary Swander comes by. You know her? I could bake a chicken. Mary's husband brings me one by on Sundays." She put the cookies in the oven, wiped her hands on her apron and sat down. "I know. I know. It's Sam you come about. Not supper." She leaned back in her chair, looked at the window as if she were expecting someone coming down the road. "Sam was with his father all week long before he died, wouldn't go to school or eat or talk to the rest of us—acting like we had done it to John Taylor and what with all he'd done to us. He died like a drunk with Sam Taylor holding his hand. Drowned is what he did. I was at the dry-goods store until six. They'd taken him out by the time I got home and Sam had gone to his room and shut himself in the closet and wouldn't come out. And he was so rude to the Reverend Malcolm at the funeral I wouldn't let him have supper with the family for a week."

The sun was going down, the kitchen cast in shadows, and Rosa wanted to leave. She thought of Filip and the fights they'd lately had and wanted to call him—tell him he could see Natty Taylor as much as he liked. And she was sorry about Angela, too. She'd call them both from the hotel.

"So you won't stay for chicken," the older woman said, watching Rosa put on her coat.

"I need an early start tomorrow," Rosa said, touching the woman on the wrist.

"It's not that I don't like Sammy, you know. Don't write that down in your book," Adelaide Taylor said. "We have our differences."

"I know," Rosa said. "I have children. We have our differences."

"He done well, Sammy," she said, shaking her head, perplexed as if doing well was the most surprising thing of all about Sam Taylor. "Better than the rest of them. You never know," she said.

Rosa leaned over, touched her cheek to the old woman's face, surprised herself at the instinctive gesture to another older mother.

She had hoped to be able to define Samuel Taylor without complications.

"No," she agreed with the woman. "You never know."

The sun had fallen, resting at the edge of the fields, bronze at the horizon, darkening the houses. From a distance, as Rosa drove away, Adelaide Taylor's farm looked like the farm prints in her kitchen—dark with age.

Rosa DeAngelis was the seventh and last child of Filippo and Maria—child of their old age. They were still young by any other standards, but Filippo was a miner in Nesquehonong—western Pennsylvania, in the mountains where the Poles and the Italians and the Czechs lived in clusters, gripped their individual heritage as hungry dogs hold to the gift of a bone stripped of meat. They died young. Especially the men. Filippo died at forty-five of black lung, but he'd been an old man for ten years. Maria resorted then to native dialect which Rosa could not always understand. The other children, grown long before Rosa, moved as far as Harrisburg and were working-class. They expected nothing of Rosa. She fought at grammar school with the Poles and Czechs and would not go to Mass. The teachers said that she was very smart, but she skipped school and hung around the firehouse where the men drank every afternoon. She told outrageous stories full of high excitement which older children told their parents and parents told their smaller children to get them to sleep at night. Early on Maria thought that Rosa would marry Tio Borio two houses down and accompany Maria to her old age, but she never understood Rosa from the start, and so when Rosa left Nesquehonong at fifteen, took a bus to Harrisburg and then to Washington with the money she'd saved working at Tony's Drugs, Maria said it was the will of God and was not surprised.

In Washington, Rosa got a job as a cleaning woman at the *Post*, where she earned a reputation as a storyteller. Every day a new one for the cleaning woman during coffee break, and the janitors heard about her and the newsmen and finally Eugene

Meyer himself, who called her into his office to sit down on a leather chair, and there she was in her cleaning uniform with spots on the apron and smelling strong of lye. She'd been a lovely young girl with dark Mediterranean looks, black eyes set deep and wide, full lips and warm brown skin from generations in the sun. There was a sense of humor in her gestures, and Eugene Meyer liked her. He had a story done about her and the stories that she told which appeared in the Sunday section of the *Post.* Antonio found her that way and married her when she was nineteen at the Roman Catholic church in Nesquehonong with Maria still in mourning black.

Later she began to write stories, first for the *Post* and then as a feature writer for the *News.* She had a natural intuition for making sense of human lives, and that is what she did in stories. She was honest and unsettling, with an untrained intelligence.

The bar at Vine and Main was crowded with children—enormous German families sitting in booths with children pressed like pulp fruit between adults, babies sleeping against their fathers' shoulders. It was light and noisy. Rosa sat alone. She could not get the child Samuel Taylor out of her mind. She wished that she had not come to Wisconsin. The job of retribution belonged to gods.

"You seem to be alone," the man said.

She had not seen him come. He slid into the booth uninvited and smiled at her.

"I know everybody around," he said, "and I never seen you here, so I presume that you must be a stranger."

"I am," Rosa said.

"I'm Bill Wentworth," the man said. He was not memorable except for being very fat. "I own the shoe store around the corner."

"I'm Rosa DeAngelis," she said.

"What are you here for?"

"I'm a reporter."

"Up from Madison?"

"From Washington, D.C."

"Oh," he said, impressed. "What brings you here to Manawa?"

"I've come to do a story on Joe McCarthy and another man."

"McCarthy's still a hero around here, you'll find."

"I have."

"You people down in Washington change your mind on things every minute," he said. "That's the trouble with this country —can't remember what it stands for one minute to the next except farm towns like Manawa and the likes of Manawa."

The waitress came with Rosa's dinner.

"Who's the other story about?"

"A man named Sam Taylor who grew up here."

"I know Sam Taylor."

"How well do you know him?"

The man was thoughtful. "Well," he said. "I suppose no one knows Sam Taylor well. He keeps to himself. But he tells the truth like no man I ever knew. Even as a boy he did, when none of us told the truth if we could help it."

"Does his family ever come back here?"

"His wife does," the man said. "I know his wife real well. Do you know her?"

"Not at all."

"She's a pretty woman with big dreams." He waved across the room at a friend who had called to him. "Fancy dreams." He got up then, pulling his belly out from the narrow booth. "Well, I hope you get a good story, Rosa," he said. "I've been pleased to meet you."

Filip read Johnny "For Esmé—with Love and Squalor," finished it even though Johnny had fallen asleep. He lay on his side in his pajamas, his face against the pillow, and at that angle, with his eyes shut, he looked perfectly normal, and Filip allowed himself to think about Johnny normal, about talking to him late at night when the lights were out, about playing basketball together. Part of the responsibility Filip felt to Rosa and had especially felt when Antonio was alive had to do with his compensation for a half-formed brother. In an Italian family in which the boy matters more, the future depended on him.

Johnny's eyes fluttered when the phone beside his bed rang, but he didn't wake up, and Filip sat beside him while he talked, running his fingers across his forehead. Johnny pressed against him like an animal seeking comfort.

The phone call was from Angela in Cambridge.

"Did Mama call?"

"Not yet," Filip said. "She's in Wisconsin."

"I know. Manawa. She just called me. I couldn't believe it was Mother. 'How are you, Angela?' she said. 'I called the other night and you were out'—but not a word about what I was doing out all night—just I was out and how she missed me and loved me and anything I do is perfectly all right because she has confidence in me. Jesus, Fil, I think she's lost her mind."

"What were you doing Friday night?"

"Out with a boy—you know, the one from Harvard I told you about who plays the drums."

"Did you spend the night with him?"

"I stayed at his house."

"In the same room?"

"Yes, Filip," she said, "but it's not what you think. We even slept in the same bed, but we didn't have sex. You can do that, you know."

"Oh, sure."

"We didn't," she said. "Don't believe me then."

"I don't," Fil said. "Did you try that tale on Mama?"

"She's changed. That's why I called. She's been transformed since Friday night and it gives me the creeps."

Angela was right. When Filip hung up Rosa called and she was melancholy and apologetic.

He covered Johnny with a heavy blanket, opened the window in the corner of the room just a crack and turned out the light.

When the doorbell rang he was at his desk working on trigonometry. He walked across the room to the window that overlooked the porch and looked out to see who had come to ring the bell at ten o'clock on Sunday night. At first he didn't recognize the girl under the hood. But when she turned he could tell by her gestures it was Blanche the Virgin and thought immediately he wouldn't go down. He would pretend that no one was at home or else he was at home and sleeping and Blanche would go away. He watched her for a moment, her arms crossed against the cold, and then he went downstairs to let her in.

It was not a decision. The space of time had been too short for contemplation, and Filip DeAngelis didn't make decisions, was temperamentally unsuited to choice. He simply waited for a choice to advance itself, the leader of a pack, and usually he didn't have to wait at all. Like Blanche at his front door on Sunday night.

When Sam Taylor arrived at Sibley Hospital, Natty was fine. Will Barnes had brought her to the hospital and stood outside the emergency room. The doctor there said she'd had a mild concussion, if that, and strained her back, and that she should be fit the next morning.

"What happened?" Sam asked in the car going home.

"I fell off a horse."

"Why were you riding a horse in the first place?" he asked. "You know better."

She rested her head against the back of the seat.

"You know," she said.

"You'd be perfectly successful as a scholar or a musician, Nat. You do well in school. You play the cello beautifully. Why can't you be satisfied to act on what you have?"

"I could have ridden fine. I got off balance and went too fast," she said.

"Will Barnes said someone made you fall."

"He wants to think that," she said.

Samuel Taylor looked over at his daughter leaning against the back of the seat. Her eyes were closed, but even with her eyes closed her face was set for combat. He wished she could be satisfied with quiet things, with books and music, with studying in her room and going to plays, with conversation, with an imagination which allowed her to endure with humor.

But she was internally organized for risk. She sought it out as she had that afternoon at Carter Harold's farm, almost as though she wished to set his love for her on edge.

"Will seems to like you very much."

"He does," she said. "It drives me crazy."

Like Sam Taylor. She looked out at the houses on Loughboro Road decorated for Christmas, flashing kaleidoscopic across her vision. Sam Taylor's insistent love, the nature of it, made Natty want to ride horses very fast uphill, knowing she was off balance, grateful for the sense of falling, which could at least express in physical fact the balance of her life with her father.

MONDAY, DECEMBER 20
1954

Natty dreamed of wild horses. They charged her sleep, rocking her bed like the long skirt of a tornado, racketing like cymbals in her ears. For hours she slipped crazily in and out of a dream of riderless horses with bodies shaped like bells, moving in unison on slender legs across creeks and over trees and hills, pounding dry ground or rock, shattering the fine pebbles with their horn mallets. And then the sound of them was gone, the thick round form of them was gone and she was left with the clear memory of Sunday afternoon at Carter Harold's farm.

She remembered leaning forward on the brown mare as Carter had told her to do, resting her head against her long neck, the harsh dry mane scratching her cheek, the ground beneath moving in and out of focus as though through the square lens of a camera. She had felt wonderful. Ahead of her she saw Carter Harold at the top of the hill and Will just out of her vision but to her left ahead as well—and she heard Will now in her bedroom as she hadn't remembered hearing him that afternoon. *"Watch out!"* he called. To her right, just in vision, came Dick Carr's mount in a terrible hurry, and the horse roared by like the horses in her dream. *"Jesus Christ!"* she heard Will Barnes again. She slid off the raised back of her greased mare and hit her head hard.

Will must have been right. It was intentional.

She got out of bed in the middle of the night. Outside her bedroom window the Bates' house was dark, the street was dark, except, in the shaft of light, a quiet rain shimmered, abandoned as house dust. She stopped beside her mother's closed door and listened. There was no sound. She put her ear against the door. Irrationally she decided her mother was dead and opened the door quietly, holding her breath, convinced at what she'd find as though her recent knowledge of Dick Carr on Sunday afternoon was sufficient to such repercussions.

But her mother lay propped up by pillows, surrounded by pillows, under her arms and legs and behind her shoulders, a lifeboat of pillows, cushioned for nocturnal disaster—and breathing as a cat breathes, without a sound. She did not stir, and Natty closed the door. Her father's bedroom door was shut, and she didn't stop to listen there. Beyond, at the end of the hall in the room for guests, Joe McCarthy snored like a trumpet.

At the cello she played part of Brahms' Concerto moving the bow through the air in her hand without touching the strings. The air was soundless except in her own head, where the memory of Brahms was nearly equal to the fact of sound. She flung her head back, moved her body with the modulations of a baton and played the whole first movement before she heard the glass break in the kitchen.

Her father was picking up glass from the kitchen floor. He took another glass from the cupboard, poured a drink from the bottle on the kitchen counter and sat down. He was aware that someone else in the house was up besides himself.

"Ellen," he said and without hesitation, "Joe."

Natty stood like a shadow in the dark hallway.

"Is someone there?" he called.

He looked unfamiliar in the slender light, set like an old man. She was disappointed in the way his hair had thinned, his mouth dropped at the corner, as though these were developments since Sunday.

Natty watched him finish the drink and lean back in his chair, satisfied that no one was there. Taking the empty glass, he tossed it across the room into the porcelain bowl of the kitchen sink, where it shattered.

Silently she crept up the front steps.

In the kitchen Sam Taylor ignored the pieces of the second broken glass. He wouldn't have another drink. Already his thoughts separated like oil drops in water. He stood at the kitchen sink and watched the slow and muddy changes in his reflection in the window. Occasionally, he thought, in the backward years, before this one—this month, these last few days—he had believed in dreams.

And now some central bolt had loosened, come unscrewed without proper warning; the machinery continued to operate at predictable speed, but the parts were spinning off.

Just after Sara Granger's casket had fallen off the back of John Taylor's wagon, hitting the ground with such a thud that the earthly remains of Sara Granger herself had popped out of the casket like a jack-in-the-box, just after John Taylor had lost the only decent and thoroughly likable job he'd ever had, burying people—less than a week after all this, he began to drink in earnest, steady, determined, increasing the amount consumed each day, increasing the time for consuming it as though he were in preparation for a contest he was going to win. It was not the first time—but it had about it a different kind of seriousness.

One cold Saturday morning in February at this time, when Adelaide was tearing around the house in her usual temper, getting it fit for company that would never come, and the rest of the Taylor children were busy at their chores, John Taylor took Sam to Appleton on the old milk mare, riding without a saddle, pressed over the flanks, warmed by each other's bodies.

"You won't get drunk now, will you, Papa?"

"I suppose I will, Sammy," the older man said, wrapping his free arm around Sam's belly.

"You won't get so drunk you can't walk out of the bar."

"Not so drunk."

Something in their close proximity, the coldness of the day, his father's inestimable good humor, gave Sam courage.

"Does it taste real good?" he asked. "Is that why you drink it?"

"Most days it tastes terrible." His father laughed. "That's why I drink it."

The bar at Main and Apple was crowded—Herr Schmidt was there, dour as crabapples, and Hilda, the warm-breasted proprietress, and Joe Smythe from the lumber mill—mostly regulars whom Sam had seen other times he'd come with his father and others he'd never seen before, but familiar with their rough Germanic faces, their broad backs straight as trees.

Everyone was glad to see John Taylor. They stopped their talk, clapped him on the shoulder, shook his cold hand. Hilda served him a lager "on the house," she said, and pressed her thick sweet body against him, her bright cheeks against his sallow ones.

"You been away awhile, John," she said.

"Adelaide kept me about the house," he said, "since the burying business fell off."

"There's been no music since you left." She held out her short thick fingers. "I can't play with this arthritis."

"You play for us, John," Herr Schmidt said.

"Lagers for every tune," Hilda laughed.

"I'll play," John said and smiled down at Sammy. "You didn't know I played, did you, Sammy? I used to play like an angel until my own father laughed me out of the house and said piano playing was for women and children on Saturday afternoons."

He moved over to the piano bench and sat down, Sam at his side, Hilda standing by the keyboard. He played and played. Sam had never heard such music before. And people danced, Herr Schmidt with Hilda and the others, and they sang around the piano like church choirs. Once Hilda leaned over the piano unabashed and whispered something in John Taylor's ear. He smiled at her, ran his narrow finger across her breast and kissed her on the lips.

He played serious music then—Beethoven and Chopin and ceremonial Bach from time to time. Hilda brought another lager. As the day darkened, John Taylor played more slowly, missing notes, leaning from time to time against the piano without playing at all.

It was late, nearly supper, before Sam realized that his father was in earnest drunk. The bar had emptied for supper—only Herr Schmidt and Hilda remained—and suddenly John Taylor lunged at Hilda from the piano bench like a spider monkey, grabbing her breasts, kissing her plump neck. Hilda took his hand firmly in her own, helped him to a booth.

"You best be off now, John."

"I'm spending the night with you," he said. "In your bed upstairs."

"Sammy's here, John. Be a sensible man."

He ran at her again, kissing her full-skirted belly. She lifted him up and leaned him against a post.

"Get your father's coat, Sammy," she said, and Herr Schmidt helped her put it on him. John Taylor pressed his lips against her hair, and she moved away so he was kissing air.

"Give me a hand, Herr Schmidt," she said, getting on one side of John Taylor.

They tied him on the horse and lifted Sammy on behind him.

"You'll be all right," Hilda said, handing Sammy the reins, "and your father will sleep."

"I'm sorry," Sammy had said, near tears.

"It has nothing to do with you." The round-faced biscuit of a woman took his face in her hands. "Your father makes beautiful music," she said, "Whatever else."

Adelaide Taylor helped Sammy with John Taylor from the milk mare and carried him into the house.

Two weeks later he was dead in the back room, where they had laid him drunk under a quilt on Saturday afternoon, and Sam, for a reason he honestly could not remember, held himself accountable.

In defense against that loss, he expected everything of himself. And took in drunks.

Upstairs Natty sat on her bed and listened to her mother's ritual rising, the shuffle of soft slippers against the hardwood floors. It was three a.m.

She could not fall asleep, but she wasn't worried, as she knew she ought to be, with dead cats and accidents on horses— obvious intentions. "Natalia, Natalia," she said over and over in her mind until the word was as strange to her as Arabic, like the shadow of her face in the mirror over her bed. She was unfamiliar in her own skin, as though she'd separated from it and was, like a caterpillar, in the process of becoming something else.

When she was small, even last year, everything had made perfect sense. She had an instinct for honesty in the way some people are natural athletes or artists. She had about her a sense of internal order while other girls her age bent supple as bamboo to every possibility.

"I don't worry about Natty because she grew up at six," Ellen had told Sam. "She has learned things about people because of her condition that I don't know."

Sam Taylor was not convinced.

But for years since grammar school, other children wouldn't cross Natty, much as if she were a mad dog and could charge them straightway because she knew their game.

Now this new complication. She wanted people to like her father in spite of Joe McCarthy. She wanted them to like her. She couldn't remember wanting people to like her since she was small and gave her toys away for friendship.

In fourth grade she had given Carter Harold fifty cents and a pack of cigarettes taken from her father's dresser.

They were sitting at the back of the playground, just the two of them, and she had pulled the cigarettes out of her pants pocket.

"You think I smoke?" he asked.

"I don't know," she replied. "I thought you might."

"Probably you'd like to be in our club," he said, taking a cigarette out of the pack, trying it unlit in his mouth.

"I don't care about clubs," she lied.

"Well," he said, "we'll think about it."

Later he whispered to her after math.

"Maybe if you dropped Will Barnes," he said. "We'd consider."

But Natty wasn't going to drop Will Barnes. She loved him and would not hurt him. Besides, she knew if it weren't for people like Will Barnes and Alfie with Down's syndrome and Sean Wright, she could be entirely alone.

Now, if the group insisted, she would consider adjustments for their friendship.

When Natty finally fell asleep, she was thinking of Fil DeAngelis—of calling him first off in the morning to make things right.

The sun shone in a half-circle on Filip DeAngelis' bed, and he lay in its center pleasantly awake but more tired than seemed reasonable. He felt impossibly good. Sometime in the middle of the night Blanche had left, whispered to him she was going or she'd be in trouble, kissed him soft as flower petals on the forehead—and he had stretched out to fill the place she'd left, which was warm beneath him now as her body had been. They had made love. Angela was absolutely wrong. You couldn't sleep with someone in the same bed and not make love. He wondered if Angela had done the things that Blanche had done to him. He could not imagine anything specific of Angela.

Blanche had kissed him everywhere, with lips more gentle than Rosa's hands had been when he was a child and couldn't fall asleep—kissed him places he had never thought of being kissed, and he thought he had imagined everything possible. She had lain next to him without clothes—a body soft and pale with gentle mounds of flesh around the hips and thighs, between the legs, and breasts like pillows. He wanted to consume her. He placed his face between her breasts and let them fall against his cheeks.

Now he rolled over in the sun center of his bed and closed his eyes. He would have lain there forever if Rosa hadn't called just after seven to remind him that he was having lunch with the coach from Dartmouth at one.

"Last night I talked to Angela. We thought you'd changed. She said you'd never been so reasonable about things."

"People don't change, Filip," Rosa said. "They make believe they have from time to time."

When the phone rang again Filip was sitting on the end of his bed. It rang four times before he got up and decided to answer it on the chance that it was Blanche.

"Filip."

"Yeah."

"It's Natty."

"Listen, Nat," he said impatiently, but the impatience was with himself for betraying Natty with Blanche. Now he wanted to justify it and find the blame in her.

"Yesterday this odd thing happened," she went on, ignoring his brusqueness with her. "I went riding at Carter Harold's farm and got thrown."

"Are you okay?"

"It wasn't an accident."

"What do you mean?"

"It just wasn't an accident," she said. "Dick Carr cut my horse off—maybe as a joke."

"He's like that," Fil said. "He doesn't like to lose."

"But there wasn't anything to lose," she said. "It wasn't a match."

He heard the insistence in her voice and knew that she wanted something from him he couldn't give her or didn't want to give her, confused by these new feelings about Blanche. She reminded him of Rosa, always countering her strong reasonable mind with a need to be loved absolutely.

"In yesterday's game Dick fouled me in a dirty play which almost no one saw," Fil said. "You know that."

She ignored him.

"Could I see you after lunch?" she said.

"I'll call."

"Are you sure you're not mad?"

"Yeah. I'm just tired. I had a bad night with Johnny."

In his mother's desk he looked around for stationery. He found a box of perfumed paper with roses in the corner which had never been opened. He took out four pieces.

After several false starts he wrote, "Dearest Blanche, I am happier this morning than I have ever been in my life."

He sat for a long time wondering what else to say. He took out the Washington phone book to look up her address and realized with some surprise that he didn't know her last name. Blanche the Virgin was all he knew. Well, he'd change that. "I have never known a girl more beautiful," he wrote, "or more gentle or more sweet."

Filip's high sense of himself required that he grace their sexual love and Blanche with dignity.

Had Antonio been alive to allow him the licenses of young Italian boys, had Filip not become a myth, expected by adults to maintain unreasonable standards, had he not been confused by the attention, it wouldn't have been necessary; but as it was, he had to sanctify his desire for Blanche in order to maintain his self-esteem, which was less intrinsic than bestowed like garlands from the crowd.

The telephone rang again after Elsa had come to care for Johnny. This time he was certain it was Blanche.

"Hello?" he said.

"Hello, Filip?"

It was not Blanche.

"This is Ellen Taylor."

"Yes," he said, exposed, as though she could see from her bedroom on Highland Place the letter he was writing, rose-perfumed, to Blanche.

"I'm sorry to bother you on your vacation," she said.

"S'all right."

"Natty's still asleep." Ellen Taylor laughed awkwardly. "I hope I didn't wake you up."

"S'all right," he said again. "Mother's already called from Wisconsin this morning."

"Oh," she said brightly, "it's your mother I called about. I wanted to talk to her. Something's come up. Do you know where she's staying?"

"The Drake Hotel in Manawa."

"Oh, yes, the Drake," she said. "I know the Drake."

Filip gave her the number.

"Oh, good," she said, full of breath. "Natty. Filip? Natty's here. Do you want to talk to her?"

"I did already today," he said.

"I see. I didn't know."

"I meant to tell you she wasn't asleep. I mean she called a while ago."

"So you don't want to talk with her."

"I mean it's okay," he started, betrayed by his own voice.

"Well, thank you, Filip."

"See you later," he said.

The letter he had written to Blanche was all wrong. He did not even read it over, tore it instead in small pieces and threw it in the wastebasket.

"Why were you talking to Filip?" Natty snapped.

"I needed to find his mother," Ellen said.

"For what reason?"

"About the article, Nat," Ellen said. "Honestly, I wouldn't intrude."

"It's intruding to call Filip."

"I won't again," she said, apologetic.

She left her mother's bedroom and shut the door behind her.

Natty sat on the top step of the stairs. She was losing Filip. She felt it as though it were as specific as bodily change. Without him she was susceptible. The image people had of Filip, if not Filip himself, had protected her.

Ellen waited until she heard Natty go down the back steps to the kitchen, and then she dialed the long distance operator.

THE SAMUEL TAYLORS OF WISCONSIN
BY ROSA DEANGELIS

Samuel Taylor is a small-boned, olive-skinned man with devilish Celtic eyes reminiscent of his Welsh mining forebears. He is quiet and self-contained, known for his acerbic wit, occasional flair of temper and above all for absolute integrity rare in this town. His words are generally measured, his thoughts exceedingly rational, his decisions a mark of fair play. He is by all appearances not the sort of man to take in the censured Senator Joseph McCarthy in the midst of a downward plunge.

Or is he?

Several paradoxes have been noted by this reporter in the last few weeks which bear examination if Samuel Taylor is to continue to represent the FCC in its top post.

1. He takes in drunks. Any observer may note one or two inebriated men arriving at the Honorable Sam Taylor's house in Cleveland Park on any given evening.

2. Mrs. Taylor spends most of the day in her robe and has been seen late in the afternoon on the porch in her robe talking to neighbors. There is no word that she has been ill. She does not attend public functions.

3. Several colleagues questioned about Sam Taylor say that they do not know him well at all, that he is secretive about himself.

4. Ed Marlowe, a reporter fired from several newspaper jobs for reasons not disclosed, is on Sam Taylor's private payroll.

5. Joe McCarthy and Sam Taylor knew each other as children. McCarthy is responsible for Sam Taylor's appointment as chairman of the FCC.

In the next several articles, written from Samuel Taylor's hometown in Wisconsin, I will be exploring these questions.

Joe McCarthy took a scissors from Sam Taylor's desk and carefully cut the article out. On a piece of paper he wrote, "More Bullshit," and clipped it to the top of the article.

Later Sam Taylor said the *News* was irresponsible journalism and should be ignored.

The *News* had omitted mention of Father James O'Flannigan —Sam Taylor's uncle on his Catholic mother's side, the priest of St. Vincent's Appleton, who taught the young Joe McCarthy what he knew of getting by when he was less than ten years old, poor, in trouble half the time and bad in school. He taught him you could do anything in the name of Christ and get by beautifully.

Once when Joe had mentioned Father James to Sam Taylor, Sam had said his Uncle James had done more to ruin human souls in the name of good than the devil himself with a troop of deputy assistants could do.

Father James was the most powerful man in Appleton and thereabouts. He knew the secrets of half the population. ("Bless me father for I have sinned"—young Joe McCarthy always named the minor sins like stealing milk from the larder or creeping out of the house after dark—never killing cats. That he listed nameless under "all my other sins.") And Father James used this knowledge in particular ways. He got free meals and packages of gifts at holidays and friendships granted in fear. The town would allow him anything, and when it came out that he, a priest and celibate, was carrying on with Al McGaffrey's wife, he said it was a terrible shame about Al McGaffrey's wife and the fate of lustful acts that Al McGaffrey left her with all those children and not a cent and she never breathed a word about what really happened for fear of worse. For fear of God. That was the kind of power he had.

"James O'Flannigan never believed in God for a moment or the Catholic Church," Sam Taylor had said.

"He was a priest," Joe McCarthy said.

"Some priest," Sam replied. "He believed in James O'Flannigan."

But Father James did fine. The people worshiped him like God himself and they turned out weeping in the middle of winter when he died.

He taught Joe McCarthy that a poor boy, full of secrets, could survive without a hitch.

And now Rosa DeAngelis, the widow of the hook-nosed Communist from the FTC, uncovering secrets in Grand Chute.

ss from
nsibility
knowing

ly. Or at
had told.
. He had
d out the
what he

ate in si-

up.
They have

e night for

e every pos-

nave a thing to tell her. The people in
he people in Appleton had loved Father

said to Sam Taylor when he came in.
day and better go on back tonight to
."

here," Sam said. "You can have my
r'd like to stay again, just come."

from the corner of Sam's desk and
e Christmas spirit from the *News*,"

where Natty was cooking break-

....d.

At m....... Natty. Joe McCarthy's gone."

"He won't be back tonight?" she asked.

"He says he's going home."

"Maybe we'll make it through till Christmas after all." She put boiled eggs on the table, poured two orange juices.

"You're reading an article," she said, surprised.

He looked up.

"You told me you never read that kind of thing," she said. "Or obituaries."

"I guess I did." He put the article down. "How is your head this morning?"

"Fine," she said. "I must have been knocked out, but it was just for a second."

"Do you remember what happened yesterday?"

"I fell off a horse," she said.

"I know that," he said. "But are you sure it was an accident? Will Barnes—"

"I know about Will Barnes," she said. "I'm positive it was an accident," she lied. There was, she thought, no point in going into what she knew about the accident at Carter Harold's farm.

But this was an intentional lie she realized, sitting acro
her father, watching his face for signs. Now a new respo
—lying to her father mechanically to keep him from
what was going on with her.

For his part, Sam Taylor did not believe Natty entire
least he knew there was more of a story to tell than she
But this morning he knew all that he wanted to know
made it his business as a journalist and in his life to fi
truth about things as best he could. Now, for fear o
might discover, he dismissed his concerns for Natty.

He set the article down beside his plate, and they
lence. When Natty had finished she picked the clipping

"I see someone's staked out the house," she said.
Mother in a bathrobe."

"We ought to put on a circus in the middle of th
their entertainment."

"As long as Senator McCarthy's around we hav
sibility."

She turned the article upside down without reading it.

"Are you seeing Fil today?" Sam Taylor asked.

"Dunno," she replied. "He probably hates me."

"Permanently?"

"He didn't say." She didn't want him to know what was
happening with Filip.

As Sam Taylor left the kitchen in his overcoat, the newspaper
rolled under his arm, he asked, "Does this have anything to do
with the business with McCarthy now that Fil's mother is in
Wisconsin uncovering my past?"

"Maybe." She shrugged. "But it shouldn't. McCarthy hasn't
anything to do with me."

When he kissed her she turned her head away automatically.
His breath still smelled of whiskey from the middle of the night
before.

Will Barnes had finished feeding the horses by dawn and was
sitting in the kitchen drinking coffee when Eliza crept in fully
dressed.

His relations wouldn't have a thing to tell her. The people in Wisconsin loved him as the people in Appleton had loved Father James.

"I'm leaving now," Joe said to Sam Taylor when he came in. "I'll be down on the Hill all day and better go on back tonight to get the house ready for Jean."

"You're welcome to come here," Sam said. "You can have my house key, and if you find you'd like to stay again, just come."

McCarthy took the article from the corner of Sam's desk and handed it to him. "More of the Christmas spirit from the *News*," he said.

Sam took it to the kitchen, where Natty was cooking breakfast.

"What's that?" she asked.

"Another article."

The front door slammed.

"Mother?" Natty said.

"At nine? No, Natty. Joe McCarthy's gone."

"He won't be back tonight?" she asked.

"He says he's going home."

"Maybe we'll make it through till Christmas after all." She put boiled eggs on the table, poured two orange juices.

"You're reading an article," she said, surprised.

He looked up.

"You told me you never read that kind of thing," she said. "Or obituaries."

"I guess I did." He put the article down. "How is your head this morning?"

"Fine," she said. "I must have been knocked out, but it was just for a second."

"Do you remember what happened yesterday?"

"I fell off a horse," she said.

"I know that," he said. "But are you sure it was an accident? Will Barnes—"

"I know about Will Barnes," she said. "I'm positive it was an accident," she lied. There was, she thought, no point in going into what she knew about the accident at Carter Harold's farm.

But this was an intentional lie she realized, sitting across from her father, watching his face for signs. Now a new responsibility —lying to her father mechanically to keep him from knowing what was going on with her.

For his part, Sam Taylor did not believe Natty entirely. Or at least he knew there was more of a story to tell than she had told. But this morning he knew all that he wanted to know. He had made it his business as a journalist and in his life to find out the truth about things as best he could. Now, for fear of what he might discover, he dismissed his concerns for Natty.

He set the article down beside his plate, and they ate in silence. When Natty had finished she picked the clipping up.

"I see someone's staked out the house," she said. "They have Mother in a bathrobe."

"We ought to put on a circus in the middle of the night for their entertainment."

"As long as Senator McCarthy's around we have every possibility."

She turned the article upside down without reading it.

"Are you seeing Fil today?" Sam Taylor asked.

"Dunno," she replied. "He probably hates me."

"Permanently?"

"He didn't say." She didn't want him to know what was happening with Filip.

As Sam Taylor left the kitchen in his overcoat, the newspaper rolled under his arm, he asked, "Does this have anything to do with the business with McCarthy now that Fil's mother is in Wisconsin uncovering my past?"

"Maybe." She shrugged. "But it shouldn't. McCarthy hasn't anything to do with me."

When he kissed her she turned her head away automatically. His breath still smelled of whiskey from the middle of the night before.

Will Barnes had finished feeding the horses by dawn and was sitting in the kitchen drinking coffee when Eliza crept in fully dressed.

"Is Mom up?" she asked.

"Probably," he said. "Are you free today?"

"I'm either free or I'm leaving home."

"Swell," Will said. "Pack up and I'll drive you to the city."

"Are you going in town?"

"Yeah." He took eggs out of the refrigerator and scrambled some for Eliza and himself.

"I can't eat," she said.

"You have to," he said. "You'll disappear."

She picked at breakfast.

"It's only six-thirty," she said. "Mom's still in bed probably. Why're you going to town?"

"To beat Dick Carr to chickenshit," he said.

"Oh, yeah?" Eliza pushed her plate away. "Four of you would fit in Dick Carr's trousers."

"Maybe so," Will said, "but angry I could kill him."

Eliza looked at him across the table, his hard Western jaw, his narrow lips drawn like string across his face, the way his eyes were set, and knew without admitting it to Will that angry he could do anything.

"So what's the matter with Dick Carr?"

"Did Mom tell you about Natty Taylor last night?"

"Nope," Eliza said. "Mom hasn't spoken to me for two days. It's a terrific new trick she's discovered."

"Well, yesterday we all went riding at Carter Harold's."

"Who was Carter with?"

"Nobody, Liza."

"Good."

"Natty invited me," Will said, hesitant, but anxious that his sister know he'd been selected.

"First choice over the superjock?"

"I don't know. She didn't exactly say, 'I asked Fil first and he turned me down so you're the only one around.'" He cleared his plate. "Anyway, she got thrown."

"No kidding."

"It wasn't an accident," he said. "Dick Carr cut her off and made the mare rear up."

"You're sure?"

137

"I didn't see it," Will said. "But I'm sure. Dick Carr's been raised on horses—he's half a horse himself. He simply wouldn't have that kind of accident." He poured a cup of coffee for Eliza. "There's something going on, isn't there?"

"You mean with Natty?"

"I mean with Carter Harold and Carr and a bunch of others," he said. "I get the feeling they're out to get her."

"You may be right," Eliza said. "I know something is up."

"Do you know what?"

"I honestly don't."

"You'd tell me if you did."

"Probably," Eliza said. "Carter and I don't talk much."

"So I've noticed."

Will met his mother coming down the stairs.

"I'm going to town," he said. "Can I have the truck?"

"At seven in the morning on your vacation?"

"Yes," he said. "There's something I need to get at school."

"Such conscientious behavior." Nell raised her eyebrows at him. "Is Eliza down?" she asked.

"Yes."

"Dressed?"

He nodded.

"Running away from home?"

"Maybe." He shrugged. "Talk to her."

Nell went in the kitchen, put her hands on Eliza's shoulders, kissed her forehead. Eliza pulled away.

"Lizey," Nell said sadly.

"You expect me to be full of love when you've locked me in my room for days. Sent in the maid with food like I'm some kind of bitch in heat."

"That's a fair description of how you've been acting."

"Shut up," Eliza said. "You haven't a clue how I've been acting. Spending all your time with your chickens and horses and your dead husband's memoirs, immortalizing skeletons."

"Liza."

"You've never given shit for me, just wonderful Will."

"I haven't known what to do with you, Eliza," Nell said. "One day you were a beautiful wild flower and the next you were simply wild out of my control." Nell reached over to take Eliza's hand. "Help me," she said quietly.

"I don't know," Eliza said. "I hate myself."

Nell drew her daughter, resisting, stiff as butcher paper, to her, held her against her breasts, and suddenly Eliza relaxed against her mother. "Sometimes I think you'd rather have someone like Natty Taylor for a daughter," she said.

"I'm leaving, Mom," Will called. "I'll be back by lunch."

Nell and Eliza watched Will pull off in the pickup truck.

"What did he leave at school?" Nell asked.

"He's going to town to see Dick Carr," Eliza replied. "He's going to beat Dick Carr to chickenshit for what he did to Natty Taylor."

"Oh Lord," Nell said, pouring coffee for herself.

"He won't."

"You never know with Will exactly what he'll do," Nell said.

Dick Carr was dreaming of doing things to Natty Taylor. She lay spread-eagled and naked on the floor beneath him, her black hair strung in disarray across her face, and first he kissed her with his tongue thrust as far back in her throat as it could go, losing himself in her hair—then Natty was a plucked and pimpled roasting chicken upside down, her legs spread open and bent, the center of her between her legs removed of parts. And he swooped down into the hollow center, pressing with all his might, and then, still erect, he mounted her and lifted her with his erection, throttling her again and again against the wall until she was unconscious and he could enter her soft white body without interruption.

All in pleasured half-sleep when the front door bell rang.

"You want coffee," Dick Carr asked Will after the initial accusations.

"No," Will replied, still standing in the kitchen where he'd come first off, still in his overcoat.

"It was clearly an accident," Dick said, pouring himself coffee, sitting down at the kitchen table. "What more can I say?"

"I don't believe you."

"Listen, man." Dick leaned back, assumed a kindly expression he'd learned from his father in difficult situations. "There's nothing I can say to you but the truth as I see it. I looked ahead, saw nothing and galloped up the hill with my head down. Right?"

"Bullshit."

The doorbell rang, and Carter Harold came in. Dick Carr raised his eyebrows and nodded in the direction of Will Barnes, standing in the kitchen in his overcoat.

"Hey," Carter said enthusiastically. "How're you doing?"

"That was a put-up job yesterday," Will said. "Natty's being thrown."

"Listen, Will," Carter said reasonably. "I know you think it was. You said so at the time. But as far as I know, as far as Dick knows, it was one of those accidents, and Anne Lowry saw the whole thing. We can count on her." He ruffled his brow. "Of course we shouldn't have let Natty ride in the first place."

"Yeah," Will said. "Try to keep Natty from anything."

"That's just the point," Carter said with absolute sincerity. "I shouldn't have planned a ride with Natty coming."

"Want some coffee?" Dick handed a cup to Carter Harold. "You're sure you don't want some, Will?"

"No," he said. "I mean, yes, I'll have some." He sat down in a chair, confused. He didn't believe them; nevertheless, they had made him feel as if he had an imagination fit for destruction, especially Carter.

"So I'm really sorry about the horse," Carter went on. "It was stupid of me. I called the Taylors this morning and Mrs. Taylor said that Natty was okay."

"She could've been killed," Will said.

Just as the grandfather clock in the hall was striking nine o'clock, Natty called and Dick Carr answered in the middle of the first ring.

She called to ask him to a party Christmas Eve after her cello concert at the cathedral. And Carter Harold, too, if he was there.

"Yes, he's here," Dick said, "and so is Will Barnes."

"Will Barnes is at your house?"

"Right here," Dick said. "Want to talk to him?"

"What are you doing there?" she asked Will Barnes.

"Visiting friends," he said. "What about you?"

"I'm having a party," she said.

"For horned toads?"

"No, a regular party for regular people after the Christmas Eve service at the cathedral."

"A masquerade?"

"What?"

"I'll come as the villain's assistant."

"Oh, shut up, Will," she said. "You believe the worst of everybody."

"With good reason," Will said and hung up. He put on his overcoat, wrapped his scarf around his neck.

"Is it really a masquerade?" Dick asked. "On Christmas Eve?"

"Yeah," Will replied, "but you don't have to come in costume."

"I forgot to ask about Eliza," Carter said. "How is she?"

"Swell," Will said.

"Give her my love," he said pleasantly.

As Will went out he noticed there was cat hair on the fine china Christmas wreath hanging on the Carrs' front door. It glistened in the morning sun like fresh snow.

"Well, my God," Carter Harold said, sitting across the kitchen table from Dick Carr. "So Natty Taylor's inviting us all to a party Christmas Eve." He opened the newspaper on the kitchen chair.

"She likes us," Dick Carr said.

"Of course she does."

He pushed the newspaper across the table at Dick Carr. "Did you see the article today?"

Dick picked up the paper and read it. Carter looked across the table confidentially.

"Did you cut Natty's horse off intentionally?"

Dick Carr smiled.

"Well?"

He shrugged, folded the paper in half.

"I've been riding all my life," he said, unable to keep the

excitement out of his voice. "I knew how to ride before I knew how to walk."

"So." Carter Harold slapped his open palm on the table. "Jesus Christ," he said. "I honestly thought it was a freak accident." Until that moment he had not understood exactly Dick Carr's possibilities.

"Well," he said, with new respect. "I'll be damned."

Natty practiced Beethoven sonatas all morning but without enthusiasm, sometimes losing her place and starting over again, sleeping in the hot sun shaft from the eastern window. Mostly she thought about the party after her concert and who would be included. Her friends mainly from Dick Carr's last week. Will, of course. Filip maybe. She'd wear her hair up and a long taffeta skirt.

Ellen Taylor reached Rosa at the Drake Hotel just before she left to visit Sam's sister Ravilla.

"This is Ellen Taylor," she said. "Mrs. DeAngelis?"

"Yes," Rosa replied. "Is anything the matter?"

"Well," she began methodically.

"With Filip?"

"With Filip?" she said, confused.

"I talked with him this morning," Rosa said. "Nothing was the matter then."

"Oh," Ellen said. "I understand. No, no, Filip is fine. I talked with him a moment ago to get your number. It's about Senator McCarthy that I'm calling." It had nothing to do with Joe McCarthy, but only with the ways in which he had interfered with the relationship between Filip and Natty and Ellen Taylor's dreams for it.

"Yes."

"I'm terribly sorry," Ellen said quietly.

"Yes?"

"I'm just terribly sorry about the whole situation."

There was an awkward silence. "I see," Rosa murmured, and then, understanding, she thought, why the other woman had called, that common knowledge between women of familiar fears and hesitations, as Ellen had understood her mention of Filip, Rosa said, "I'm sorry, too," and on a lighter note, "I see your sister-in-law today."

"Ravilla." Ellen laughed. "You'll find her quite eccentric," she said. "And probably drunk."

The house where Ravilla Taylor lived was a perfectly ordinary wood-frame house in disarray from the outside. Chickens roamed the front porch, pecking for feed beneath the snow blown there by a steady wind across the fields. A goat was eating a sheet hung on the line, and two matching mongrel dogs lifted their heads momentarily as Rosa walked up the front steps. Then the front door flew open, jet-propelled, and there was Ravilla Taylor in a wide-brimmed hat with streamers and a summer dress from her grandmother's trousseau, handmade in yellowed lace with a flounce at the back and a waist the span of her fingers.

"Hello, Rosa," she said, grabbing her by the arm, swinging her into the house. "Welcome," she said. "Come in immediately or you'll die of the cold."

Another mongrel dog, matching exactly the ones on the front porch, lay on a velvet couch in a living room cluttered with sculpture wildly painted in deep purples and rose, hothouse pink —and chairs, strangely conical in shape, like inverted cups. In the corner of the room was a donkey or an ass—something smaller than a horse, but similar—who looked at Rosa straight on.

"Rufus," Ravilla said, nodding toward the donkey. "He hates the winter," she said. "You call me Belle. Mother called me Ravilla after the minister's daughter, hoping for favors, but I call myself Belle."

She sat Rosa down on a velvet couch next to the dog, and she pulled up an inverted cup across from Rosa.

"Furniture," she said, throwing her arms about the room, indicating the sculpture, which from the vantage of sitting with Rufus out of peripheral vision seemed quite agreeable. "Whatever Mother says, I'm fundamentally utilitarian." She took off her hat with streamers and laid it carefully on the floor beside her. "I wanted to be an actress, but Mother said no, absolutely no. Only women of ill repute and fools are actresses and I should stay in Manawa and marry and be a schoolteacher. Can you imagine?"

Rosa could not imagine.

"They all laughed at me like they laughed at my poor father and his piano. Did Mother tell you that?"

"About your father's piano?"

"He was a wonderful musician," Ravilla said. "I'm sure she didn't tell you that. She probably told you he dropped Sara Granger's corpse off the back of the wagon. Mother is crazy about tragedy. And that he drank." She leaned forward and Rosa could see in the deeply wrinkled face, the haunted Welsh eyes, the ghost of a beautiful child. "I drink too," she said.

"I was told that."

"That I drink all the time?"

"Well . . ."

"But," Ravilla said, holding up her hand for silence, "I take perfectly good care of myself, which my father didn't. Will you stay for lunch?"

"You are kind," Rosa said. "But I have a lot to do. Let's see how far we get."

"I put up soups and fruits," she said. "Boring, putting up. And I paint. I've never sold a thing. Not in Manawa. Do you like soup?"

Rosa nodded, although she suspected botulism, imagining Ravilla in her grandmother's trousseau, lavender paint still wet between her fingers, forgetting to boil the canning jars. Already she was thinking of excuses.

"We'll have some soup," she said. "So you've come about Sammy and Joe McCarthy. Mother rang up this morning. She said you were Jewish."

"Italian."

"One and the same. Mother only knows Catholics."

"I am Catholic," Rosa said.

"German Catholics," she said. "They aren't a bit of fun," she said. "I can't tell you much about Sammy."

"What do you remember?"

"Absolutely nothing," Ravilla said. "He took care of my father. That was his job. I was very busy with boys in town at the time," she said. "I had a reputation."

"For bad behavior?"

"For," she stretched her arms, turned her wrists up, examined her slender fingers, "perfectly normal but unacceptable small-town Midwestern behavior in 1918." From a small velvet purse attached to a chain around her waist she pulled a flask and laid it on her lap as if it were a challenge. "Would you like tea?" she asked.

"No," Rosa shook her head, "thank you. I want to know what you remember about Joe McCarthy."

"I remember Joe McCarthy well," Ravilla said. "I was going to be married to Andrew Burden, whose father was a doctor and very respectable, so Mother thought it was wonderful and made me an elegant dress and spoke to me of God and purity and germs—Mother's particular favorites at the time. Even I was happy, since I knew it was likely I'd never get to New York. And then the war came. Andrew Burden went away a hero and returned a corpse. So Mother packed the gown in mothballs and told me to maintain my virginity or no man would have me." She got up and motioned to Rosa, who, with Rufus, followed her to the kitchen.

"I'm famished," she said. "And I was past twenty and not a virgin as was well known and drinking then. I moved in this house with my grandmother, who died immediately, and Joe McCarthy courted me in this living room. He was sixteen years old and I didn't much like him, but there he was and Andrew Burden gone. So. Soup!" She produced a jar from the cupboard. "I suppose you're wondering about Rufus."

"Rufus?"

"He's trained," she said. "He goes outside. See?" She opened the back door. Rufus turned his head, looked at her quizzically and didn't move. "He doesn't need to go now," she said, lifting the top off the jar of soup. "That's what he told me." She smiled

145

at Rosa. "You're worried, aren't you?" she said. "You've heard
I'm crazy and put up bad soup and drink too much." From the
refrigerator she pulled a loaf of bread. "Herb bread," she said.
"Homemade. I baked it last night when Mama rang up to say
you'd be coming." She pulled off a piece and handed it to Rosa.
"There's nothing you can do to ruin bread."

"It smells very good."

She set the table with linen napkins and china.

"No one ever comes," she said. "This is an occasion."

"You were saying about Joe McCarthy."

"I was saying he was impotent," she said. "But don't write that
in your paper." She put the bread in the oven, put on the fire
under the soup. "It's not a fair thing to talk about no matter
what worth you give a man, and I give that man nothing." She
put two stemmed glasses on the table. "Wine," she said. "I have
some hidden away for royal moments." She pulled a chair for
Rosa. "Sit down," she said. "So I was glad to be Joe McCarthy's
lover for a time. I had no scruples about that, and I was plenty
lonely after they buried my chances with Andrew Burden. But
Joey couldn't do it for the life of him. And we tried everything.
One time I danced naked to the gramophone with candles lit in
the bedroom. Nothing. Poor old Joey. It made him so mad of
course he said it was my fault and told everyone around that he
had done it to me and about the candles. Oh, well. Mama said it
was for a bad reputation no one would marry me. But I think I
wasn't meant to be married. Not in Manawa, Wisconsin, at least.
Maybe in New York."

Rosa ate lunch, forgetting the botulism, caught by the odd
charm of this lonely woman as though she'd been invited to a
private opening of a one-woman show. Only later back at the
hotel did she remember the poisoned soup and lie on the bed
waiting for the pains and think about calling Filip to talk to him
just in case. But then he was with the coach from Dartmouth and the wine from lunch put her to painless sleep.

"But it's really Sammy you've come about," Ravilla said.

"I'm writing articles about your brother as a boy and his relationship with Joe McCarthy."

"They were never friends," Ravilla said. "Joey and my other brother, PDQ, were friends. Sam never approved of Joe at all. Or PDQ for that matter. Only at one time Sammy and I were very close. We knew things about the other without talking. But when my father died, Sam turned black and didn't have the time of day for me. I don't know what it was," she said. "We were my father's children, Sammy and me. I was like him and Sammy loved him. It was something more than our father dying. Even Mother, who hasn't a sharp eye for matters of the heart, says there was something to my father's death the rest of us don't know that turned Sammy in on himself like a snail." She leaned over to Rosa. "Does he mention me ever?"

"Sam Taylor?"

She nodded.

"I don't know Sam Taylor."

"You don't know him and here I am telling you private things as though you love him." She threw up her hands. "You probably hate him. For all I know the articles you're writing could hurt him."

"No," Rosa said. "I understand how you feel about your brother. I wouldn't intrude."

"I don't cash the checks he sends me," she said. "I live simply and take in sewing and laundry." Then she smiled with a distant memory. "He's done very well, hasn't he? It's funny. Everyone thought it was wild Belle who would be someone—go off to New York and paint or act or marry a wealthy banker. But it was Sammy did. Like my father, I was too scared to leave Manawa in spite of dreams. And here I am. Did you like lunch?"

"It was wonderful," Rosa said honestly. "Thank you."

"No one comes by," she said. "You'll come again?"

"Probably not," Rosa said. "I have to be back in Washington on Tuesday night."

"You're not going?" Ravilla said. "I have paintings to show you. It's only one o'clock. Here. Come see my bedroom. There's a painting I did of Sammy."

The painting she had done showed Sam Taylor as a young

147

man with a full head of hair, and it hung over her bed in a heavy wood frame.

"I did it from memory," she said. "I haven't seen him for years. And that," she said, pointing to another picture over the dresser, "is my father at the same age."

The pictures as near as Rosa could see were of the same young man.

Outside, as Rosa left, the goat had finished the white sheet and dug absently at the ground with his hoof. On the front porch Ravilla stood in the winter sun, in her grandmother's dress, holding the wide-brimmed hat, waving to Rosa.

"It was wonderful to see you," she called bravely. "Come again," she said as though it had been a common afternoon.

Carter Harold made arrangements early Monday for Sam Taylor to be followed after work. Certainly Sam Taylor did unexpected things, and he wanted the sense of control it would give him to know Sam Taylor's daily habits. If, for example, there was a woman he met after work—that would be something.

It was also a way to keep Al Cox away from Paulette Estinet, and Carter knew that kind of responsibility would appeal to a man who dropped his trousers for entertainment at Harvard.

"What do you expect him to do?" Al asked on the other end of the telephone.

"Nothing in particular," Carter said, "but just in case, we need to be on top of things. This morning both the *News* and the *Post* mention that Rosa DeAngelis is in Wisconsin uncovering information. I'm sure the *News* has someone on him now."

"And I'll follow the guy from the *News*," Al said. "Terrific."

"It will be a great help in our plan."

"What's our plan?"

"As it develops," Carter continued.

"Yeah," Al said, secretly pleased with the possibilities. "Well . . ."

"We're meeting back at Dick's this afternoon around five."

Al Cox looked up the address for the FCC immediately, got dressed, trying on several outfits, settling on a fishing hat of his father's and his brother's glasses without the glass. Tomorrow if he had a chance he'd buy a plastic nose at the five-and-ten.

"I'll be in and out of the office today," he told his father at breakfast.

"That is nothing new."

"I'm looking for a regular job," he said. "That's why I'll be out."

"Four days before Christmas?" his father asked.

"As a Christmas angel," he replied and slammed the front door.

Al was convinced his father enjoyed his sons in equal proportion to their successes. Which made Al the least pleasurable of the Cox boys.

It occurred to Al while walking to the bus stop on Massachusetts Avenue that following Sam Taylor might lead to something. The Syndicate could be successful, make the front page of the *Post*, and then the distinguished Buddy Cox of Nathaniel Cox and Cox could smother in his stuffed shirt.

He was smiling when he got on the bus.

Sam Taylor was late to work.

"The President's office called," his secretary said.

"I'll get to that shortly," he replied. "There's something pressing."

"More pressing than the President?" Ed Marlowe asked.

"You're here early," Sam said.

"It's after ten."

"Anyway," Sam said. "I saw the President on Saturday. His office needs information about regulations, but not until noon."

He stopped as he opened the door to his office. "Ed," he called to the older man. "Do you remember the name of the young man with us yesterday?"

Ed followed him into his office. "Do you?" he smiled. "I didn't think you drank."

"Occasionally," Sam said without humor.

"I don't remember," Ed replied. "But the other man is Joe Fox."

"With the *Times*."

"That's right," he said. "Why do you ask?"

"The other man, the young man," Sam began awkwardly, making up excuses as he talked, "knows a friend of mine whom I haven't seen for years."

He closed the door after Ed had left his office.

All night he had had waking dreams of the young man who reminded him of his father.

When he called the *Times*, Joe Fox had not arrived.

"I'll take your name," the woman at the other end of the line said.

"Samuel Taylor," he said. "Chairman of the FCC." It was automatic. He'd never used his title before. "Please have him get back to me immediately."

Sam got to the business for the President's office and the stations on the West Coast and was in a meeting with a newly appointed commissioner when the telephone call came from the *Times*.

The young man's name was Andrew Slaughter, and as far as Joe Fox knew he had left for Toronto Sunday night after they had lunched in Washington. In New York he lived alone and was seldom home. He might be staying at the Hotel Dominican in Toronto. Sam called the Hotel Dominican. They had an Andrew Slaughter from New York registered, but his room didn't answer.

Sam left his name and number. He said that he was chairman of the Federal Communications Commission and wanted to be in touch with Mr. Slaughter. Would he call as soon as possible?

He ate lunch alone in his office and requested that his secretary put through no phone calls at all except Mr. Andrew Slaughter from Toronto.

"Who is Mr. Slaughter of Toronto?" his secretary asked Ed Marlowe.

"Beats me," Ed said. "Has Mr. Taylor been himself lately?" he asked.

The secretary had been with the government for thirty-one years, with Samuel Taylor since he was appointed chairman in 1947.

"I really don't know," she said carefully. "I'm just his secretary."

"Well," Ed Marlowe apologized, "I was thinking about him. He's a special friend."

Sam Taylor was thinking about himself as well. He sat with his feet on the desk, his head against the back of his chair—and wondered what was going on. He had always been predictable in habits. Even as a small child when it had been his job to look after John Taylor.

The young man from New York had reminded Sam of his father's dying. Near as he could remember. A memory set aside years ago, without tendrils into the present to lead him back—as if the moment had been cased in a hard-shelled seed—and all that Sam recalled was that his father had died in a room in the back of the house and that he'd been with him for many days. Now he saw the room with a black-haired Andrew Slaughter lying on the couch propped up by horsehair pillows, sleeping with his eyes open. From time to time, Sam takes his hand and strokes it. Andrew Slaughter's lips move and nearly smile.

His father, then, must not have looked as old as he remembered if the young man from New York could take his place in a memory unavailable to him for forty years.

He answered the telephone on the second ring.

It was not Andrew Slaughter.

His secretary said that the Dominican Hotel had returned his call to say they were mistaken. Mr. Slaughter had checked out that morning and had not left a forwarding address.

There was no answer at the apartment in New York where he lived alone.

151

Joe Fox at the *Times* appeared impatient. He gave him Andrew Slaughter's number at his office in New York and said he
had a mother who lived in Putney, Vermont, whose name was
also Slaughter. He said it was unlikely he would see Andrew
Slaughter in the next few days but if he did he'd pass on the
information.

The operator in Vermont gave Sam the number of three
Slaughters. Mrs. Ellery Slaughter at the third number said she
had a son named Andrew Slaughter and he'd be spending
Christmas with her but she had no idea where he was now or
when he would arrive, sons being what they are, you know.

Sam gave his number and said that he was chairman of the
FCC.

After lunch with the coach from Dartmouth, Filip stopped in
Georgetown for ice cream.

He could play tailback, the coach had said, and would get an
adequate stipend for spending money, more than Princeton had
offered. Harvard never did that kind of thing. Of course he
would play professionally. Football was important in college, as
Fil knew, but the coach agreed that pro baseball would be fine
as well. There'd be time for that decision. At dessert the coach
brought up his father.

"It must be tough making this decision without a father," he
said.

"Yeah," Filip agreed.

"I suppose your father played ball with you a lot," the coach
said. "Was he an athlete?"

"No," Filip said, remembering his father in a business suit,
leaving the house without breakfast at seven. He seldom saw
Antonio at night. Occasionally he came to games, but never in
the year before he died.

One night the winter of Fil's junior year after he had gone to
bed, Antonio came in and sat down next to him on the bed.

"My father used to come home for lunch," Antonio said. "I'd
tell him about school and any trouble I'd been in that day."

"I understand," Fil said, not wanting apologies from his father, embarrassed by them. "I know you've got a lot to do."

"It's no excuse," Antonio said. And then he talked about Filip's responsibility to Rosa in formal terms.

"It is the custom in Italian families for the eldest boy to take responsibility for his mother," he said.

"For Mother?" Filip asked, surprised.

"I know Rosa seems to be able to take care of herself," he said, "but she will need you if anything should happen."

Of course he was talking about prison after the investigation by McCarthy's committee. He had not intended to die.

"Sure," Filip said. "Don't worry. I'll be okay."

"The good thing about athletics when you've lost a father," the coach was saying, "is that the team replaces him in spirit."

"Yeah," Filip said, and he turned the conversation back to the problems with the single wing.

Sukey Moorehead made up Santa Theresa of the Hills and played her regularly walking down the streets behind the Capitol or at the 1st and E Street market picking up milk and oranges, at the Calvin Coolidge High School in the back of the classroom dreaming of sacrifice and spiritual victory over impossible odds. Like Jeanne d'Arc, Santa Theresa heard voices, and these begged her to lead the children of Provence out of the valley to save them from the onslaught of the plague. Which in the person of Sukey Moorehead she did and they were saved. Sukey played the scenes out verbatim in her head, played them now as she walked down P Street in Georgetown, headed for Dick Carr's house.

She recognized Filip DeAngelis coming out of Swenson's Ice Cream Shoppe after he had passed, and she would have gone on without acknowledging had he not called to her.

Fil DeAngelis had known Sukey since grammar school, had gone to school with her when her father was assistant minister at St. John's, Georgetown. Before Father Moorehead had designs of reformation. When Sukey was simply distant as a fawn and unpossessed.

Now there was an intensity about her at once unsettling and imposing. Filip knew that she could see the full and bare-breasted body of Blanche across his chest.

"Hello," she said. "I didn't see you at first."

They fell in stride.

"I'm going to Dick Carr's," she said. "I think Natty'll be there. That's what Dick said. Natty would be there."

"Yeah?" Filip said. "Natty seems to be spending a lot of time with Dick Carr. She was there yesterday."

"No, yesterday she was at Carter Harold's farm. I couldn't be there," Sukey said. "I had to be at church."

Filip had been afraid of that. "At church," he said as if to actualize the presence of the place. He was certain that Sukey knew everything about Blanche.

"Anyway," she said. "I heard that you and Natty were sort of kaput."

"Oh?" Filip said. "I don't know. I mean as far as I'm concerned we're not."

"Someone said that you and that girl from Wilson . . ." Sukey went on. "Blanche, y'know."

"No."

"Anyway, you were at the Poviches' with her."

"Yes," he said, "but there's nothing at all." Blanche sat boldly in the corner of his mind without clothes.

"So," he said, not having more to say. Sukey thought they had slept together, he was sure. She could see through his brain as though it were clear glass, not only what had happened, but what more he wished to happen as well.

"What?" She looked perplexed.

"I mean you obviously think there's something between Blanche and me," he said fiercely. "Well, there's nothing. She's a very nice girl and that's all."

"I don't even know her," Sukey retreated.

"And you can tell Dick Carr as well."

"About what?"

"About Blanche."

"Being a nice girl?"

"No," he said, exasperated. "About Blanche and me having nothing between us."

"Jeez." She wished he would go away.

"Okay."

She nodded. "Natty was thrown from a horse," she said. "Yesterday at Carter Harold's. She had to be taken to Georgetown Hospital," she went on, anxious to change the subject.

It was only later when Filip was having a Coke that he realized he hadn't asked Sukey anything more about Natty. And he imagined Sukey turning left at Dick Carr's thinking of him and Blanche the Virgin lying naked on the Poviches' daybed with her large white breasts spilling over his ribcage.

Natty and Anne Lowry and Paulette sat in the study at Dick Carr's. Dick Carr was there and Peter von Trotten; Choo Choo came in late with Sukey, whom she'd met at 30th. Alexander Epps sat on the floor with his eyes closed, drinking a glass of warm bourbon, dreaming of disasters. Al Cox would be there later, Dick said. This meeting was intended to be a gathering of consequence, but they would not wait for Al Cox. Carter Harold brought in pizzas.

"So," Dick Carr began. "We really wanted you here," he said to Natty. Some of the conversation had been prearranged.

"It's for your own good."

Choo Choo spoke up first. "Do you know what McCarthy did?"

"Of course," Natty said.

"I mean really," Choo Choo said. "Do you know what happened to people like my father?"

"Your father got a terrible deal," Natty said. "So did a lot of others."

"He'll never be able to work again," Choo Choo said. "At least as long as there's a blacklist."

"It's sinful," Sukey said. "Innocent people were hurt."

"Listen," Natty said, sensing the unity of the crowd against her and ready instinctively to fight.

"What concerns me, Natty," Carter Harold said with practiced resonance, spreading out on the couch to assume magnified proportions, "are your own convictions and do you have any."

"Of course I have convictions," Natty said angrily. "McCarthy was wrong. Terribly wrong in every way."

"But," Dick Carr pointed out, "it's perfectly right for him to be a guest at your house."

"He's not my guest," she said. "He's not a guest at all." And then, her head clearing from the unexpected attack, she said, "McCarthy was wrong and now he's absolutely nothing. He couldn't hurt anyone."

"But he did," Anne Lowry said. "It's immoral," she said, drawing on the word without mercy.

Carter Harold crossed his arms behind his head and stretched.

"It's as though your family accepts the existence of evil as the natural condition of our lives," Sukey said.

"Shut up," Natty said, getting up.

"Supports it even," Sukey added.

"Just a second, Sukey," Carter interrupted. "There're other things to get out in the open tonight, Natty."

"Like what?" she snapped.

"Like Fil DeAngelis."

"What about him?" she said, furious at them all, but not willing to leave without a fight.

"Fil DeAngelis is someone; everyone in the whole town knows him. He's a regular bullshit hero, a kingpin, better known in these parts than Jesus Christ," Dick Carr said.

"It's not a bad deal for a girl like you with liabilities to tie up with Fil DeAngelis," Carter Harold said.

"Basically," Sukey said slowly, "it's insincere."

"What about Will Barnes?" Dick Carr said. "What do you want from a poor sweet guy like that who worships the ground you walk on?"

"You guys," Natty said, "are full of crap."

"It's for your own good, Natty," Carter Harold said. "To see a perfectly decent family like the Taylors fall apart."

"Keeping Joe McCarthy as a house guest."

"And to see what's happening to you," Sukey said.

"You know?" Dick Carr asked.

Natty left the room.

"Proof of the pudding," Dick Carr said without hesitation.

Carter Harold followed her out of the living room. She stopped at the lavatory door and slapped his face.

In the mirror above the sink she did not recognize her own face, as though she had been translated in form to another language. She got up close to the mirror and stuck out her tongue as her mother used to have her do when she was pale as a child. Her tongue was coated gray and thick as oatmeal.

"You've got *something* wrong with you," her mother would say, seeing a tongue like that. "Pretty soon, you'll come down with it and then we'll know what it is."

Later they apologized, even Carter Harold, and she practiced cheerleading with Paulette and Anne in the Carrs' recreation room. She did not forget what had happened, but she didn't want to talk about it either.

Sam Taylor had called Mrs. Slaughter in Putney, Vermont, once more before he left his office at five.

"No," she said. Still no word from her son, but—she laughed— you know Andrew and his piano.

He didn't know that, Sam said quickly, astonished at this new information. He had only met Andrew once, he said, and that in Washington. This was essentially a business call. Did Andrew play the piano?

"Blues," Mrs. Slaughter said across the wires of New England to the office where Sam Taylor stood. "And jazz," she said. "He's very good, but occasionally he'll begin to play at a pub and just go on and on."

"Well, thank you," Sam said. He gave Mrs. Slaughter his number at home and said her son could call him anytime.

"I'll have him call," she said.

He copied down the number in Putney and put it in his breast coat pocket.

Ramona's was a bar behind the *Post* where reporters went, and Sam stopped in now on his way home from work. He had never gone in alone before, and only a few people recognized him. He ordered a double bourbon and drank it straightaway. And then another, which he drank more slowly and felt. Al Cox, standing on the corner of 15th Street, saw him come out, lean against the office building next at hand, rubbing his head, taking off his hat. It was obvious when he walked down 15th Street that he'd had too much to drink.

"I was downtown," Al Cox now said to the group assembled in Dick Carr's study. "Doing a bunch of things," he was careful to add. "And I saw your father," he said to Natty.

"It must be later than I'd thought," Natty said. "If he's left work."

"He was drunk," Al Cox said, trying to make his voice as kind as possible.

"But he doesn't drink," Natty said. "Only a little, at parties. Not regularly."

"Perhaps," Al said, reaching over to Paulette, taking the cigarette in her mouth and puffing it grandly, "but he's been drinking today."

"Jesus," Natty said. "I wonder if something's the matter," she said. She put on her coat. "I better go home. It must be nearly six."

"Do you want a ride?" Dick Carr asked.

"You're sure about my father?" she asked Al Cox.

"Dead sure," he said. "I'm sorry, Natty. I just thought you'd want to know."

"Jeez," she said again.

On the way home Dick Carr left his hand between their thighs on the front seat. Natty was aware that it was there and didn't move away.

———

Joe McCarthy was not there. Natty had a light-headed sense of his absence when she walked in the front door and checked quickly through the dark downstairs to be certain.

Upstairs she heard her parents arguing. It was after six by the clock in the kitchen, and there was no familiar smell of dinner cooking.

She took off her coat, lit the light in the study and brought out her cello. For a long time she sat in the straight-backed chair with the bow across her knee. She was becoming someone she did not understand—as though her new self divided had stepped out into a cold night without wraps and the familiar warmness of her own body had fallen away like a comforter. Things which had been clear to her since childhood no longer made sense. Above all she wanted friends to think well of her, and they did not. She didn't think well of herself. Something had happened which she could not identify as fact but knew as she knew rottenness in the perfect fruit, soft beneath the skin. It had to do with Joseph McCarthy.

"You've been drinking," Ellen said, wrapped up on the chaise, a romance folded face down in her lap. "Haven't you?"

"Yes," Sam said. "I have. I was picked up for it. That's why I'm late."

"What do you mean picked up?"

"I was very drunk," he said. "I was arrested on 15th Street and booked for disorderly conduct."

He had swung at the policeman. That he remembered. He'd been resting against a lamp post or a building, something hard which supported him, and a policeman had come up to him, perhaps only noticing he was drunk, inquiring after his well-being, but Sam had swung at him before the officer had a chance to speak. It was entirely a reflexive action.

"How did you get home?" she asked.

"By taxi."

"Will it be in the papers?" she asked, not wanting to press him, not wanting to know.

"It's doubtful. But, of course, as long as I've been booked, I'm fair game for any reporter."

In fact, he was pleased to have been caught, to know there were limits to the recent chaos in his life. He was a public man who had abused the law. His arrest was a warning to him to require laws in his private life as protection against greater chaos.

"You haven't had that much to drink," Ellen said hopefully. She dismissed circumstances out of her control, secreting them away in a bottom drawer under sweaters and old sachets, out of sight. It was only specific emergencies which she could handle, and Sam Taylor's drinking was not one of those. Like termites, eating at the interior of houses, visible too late after the damage is done, Sam Taylor's drinking was a sign of damage beyond her reach. It was not in her temperament to be angry or rail at him for his public exposure, only to pretend he had not been arrested. She tried not to read the papers anyway. She didn't like bad news.

"I feel certain this drinking has to do with Natty," Sam said.

"There's nothing wrong with Natty," Ellen said, "except that Senator McCarthy is breaking up her romance with Fil DeAngelis."

"Nonsense," he said. "Joe McCarthy hasn't the capacity to break up anything any longer."

"Rosa DeAngelis is in Wisconsin—"

"I know." Sam Taylor could not concentrate on the dusky colors of his wife across from him. She was indistinct as an Impressionist painting of flowers.

"I'm terribly sorry, Ellen," he said to her.

"Shh," she said.

"I've had too much to drink to make sense of things."

She put her fingers to her lips.

"Listen," she said.

Natty was playing. For a long time they listened, sitting across from each other in Ellen's room.

"Does she sound off to you?" Sam asked. "Or is it my head?"

"It's off," Ellen said. "She sounds terrible."

Sometime in the middle of the night Natty heard a crash under her bedroom. She got up and ran to the head of the stairs.

The hallway below was dark except for the blue light at the bend of the stairs, the blue light in the living room—sufficient light to recognize the form of Senator Joe McCarthy struggling to his feet.

"What is it?" Ellen Taylor whispered, coming up behind her daughter.

"What do you think?" Natty replied, turning back to her own room.

Ellen looked down the stairwell. Joseph McCarthy was standing now, brushing off his suit. He'd thrown his overcoat on the library table in the hall.

"But how did he get in?" Ellen asked.

"He has a key."

"From whom?" she asked.

"From Daddy," Natty replied, "of course." And she shut her bedroom door.

TUESDAY, DECEMBER 21
1954

Carter Harold was certain that Natty would do anything.

"Anything," he said to Paulette, who danced alone and without music around the Carrs' living room.

"Three days of dress rehearsal." Dick Carr laughed, stretched out in his shoes on his mother's peach velvet sofa. "Three goddam days."

"If you knew Natty like I know Natty . . ." Alexander Epps danced around the room, knocking over a basket of silk flowers.

"Oh, oh, oh, what a gal. There's none so classy as that fair lassie," Dick Carr chimed in, raising a glass with Al Cox.

"So." Paulette folded like a robe on the chair by the fireplace.

Carter Harold was in the bathroom pretending to wash his face.

In the mirror over the sink he looked absolutely the same. Feeling otherwise, feeling an unfamiliar power beyond his conception of himself, he had gone to the bathroom to be certain. But there was the same thoroughly American face, with features meshed together like pastels losing their primary colors—his eyes too small and close together, his nose thick at the bridge, his fine long lips interrupted by a clown's chin and a neck so short it disappeared into his collar. He was not offensive-looking but not attractive either, and certainly not distinguished. Mediocre, in fact. And to contain within that head, shaped as imperfectly as a pear, marked by hair thinning before twenty, a brain so sharp and original and categorically arranged to overturn the top officials in government. Well, he was impressed. A plan began to formulate itself in his mind.

It continued as in the mirror he could see Paulette, dancing again, moving across the room, her eyes half closed. This night he wanted to design such a plan for the Syndicate as to turn the French girl's head—and set her to thinking of him as he thought of her.

But he retained enough good sense even in the hours after midnight to know the danger of this new vanity.

"So what?" he asked Paulette.

"So what do we do now we have Natty Taylor in the palm of our hand?"

Carter sat down, picked up the silk flowers on the floor and crossed his legs.

"Kidnap Natty," he said.

"Terrific," Alexander said. "Can we use masks?"

"With her permission," Carter went on.

Paulette stopped dancing and sat down on the couch with Dick Carr, moving his legs for room.

"What for?"

"We have the possibility now to force Sam Taylor's resignation," Carter said. "To really accomplish something."

"Of value to the country," Al Cox said sardonically.

"Exactly," Carter went on, ignoring Al Cox's tone.

"Natty would be devastated if it came out in public that her father had been drinking."

"Drinks," Al Cox added.

"But do we know he does?" Sukey asked.

"We know," Al Cox said, assuming his new posture. "I saw him drunk."

"Drinking."

"After drinking," Al Cox rejoined.

"It's a small point," Carter Harold said. "The real point is that we know he's irresponsible in other ways."

"Because of Senator McCarthy," Choo Choo said quietly.

"Absolutely."

"If we kidnap Natty," Carter Harold said, "if we make her return to her family conditional on Sam Taylor's resignation, he'll resign. He's got to."

"How do you know?" Paulette asked.

"How many kids does Taylor have? You think she's not the apple of his eye? There're things you simply know," Carter said absolutely.

In the bathroom Choo Choo sat on the closed toilet seat and wept. No one saw her go in but Eliza Barnes, who followed her.

"What's the matter?" Liza asked, peering in the door.

"We are," Choo Choo said. "All of us. Wrong as McCarthy ever dreamed of being. It's crazy."

"Choo Choo's crazy," Carter told Eliza going home in the car. "Really crazy. She sees Dr. Baer twice a week. Someone told me she hasn't even got her period yet."

He reached over and rubbed Eliza's thighs. "Have you?" he asked.

"Shut up." She brushed his hand away.

"Liza," he said softly, reaching up to her face, glancing his hand across her cheek.

"That's all you want," she said.

"What's all I want?"

"To put your hand between my legs," Eliza said, moving against the door. "That sort of thing."

"No, Eliza," he said, careful in his approach.

"I can tell about Paulette."

"What about Paulette?"

"There's something between you."

"We're friends," he said.

He did not try to touch her when they stopped the car at the end of the road to the farm. He kissed her and held her hand.

"I'm sorry you think that, Liza," he said.

"You really have a thing for Paulette," she tried again.

"I respect her," he said. "And like her a great deal."

"And me."

"I could fall in love with you." He was careful to concern himself with possibilities, to seem reliable and sincere. It wasn't possible for her to disbelieve him, even though she knew he must be lying to her.

"Don't tell Will under any circumstances," he cautioned, "and don't fret." His lips brushed her forehead and her hair.

She wanted to be naked in the back seat, to open her legs for him. It was all that she could do to walk up the path to her house.

Will was sleeping. Eliza turned on the small light at the end of his bed, watched him wake up, stretching first and half sitting, face her through the darkness.

"Liza?"

"Yes."

"Jesus." He flopped back down, made a hill of his pillow and leaned against it. "What time is it?"

"Nearly morning. Four, I guess. I just got home."

"Mom must be ecstatic."

"She was waiting up. I called and said I would be late."

"Been screwing with Little Boy Blue?"

"That's all he wants from me."

"Ah, Liza, what a brain you're growing," Will said sitting up now. "Carter Harold is not a man of great imagination."

"I think he likes Paulette."

"Paulette's soul and your freewheeling body."

"I've never."

"Never? Tell the truth."

"I wanted to tonight."

"But you didn't."

"I've let him do a bunch of stuff," she said. "Not everything."

"But you would. Right?"

"I shouldn't," she said. "You think I want to be with him while his eyes are closed seeing Paulette's little yellow curls and pink cheeks?" She was crying. "I just don't know what else to do."

"Don't go with him again."

He watched his sister walk in the dark to the door. It was as if they were real twins and the egg had split in half at conception, leaving them both incomplete and vulnerable in impossible ways. "You didn't have anything to drink?"

"You think I want to spend the rest of my life in my room?"

"Was Natty there?" he called.

"Nope."

"Did they talk about her?"

Eliza didn't answer.

"They made new plans, I guess." He lay back against the pillow. "You wouldn't tell me if you knew, would you?"

"Maybe not," she said.

He listened to Eliza's bare feet thump on the carpet to her room, listened to his mother get up, turn on the light, take down a book from the library, climb back in bed.

In his mind he pictured Carter Harold rolled flat as a paper doll, cut in small strips and scattered. The Carter Harold paper doll looked like pieces of an ordinary boy of indiscriminate size. He did the same with his mind's picture of Dick Carr, rolling him flat, cutting him in narrow strips, but even a strip of Dick Carr, including an ear, part of an arm, torso, leg, was identifiable.

Down the hall, Will heard Liza weeping. His mother shifted against the wall, got up, walked over to the door and stopped there. He heard her sit down on the bed.

He turned over, covered his head with his blankets. He wanted to cut out his mother's slim advances, his sister's losses, but he was, even in a silence without reminders, too angry to sleep.

Dick Carr was awake but in pajamas when Carter Harold came back.

"Everybody gone?" Carter asked, walking in the front door, throwing his coat over the banister.

169

"It's four in the morning, for chrissake," Dick said, walking upstairs.

"Paulette?"

"Yeah."

Carter followed Dick into his bedroom.

"With whom?"

"With whom what?"

"Did Paulette go home?"

"Oh, yeah." He flopped down on the bed, disengaging slowly, like a block tower. "I took her. Her parents called. Paulette, they said. It's sooooo late. So I took her," he said. "You've got a thing for her?"

"No."

"You lying bastard," he said good-naturedly.

Carter shook his head, lit a cigarette and drew on it slowly.

"What about Eliza? That's finished. Right?" He shut his eyes against the light over his bed. "Easy lay. Right?"

"Wrong."

"Well. Paulette's not."

Carter watched the fallen body of Dick Carr like a giant in paisley pajamas, his bare feet at right angles with the end of the bed, his arm thrown over his eyes.

"God, I'm tired," Dick Carr said. "Don't you ever get tired?"

"Have you ever slept with anyone?" Carter asked.

"You mean really?"

"Precisely."

"Have you?" Dick Carr hedged.

Carter didn't answer. Instead he watched the enormous head lift off the pillow, the arm come down, Dick Carr shift to his side, hold his head like a basketball in the palm of his hand.

"Well?"

"I was just noticing earlier today that Natty Taylor didn't mention Fil DeAngelis once."

"Yeah."

"In fact, she seemed interested in you," Carter said.

"No," Dick Carr protested. "Not me."

"I wouldn't be so sure."

"How come you say that?"

"I could tell," Carter said, getting up, going to the mirror, arranging his hair with his hand. "I have an eye for those things."

"I guess you do," Dick Carr said thoughtfully.

"Well," Carter said. "I better be going."

"Listen," Dick called after him. "Do you think this whole thing will be over by Thursday? I got a call from my parents and they want me to fly out to Oklahoma for Christmas on the twenty-third."

"By Thursday night Sam Taylor should resign," Carter said. "You can leave on Friday."

"Man," Dick Carr murmured. "That's something. I guess you can do anything you set your mind to. That's what my father always said." He imitated the gruff oratorial voice of Senator Carr. "The American dream, son. To do anything a man sets his mind to doing."

They laughed.

"Wait till it hits the papers."

"Hell, yes," Carter said. "If Sam Taylor resigns."

"Jeez," Dick Carr said. "We'll be regular heros."

Carter Harold stopped at the door.

"Did Paulette say anything to you tonight when you took her home?"

"Like what?"

"About the Syndicate or anything."

"Well . . ." and Dick Carr laughed, his bassoon laugh, tossed a pillow at Carter. "You mean about you, right, Harold?"

"No," Carter retreated. "I simply wondered whether she made any comment about what we're doing."

"She's having a swell time," Dick said. "You can tell that."

"I'm sure she is."

"I could tell she really liked you," Dick Carr said.

"Bullshit," Carter retorted.

"Well, I know she does."

Dick Carr turned off the light and dreamed of floating down the basketball court like a bird, tossing ball after ball through the center net. He dreamed of Fil DeAngelis shrinking to the size of a gray squirrel, skittering across the court between his legs. Squashed by the feet of another player. He dreamed of dropping Natty Taylor through the net again and again, catching her before she hit the ground and tossing her up against the backboard. Swish, flopping through the net again.

Carter Harold drove by Paulette's house, next to Dumbarton Oaks. It was dark except for one light in the back of the house, which he imagined to be her bedroom, and he drove once around the block with the vague hope of catching a glimpse of her in her nightgown before his rational mind took over and he drove straight home.

Natty got up at six and couldn't practice. She had gotten up at six because she couldn't sleep. She had locked the door to the library, put up her music in the corner of the room to catch the shadows from the pale sun of early dawn and sat. From time to time she moved the bow across the strings, back and forth, without melody. Mostly she thought about her friends, of practicing cheerleading for the Friends–Episcopal game. Of Dick Carr in a yellow crewneck sweater, huge as a bear, and how the sweater looked against his dark skin. Of Paulette Estinet. On Paulette flesh around the hips looked well, she thought. She stood far back in front of the mirror above the piano so she could see herself from the knees up. Her hips in corduroy pants were flat and sharp as spatulas.

She looked in the mirror at her face, dark and sallow, uninspired as a crow's.

She had, as a child, wanted to be famous. An actress or the first woman military hero—front and center. She wanted the applause. She was temperamentally unsuited to team sports. Her imagined world was one of high excitement, and if not more real, it was at least more attractive to her than the ordinary world in which she lived. But she was a realist as well and wanted to be famous in fact. And so she had for years balanced carefully as a young gymnast between her own requirements and the demands made to belong.

Now the balance had altered and she was concerned with

merging undistinguished as part of the whole as though the color of the group had been mixed by the addition of Natty with its own exact depth and was unchanged.

She worried now about ordinary things like appearances and whether she expressed them suitably. Since Sunday she had stopped imagining.

At seven she put the cello back in its case, and then she heard Joe McCarthy in the kitchen. Later after the game that afternoon, she would practice again.

"Will you have breakfast with me?" Senator McCarthy asked, seating her with a flourish. "Here, we'll share it equally, like old comrades." He split the scrambled eggs down the center, half on a separate plate, poured coffee, gave her half his toast. "An early-morning arrangement," he said and smiled at her full in the face. She had never seen his smile before, and something about his eyes engaged her.

His eyes, opaque this last week, wandering, as if detained by some activity in another part of his brain, were clear this morning. Their black centers held Natty in place. He was different than he had been, and Natty sensed in her response to him an alteration.

"So," he said. "You play the cello. A musician like your grandfather used to be."

"You knew him?"

"I heard about him," he said. "John Taylor had a reputation and died young." He finished his coffee. "It could be a song," he sang to the tune of "Jesse James," "John Taylor had a reputation, a reputation had he."

"What was his reputation?" she asked, conscious of the way McCarthy looked at her, conscious of a kind of danger in it, but liking it just the same—like a game she used to play on the curb as a child, walking on the edge of the curb, spilling half over the edge, making believe that the street just below was fire or water, a tunnel to China. Unsafe at any distance.

"Drinking?" she asked.

"Yes," McCarthy replied. "He had a reputation for drinking and music. He made wonderful music. Wonderful music." He imitated the Midwestern Germans as they might have spoken of John Taylor. "Such a terrible vaste."

"You mean to drink?"

"That's what the people in Wisconsin meant. That he was a talented man who drank his life away."

"Well," she said, testing, "is it a crime to drink?"

"I am a talented man drinking my life away," he said. "And your grandfather told wonderful stories," he went on. "They're still around Manawa. I heard one when I was back last month sitting in the bar on Main and Apple drinking with your mother's first husband."

"I know about him."

"Hilda, who runs the bar, told me the story from her father and it was a story John Taylor used to tell about my father."

Senator McCarthy settled in the chair, leaned over his arms on the table, and Natty was silenced by an energy in the man as though she were a photograph or still life whose existence somehow depended on his making of it. The way she had felt with older people when she was very young, occasionally felt now with people. Carter Harold lately. Filip once, and certainly her father.

She wondered if she looked pretty. If her hair fell softly across her forehead, if her lips were damp.

"Tell me," she said, conscious of unnamed developments.

He told her the story, drawing her in with his voice, in the curious manner of a sorcerer lifting her up, not in the story or even the words of the story, but in the tone and shape of them, a kind of melody like music that catches you unaware, sets you dancing.

"My father was a poor and unsuccessful Irishman, full of tricks but with a vision of courage and nobility that he'd inherited from a long line of deceits."

Natty had never been conscious of looks—not her own nor the looks of other people. Until lately. Now the morning sun lined Joe McCarthy's middle age, made the darkness of his face blacker, his hair retreating thinner, his dark eyes striped with pale yellow. A surly punkish man in daylight, he was handsome to her this morning, and only the night before he had been too terrible to look at full in the face. There was a new clarity in his voice.

"My father had been told by his father," McCarthy went on, "when he was a young boy still in Ireland about his father's military prowess, his great courage fighting the British for the Nationalists, his medals of honor and commendations, his war injuries. He had been told about one particular battle in which his father, my grandfather, saved a good Catholic family, a mother and eight small children, singlehanded after the children's father had been killed. All my grandfather's children used to marvel at these stories and at their father's heroism and dream of their own chances."

She had heard stories about Senator McCarthy for years from her grandmother and Uncle Paul and people in Manawa, in Madison where they had lived—and in Washington during his brief reign. What a hold he had on people. Even Sam Taylor had said he had a power which seemed to multiply with recognition like self-dividing cells. But the man who had fallen through the front door late last summer, haunting the Taylors' house on Highland Place, gave no evidence of that power, except occasionally the intrusive evidence of ghosts, a banging of doors on windless nights.

Natty had feared Senator McCarthy because he had a reputation for doing harm and drank too much, because of the inexplicit sense of doom that comes when a family acknowledges that its house is haunted.

Now this new Senator McCarthy honoring the myth about him, filling the kitchen like the morning sun over the window ledge with the magic of his voice.

She wondered if he had changed overnight with a good sleep or if she, with this new self-consciousness invading, was suddenly susceptible to his stories.

"And then," he was saying, and Natty was caught by the sound of his voice, "my father came to America at fourteen after his father had died, to Wisconsin, and enlisted when I was young to go to the First World War. We were all thrilled that our father was going to this great war. And he went and came back a hero. I never saw any medals or letters of commendation from the President or any war injury evident on the body of my father, although he was thinner than when he'd left and had a vacant look about his eyes. But he told us stories of his great bravery in this war, how he had been the one to go into the front lines with hand grenades, the first to advance against the enemy —how they'd been gassed and he had in spite of the odds found a means of escape for his company and led them to safety after their commander was killed. We would sit in the farmhouse the first winter after the war listening to these stories which changed in the telling from night to night and dream about the war we were going to get to fight."

Natty imagined Joe McCarthy a war hero. Imagined his brown face and black eyes as a young man without the skin pockets and pencil lines across his brow, the quiet attack of years. She imagined him her age and wondered how the neckline on her robe looked from his chair.

"When our war came we went with visions of ourselves as heros, knowing we had a lineage of heros our efforts wouldn't match. Nothing less would do."

He settled back, poured more coffee for them both. Natty hoped Sam Taylor would sleep late this morning, that the telephone wouldn't ring until after eight.

"But the story that John Taylor told about my father was that he had never left Washington, D.C., that he'd come down with tuberculosis two weeks after he'd enlisted to go to Europe and spent the remainder of the war in a sanatorium in Maryland. And that my grandfather had not fought with the Irish Nationalists either. That he had had a bad heart and couldn't bear arms. But his own father had told him such grand stories of victory that, like my father, he felt a responsibility for the history of his family and made up lies. So," he laughed, "your grandfather was full of stories."

He stretched, got up, picked up the telephone to dial and then thought better of it. The day was clear as winter days are seldom clear in Washington, and looking out the kitchen window at the new details of black branches and trash cans piled with trash against the old slat porches like the slat porches of Wisconsin farmhouses, Joe McCarthy felt himself again for the first time since August.

"It was nice to talk to you," he said to Natty in a voice both courtly and familiar.

She smiled and walked out of the kitchen with a sense of his eyes on the back of her. She was conscious of her lack of grace.

Sam Taylor stayed upstairs until just before eight, although he'd been awake for hours and had slept fitfully. At eight he called Mrs. Slaughter in Putney, Vermont. The telephone rang several times in Putney, and when a woman answered in an unfamiliar voice, perhaps the morning voice of Mrs. Slaughter, he hung up without conversation.

It was Tuesday, after all, he told himself. Still too early for Andrew Slaughter to have reached his mother in Putney.

Once, as a boy, he'd been possessed by a craziness similar to this business with the young man from New York. When he was thirteen and delivered the milk route before dawn to the houses in Manawa, he would imagine his dead father as a boy sitting in the milk wagon next to him, full of conversation, teasing the young Sammy Taylor with the possibility of his presence—for every time Sammy looked over at the seat where he felt his father was sitting, the boy John Taylor was gone and in his absence was the memory of human shape so nearly tangible that Sam from time to time reached out expecting to feel the invisible soft flesh of a child.

John Taylor died on a day of unexpected spring the first of March. Sam had slept with him on a blanket beside his bed, waking through the night to his unsteady breathing, spaces of silence punctuated by a long drum roll from deep in his father's chest. Sam got up in darkness, wrapped the blanket around himself and watched the cautious sun move across the floorboards, up the bedpost, over the sleeping form of his father.

His father's eyes were closed, but Sam knew he was awake by his consciousness about the room, as though the body's waking soul had another and separate life.

"Are you sleeping?" Sam asked, expecting no response.

"I am dreaming of playing music to a crowd so large I cannot see the end of it," his father said, moving his hand with an imaginary baton, "and they are cheering."

"What are you playing?" he asked.

"I can't hear the music," John Taylor said. "Only the cheering." He struggled up in bed, leaned against the pillow. He was wearing a workshirt and a heavy sweater and a muffler that Adelaide had made for something to do with her warbling fingers while she sat by the wood stove in the evenings. It was a constant argument Sam had with his father.

"You'll strangle wearing a muffler to bed," Sam would say.

"Not a bad way to die," John would answer. "Adelaide Taylor's husband died by his own muffler in bed this morning. He was found peaceful as a kitten by his sweet wife at eight a.m. when she brought his usual morning tray of her bad temper."

"It could happen, you know," Sam said.

"Although Mrs. Taylor made the muffler by the labor of her fingers, the death was ruled accidental."

"So," he said this morning of the day he died, "I have survived another night without strangling on the muffler. I am beginning to have unshakable faith in Providence."

Sam propped him up, covered him with blankets, brought him tea, which he did not drink.

"Sing to me," he said.

"I have a bad voice," Sam said.

"Sing to me anyway," he said.

So he sang all the songs he remembered that his father had taught him, and off and on, John Taylor slept.

Toward noon Sam brought him another cup of tea, and standing beside him, looking at his face in the open sun of midday, he saw the skeletal mask of a dying man rise up as sea debris rises when the water stills.

It was Sam Taylor's last visual memory of his father alive, and through the years when he thought of this March day the picture that rose like the bones behind the flesh had risen was the one of John Taylor dying.

He had died at three o'clock. That memory was factual, for Sam had noted on the clock that it was three when he went to get the doctor. But something had happened between noon and three that day which struggled inside his head as a bird in captive hands struggles to take wing.

Again and again last night, waiting for the morning to call Andrew Slaughter's mother in Putney, Sam had rehearsed the morning of the day of his father's death as if for a performance, knowing that something eluded him as the ghost child John Taylor had vanished incompletely on the milk-wagon rides when he was thirteen.

He must take hold, he told himself, packing his briefcase, reordering the piles of incidentals on his dresser.

"Joe," Sam Taylor said, coming down the backstairs to the kitchen. "You've come back."

"Remember," McCarthy said, looking up from the newspaper spread out on the kitchen table. "You said anytime."

"I did." He poured orange juice, sat down across from McCarthy. "News?"

"Of us?" MCarthy shook his head. "Not a word in the *Post*. In fact, not a word about me in the paper unless Allen Saunders is referring to me as the lover in *Mary Worth* this morning."

"How was the Hill yesterday?" Sam asked. "Anyone still around?"

"As you can imagine, there was a huge welcoming party. Brass bands in the rotunda."

"Great."

"Welch was carrying a placard with 'We Love Joe' in green and they served cranberry juice, knowing I stay clear of booze." He leaned across the table. "Do you remember Andy O'Leary from Manawa?"

"He was a redhead."

"Bright red hair and freckles but ordinary as peas. He could have been a Senator from any goddam state in the country, either party."

"He made it yesterday to the cranberry reception at the Hill?"

"No," McCarthy said, "but I was reminded of him. I used to watch him adjust to positions as though he'd invented them. I remember thinking when I ran for president of my high school class that with O'Leary on my side every guy around would think I was anointed and if I lost, O'Leary would forget my name if he met me on the street. Which is how it happened." He stood up, assumed a posture of dignity. "So I go up to the Senate chamber yesterday. Hello, Clay, I say to Senator Fust— remember, my big buddy during the hearings. 'Oh,' says the Senator," McCarthy minced across the room, "vaguely recognizing my face like some grade school buddy years ago for chrissake. 'Hello.' And Senator Hooper, the jackass who ran on 'Honesty Is My Policy' from the cornbelt," McCarthy stiffened, bent forward like a mannered British butler, rolled a newspaper under his arm. "Hell, I say, 'Good to see you, Hooper.' '*Mmmmm*,' Hooper says, moving like an arthritic rhino across the floor, '*Mmmm*,' as though we talk through our throats and I haven't got a name. 'Hey, James,' I say to Scott—pretending all my friends are simply absent-minded." McCarthy crouched in a football center's position. "James looks as though he's seen the devil—dashes off across the floor as if I'm after him in hot pursuit." He imitates James Scott. "Poor old deaf Abraham, the East Wing janitor, said, 'Morning, Senator,' but he'd say 'Morning, Senator' to Andy O'Leary or my mother."

Sam Taylor laughed. "You need a new cause, Joe."

"You're right. I probably do."

Sam was pleased by the live memory of the old McCarthy masquerading in his kitchen—teased by it even as a boy when McCarthy could use that familiar voice which had persuaded centuries of men to follow banners—that accidental self-mockery which caught a man off guard, drew him into the game, for that's exactly what it was, with all the high spirits and secretness of games, and it made what happened acceptable because it happened in good fun.

In September 1953, Sam Taylor made a public statement against Senator McCarthy in a speech to broadcasters at the Press Club in which he said that Joe McCarthy was a metaphor for the absence of belief, that if a man without conviction could terrorize a people on slim evidence, then the American people had lost their memory of our black moments in history and assumed no responsibility for our future. We could go after witches in Massachusetts and Jews and niggers in the South and Communists. And you and me. No one whosoever was protected from the turn of events in his favor or against it. Whether belief in something is illusory or not, it is essential to our preservation or we'll die like Melville's sailors in our pursuit of white whales.

The next morning Joe McCarthy had seen Sam Taylor at breakfast.

"Sam," he'd said, coming up behind Sam Taylor. "I heard about your speech. How come you're mad at me?"

"Christ, Joe . . ." Sam shook his head. "I'm mad at all of us," he said.

He could be a dangerous man, insidious as a wood tick creeping in soft hidden places of the body, sinking his head beneath the skin until white and fat and full of human substance he drops off and rolls around the ground, innocuous as pebbles.

There was a change in atmosphere when Sam left the house to drive to work. The day warmed uncomfortably for December and darkened. It began to rain invisibly so his clothes were damp, but he couldn't see the water drops. At Wisconsin and Newark a red convertible ran the stoplight. Twice he had to pull over for ambulances on the way to Georgetown Hospital, and at the corner of Wisconsin and M Street a morning drinker tripped and fell in the street in his attempt to board the streetcar for downtown. The conductor came to the door, spoke to the fallen man and drove on before the man had struggled to his feet. Sam Taylor waited through a light to see him get across the street.

In his office building the elevator was stuck between the fifth and sixth floors. "Is someone on it?" he asked one of the engineers working to fix it.

"Full of people," the engineer said ominously.

Once Sam had heard of a man who'd walked through the open doors of an elevator before he'd realized that the doors had opened in advance of the arrival of the elevator and the man had fallen down the shaft, crushed, as Sam recalled, by the elevator in its descent.

He would have to remember to take the stairs from now on. He thought about heart attacks. Whether climbing stairs could cause them after fifty.

It was early and his office was dark. He did not bother with a light but called Joe Fox at the *Times*.

"I don't mind telling you what I know about Andy," Joe Fox said, "but do you mind telling me why?"

"It is irregular," Sam admitted.

Joe Fox agreed.

Sam wanted to tell Joe Fox about his father and how Andrew Slaughter called his father to mind, but he could imagine how crazy it would sound to the professional voice at the other end of the line.

"I am interested in recommending him for a job."

"In Washington?" Joe Fox asked.

"Yes," Sam said.

"I know Andy personally, not professionally," Joe Fox said. "I presume he's good at what he does or he wouldn't be doing it. He's also a musician, which is how I met him, and I'm sure that it's on record somewhere that he used to drink too much." He hastened to add that Andrew Slaughter no longer drank, as Sam had no doubt noticed, and had given up jazz piano except for pleasure. He was, in other words, accountable.

Sam Taylor could see the Capitol out of the window of his office. Half of the dome was lost in mist this morning, and across the darkness hiding the missing half was the shadow of the statue of freedom facing east.

Natty sat down at her mother's dressing table and unscrewed the pastel tops of bottles. Liquid powder, beige cream foundation, mustard-colored eye grease, mascara for extra-thick lashes, tubes of peach and pink and coral lipstick. Ellen Taylor had the natural blush of the rainy season in southern Ireland and did not paint her face. But she bought makeup all the time. Her dressing table was crowded with possibilities.

Natty put on tawny beige, glazed her face like pottery and brushed her cheeks with rouge. Carefully she lined the bottom of her eyelids and put on black mascara, extra thick. Like her mother, she did not wear makeup except occasionally Revlon coral lipstick from her mother's makeup tray. But Paulette wore everything, including blue stuff on her eyelids. She smelled of drawing rooms. Even Anne Lowry had her hair done at Roi of Georgetown and lined her eyelids with pencil for school.

"You know," Natty called to her mother, who was reading on the chaise, "people are wearing nail polish."

Ellen Taylor looked up. "What about nail polish?"

"People are wearing it."

Ellen looked at her daughter's face in the mirror across the room.

"Ask if you want to use my makeup."

"I did."

"I didn't hear you."

"You were reading." She turned around and faced her mother. In the gray daylight she looked like a painted Indian doll made out of plastic.

"What did you say about nail polish?" Ellen Taylor asked again.

"That *everyone* at school is wearing it. And eyeshadow. You can get iridescent green at Murphy's."

She stood up, went over to the long mirror on her mother's bathroom door and looked at herself from several angles. Front on, she decided, was the best view.

Ellen Taylor was sitting on the bottom of the chaise now, watching the back of her daughter as Natty shifted her weight, pulled her left leg behind her like a walking stick, assumed an expression of boredom as she examined her face.

"Natty," she said, perplexed as a mother is when her predictable child changes perceptibly and without warning. "What are you doing today?"

"Going to cheerleading practice and then a game."

"Like that?" She gestured at Natty's face.

"Like what?" Natty turned around. "Do you think I'm getting fat?"

"No, you're not fat," Ellen said. "Made up is what I mean. Are you going out with all that makeup on?"

"Why not?"

"Well . . ."

"Everyone does," she said.

"You don't look like yourself," Ellen said. "You haven't played at masquerading since you were six."

"I don't feel like myself either," Natty said, but she was not going to pursue that development with Ellen Taylor, whose understanding of people came from Victorian English romances.

When Natty's body first began to change at nine or ten she remembered lying in bed at night feeling the pain in her breasts as though they were growing with such speed that she would awaken in the morning lying on her back unable to see her feet for their obstruction. That kind of change was happening now. Nearly physical in its explicitness.

She watched herself go by two mirrors on her way to the phone in her father's study.

Filip wasn't home. He had gone to practice and had a game this afternoon. If a girl called, Elsa was to tell her to meet him at the game.

"What girl?" Natty asked.

"Why you, I suppose," Elsa replied. "How many girls do a young man have?"

"I don't know," Natty replied. "My name's Natty Taylor. Did he give the name?"

"Well," she said after a moment. "I guess he did."

"And it wasn't Natty," she said quickly.

"Natty. I've heard that name Natty around here," she said. "But I don't think it's the name he gave me this morning."

In her father's bathroom she washed off the makeup, scrubbing her face with his washcloth until it was raw.

She had not noticed her mother standing in the doorway until she spoke.

"Are you and Filip—"

"I asked you not to mention Fil DeAngelis again," she snapped. "Or me."

"You took it off," her mother said with a small laugh, trying to change the conversation quickly.

"Yes," Natty said, drying her face. "I did."

Ellen wandered through her husband's study.

"Has Daddy gone?" she asked.

"Who's here?"

"I don't know."

"Someone's in the kitchen," Ellen said.

"Joe McCarthy."

"Oh." She pulled her robe around her, twisted her hair up on the back of her head. "I had forgotten he fell in the front door last night."

"You know," Natty said, shutting the bathroom door behind her, standing in front of the long mirror, pulling up her socks, adjusting her skirt, "Senator McCarthy's not so bad."

Ellen sat down at Sam's desk.

"Oh," she said, lifting her eyebrows.

"He's not. He's pretty funny really." She pulled her sweater over her head, put on her coat. "I had breakfast with him this morning and liked him in spite of everything." She took her megaphone out of the closet and some records. "Daddy's probably right. See you," she called going down the stairs. "I'll be at the Carrs' for practice and then at the St. Albans gym for a game."

Ellen did not go back to the English romance face down on the chaise. She dressed instead in a woolen skirt and sweater, made her bed, pulled up the blinds, opened the curtains and went to the attic to get down the Christmas ornaments.

A new energy after days of reading in a darkened room; familiar in emergencies.

"If someone's ill," her grandmother used to say of her, "our Ellen can stay up nights without sleep."

"In emergencies," Aunt Sally would agree, "Ellen can be counted on absolutely."

It was a special energy Ellen Taylor had in response to situations. It did not have an independent life. Like a camel, she stored it in pockets, letting it accumulate in downspouts available without effort in the dry season.

Once in anger Sam Taylor had said to Natty, "If I had terminal cancer, your mother would be heroic."

"She is good in emergencies," Natty agreed.

"It is always an emergency," he said, pulling on his coat, unable to listen to Ellen Taylor's aimless morning putterings in the room above him.

Now, lifting the boxes, carrying them downstairs, unpacking the ornaments, ironing ribbons, making lists of things to do for Christmas Eve and Christmas Day, lists for Natty's party after her cello recital, making cookies in the shapes of trees and bells and pumpkin pies and mincemeat in a sudden rush of energy that made the gloomy Tuesday morning full of sun, she wondered what secret emergency which her cells understood had unleashed this thumping of blood. Natty painting her face, unfamiliar as a plastic Indian doll, must have provoked her, and she had responded like an animal to danger.

PDQ ran an auto mechanic's shop in Appleton on Grove Street, and Rosa met him there in the back of the shop in a room heated by a wood stove and electric burners with high school pictures of his wife thumbtacked on the wall beside the hook for ACCOUNTS RECEIVABLE. There was one chair, and he sat on the desk picking his nails with the blunt end of a pencil.

He was a disappointed man. Rosa knew it by the way he talked about his wife gone gray and arthritic in the hands, about his sons who had left Appleton and never had an interest in the machine shop, about the dental work he was having done and what a cost it would be, as though the predictable shortcomings of growing older had been unanticipated. He had not expected the yearbook picture of Mrs. Taylor on the wall to ever be out of date. But his disappointment was unimpressive and led to gloom instead of anger. PDQ was not an imaginative man. Only Sam Taylor had suggested that there was life beyond the farms of central Wisconsin, beyond the machine shop in Appleton, and PDQ had dismissed that as possible for the likes of him because everyone knew that Samuel Taylor was smart.

"You want to know about Sammy," he said to Rosa. "Don't take all this down. You'll probably tell him."

She put the notebook on the desk beside him.

"Well, Sam was smart," PDQ said. "Smart as a kid and smart now. So that's how he gets these jobs he gets. That and luck. Which is something I've never had," he added without bitterness. "Some do and some don't," he said with conviction.

When the phone rang, he told the person on the other end that he had an important person in his office and was being interviewed for the newspaper in Washington. He said important twice. He asked Rosa if she'd brought a camera.

"And Joe McCarthy." He smiled. "Joe McCarthy was one of my best friends growing up. He used to go around with Mrs. Taylor back then. My wife," he said and cocked his head, looked down at Rosa, hammering on the pipe between his teeth, moving it to the corner of his mouth. "You know, Joey McCarthy was the first boy that Mrs. Taylor ever kissed," as though to share the child in his wife with Senator Joseph McCarthy gave PDQ Taylor dignity.

"Were Joe McCarthy and your brother Sam good friends?"

. "Like what?" PDQ asked, distrustful.

"Like you and Joe McCarthy."

"I was Joe's best friend," he said. "Mostly Sammy didn't bother with us."

He stepped to the door, told his assistant to turn off the machines. They couldn't hear each other think, he said.

"Sorry about the inconvenience," he said to Rosa, back on the desk. "You know," he said, "I've never been interviewed before. Once they came when Sam was made whatever he is at the FCC, but they talked to Mrs. Taylor and she told them he was a wonderful brother and how he'd looked up to me and how we'd both done well in school, which wasn't true. In the article they called her an older woman and she was forty-two. So she wrote a letter to the editor saying if forty-two was elderly, she hated to think of all those old men running the country in Washington." He laughed. "That's how Mrs. Taylor is," he said. "And she wouldn't send those people down to see me in the shop because she said I don't look decent when I'm working and they might have wanted a picture."

"So, Sam and McCarthy weren't friends," Rosa pressed on.

"Nope, not friends. But . . ." He looked at Rosa with his close-set German eyes, centered on her without embarrassment. "I could tell you a story," he said, checking her for imperfections as though internal ones might be visible on the clothes she wore. "Ravilla thought you were wonderful," he said. "But Ravilla . . ." He rolled his eyes.

"Ravilla's sweet," Rosa said.

"Sweet!" He shook his head. "And Mama thought you were all right," he said. "Mama's got good sense for the most part."

"I'll let you see the story before it's published," Rosa said. "You can censor what you like."

The story PDQ told was about the crippling of Martha Lacey Brown the summer PDQ was sixteen. The days were unusually hot that summer and lasted too long, with work around the barns and in the fields. Even without the steady heat thick about their shoulders until evening, they would have been restless because they were sixteen and there weren't any girls around. No one but Ravilla, who already had strange ways for a Catholic farm girl. And Martha Lacey Brown—named Martha for Mrs. George Washington, of course, and Lacey for the thin fine stuff on the edges of sleeves and hems, and Brown for the only Negro family in Manawa or Grand Chute or Appleton or any of the spaces in between. Martha Lacey Brown was smooth, the color of milk chocolate, with long black braids woven tight and a small compact body, supple as a birch branch. She came to the Taylors' with her father when he worked the fields. Occasionally she scrubbed out the bathroom or did the kitchen floor for Adelaide. Mostly that summer, she lazed up against the barn where Joe McCarthy was working, humming a little tune to herself, dancing in a circle of sun.

She'd have her lunch with them out behind the barn and lie back against a tree, pick up her long skirt, "Just a space," she'd laugh, "so the wind can blow through and cool me down."

"Your hands are pink," PDQ noticed one noonday picnic, picking up Martha Lacey's brown hand, turning it palm up. "Pink and brown like a wild rabbit."

She laughed, turned over on her stomach, tilting her hands back and forth. "You don't know from nothing, PDQ," she said, again and again. "That's all I can say."

And she'd sit up between the boys, draw up her legs and smile at them with eyes half closed against the sun.

Sam was there too. He was lonely that summer, with too much work to do and no friends around, so he stayed with PDQ and Joe McCarthy as long as they would let him.

"What d'ya think Uncle Lew'd say if the first time I had it was with a nigger girl?" PDQ asked pensively one day.

"You've never had it?" Joe McCarthy asked.

"Are you gonna tell me you have?"

"I'm only fourteen, Paulie, and a good Catholic boy."

"Bullshit," PDQ said in high seriousness.

"If what you're thinking of is messing around with Martha Lacey Brown, you can't," Sam said.

"That so, sweet pea."

"She's twelve years old," Sam said.

"She's older than God no matter how many years she's been on earth."

"You can't," Sam said. "That's all."

" 'Cause you'll tell," PDQ said. "You're a wonderful brother, Sammy. I don't know what good things I did in my former life to deserve you."

So the summer went on with Martha Lacey Brown giggling over lunch behind the barn, climbing the oak tree by the hay field and flipping over her long skirt, unfolding like flowers her bloomers white as clean sheets.

"She's a baby," Sam said one night to PDQ after the lights were out in their bedroom. "She doesn't know what she's doing."

"Provoking is what she's doing."

"By accident."

PDQ pulled the cover over his head and wouldn't listen.

He and Joe McCarthy had a plan. They didn't tell Sam Taylor about it. August 15 if it was a fair day or the 16 or 17 if there was rain. They'd take their lunch to Peah's Hill—a rock ridge beyond the meadow, and though only a short walk from the farm, it was remote. They'd do it then. First PDQ. Then Joe. Imagine. Their first coming with a girl the color of caramel, with a twelve-year-old virgin closed tight as a morning glory. PDQ couldn't sleep for thinking of it.

"Do you think she's got breasts yet?" PDQ asked one afternoon.

"Yeah," Joe said. "I think she has."

"Look."

Joe did.

"She has them," he said. He held his palms apart. "That size."

"You don't suppose she's too small?"

"For yours?" Joe McCarthy laughed. "The head of a needle's large enough for yours."

The truth was Martha Lacey Brown did not know what she was doing lifting her skirts and lying on her stomach, stretching her body out thin as a snake—so when PDQ jumped on her on the top of Peah's Hill before they even sat down for lunch she ran faster than she had ever run before straight in the direction from which they'd come, caught her foot on a tree root raised above the earth and plummeted over a ledge. It was not a long fall, but she landed on the back of her neck.

When Sam Taylor, who knew that morning something was up, watching PDQ washing under his fingernails, catching the mirror each time he passed it, reached the top of Peah's Hill he found her lying in a heap, her skirt up over her face, her bloomers streaked with black mud from where she'd fallen.

Later it was Sam who told PDQ that Martha Lacey would never walk again and would have to be carried places.

"You and Joe McCarthy did it," Sam said quietly.

"We done nothing," PDQ said. "We weren't there."

"I don't believe you," Sam said. "You wanted to have her. I bet you chased her and she fell."

"Bullshit," PDQ said.

Sam stayed alone from then on that summer. Read books in the loft, whittled over the back steps, watched Joe McCarthy and PDQ whispering. That fall he moved his bed into the back room and PDQ went off to Appleton to find a job without finishing school.

Once Sam asked Martha Lacey if PDQ and Joe McCarthy had been around when she fell.

"No," she said carefully. "I was by myself," she said. "Just walking along and fell across a root."

One other time, he caught her unawares.

"Are you afraid of Joe or PDQ or both?" he asked.

She hesitated, looked at him with eyes black as crows.

"Joe McCarthy," she said quietly.

That Christmas, when PDQ was home from Appleton, Sam said to him, "You'd do anything to get McCarthy's favor."

He nodded.

"You'd be okay alone," Sam said, but his brother's fist connected with his nose and sent him tumbling over the back of the bed.

"Some story," PDQ said, smiling. "Though it's a shame about Martha Lacey Brown."

"It is some story," Rosa agreed, and she could tell in his attitude that PDQ saw himself as the wise hero of the story and Sam as the young innocent who is initiated.

When Rosa got back to the hotel it had started to snow. She packed quickly and left without making final telephone calls to Joe McCarthy's history teacher and great-aunt in Manawa. To the man who had worked for him on his chicken farm before he went to law school. It didn't make any difference. The trip to Wisconsin for the *News* was nothing next to a sudden sense she had of immediate danger. Not the old familiar fear that Filip would be hit by a streetcar on Wisconsin Avenue or come down with a devastating virus of an unknown strain. But a new sense more perilous than accidents, that Filip would not advance beyond the promises of youth and was susceptible. As PDQ had been to Joe McCarthy.

On the plane from Chicago, Rosa sorted her notes. It made sense to her, in retrospect, that she was not the first one to hear the story PDQ Taylor had told her about Martha Lacey Brown.

In fact, she guessed he had told anyone who would listen, as though what happened gained respectability in the telling.

The All Metropolitan All Stars were playing in the St. Albans gym for a demonstration game to benefit the March of Dimes. Filip was on the bench with three fouls against him in the first quarter.

The visiting coach had snapped his thumb in the direction of the bench, and Filip sat down, replaced by a lean, gliding Negro boy from DeMatha with a cross the size of his number 43 around his neck.

"So what's up?" Fil's coach asked. "What the hell is up, Fil?"

"Dunno," Filip said, leaning over in the posture of bench players, his back horizontal, his head at a level with his knees. "I'm tired out."

"Tired out?" the coach repeated. "Tired out?" as though that was not a condition to be considered.

"Do you know who's here?"

"Yeah, yeah," Filip said.

"The coach from Dartmouth," he said through his teeth.

"I know."

"You've never fouled before. I mean once or twice, but in one game. My God." The coach held his head in his hand. "Probably Dave Bean is here from Harvard."

"Yes."

"You saw him?" The coach's head shot up, scanning the crowd, mostly scouts, professionals, college scouts from the state universities, the Big Ten, from the Ivy League, spending Christmas week in Washington selecting for their next year's freshman team.

Filip DeAngelis was on the All Stars team—the starting five. It was the first time in the history of the All Star team that there'd been a boy from private school—not parochial, where the classes were large and the boys tougher than the public-school boys, even the Negroes from Roosevelt and Coolidge—but the private schools, the small clubs of gentle boys, hangovers of America's slender aristocracy, which did not raise a band of athletes—boys sound in mind and body surely, Christian boys secure in their sense of themselves, tested in small arenas where the old boys, smelling of pipe tobacco, gather in civilized ways. Now Filip DeAngelis, the Italian boy from St. Albans, was Big Time.

Rosa had insisted on private school for Filip when he was nine.

"Honestly, Rosa," Antonio had said. "What pretenses you have in store in future years. We didn't need private school to do well."

"I want the best for my children," Rosa had argued. "Every opportunity. It is not pretense and he can still be Catholic. He'll go to Mass before the service at the cathedral."

"You want to give your child something different from every other kid on the block," Antonio said in disgust. "No neighborhood boy will speak to him."

"They're scared of him now," Rosa said, "because he's strong. They'll speak to him whether they like him or not because they're scared." She was right. If any of the neighborhood children was inclined to call him sissy when he came home in his blue blazer and red-striped tie, they never did, and St. Albans was glad to have this young Italian boy who sang soprano in the cathedral boys' choir and made news for them on the sports page. After his voice changed, they made him an acolyte for the cathedral so that he could maintain his scholarship. He had made them a democratic institution.

"Think when they put you back in the game," the coach said as though thinking was an entirely foreign experience. "Think."

"Yeah, I will," Fil said. "I'm really sorry," he said. "I don't know what happened."

He did know what had happened. All night last night, he had lain in his single bed with Blanche, under the football and baseball pennants, the blue STA letters in black five-and-ten-cent-store frames, the letter from President Eisenhower, who had met him once and said that Fil reminded him of his son, before John, who had died.

Now over in the corner of the bleachers, just in view, Blanche sat alone like an angel in a camel's-hair coat. He could not take his eyes off of her.

Natty had intended to go straight to cheerleading practice at Dick Carr's house, but walking through the grounds of the Washington Cathedral, through the Bishop's Garden, up the road to the Peace Cross where the federal city of Washington, suspended in winter fog, rested like an abstract just beyond the gymnasium, she thought of Filip with a memory of their early love, gentle as memories of childhood. She stopped by the gymnasium because she knew he would be there.

Filip was called back in the game at the beginning of the second half. He could not concentrate. He heard the crowd on either side of him and saw his coach sitting on the sidelines. He saw Blanche watching him and the coach from Dartmouth in his green-and-white parka just behind the bench. He saw Natty Taylor come in the side door of the gymnasium. The scenes divided into pieces like a jigsaw puzzle which fitted in and out as he moved up and down the court.

He knew before it happened that he would foul out.

"So," his coach said.

"I'm really sorry, Al."

"It's such a waste to mess up on the one important day."

"I looked bad, I guess," he said.

"Terrible," the coach said. "Terrible," he said again as though he could taste it.

"Fil DeAngelis has never fouled out," Natty said to the boy next to her, whom she had never seen.

"Yeah," he said. "Well, tough shit. Better luck next time."

"Do you know him?" she asked.

"No," he said. "I came here to see Larry Luce. He's high scorer," the boy said. "The other guy, DeAngelis, has had a lousy game."

"I've never seen him foul before," Natty said.

"So you said."

"I said . . ." But she didn't go on to explain to this foreigner in the St. Albans School gymnasium what she had said.

She watched Filip on the bench with his head down, a white towel like a collar around his neck, and tried to call up what she had felt for him. Just last Sunday. She felt terrible that he had fouled out of the All Star game, as though the fact of fouling out was significant to them both.

Ellen was decorating the house for Christmas when Will Barnes came in—clipping the holly sprigs in little silver bows, winding the balsam fir into ropes tied together with red taffeta, thin now with the tyings and ironings of past Christmases. The Cleveland Orchestra's *Messiah* was on the radio, and she turned it up as a warning to Joe McCarthy.

Joe McCarthy answered the door and laughed when he saw Will Barnes in his jeans and jacket and cowboy boots smelling of cattle.

"Jesse James," McCarthy laughed, "back from the dead without bothering to take a bath."

"I'm Will Barnes, Mr. McCarthy," Will said without humor, kicking his boots against the doormat, dislodging black clay in wet lumps on the Taylors' front porch.

McCarthy took Will by the shoulders and examined him for recognizable signs. "Nell Barnes' son," he said, squinting and then slapping Will gently on the back. "Nell and I are not good friends."

"I guess not," Will said.

"Which is no reason why you and I can't be good friends." He threw a burly arm around Will Barnes, as comfortable in that gesture as if he were a professional comedian given to artificial intimacies as part of his act.

"You've come to see Natty?"

"Is she home?" Will asked.

"I'm not sure," McCarthy said. "I've only been working at the Taylors' for a week now." He escorted Will into the study, offering him a large leather chair, a straight-backed chair, a two-cushioned couch with a sulking orange cat. Will declined, preferring to stand, he said.

"Difficult to please," McCarthy said. "Like your father. I liked your father. He was a cantankerous, bad-tempered man who kept his hands clean," he said. "Which is more, I notice, than his son does." He swung his leg over the desk, examining Will Barnes as though his body chemistry carried old-fashioned weapons.

As a young boy Will Barnes had memorized the gestures of cowboys. He spoke roughly and used poor grammar with intention. He walked from his hips as though his legs were tied to stilts and carried his shoulders like rectangular boxes, angling beneath his neck. People laughed at him as McCarthy had done —but carefully. Something in the bearing of Will Barnes, in his assumptions, suggested that the dress and carriage were hints to the secrets of a boy who understood substantially the violent spirit of the outlaw in the old American West.

Ellen gave Will Barnes hot chocolate and a sampling of the cookies she had made that morning. She asked him about his mother and how was she since her last heart attack and about Eliza and was she going to college and what did Will do in the summers, stringing the questions together in sequence, ending with the only question which interested her at all. Did Will know what had happened to Natty and Filip DeAngelis?

No, he said, he didn't.

"I think Fil has a new girl," Ellen said.

That he had heard, Will agreed.

"But I'm not around much," he said.

It was not that he didn't like Ellen Taylor, he thought to himself. There were things about her that touched him—the way right now her hair fell out of a clumsy bun, the way one button of her blouse that pulled across her breasts had struggled free. She was open to injury in a way, for example, that Nell Barnes was not. He sensed a heart attack would strike Ellen Taylor dead on the first round.

But there was something he did not trust. She must have learned subtle ways to defend herself against direct attack.

Specifically he knew that Ellen Taylor did not like him as a replacement for Fil DeAngelis. That kind of direct attack.

"Well," she said. "I guessed that." She got up and washed out the cups. "Young fickle love." She laughed. "I'm glad I'm grown."

Will sensed he ought to say "I'm sorry" as if there had been a death.

At the door Joe McCarthy gave a rakish military salute.

"The Mrs. says come back again," he called to Will. "Give your sweet mother a hug for me."

"You know Bill Barnes' son?" McCarthy asked Ellen after Will had left. "I wouldn't touch him with a ten-foot pole."

"It's crazy," Will said later to Natty. "McCarthy wandering around your house and your mother doesn't even speak to him."

"He's like a ghost," she said.

"He's too dangerous to be a ghost."

"Will," she laughed, ringing her arm through his. "He's absolutely harmless."

She would ask Fil DeAngelis to dinner after Christmas, Ellen thought. Rosa and his sister and brother. All of them. They'd use the Italian lace cloth and have wine. She could make cranberry tarts and decorate the table with white grapes dipped in sugar. She'd wear the new rose silk dress gathered at the breast in tiny pleats, gotten for a dinner at the White House and then she had been too tired to go. Filip would sit next to her and she'd talk to him quietly, wear her hair down. The scene was set in color in her mind. She played it out against the last of the *Messiah*, turned up as high as it would go. She did not even notice when Joe McCarthy came in the kitchen and washed out his glass.

Choo Choo had on white lipstick, and a lavender heart was painted on her cheek. She wore her mother's raccoon coat from college, and her hair wound in crochet caps around each ear.

197

"Hello." She edged down toward Natty sitting on the bench. "Aren't you going to practice at Dick Carr's?"

Natty nodded. "I just stopped by the game," she said. "Poor Filip."

"Yes," Choo Choo agreed. "Poor Filip." She had not come to see the game. She didn't like games. She had come to be in a roomful of people instead of by herself.

"Were you here when he came?" Natty asked.

"You mean did he come with Blanche," Choo Choo said, truthful in the way of people whose ordinary restraints have been broken down and who can tell the truth without embarassment.

"Well," Natty said, "yes. Did he come with Blanche?"

"He's always with Blanche," Choo Choo said. "That's what I hear."

"*What* do you hear?"

"That," Choo Choo said, hesitating at Natty's sharp voice. "Don't be mad."

"I'm not mad," Natty said.

"You're sure?"

"Yes," Natty said. "I'm sure. Do you think they're really involved?"

"So I hear."

"From who?"

"From everyone," Choo Choo said. "From Dick Carr."

"Who else?"

"You know," Choo Choo evaded. "Everyone."

"That's what I thought."

"I guess Blanche is like you," she said, "and wants to look good. Important."

"Maybe," Natty said, exposed and feeling sick. "I never thought so myself, but that's what people told me at Dick Carr's last night."

Perhaps that's what it had been. The sense of floating halfway between the ceiling and the floor, that flying just above the trees. And she had thought she was in love with Fil DeAngelis. Innocent, of course—for all her common sense, she had not got that kind of clear line on herself to see that all along she had been falling in love with herself.

"Jesus," Natty said to Choo Choo without vindictiveness. "You're probably right."

She wanted to ask Choo Choo what it was like to be crazy—whether you knew it when it happened, whether all of a sudden at a given time, the sections of tomatoes and radishes and onions and cucumber and mushrooms and artichokes in your dependable brain were tossed and clouded with some kind of oily dressing and you were no longer what you thought you had been. The veins of your hands receded, your knuckles grew plump, the nails turned automatically blue. Whose hands were these attached to the familiar arms? Whose face in the mirror which had been as predictable as the sun? Did Choo Choo know that she was crazy? That people didn't paint lavender hearts on their cheeks or speak without reservations? When it happened that a mind went, was a mind gone as ordinary as the neatly sectioned mind you'd grown accustomed to?

Natty wanted to tell Choo Choo that out of the blue she had turned bad, as though a girl were like a playing card with two sides. Until these last few days, the right side had come up in the toss. Now this stupid change.

"Listen," she said to Choo Choo, moving closer so the boy from Gonzaga couldn't hear her. "What's it like to see a psychiatrist?"

Choo Choo looked at her without expression.

"For migraines," she said simply. "I see Dr. Baer for physical reasons," she emphasized. "That's all."

"I'm sorry," Natty said, aware she had intruded, but pleased as well to know there were limitations even to a craziness like Choo Choo's. It promised that this new vision of herself was not irreversible.

"I don't see why you like Will Barnes," Choo Choo said when

they both saw Will come in the side door of the gymnasium and sit down on the end of the bleachers. "He really smells bad."

He smelled like a perfectly ordinary boy in the back seat of Nell Barnes' car, where they were lying after the trial game, after lunch at the Hot Shoppes. If Natty closed her eyes, she could pretend that he was Filip. The same thick hair that curled slightly at the neck, though the body was longer, stiff as a two-by-four and lighter against her body. First she thought of Filip kissing her, and then she imagined Filip watching in the back window of Nell Barnes' car, only it was Larry Luce on top of her and not Will Barnes. Someone as famous as Filip at least, worth his anger as he banged on the back window, kicked the chrome fender, demanded Natty back immediately or he would overturn the car.

Will Barnes looked down at Natty, her eyes closed.

"What are you thinking about?" he asked.

"Mmmmm." She opened her thighs, kissed him on the neck with her tongue.

He dropped between her legs, and fully clothed they lay together—Will Barnes dreaming his dream of Natty behind the hay he had stacked last spring, knowing in the way we know the truth of things that as his own mind's picture of his body was replaced by the body of Fil DeAngelis, so was Natty's as he kissed her.

He raised up again.

"Nat," he said.

Her eyes were tight closed.

"You're different."

"Yes?" It was a question. "How come?"

He sat up and she scrambled up on the seat beside him.

"What are you doing this for?"

"Doing what?"

"You know," he said. "Doing this," he said. "With me."

"I want to," she said.

He opened the back door of the car, got out, brushed off his pants and straightened them around his belt.

He knew that something had happened to Natty Taylor the same as if she'd dyed her hair blue-black and replaced her withered leg with one as ordinary as a dancer's.

Natty walked to Georgetown down Wisconsin past the shops, done up in bells and scarlet velvet for Christmas, past the genteel ladies with their packages and small annoying dogs. The women arm in arm in daytime black and businessmen late from lunch, occasional familiar faces, familiar not because she knew them, but because they were eighteen and wore their short hair in curls around their faces, chattered in familiar voices.

And in that accidental settlement from walking without trying to think, she knew she could do anything without remorse. She went over the possibilities like a Christmas list. She could cheat in French class if she did not know the answer, she could drink until she fell over in a chair, she could lie straight out to anyone except her father, she could deceive Will Barnes and kiss the lips of boys whose faces were unknown to her.

She could even, she thought, lie to her father. In fact, she already had about the accident at Carter Harold's farm.

At the Little Tavern she turned left to Dick Carr's house. She was, she decided, capable of doing harm.

Rosa's story about John Taylor was on page 35 of the *News* with an old photograph too obscure to identify generally, but Sam recognized it as one which sat on his mother's dresser.

Sam didn't read the story until after lunch, after the business of the day, the meeting with the North Carolina broadcasters, with Philip Graham of the *Post* about some lobbying problems.

JOHN TAYLOR, the headline read, BORN OUT OF SEASON.

The story was neither surprising nor upsetting about John Taylor's drinking and his shiftless ways, his music and his wit, his incompatibility with Adelaide Taylor, his peculiar favoritism for the young Sam Taylor. Until the end, which struck Sam Taylor like soundings trying the ocean's depth, finding to one's astonishment that the depth can at a given and impermanent

moment be measured. It read: "There are men born out of season who cannot find a place in their own time but whose spirit,
generated through their children, recollected in another form,
may find shape in more congenial places. Perhaps Sam Taylor is
what his father could not be. Perhaps Sam Taylor's daughter will
be. In any case, I found a music maker in Wisconsin, dead forty
years, whose imagination was sufficient to survive generations.
R. DeAngelis, Manawa, Wisconsin."

He would write to her, Sam thought, and tell her how
strangely affecting he thought the article was. He would call her
instead, immediately, when he got home.

Andrew Slaughter had arrived at lunch, his mother said, and
was out now in the grove behind the farm chopping wood. She
had given Andrew the message, she said, but he did not seem to
remember a man named Sam Taylor in Washington. What was
it he said he did?

"Chairman of the FCC," Sam said and gave Mrs. Slaughter
several numbers where her son could reach him when he got
in.

He couldn't get his father out of his mind. He wanted John
Taylor back complete. His memory was missing parts; it had
no flesh.

Irrationally he thought of digging up his father's grave in
Manawa. How carefully was the job done then—the blood
drained and the body injected with the fluids preserving death.
Would be find bones familiar as the fleshless memory in his
mind? Could he recapture something if he gathered up those
bones and held them in his arms?

"Jesus," he said, putting away the things on his desk, dressing
to go home. He was a man of practical good sense, not given to
such ramblings of the spirit.

Lafayette Park, located in front of St. John's Episcopal Church,
across the street from the White House, was a gathering place
of homosexuals. People crossed the park or passed by it on

either side, but they did not sit down on benches, accepting that the park was covenanted land. Sam Taylor crossed the park many afternoons on his way home from work, crossed it this afternoon, and without conscious decision, sat down on a bench in the center of the park and opened the *Evening Star* and began to read

Al Cox watched Sam from the steps of St. John's Church. He had followed him from the FCC at 12th and Pennsylvania, watched him sit down, open up the newspaper which had been rolled under his arm, watched the thin, high-hipped young man in a red muffler pass by Sam once. Stop, look back and then join Sam on the bench. Sam put down the newspaper and spoke to the man on the bench beside him. It was—Al Cox concluded quickly, with the sharp energy of discovery—an arrangement.

Al Cox waited, but the two men did not move. Their conversation from that distance seemed intense. Sam leaned his head toward the younger man and gestured with his hands.

Al Cox could not wait.

He shouted it in his head, running to the trolley stop on Pennsylvania, catching the Friendship Heights to Georgetown. "Jesus," he thought, hardly able to wait as the bus ambled up Pennsylvania onto M Street. "This is some goddam news," and all the way to 31st and N, running down N from Wisconsin Avenue, he rehearsed his story for Dick Carr.

The man who sat down next to Sam Taylor asked him if he was meeting someone.

"No," Sam replied, conscious of physical acceleration.

"Do you work near here?" the man asked.

Sam agreed that he did.

"And you're not waiting for someone?" the man asked.

"No," Sam said. "I stopped to read the paper before I took the bus home."

"You're not new to Washington."

"I've been here ten years," Sam said.

"You know about . . . ?" The man gestured around the park.

"Yes," Sam said, knowing he was taking chances, but knowing that the real chances were with himself in ways that eluded him except as a brushstroke here and there across a stretched white canvas. Something was missing in the picture to connect the planes. Some definition.

"I think you are taking a risk," the man said, not without sympathy.

"Yes," Sam said.

"It suggests an arrangement," the man said, "your being here."

Sam smiled at him, got up without hurrying, slid his paper beneath his arm.

"You have wonderful hands," the man said, as though to ease Sam's possible embarrassment.

"Thank you," Sam said and he walked out of the park as slowly as if he'd invented it—conscious that the younger man in the red muffler was watching him, unaware of the cold.

"He must be queer," Al Cox said to Dick. And he told the story. He told it straight the first time and the second time completed it with his own conclusions.

"So," he said. "You begin to see the whole picture."

Dick Carr knew one homosexual in Oklahoma, none in Washington. But the one in Oklahoma worked on his father's ranch, a tall man, a cowboy, thin and supple as sugar cane, with full lips and narrow eyes, slits of color beneath his hat. Whenever Dick thought of him, whenever Dick thought of what he did with other men, it made him sick. He wanted to do terrible things to the cowboy, loathsome to him as German roaches— squash him with the heel of his boot, run him down with a stallion. Now at the mention of the mere possibility of Samuel Taylor—of Natty Taylor's father—he was too sick to finish his beer and poured it out in the sink.

"I'd like to kill him," he said in disgust.

"Too extreme," Carter Harold said, leaning back in his chair, gently titillated by this new development.

"We've got to do something," Dick said in a heat.

"We could," Carter said, hesitating, as though ideas sifted slowly in his mind, "call the city desk at the *News.*"

Al Cox whistled.

"Just what in God's name is calling the *News* going to do?" Dick Carr asked.

"Personal feelings aside, Dick," Carter began, "we should feel a sense of responsibility. It is dangerous to have homosexuals in the government," he said.

"Absolutely," Dick Carr agreed.

"However we feel about the man himself."

"Absolutely," Dick said again. "Let's call DeAngelis' old lady."

"Hell no," Carter snapped. "If we call the city desk and tip them off on Sam Taylor—say we had been in Lafayette Park— they'll follow him and expose him. Don't you see? You don't call a columnist on something like this."

"Yes, I see," Dick Carr said slowly. "I'm sure you're right."

Carter Harold called the city desk. He was careful about it. He said that in fairness to the man's daughter, whom he knew and respected, he did not want to be involved. The man on the city desk was guarded.

"I wonder," Dick Carr said after Carter had hung up the phone, "if that's why Joe McCarthy's at the Taylors' house."

"What?" Carter asked.

"You know."

"You mean McCarthy and Sam Taylor?"

Carter shrugged.

"Jesus," Dick Carr said. "Jesus Christ."

Rosa could tell that Filip was not alone in the house when she came home from Wisconsin Tuesday afternoon, and by the time she'd dashed up the stairs Filip was sitting at his desk in jeans and bare feet.

"I didn't think you'd be home," Filip said, white-faced and shaken. "We weren't expecting you until tonight," he said.

Rosa stood in the door to Filip's room and looked from her son to Blanche, recognizing in the other woman the visual residue of spent desire. And Filip's shame.

She left the room without speaking.

In her own room she thought of Antonio. There was some soft center, some perceptible mutation in the genes passed through Antonio and herself to these children, that she did not recognize as the hard core of her own being. Angela probably lying in some unmade bed with a rich and mindless Harvard boy— Johnny stunted at birth, now Filip on whom she had counted.

She opened her suitcase and unpacked. Down the hall she could hear Filip and the new girl whispering.

The thought flashed through her mind that Antonio had been a Communist after all and had lied to her about it.

After Rosa left, Filip was too sick to move.

"You got to go," he said to Blanche without looking at her.

"Yeah," she replied. "I'll say."

"I'll call you tonight," he said. "We can still go Christmas shopping tomorrow."

He listened to her creep down the front steps, heard the front door open and quietly shut.

Filip had been a model son for years. He had been good in the conventional sense of the word and extraordinary in unexpected ways. Even as a young child he could not remember doubting himself or fearing what might happen in the future. Good fortune had seemed to him predictable, and so the shame of these last hours was intolerable. He had never anticipated failure. Now he would have to face Rosa over dinner. He locked the bedroom door, pulled down the shades and climbed into bed. Instead of Blanche, he dreamed about his father.

When he awoke to Rosa's knock announcing dinner he could not remember the dream. All he knew was that he felt like dying —or sleeping until school was out for the summer.

———

Carter was enormously kind to Natty when he told her about her father. He did not even mention the possibility suggested by Dick Carr with Senator McCarthy. He made her feel as if the kidnapping were her own idea.

"It's not true," she snapped. "He had too much to drink yesterday. Big deal."

"Al did see the whole thing," Carter said gently. "We're trying to help you."

"What is Al Cox doing that he happens to see my father drinking?"

"He works downtown."

"Listen, Nat," Dick Carr said. "It could be in the papers."

She put on her coat. "Shut up," she said.

Dick Carr took her by the shoulders, and she wrestled away. "Your father was picked up yesterday for drinking."

"Arrested?"

"Yes," Dick said, "and now the newspapers are free to write anything about him."

"Leave me alone," she said.

"Nat." He dropped his hands from her shoulders. "We're trying to help."

Natty backed against the front door, glaring at them.

"You're being terrific," she said without expression. "I'd like to kill you."

"If something happened to you," Carter said thoughtfully, "your father would do anything. Don't you think?"

Carter Harold was right, of course, and in the confusion of the moment, the growing confusion of these last days, Natty was willing to do anything.

If, she decided, she was kidnapped and her return was conditional on his resignation, then possibly this new story about his private life would not have to come out. There was no need for the Syndicate to identify themselves, they agreed. They would take her that night to the Senior Shack behind Friends School, which was deserted because of Christmas vacation.

They all agreed it was a sensible solution and would in kindness protect Samuel Taylor from disgrace.

—————

"I hate you," Natty said to Carter Harold as he walked with her to the sidewalk.

"It's a shitty deal," Carter agreed. "I don't blame you for being mad."

"You can rot in hell," she said and walked up N Street without looking back.

"My God," Dick Carr said after Natty had left that evening, "we're going to force Sam Taylor out."

"It has been extraordinary," Carter Harold agreed, his eyes half closed, watching the smoke from his cigarette trail streamers toward the ceiling.

They could be right, Natty thought. On the way down Wisconsin she remembered that last summer Sam Taylor had moved from the room he shared with Ellen, and lately, just this last week, some sense she had of her father had given way as though she were standing in an old house unpredictable in storms.

WEDNESDAY,

DECEMBER 22

1954

Natty lay in her dark room under the covers fully dressed. She lay on her back with her eyes open looking at the ceiling as though entertainment would materialize there. At two a.m. the Syndicate would meet her at the corner of Highland and 34th Street. At one-forty-five she would get up to leave, allowing time to listen to the sleeping house before she left, to determine she was not going to be discovered missing immediately.

At dinner her father had seemed old to her. In the obscure light of the dining room it looked as if the skin fell away from the bones on his face, like clothes separating from the body. She could imagine him eighty, his hair gone, the skin tight and mottled on his skull and hanging in graduated folds around his eyes as though he were in the process of shedding it. She imagined him dead with no skin like Suzie Bones in sixth-grade science at Sidwell Friends. A skeleton without distinguishing features, this high with arms this long and sockets where extraordinary eyes might have been. She sat at the table watching him eat, relieved at his death as though it were absolute. And then she shook out the funeral—she was standing with her mother and her mother's first husband and her stepbrothers, Adelaide and drunken

Ravilla, Uncle Paul in greasy pants—shook it out of her head, fearing that the power of her thought could kill him. Especially vulnerable as he was now, looking eighty.

"You're not listening," Sam was saying.

Natty looked up. "I didn't hear you," she said.

"You haven't been practicing for Christmas Eve," he said.

"I know it," she said. "I know what I'm playing down pat."

Sam raised his eyebrows. He did not criticize, only an occasional shift of posture, like this evening, which told her he expected everything of her.

"I do," she snapped. "Beethoven's Sonata in G minor. Dum de dum, dum, dum," she exaggerated. "I could play it with my feet."

"Perhaps," he said, "you'll have to play it with your feet to compensate in tricks for your lack of skill."

She thought of leaving the table, throwing her chair back against the wall and storming to her room. But she wanted him to know it didn't matter what he said.

"Sam," Ellen chided.

"Perhaps," Natty replied coolly and the moment passed.

Ellen chattered about Christmas Eve with the Goodwins, the party for Natty after the concert, about what special things she'd made that day for the Armands' children and Aunt Nettie down the street. She said she was thinking of having the DeAngelises for dinner over the holidays.

"Think again," Natty said.

"You look wonderful," Sam said to Ellen, and Natty noted that her mother did look well, dressed for the first time in weeks. There was an unfamiliar sense of expectation about her.

The second time Sam Taylor brought up cello practice Natty did leave.

"I'm concerned that you're giving a concert cold," he said, "not so much for its own sake but for what it suggests about you."

"It suggests that I'm busy with other things," she said. "I'll be fine Christmas Eve."

"I heard you practicing last night," he said. "You weren't fine then."

She left. In her room, she put on the station playing popular music top volume, lay down on her bed and put her feet up against the wall. She couldn't ever remember listening to the Top 60 by herself.

Her father came in again. She heard him come in but she didn't move, didn't take her legs down from the wall where they were beating time to the music, didn't remove her arm from across her face. She knew it was her father.

"Natty?"

"Yes."

He turned down the music. She could feel him sitting down in the chair beside her bed.

"I haven't been working lately either," he said. "There is a personal cost."

"I'll practice," she said. She wanted him to go away.

"Is it your friends?" He leaned over, resting his elbows on her bed.

"Is what?"

"I know things have fallen apart with Fil DeAngelis," he said, "because of Joe."

"Maybe," she said into her sweatered arm.

"I'm wondering if it's these friends of yours who decorate their houses with the corpses of cats."

"If what?"

"This change," he said.

"In me?" She took down her arm, rolled over on her side, rested her chin in her hand and looked at him. "I *like* my friends," she said. "I like them and they like me."

"Well," he said and got up, stiff-legged like a war veteran, rubbed his eyes as though in hope the scene might change when he focused again. "I hope you'll try to practice tonight."

She had. She had practiced for forty-three minutes. Once through her solo concert, once through the ensemble, watching the clock in the study. And then she'd stopped. In the kitchen, she made a peanut-butter sandwich and ate it in bed with the lights off. In the darkness she remembered Dick Carr kissing her last Friday night and wondered whether he would kiss her again.

It was nearly one by the clock beside her bed when she heard the cello. At first she thought it was outside, next door, and then that she was imagining it, but it was her own cello playing Beethoven, halting but clear, and she wondered who was playing in the middle of the night.

She put a bathrobe over her clothes to conceal them and went down the back stairs. In the blue light from the study Joe McCarthy slouched in a chair with his mouth open—and in the corner of the room, Ellen Taylor with her back to McCarthy played the music by the lights from the Christmas tree. She was still fully dressed.

Natty slid into a chair unobserved. Ellen Taylor looked like Natty's image of herself, though she had never seen herself play except once in the hall mirror. Her head and shoulders were bent, her fingers high on the bow, strutting. For an amazing moment, before Ellen discovered Natty in the chair, she saw a connection between her mother and herself as though it were visible.

"Nat?" her mother said, turning, catching the shadow of Natty traced in blue light. "I thought you were sleeping."

"I was," Natty said, "and then I heard you playing."

"I couldn't sleep," Ellen said. She put the cello in its case. "Do you want tea?"

Automatically she picked up the brandy and then changed her mind. "I think I'll have tea, too," she said.

"I didn't know you played," Natty said. "I knew you used to."

"When I was small," Ellen said. "Sometimes, when you're not here, I play," she said. "I don't like people to hear me."

"But if you practiced . . ."

"People were better than me," she said.

"People are better than me too."

"But I was in Manawa, Wisconsin," she said, sitting at the kitchen table, sipping hot tea. "If there were people in Manawa better than me, I knew I hadn't a chance."

"You quit?"

"When I was fifteen." She remembered a time playing in her bedroom at her grandmother's house in a velvet dress with a lace V neck, long and narrow as a snake, a waist reed-slender, her hair done up in ribbons. She played to the walnut mirror on her door in the guarded light of early dusk, played

Beethoven's preludes to a full house at Carnegie Hall—diminutive as wild flowers from the enormous stage. "I wanted to be very good," Ellen said softly, exposed by this late-night discovery, by the feeling of music in her hands again. "It was a dream I had, to be famous." She poured them both another cup of tea. "The trouble is I never learned to get beyond the dream." She glanced at Natty shyly. "Do you ever dream of being famous?" she asked.

"Sometimes," Natty said. "Mostly I just do the next thing."

"Like your father," Ellen said.

"He dreams of being famous."

"But he's practical about it."

"Would you like me to be something?"

"I suppose I would," Ellen said. "All mothers would, but I haven't wanted to impose."

"Which is more than Daddy's done."

"He can't help it."

"Maybe," she said, realizing something about Ellen Taylor she had not known before—this mother she had thought too tired for a second set of children, too strung through the tapestries of her dreams to recognize the possibilities of flesh. All along, all these years of living together in the same house, she had passed on to Natty the chances for a life, but passed it on as a secret that carried with it no responsibility for Natty to be this woman or this musician or this flesh form of Ellen Taylor's dream.

Natty wanted to touch her mother, brush her face with her own, but the knowledge was greater than physical expression. So she took it as a secret back upstairs.

Leaving was simple. She went down the front stairs in stockinged feet, through the living room to the door that led to the side yard, and although she heard Joe McCarthy rattling like metal trash cans in the study, although she knew she was clear as the furniture in the blue light of the living room, she did not hurry. She knew the house was preoccupied with itself, her mother reading on the rose chaise, her father turning from one side to the other in his bed, waiting for sleep as though it traveled motorized down determined paths. And Joe McCarthy drunk again.

Dick Carr was waiting on 34th Street at the end of Highland, with Anne Lowry in the back seat and Carter Harold in the front.

"Any trouble?" he asked, lifting up the seat so Natty could crawl back with Anne Lowry.

"No, it was easy," she said.

They drove through the blinking red lights on 34th Street up Porter to Wisconsin and down the Post Office driveway to the back parking lot of Sidwell Friends.

At one time, when Friends School was a farm for summer residents in Washington, the Senior Shack in all probability housed small tools for crops—shovels, scythes and rakes, a hand plow perhaps and leather strappings. It was frame like the school, exactly square, painted white with two windows on either side just under the roof and a front door secured by a combination lock. Every senior at Friends School knew the combination, and it was a point of honor to tell no one else. Each year the combination lock was changed for the new senior class.

There was one room inside, with furniture donated years before by Anne Lowry's mother from her summer house in Mississippi. The walls were painted lavender and decorated with messages kept within the bounds of propriety. The class of 1950 had been denied the use of the shack from January on because one senior had written FUCK on the wall in white oil-base. There were rules, of course. No smoking, no drinking, no sex and no use on the weekends when the school was empty, but the rules were cautiously broken year after year by an elaborate system of checks and balances whereby the people having sex or a cigarette on the white wicker couch from Biloxi were protected by appointed class agents. The one rule maintained through the years was that pertaining to the use of the shack on weekends. Sometime after the war and before 1950 a group of seniors had been discovered at the shack on Saturday night, and whatever the actual repercussions, the stories about it grew from year to year. No group since then had bothered with the shack on weekends.

Dick Carr turned off the engine.

"Well," he said.

"We'll stay here for a few minutes," Carter said, "to see if anyone comes."

"Paulette is coming with Al Cox," Dick said.

"Here?" Carter snapped. "I didn't want complications."

"Well," Dick said, "I thought we might be having a meeting," he said. "You know, to decide what's next."

"At your house, Carr," Carter said. "Not in the middle of the goddam parking lot at Sidwell Friends."

They waited ten minutes on the car clock in a silence active with Carter Harold's bad temper. And then Natty with Anne Lowry crept up the hill to the back of the shack and went around it and in. Dick Carr waited until they were no longer visible, then he started up the car, driving down the driveway without headlights.

"Drive off," Carter had told him.

"What about Paulette?" he'd said. "They'll come and we won't be here. It could be disastrous."

"A thought that didn't cross your mind when you suggested they come."

But they waited at the end of the Post Office driveway until Al Cox drove up with Paulette, and then they made arrangements to meet the other car at Dick Carr's right away.

"We've got to stay together in this," Dick Carr said while they were waiting for Al Cox. "You and me. I mean we planned the whole thing. We can't have a fight."

Carter didn't reply. He looked out the side window with great interest, as though he expected a parade.

"Listen, Carter," Dick said, frightened by discord, unequal to the situation without the predictable arrangements of Carter Harold. "I'm really sorry," and then, stupidly, "Do you have a thing for Paulette Estinet?"

"What thing?" Carter asked coolly.

"Nothing," Dick said. "Nothing at all. Jesus Christ."

On the drive down Wisconsin Avenue to Georgetown, Carter said, "Forget it." By the time they had parked and gone in the Carrs' house, by the time Paulette had arrived with Al Cox, he was himself again, and although he wasn't especially good-humored, he was decent about things.

The plan was that someone would be with Natty all the time in case she was inadvertently discovered by the school janitor or bus driver or post-office employee or even another senior—they would appear to be playing cards.

On Thursday, after the Taylors had a chance to discover her missing and to look for her in the usual places, after the newspaper story on Samuel Taylor's homosexuality had broken, Natty would send a note to Sam Taylor asking him to resign because of the humiliation. Saying that her return was dependent on that.

"After all," Carter said easily, "this has been Natty's decision. In the last analysis we are in no way implicated."

Carter noticed that Paulette had followed Dick Carr into the kitchen after the Syndicate meeting. He finished his cigarette carefully, putting it out in the crystal ashtray. And then he followed them.

"I'm taking you home now," he said to Paulette. "It's three in the morning."

"So?" She shrugged. "I told my parents I'd be very late." But she followed him anyway and told Dick Carr she'd see him in the morning, maybe they'd all have lunch after cheerleading practice, and was he playing in the game on the twenty-third?

In the car Paulette put her feet up on the dashboard and closed her eyes. She had blond ringlets carefully done every morning, incongruous on a face already old.

"You don't need to walk me to the door," she said.

He walked her anyway. "The trouble with Dick," he said, walking up the steps to her house in Georgetown, "is that he's not very smart."

"Oh, well," she said. "Who cares? He's like a big brown bear."

"A stupid big brown bear," Carter said and was immediately angry at himself for that lapse.

Down Wisconsin Avenue to Massachusetts Avenue he pretended that Dick Carr had just stepped off the curb making a dash for the other side and Carter, without time to brake, ran over him completely. He could imagine the enormous body thudding against the underside of the car.

Anne Lowry sat on a floor pillow and watched Natty, who was wrapped in her coat, trying to sleep on the wicker couch. It wasn't, she decided, that she didn't like Natty. Although she had problems with imperfections like Natty's. She also had trouble with people who had crooked hands, immovable glass eyes, faces deeply marred from acne or smallpox, mongoloids, even very old people, especially if they were, like her Grandmother Lowry, incontinent.

"Annie's so sensitive," her sweet-voiced Mississippi mother would say, "she just can't bear to see anyone in pain."

Which was to say she did not care to be in pain herself.

The fact was Natty Taylor frightened her, although that fear translated as disapproval. Anne Lowry lived by an absolute code of behavior, according to a system of right and wrong. It was, for example, absolutely wrong that Joe McCarthy should be harbored by Sam Taylor and right that she should do everything possible to correct the situation. She accepted this kind of responsibility without humor.

Something about Natty Taylor ridiculed her, even her crippled leg, as though its strangeness promised equal dangers for those around her.

"Where did you tell your parents you were tonight?" Natty asked with her eyes closed.

"At Sukey's," Anne said. "Sukey knows."

"Jeez, Anne," Natty said. "I thought you never lied."

"Well," Anne hesitated. "Usually. I mean you have to make those decisions."

"I guess," Natty said and tried to sleep, but the picture of her father at eighty rested against her inner lids in black and white and kept her from sleeping.

Senator Joe McCarthy stepped carefully up the back stairs from the kitchen at the Taylors' to the guest room on the second floor. The stairs were too short and painted orange and curved in a circle, each stair being a different shape—like the stairs in the farmhouse at Grand Chute. He held tight to the rail.

"Did you bring in the cows, Joey?" his mother used to call as he went up those twisted stairs dog-tired to bed.

"And shut the gate, Joey?"

"Is the chicken house locked from the cows, Joey?" Her voice chanted instructions like the priest at Mass.

"Say your prayers before you go to bed, Joey. On your knees," she called. Generations of Catholic mothers with their instructions, over and over the same ones as if they were stuck in first gear. "And be up early. Not after five like this morning, you hear?"

"I hear," he called. "Yes, Mother, I hear." His knees hit the hardwood floor. "Holy Mary, Mother of God . . ." He pulled himself across the bed. "Amen, amen." He fell asleep dreaming of being crowned by the Father Almighty halfway between heaven and earth but visible to all the folks in Grand Chute like his mother.

All those rules. Don't talk back. Clean out chicken coop. Sit up straight. Be humble, grateful, loving, kind. Don't let God see you messing with yourself after lights. Scrub your hands with lye—cleanliness is next to godliness. All the McCarthys went every Sunday and Holy Day to the Chapel of the Little Flower in Manawa. One Sunday Joey went as usual, scrubbed behind the ears, dizzy without breakfast. The cold in the chapel was absolute. This Sunday when the bell rang and the incense rushed through the dark space, he saw God standing right beside his pew next to his relations. And he felt his flesh electrify.

"So," he said to his good friend PDQ Taylor. "I seen God in church on Sunday."

"So," said PDQ Taylor. "I seen Wild Bill Hickok, Thursday last. He come for supper."

"Someday," he said to PDQ Taylor, "I'm thinking of going to war."

"You might get hurt bad."

"Yeah," McCarthy said. "I might get killed," he said. "But I'd get a decoration, too."

"A lot of good it would do you dead."

"Someday," he said to PDQ Taylor, "I'm thinking of playing baseball in the minors or else be governor."

Joe McCarthy stumbled over a bed before he realized he was in the wrong room. He was sitting on the end of Natty's bed when Sam Taylor turned on the light.

"You seem to have woken me up," McCarthy said.

"Where's Natty?" Sam asked, noticing at once her empty bed.

"You must be mixed up."

"Ellen," Sam called to his wife. "Natty?"

Ellen Taylor in her robe came up the stairs. "No one else is downstairs," she said.

"Well, Natty isn't in her room."

Ellen walked into Natty's room, ignoring McCarthy, who had fallen across the bed, his head hanging from his upright torso as though it were attached by strings. She walked through the room lifting papers and letters and pieces of clothing and a nightgown as if expecting a diminutive Natty to be underneath.

"Ellen." Sam followed her to her room.

"Shh," she said.

"We have to do something," he insisted. "I knew this was going to happen."

"You knew what was going to happen?" she asked quietly.

"This," he said. "What has happened."

He sat down on her bed. "Call the police," he said.

"Sam."

"Call the police right now."

"Let's think," she said. "We don't even know she's not in the house," she said. "We haven't checked."

"She's left," he shouted, out of control. "It's perfectly obvious that she's left."

"I'll check downstairs."

"She's run away," he said. He picked up the phone for the police. "I knew that she would." He told the police that Natty

221

had disappeared. He did not mention the possibility that she might have run away.

"She's not here," he said when Ellen came back from her search downstairs.

"No," she said.

"I did call the police," he said.

Ellen looked in her phone book and called Will Barnes without success and then Dick Carr, who answered on the second ring.

"He had not been sleeping," she said, "and it's three o'clock."

"Had he any idea?"

"No," she said. "None whatsoever."

Sam followed her into Natty's room.

"Natty's group of friends doesn't seem to require any sleep at all. Here." She pulled McCarthy up on Natty's bed. "Help me."

"Are you going to leave him in Natty's bed?"

"Unless you want to carry him to the guest room."

She put a quilt over Senator McCarthy and turned out the light.

Downstairs they sat in the living room and waited for the police.

"Joe McCarthy will have to leave," Ellen said.

"I'll see that he goes," Sam said.

"Today," Ellen said. "As soon as he wakes up."

She did not mention the trouble since McCarthy had moved in.

"He'll move today," Sam said quietly.

Sam Taylor was afraid that in a final crisis he would run. Or else in that moment of adrenalin, the energy for action turned inward would well up and spill over like a dammed creek, the best of it seeping into the black earth. Which is how he felt right now, welled to bursting, but without the possible release for forward movement. He wandered through the blue-lit house after the police had left, going from room to room adjusting clocks which told him that the day advanced like a foreign army.

In his study he rearranged the papers on his desk. He called the weather, which promised snow or freezing rains with clearing by Christmas Day. Finally he called time, which reported it was four minutes after five a.m. He thought of Andrew Slaughter and tried to reproduce the young man's face, but he could only reproduce John Taylor, and that indistinct and mixing like water color with the memory of his own face.

Once again he was thinking of the day his father died in the back room of the farmhouse in Manawa—the insufficient memory returned accidental as the paths of a tornado on the plains.

Will Barnes had black dreams of Natty all night. He slept too late and ached when he got up. When he came in from feeding the livestock Nell was downstairs and already dressed.

"You're late," she said without looking up from the book she was reading.

"Yes," he said, kicking the dirt off his heels on the side porch. "I had nightmares."

"I didn't think you had dreams."

"I don't," he said. "But I did last night."

"Mrs. Taylor called for you last night," Nell said. "Melvina answered the phone and said you were sleeping. She didn't say what she wanted."

He waited until eight o'clock exactly and then he called Natty.

"Natty Taylor's gone," he said to Nell when he hung up the phone. "Goddam," he said, shaken by the proven premonition of his dreams. "They think she's run away."

"Is that what Ellen Taylor said?" Nell quickened, her chest tight with familiar pains, but she contained herself, knowing Will's intemperance, not wanting to chance his reaction.

"She said that *she* would have run away if she were Natty, given the circumstances." He took a piece of toast off his mother's plate. "She didn't say that Natty had."

"Will," Nell Barnes began in a reasonable voice, "I'm sure that the Taylors have things in hand."

"What do you mean?"

"I mean that I don't want you running off to Washington searching for Natty Taylor like a chicken—"

"With his head cut off." Eliza danced into the kitchen.

"Shut up," Will said to Eliza.

"It's serious," Nell said quickly.

Will told Eliza about Natty.

"You can call the Taylors later to keep track of developments."

"Do you know anything?" Will asked Eliza.

"I don't know anything," she said.

"You're sure."

"Yes," she said, getting breakfast. "Of course I'm sure."

"There are several things I want you to do," Nell said, helplessly filling up the list in her spiral notebook to detain him as long as possible. He took the pad and read through it quickly.

"The storm windows are up on the back of the house," he said. "Honest to God, Mom, I'm not going to paint the porch in December." He handed back the pad. "I'll do the first four things on that list and leave by twelve," he said.

Nell Barnes was not an anxious woman. She had accustomed herself to the chance of another heart attack at any time, as though the heart muscle were located in the ankle and that inessential.

Now she sat at the kitchen table and waited for the pains to pass, confident that if they did not, she could take a pill and that the pains probably meant nothing. Confident, too, that if she wanted, she could detain Will at the farm all day with her heart pains.

She heard his boots on the hardwood floors above her, heard him clatter down the front stairs and through the hall and dining room. She was still undecided when he came into the kitchen.

"Done," he said. "The screened porch has plastic all around now and the hole in the bedroom wall is fixed so the squirrels can't get in." He washed his hands. "I just don't think it's Natty's style to run away." He sat down across from Nell.

"Where's Liza?"

"Dressing."

"Still?" he said. "I want her to come."

Nell was conscious of showing pain in her face and was surprised at this sentimental lapse in herself.

"You don't want me to go," he said.

"Of course I don't."

"How come?" he asked, putting his feet up on the chair.

"For all of your good sense, you have a crazy streak," she said.

It was not a crazy streak, she knew. Will Barnes, by instinct, acted on principle as though his world of absolute justice could be invisibly linked to the world at large, whose natural laws were filtered through systems. But it didn't work that way and in the ordered civilizing of an outlaw land, he had a crazy streak.

"I feel odd about this," she said. "What are you going to do in town?"

So he told her about Dick Carr and his suspicions. He told her about the dead cat and Joe McCarthy, about Natty and the horse. He even told her about the change in Natty when he kissed her and how she'd never been like that before.

"So?" he said, leaving the question open.

"What do you expect to find?" she asked, organizing the spices on her shelf, washing apples for Christmas pies.

"I expect some kind of foul play."

"Why don't you tell the Taylors what you've told me?"

"I will," he said. "That's why I'm going into town."

"You don't need Liza to tell the Taylors, Will Barnes," she said. "All you need is a telephone." She carried her dishes to the sink, standing at it rubbing her arm above the elbow.

"If it's high drama you want," she said, "I haven't got respect for that."

"Does your arm hurt, Mom?" he asked, ignoring her comment. "Are you okay?"

"I'm perfectly fine," she said.

Upstairs she listened to the truck drive out of the driveway. The pains were worse now in her arm and across her chest as well. She couldn't distinguish whether they were physical or invented as a protection against her son's intemperance.

There was a brief notice at the bottom of the late edition of the *Post*.

"Natalia Taylor, daughter of FCC Chairman Samuel Taylor, disappeared from her house at 3204 Highland Place sometime

225

after midnight last night. Although the house did not appear to have been burglarized, a side porch door was ajar, and police are not dismissing the possibility of kidnapping."

The notice was outlined in double-width black lines, and Rosa noticed it first off when she opened the paper on the dining room table.

"Filip," she said quietly. He was sitting on the other side of the table reading the sports page. There was a center picture of the first five of the All Star basketball team selected in the game from the previous day.

"Hell," he said. "Larry Luce from Wilson made first string," he said. In the last paragraph of the story it said that Fil DeAngelis of St. Albans School had fouled out in the third quarter. "Damn," he muttered.

"Look," Rosa said, throwing the front page of the *Post* across the sports page.

"What?"

She pointed.

"Jeez," he said.

"Poor girl," Rosa said. "Do you think she could have run away because of this publicity on her father?"

He got up from the table quickly, so Rosa couldn't determine his expression and react to it. He poured out the rest of his cereal and put a full glass of juice back in the refrigerator.

It was his fault. For making love to Blanche, for fouling out of the game, for falling apart so easily. He felt as a child feels when all of a sudden in a way unprepared for, someone, even an animal, dies and the child wonders how he could have caused it to happen.

"How do you feel, letting her down like you did?" Rosa said, suddenly angry.

"How do you feel going to Wisconsin finding out stories to screw her father?" he shouted at her, out of control.

"I found out he's a decent man."

"I told you that," he said. "I told you that a hundred times."

"You haven't an idea what decent means," she said.

He ripped the paper with the announcement about Natty and threw it across the table.

"Decency's not one of your strong points either," he said.

"So," Rosa said, going upstairs, where Elsa was bathing Johnny. "You drop Natty Taylor just when she needs you and take up with this . . ." She didn't finish.

"Shut up," he said.

He followed her now into her bedroom, into the bathroom.

"Please get out," she said, locking the bathroom door.

"You've run every bit of my life since I was born," he called at her behind the closed door.

"When you couldn't," she called back, unable to restrain herself.

"How could I do it?" he said. "Anything I've ever tried to do, you have done for me. Here, Filip. Not like this, Filip. That's not right. Let me," he mimicked. "I'm older. I do everything a little better. Let me get into college for you and do your papers for you. Mom?"

Rosa didn't reply.

"Do you hear me?"

"Of course I hear you, Filip," she said. "You are shouting."

"And I'm right, too."

She sat on the toilet seat with her head in her hands and waited until she heard him leave.

"Leave me alone," she said.

On the streetcar downtown Rosa sat in the back seat alone and watched the Christmas shoppers in Georgetown. She thought of Filip as terminal. As though she had been told that morning that he had months at most.

At the White House she got off and walked—and walking through a thin, dark rain without an umbrella, cold behind her neck, she turned her anger at Filip on herself. Rational as an accountant tallying columns, she listed her mistakes.

First off, the one he'd mentioned—standing in for him so he could not possibly fail himself. He must think then with such a fuss as she had made that any failure was absolute without a second chance.

She saw herself as though she were Filip standing on 19th and Pennsylvania watching a middle-aged woman in an ordinary trench coat whose dilated black eyes foreshadowed disasters at every corner. Angela ruined by the boy from Harvard. Filip run over by a moving van at Calvert and Wisconsin. Johnny living unchanged but forever in the row house on 39th Street. And Rosa herself teetering as if drunk between crises.

They, Filip especially, had lost in the diffusion of genes their source of strength that allowed hot-blooded people unimaginable courage and self-containment in real crises, spun off like excess oil in imaginary ones to contain the surfeit of feeling as protection against the real thing.

Her children must believe what they had heard from her. She had misrepresented herself as a woman who would jump off the Calvert Street Bridge on slim provocation when in fact she knew with certainty that the middle-aged woman walking down 19th Street would not jump anywhere.

If Filip believed he was terminal, then what difference did it make? Of course he'd choose Blanche, with her enormous breasts and empty brain.

She did not have time to think of how she'd tell her editor the story in Wisconsin wasn't there.

"Christ, Rosa," was all he could say. "It cost a bundle to send you out there."

She shrugged.

"I never knew such reservations in you before, Rosa," he said.

"You don't know me at all then," Rosa snapped. "I'm full of reservations."

"No story?" the editor asked. "No story at all?"

"There is a story."

"I'm listening."

"I'll write a story," she said. "But it's a boring story about a good man."

"We had planned for it to be the major story break next week."

"You'll have a story."

"I don't particularly want a boring story," he began, but the city desk editor came up then, took the editor and Rosa aside and told him about the tip he had received and that Sam Taylor had been arrested drunk for disorderly conduct.

The editor was stunned.

"There are some suspicions about McCarthy's relationship to Sam Taylor," he said. "That it's . . . you know," and he gestured like a dancer, twirled his hips.

"Goddam," the editor said.

"Garbage," Rosa said instinctively.

"I've sent Simms to Lafayette Park today," the city desk editor said. "What's got into you, Rosa? You follow leads. Any decent journalist follows leads."

Rosa put her coat back on and tied the belt.

She took the elevator down to the first floor and bought coffee. She had intended to go back up to her desk but left the building instead, putting up the collar of her coat against the steady rain, and headed toward Lafayette Park.

Filip walked to Georgetown to meet Blanche at noon for Christmas shopping. Occasionally he clicked his heels, hopping in the air, snapping a winter branch.

He wanted to buy her a silver friendship ring engraved with hearts to wear on the ring finger of her left hand, alerting everyone that she belonged to him.

He'd seen a pale-blue cashmere sweater at Raleigh's, and the thought of Blanche in it, of touching her breasts beneath the soft wool, sent him down Wisconsin from Reservoir Road at such a clip the people on the streetcar, like the man who'd recognized him the night he'd met Blanche at the bar on M Street, would not have had a chance to see his face, to say to the passenger in the seat next to him, "Hey, that's Fil DeAngelis. Y'know?"

It seemed altogether possible that he could win a gold medal in the 1956 Olympics, and he walked down the hill from S Street humming the "Star-Spangled Banner," watching the judge place the gold medal around his shoulders.

He would marry Blanche, he thought, half aware of his self-deception.

Once he thought of Natty. Looking in a gift shop at Q Street he saw a gold barrette, similar to the one he took out of Natty's hair when he kissed her. Counting back, he realized with mild

229

surprise that he'd last kissed Natty only six nights ago on her front porch. Things change, he thought to himself, but it was unsatisfactory. Until yesterday he'd believed in a kind of optimistic fatalism in which things usually went well and if they did not, he was innocent of blame.

He expected that Natty had run away and was staying at a friend's house, and dismissed that sense of her from his mind by the next storefront window.

He was to meet Blanche at noon at L'Aerodrome. She wanted to buy him a pin-striped shirt with a small collar, she had said, and an identification bracelet with his initials on one side and on the other, "Love forever, Blanche." She said she did not like surprises.

Filip saw her first, and then Larry Luce. He was walking on the east side of Wisconsin waiting for twelve o'clock and he saw her in Fancy Togs. Her white hair was pulled back in a ribbon and she had on a navy pea jacket. Larry Luce was standing next to her in his Wilson letter sweater, and they were leaning, with their backs to him, over a low table. Blanche had her arm over Larry Luce's back and her hand was in his back pocket.

Filip met her in front of L'Aerodrome at exactly twelve. She was alone standing against the wall.

"What were you doing with Larry Luce?"

She looked confused.

"I wasn't with Larry Luce," she said.

"The hell you weren't," he said. "You were standing in some shop with your arm around him and your hand in his back pocket."

"Filip," she hedged. "Oh, that," she said. "I completely forgot. Larry Luce and I are old friends. I just happened to see him."

"I bet."

"Listen." She grabbed his arm. "You don't own me anyway."

But he pulled away and ran down Wisconsin. At N the street-car was stopped at a light. He hailed the driver and got in.

When he looked up Wisconsin Avenue he saw Blanche just

where he'd left her. He kept her in view until the streetcar turned at M, and then he got off and ran the side streets of Georgetown uphill to Glover Park where he lived, stopping only once before he came to his house.

Ellen Taylor had gone over every possibility with the detectives from the Eighth Precinct. By nine that morning the house on Highland Place had been surrounded by the unmarked cars of plainclothesmen and ordinary cars with press cards in the back window.

"We have no information," Ellen said to the young reporter from the Washington *Post*. She answered the door and spoke to him herself, although the detective said he'd be glad to and she was perfectly within her rights.

When the reporter asked about Senator McCarthy, however, she said, "Thank you very much," and quietly shut the front door.

The general conclusion was that Natty had left home shortly after one a.m. of her own accord.

"I was awake reading," Ellen said. "I would have heard any slight commotion."

She did tell them about the dead cat and the accidental fall from the horse. She mentioned the problems with Fil DeAngelis and the obvious developments since Senator McCarthy had come to stay. There was nothing necessary that she left out in her report to the police.

"We never find them honest like you've been," the one detective told her. "Especially if their kid has run away. We ought to get to the bottom of this quickly, because you've told us everything."

Ellen had not told them about Sam Taylor except to say that he had gone to work because of a meeting with the Secretary of Commerce which he couldn't cancel. Besides, she said, there was nothing he could do at home.

In fact she had called Ed Marlowe just before the police came and the people from the newspaper, because, she said, careful not to betray him, he would be better off at work than waiting for developments.

She had sat in the kitchen with him drinking coffee and watched him stand at the window, his back to her, and drink down two bourbons in a tiny silver cup.

"Sam," she said.

"Don't say a word to me," he said, sitting at the table with her, spreading out the newspaper. "If something has happened to her," he said, "I'll die."

"Nothing has happened to her, Sam," she said. "I am convinced."

"You'd be convinced of our ultimate safety if you stood in the center of a flaming house," he said.

Once on a night trip to Madison early in their marriage, Sam had turned the old Ford coupe off the road into a ditch in order to avoid running over a paper bag.

"Sam," Ellen whispered. "What did you do that for?"

"I think," he said in dead earnest, "there's a baby in that paper bag I nearly hit."

For a startled moment, she actually believed him and got on her knees to watch him retrieve the paper bag from the highway.

"Well," she asked as he got back in the car with an empty paper bag large enough for groceries.

"It could have been a baby," he said, putting the paper bag in the back of the car and driving very carefully to Madison.

They had laughed many times in the years since about the baby in the paper bag, but always with care given to the fact that Sam believed we live in a state of emergency.

At six, the house dusty gray, but light enough to see without blue bulbs, Ellen had gone upstairs and found Sam in Natty's room watching a sleeping Joe McCarthy's periodic thunder.

Ellen went over to him, sat down on the floor next to him.

"You must stop punishing yourself for this," she said.

"It's my fault," he said evenly. "For having Natty count too much. And . . ." He motioned to McCarthy on the bed. "For sentimentalism."

"It was with good intentions," Ellen said.

"Sentiment, Ellen, is false intentions," he said, "and mine were false."

After Sam had left, Ellen found McCarthy in the guest room on his back with a quilt over his legs. She supposed that Sam had moved him out of Natty's bed himself.

By ten in the morning Sam had called six times. The last time he called, Ellen noticed he had been drinking again.

"Nothing," she said each time and then, "I'll call you if there's any word." But still he called back regularly.

There had been word by ten-thirty when he called again.

She hesitated. "Nothing," she said, but he knew her well enough to hear the hesitation in her voice and pressed for information which she gave in part.

When she had let the dog out just after ten, there had been a note pinned to the front door.

"Dear M, I have left because of McCarthy and because of the craziness with Daddy this last week. L, Natalia."

Ellen called the police immediately.

"Do you have any idea where she could have gone?" they asked.

Ellen gave the detective a list of Natty's old friends, including Fil DeAngelis and Will Barnes and Sukey and several others whom she had not seen lately but who had been friends.

She also mentioned Dick Carr and Carter Harold, with whom Natty had been spending so much time this last week.

"If she's sending notes like this," the detective said, "we'll have her found by nightfall."

McCarthy was still asleep when Ellen left. She put a note on the kitchen sink next to the orange-juice pitcher.

"Joe," it read, "the house may be surrounded by the police and press because Natty ran away from home last night. I would be grateful if you'd stay until I get back. Ellen."

She had a mental picture of McCarthy wandering out to the front yard giving a press conference on Natty and how well he knew her and his childhood relationship with Sam Taylor.

Dick Carr answered the door with half a face of shaving cream—a circus clown on stilts.

"I'm Ellen Taylor," she said. "Natty's mother."

"Yeah," he said. "Well." He stood back from the door. "I'm shaving."

"So I see," she said. "Finish and then I'll talk to you."

"Yes," he said. "Well, come on in."

She stood in the hall while he finished shaving.

It was the first time she had been out since August, taken herself out, that is, with a decision to act of her own accord, and she was surprised at the calm she felt, the new energy clear as a winter day.

She was, as people had always told her, extraordinary in crises. But these last few years had made no demands. She was ordered by nature to respond to situations, at a loss without them. And now this sense of purpose in Dick Carr's living room, almost as though it were necessary for her family to fall apart for Ellen to find reason to survive.

When Dick Carr came down and sat on the soft couch, looking thick as sacks of peat moss, his tiny eyes shifting back and forth as if they were dots recording his heart beats, she suspected he knew everything.

"I have no idea," he said, looking past her at the archway, at the yellow flowered chair in the corner of the room, out the window. "Yeah," he said. "She came over for cheerleading practice yesterday. I mean, you know, with a bunch of people like Paulette. You should ask Paulette."

"I don't know Paulette," Ellen said.

"She's French," he said emphatically, as if that explained everything.

"Who else?" she asked.

"Carter Harold." He sat up a little on the couch as if the mention of Carter Harold promised his salvation in this moment of danger. "That's exactly who you should ask," he said. "Carter Harold. I've got his phone number right here."

"You haven't seen her since yesterday?"

"No," he said, "but maybe Carter'd know," he said, writing down a number and handing it to Ellen Taylor. "You know," he said, "Carter and Natty have gotten to be real good friends."

"No," she said. "I didn't know."

"Shit," Dick Carr said when he telephoned Carter Harold. "Natty's mother just came over."

"Good," Carter said. "Have her call me."

"I did," Dick said. "I thought you'd want me to."

"Ha." Carter laughed. "You're a bloody chicken, Carr," he said and hung up before Dick Carr had a chance to respond.

Dick Carr had lied to her, Ellen thought as she started the automobile and headed back to Highland Place to keep Mc-Carthy from courting the press on the front lawn of the house. When she got home there was only one press car left and an unmarked green car with two men inside.

"Here," one called to her, handing her an envelope with "Ellen Taylor" on the outside.

"Dear M," it read. "Yesterday one of my friends saw Daddy in Lafayette Park with a guy who hangs around there. He had been drinking, the friend said. He couldn't even walk straight. So, you can imagine. I feel terrible about this. L, Natalia."

The man in the car had his hand out for the note.

"No," Ellen said.

"Wait," he called out to her as she went into the house. "We need all the information possible."

"It's personal," she said.

When she called Sam's office he had left.

"He's had one meeting. I don't know if he's coming back," his secretary said. "He didn't say. I'm sorry, Mrs. Taylor. I heard."

"Thank you," Ellen said.

"If you see him before I do," the secretary said, "please tell him I have another call in to Andrew Slaughter in Putney, Vermont."

Joe McCarthy was still sleeping in the guest room. She shook him hard.

"Joe," she said. "You have to get up."

He rolled over on his side.

"Joe." She shook him again.

Then she went downstairs and asked the two men in the unmarked car to help her carry him.

"I have a man upstairs—an old acquaintance of Mr. Taylor's," she said. "He's too drunk to awaken. I want you to help me carry him to my car."

If the two detectives recognized Senator McCarthy, they did not mention it.

Ellen Taylor got in the front seat and drove McCarthy to the emergency room of Doctor's Hospital. She called his wife in Wisconsin, who said she would be on the next plane home and was sorry, but the pressure on him had been just terrible. Ellen waited in the emergency room until he was admitted and his personal physician arrived.

By the time she arrived home at two o'clock there had been another note and the street was once again full of unmarked cars and press.

"Dear M—Unless Daddy resigns as chairman, I won't come back. Natty."

She handed the note over to the man in one of the cars.

"A little boy about six who lives in that house," he pointed, "brings these notes. He says a teenager with thick glasses who drives a red car has been giving them to him and paying a quarter to deliver them."

"Gerald," Ellen said vacantly. "The little boy's name is Gerald."

Inside she bolted the front door.

———

Sam had one more drink. One more, he told himself, and then he'd leave the office so he wasn't tempted to call home about Natty. One more, which he drank slowly while he outlined the points for the Secretary of Commerce so the yellow legal sheet read:

> Sec'y of Commerce: re: Anti-Trust
> I. Regulations on single station ownership.
> John Taylor
> John Samuel Taylor
> J.S.T.

(On his headstone it read, "John Samuel Taylor. May 18, 1886—March 1, 1926." The headstone was black granite and had a small pine tree behind it.)

> Natalia—Natalia—NAT   AL   IA   TAYLOR.

He left the office at eleven-fifteen, turning the legal sheet face down on his desk.

"Call the office of the Secretary of Commerce," he said to his secretary, "and tell them about Natty."

"Do you want to make another appointment with him?" she asked.

"No," he said. "I don't."

He met Ed Marlowe going down in the elevator.

"You look like hell," Ed Marlowe said. "Let me take you home."

"No," Sam said. "I'm taking a walk."

"Let me go with you then."

"I want to go alone."

Ed stopped at the coffee shop on 13th and Pennsylvania.

"At least have a cup of coffee, Sam."

"You have a cup of coffee for me, Ed," Sam said and walked on, feeling the older man's eyes on his back and wondering, detached from his bodily self, how an old drunk must feel watching the dependable Sam Taylor unsteady on his feet.

By 14th and Pennsylvania he had lost all sense of place, and in spite of the heavy traffic on Pennsylvania, the people clustered on the sidewalks, the imposition of city sounds, he was back in rural Wisconsin in the winter and even smelled the black pine behind the house where he had grown up. At Lafayette Square he slid into the first park bench just off Pennsylvania and lapsed into a waking sleep, like dreaming because it persuaded him to follow its course—but he knew he could not be sleeping.

In the distance he saw the man with the red muffler he had seen the day before.

This then was how John Taylor had felt when he was drunk, Sam thought, moving down on the bench so the back of it held his neck—this opaque sense of the outside world, this clutter of the brain as though its compartments had been emptied on the mind's floor and were distinguishable as single elements, but unrelated to any whole. This sense of irretrievable loss. This then was how his father had felt in waking moments on the milk mare riding back from the alehouse that last evening he was out in open air.

John Taylor lay on the day bed in the front room. A quilt pulled up to his chin, his slender fingers tight around its corners. He was the color of light-gray slate and made noise when he breathed. Sammy knew that he was dying and pulled up a stool beside his father's bed.

"Sammy," John whispered. "Run down the street and get Dr. Richards, will you?"

Sammy didn't move. He sat on the embroidered stool and watched his father's face for final signs.

He wanted him to die today. He did not want another day of watching the person he loved more than any other slip in short graceless movements away from him. He did not want another afternoon of Adelaide Taylor banging "shiftless" and "drunkard" and "no good" as she slammed pots on the wood stove and "you and your father" as though the house supply of roaches had multipled at the mention of their names. He did not want another chance at silent laughter as the drunken John Taylor was flung like sacks of flour over the back of the milk mare. He wanted him dead this March afternoon because the responsibility of his living had gotten too large for a young boy to assume.

"Sammy?"

"Dr. Richards is gone to Grand Chute running calls, Dad," Sammy lied. "Can I get you something?"

"No," his father said. "I don't need anything."

"I saw Dr. Richards this morning," Sammy said, "when I fed the horses. He told me he was going and would be back by dark."

"You'll stay here, Sammy."

"Yes," he said. "I'll stay."

John Taylor drowned, or that's how it looked to Sammy, who watched him even though he wanted to run out of the room when his father began to struggle, to crawl under the bed so he didn't have to watch it, but he made himself watch the dying as punishment for having let it happen.

Dr. Richards was in his office back of his house next door tending to Mrs. O'Malley's bunions. On the way over, Sammy convinced himself that Dr. Richards had indeed said that morning that he was off to Grand Chute, and so when he walked in the office and saw Jermyn Richards with Mrs. O'Malley's big bare feet on his lap, he was startled.

"You better come on over to my place," Sammy said, and Dr. Richards laid Mrs. O'Malley's feet down and followed Sammy across the field.

Sammy wanted to ask him if he could have saved John Taylor had Sammy gotten him in time, but instead he just said "Thank you" for sending the wagon for the body and "I'll run over and get Mama at the shop." He was afraid to find out.

He let go the moment of his father's dying—soft-packed in newspapers like hand-cut family crystal, stacked in boxes during the dark years, to be recovered years later, carefully unpacked and washed to transparent glitter—exactly as it had been.

Rosa arrived after eleven at the corner of Pennsylvania across from the White House, where the broad expanse of park called

Lafayette connects to St. John's Episcopal Church. She recognized the press car with a reporter she did not know sitting in the front seat with the door open. The photographer from the *News* got several shots, but just as she approached the car, a young man who had been sitting on a park bench knocked the camera out of his hand.

"What do you think we are?" he shouted at the photographer. "A traveling circus?"

The photographer stepped back, readjusted the camera. "It has nothing to do with you," he said to the young man. Several other men approached and stood watching.

"That must be Sam Taylor," a young man said to Rosa, flashing his press card from the *Post*. "Are you the press?"

"No," Rosa said. "I'm not."

Sam Taylor, awake now, his mind cleared in an emergency, but still unsteady on his feet, got up.

"Are you Sam Taylor?" the man from the Washington *Post* said. The reporter sitting in the press car jumped out and ran over.

"I am Sam Taylor," he said.

"Sam," Rosa called, clear in what she had to do. She pushed her way through the regulars at Lafayette Park, gathered now to protect their privacy, through the reporters moving around Sam Taylor, who was too full of drink, too silenced by his personal odyssey of the last few hours and shaken by Natty's disappearance, to protest.

"I didn't know whether you'd be here on time," she said, "and Ellen says you have the flu." She took him by the arm. "I'm sure you were up all night because of Natty," she said. "You look very ill."

At Pennsylvania Avenue she hailed a cab and told him to get in the back seat first. "I'm Rosa DeAngelis," she said to the reporter from the *Post* who had run after them, "a family friend," she said. "There is an emergency at home."

The reporter from the *Post* pulled the man in the red muffler aside because he looked reliable.

"Can you give me your name?" he asked.

"Sorry, son," the young man said. "I can't."

"You know this park?" the reporter asked. "You've been here before?"

"Yes," the man in the red muffler said.

"That gentleman who just drove off was Samuel Taylor," he said.

"I see."

"He's very high up in the government and was arrested yesterday for drunkenness and disorderly conduct," the reporter said, hoping to exact information with that revelation.

The man in the red muffler looked askance.

"Have you ever seen him before in this park?" the reporter asked.

"I have never seen him before in my life," the man in the red muffler said.

"I'm Rosa DeAngelis," Rosa had said. "Fil's mother."

Sam Taylor looked confused.

"I don't know you?" Sam asked.

"Not specifically," Rosa said. "I work for the *News*," she said. "I knew that reporters had been told you were at Lafayette Park."

He shook his head.

"Making arrangements," she said. "Personal arrangements."

He didn't seem to know.

At Highland Place Sam got out the far side door.

"Come in," he faltered.

"No," she said. "I have to go back to work."

He walked around the cab, tapped the window at her side. "Thank you," he said.

She could barely hear him through the glass.

Will and Eliza arrived at Dick Carr's house in midafternoon. The entire Syndicate was there except Alexander Epps, who was with Natty.

In the living room Paulette was practicing cheers in front of the long mirror, practicing keeping her back straight while she bounced up and down in a crouched position. She looked at

241

herself without expression, her chin pointed, her eyes narrowed in mild self-contempt. On the couch Anne Lowry sat crosslegged knitting a sweater, the slender needles snapping like branches. Sukey was lying on the floor with her feet on the fireplace.

"What's that?" she asked when she heard the front door shut.

"Will Barnes." He stood in the archway to the living room. Paulette looked at Will and Eliza in the mirror.

"Hi," she said. "Carter," she called without breaking position, her straight back, her leg stretched out behind like a baton, her arms circling an imaginary form. "Someone's here."

"Will Barnes," Will said again.

At first he had not seen Dick Carr, who was dressed today like an Oklahoma cowboy with dark-blue jeans high on his hips and a string tie like an incidental thread on a neck so thick. He was playing poker with Al Cox at a table at the far end of the living room.

"Do you know what's happened to Natty?" Will asked.

Anne Lowry shook her head, her face in plastic tranquillity as though she were rehearsing for the part of the Virgin in the Christmas pageant.

"No one knows," she whispered. Sukey turned over on her stomach.

"We thought she was with you," Sukey said.

"Yeah," Dick Carr said, brightening. "That's what we thought."

"It's a terrible thing," Carter said, coming into the living room from the study. "Hello, Will," he said. "We just heard about it this morning."

"She ran away from home," Dick Carr said. "That's what the word is. Carter talked to her mother this morning."

"I don't believe it," Will said.

"Listen, Barnes," Dick Carr said. "You don't believe anything." He slammed down his poker hand. "Got you," he said to Al Cox.

Will and Eliza followed Carter to the kitchen.

"Want a Coke?" Carter asked.

"Nope."

"Will thinks it's you guys," Eliza said with warning.

"What is?"

"Natty's running away."

Carter sat down on the kitchen stool across from Will.

"What do you mean?" he asked.

"Something's just obviously been up these last few days," Will said. "Natty's been different."

"Precisely," Carter agreed. "I've noticed that myself. All of the pressure on the Taylor family because of Senator McCarthy."

"It's not like her to run away. Whatever the situation."

"She's never been under this kind of pressure before," Carter said. "These articles in the newspaper and Fil DeAngelis dropping her. Then yesterday I heard a story about her father. . . . Look at Choo Choo. Look what happened to Choo Choo because of her father."

"Choo Choo was always crazy," Will said. "Probably born crazy. Natty's solid as trees. You know that, Carter."

Carter Harold took Eliza's hand, played with her fingers. He could barely see Paulette Estinet from his seat on the kitchen stool. Only an occasional outstretched leg as she skirted his vision.

"Where is she, Carter?" Will asked, angered at the precision of the young man across from him, at the careful way he played now with Eliza's hand.

"You know what I can't understand about you, Will, is how you put up with Natty."

"I didn't ask for judgments."

"You're like a lackey," Carter said, putting the tips of Liza's fingers on his lips, "a tall, slender, bad-tempered nigger boy."

Will did not hit him. Carter must have known that he would not, careful as Carter was about personal risk—but Will left by the back door and hit the concrete pillar on the porch so his knuckles bled.

"Whore," he called to Eliza, but she could not hear him. He did not know a word sufficient for Carter Harold. "Whore!" he called again, shouting it this time as loud as he could.

All afternoon he walked up and down the back streets of Georgetown, unconscious of the Christmas shoppers snapping by him, unconscious of the shops rich with the smell of butterscotch and pine . . . charting Natty's decencies.

He had known her for years and she had always been, like Nell Barnes, accountable as spring.

Still that doubt. As he crossed 31st into Dumbarton Oaks, black and gray in winter as an old photograph, sat down on one of the benches high above the gardens—doubt creeping like moisture through the walls of houses in wet weather, chilling his neck and shoulders, that Carter was right and Will had misinterpreted Natty all along because he had counted on her for dreams.

It was dark when he went back to Dick Carr's house to pick up Eliza and take her home. They would go first to the Taylors', he decided, and then home.

He did not see Choo Choo until he had passed her sitting on the first step of the Carrs' porch.

"Hello," he said. "What are you doing here?"

"Sitting."

"Without a coat."

"I'm hot," she said. "I'm really not cold. Listen." She pulled him down beside her. "Can you take me home?"

"Sure."

"I'm scared of the dark."

"It's okay," Will said. "I'm just getting Eliza. Then I'll take you."

"I don't want to go back in," Choo Choo said. "It's creepy in there. Like . . . I don't know. Secrets."

"Yeah," Will said. "I've noticed."

Choo Choo wrapped her arms around herself.

"You are cold," he said. He took his jacket off, threw it over her shoulders.

"Just a little."

"Is your coat inside?"

"Don't get it. Promise you won't get it. I don't want them to know I'm here."

"Okay." He knelt down beside her. She was frightened, her pupils dilated like a wood creature's, and she was shaking.

"Listen," he said. "What happened?"

"It's creepy," she said.

244

"I bet." He sat down with her, knowing that Choo Choo could tell him things. "Do you know where Natty Taylor is?"

"No."

"Choo Choo."

"No, I don't know."

"She didn't run away. I know she didn't run away," Will said. "She's not the type."

"I'm the type," Choo Choo said. "I ran away twice. Once to Los Angeles by plane. I emptied my savings account."

"Listen, Choo Choo," Will said, leading her back cautiously. "Is Natty here in town?"

"I don't know," she said. "Maybe." She hesitated. "Maybe anything."

"I know they've taken her someplace," he said, certain of his instincts. "I just want to know if she's in town or not," he said. "Like near here."

"Maybe."

"But not inside at Carr's."

"Don't ask me questions like this," Choo Choo said. "It's creepy."

"But near here," Will said.

"Yes yes yes yes yes," Choo Choo said into the sleeve of Will's winter jacket.

When he came out of Dick Carr's house with Eliza, Choo Choo had gone and his jacket was nowhere in sight.

Dick Carr took a bottle of wine and a candle to the Senior Shack. He had a plan. It had been spreading like moss since last autumn when Fil DeAngelis had first disgraced him. Now on the second night of winter, he had wine and a candle and Natty Taylor alone in a small house behind a vacant school. It was an impossible stroke of fortune, and his heart beat like drums in anticipation.

They sat on the wicker couch with a candle on the table in front of them and drank the wine.

"What time is it?" Natty asked.

"Seven-thirty," Dick Carr said. "Have you eaten?"

"Alexander brought lunch from the Hot Shoppes. A lot," she said. "I'm not hungry." She moved down on the couch, put her legs up on the table and crossed them. "It's dark early," she said. "It's been dark forever."

"Yesterday was the shortest day."

"I'll say," Natty said quietly. "The longest night."

"Yeah," Dick said and they grew silent again, letting the wine warm their chests, run their thoughts together.

"Wine makes me warm," Natty said. "You know?"

"Yes," Dick Carr said. "I know."

All day Natty had felt like a paper doll pasted back to front which separates down the center with use and becomes two dolls, the front and the back, distinguishable as separate and one. And she had felt herself pliable, with parts fragile enough to be broken in a single false move.

Now she watched herself with the huge bulk of Dick Carr. She was light-headed, gently burning through the center of her body, mellow as autumn, and she was Blanche the Virgin, provoking Filip. She felt her breasts fill, her legs fold open, her arm fall as though dropped across Dick Carr's thigh.

It was not that she wanted Dick Carr specifically. But that she did not care at all.

It was as though all her familiar edges had been filled and leveled to a single smooth and undistinguished line. Dick Carr grabbed her hips with his enormous hands familiar with the coarse rubber surface of basketballs and kissed her with his mouth open.

Will Barnes searched Washington methodically. First Anne Lowry's house, where Senator Lowry said it was a "terrible business" but the business of raising children anyway was terrible. And then the Taylors', where there was still no word, but Ellen Taylor, in a surprising motion, kissed him on the temple and thanked him.

All along Eliza was saying that she honestly believed Carter was interested in Paulette Estinet.

"He kissed your hands for an appetizer."

"Shut up," Eliza said.

"I want to check one more place."

"And then home?"

"Yes," Will said.

"What do you think about Carter?"

"I think he's a jackass."

"I *know* that, Will," she said. "But do you think he's interested in Paulette?"

"Nope."

"In me?"

"Nope," Will said. "In no one."

"But if it had to be someone," Eliza insisted, "which one of us would it be?"

"Jesus, Eliza."

Driving down Wisconsin Avenue toward Maryland, Will thought of the Senior Shack.

"You know," he said, "she could be in the Senior Shack."

"Who?" Liza asked.

"Natty, for chrissake."

"I don't know why I like him."

"Dick Carr?"

"I hate Dick Carr," she said. "Carter Harold. We were talking about Carter Harold."

"Not me," Will said, pulling his car into the parking lot beside the Post Office.

"He thinks Natty uses you."

"So he said."

"He thinks you're a sucker."

"Listen, Liza," Will said, getting out the car door. "Are you coming?"

"No," she said. "I'm staying here," she said. "Carter thinks Natty really likes Dick Carr," she added for emphasis.

"Shut up."

"That's what he said."

"I don't want to know what Carter Harold says." He shut the car door. "I'll be back," he called.

———

The Senior Shack appeared to be entirely dark until he was very close to it, beyond the old farmhouse which was the high school, above the science building, and then he saw a light which was small and unsteady. He walked up and stopped just short of the window in the rear of the building so he could see in but could not in all probability be seen. What he saw was Natty Taylor—her legs crossed and resting on a table, her black hair like a pillow underneath the enormous polar-bear head of Dick Carr, who was stretched across the rest of her like a hulking, thick, leather-skinned rhinoceros.

And something overtook Will Barnes—the splintered anger loose in him like bits of mercury separated from the whole, collided and grew, instantaneous as sea storms, to a single silver ball which measured his body temperature above the level of danger.

He only hit Dick Carr once, but such a blow as to throw him back against a chair shaking.

He had rushed in the room, lifted Dick Carr by the left shoulder with one arm and with the other connected with the side of Dick Carr's enormous intractable head, hitting him with the same hand he'd beaten against the cement pillar that afternoon.

Dick Carr made a motion as if to stand, then fell over with his arms beneath him. For a moment, his body riveted in motion as a car engine set in high will do after the ignition is turned off, throttling his life out in short staccato movements as if in a brief attempt to reverse the final decision.

THURSDAY, DECEMBER 23
1954

Natty and Will were not aware of holding hands. They sat together on the white wicker couch and stared at approximately the same place on the wall. The only light in the room was candlelight, which threw into mobile shadows everything beyond its circle. Dick Carr was beyond the candlelight. Will and Natty did not look at the space of floor where he was lying. They did not mention his name. Instead, they breathed single deep breaths consciously taken as an act of defiance against dying, because in the initial moments of shock, their dying was the only possible solution.

"Should we turn on the light?" Natty said finally.

"No," Will replied.

"Well," she said, her mind moving slowly, but moving now at least in some recognizable direction. "What should we do?" she asked.

"Tell," Will said simply.

"Tell?" she asked.

"Tell," he said again. "Eliza's in the car."

"Tell Eliza?" she asked, confused. "Should I turn on the light?"

"No," he said. "You go."

"Tell Eliza?"

"Get Eliza and tell the police."

"Oh," she said, and at the thought of moving out of the wicker couch, across the room, she had to breathe intentionally again. "Will you go?"

"No," he said. "I'll stay here."

"Here?"

"I have to," he said, clear that the one responsibility he had was to remain in the room with the evidence until he was discovered.

Natty got up.

"Should I call the police or go get them?"

"I don't care."

"Do you want me to turn the light on when I leave?"

"No," he said, impatient.

"The candle might burn out."

"Then I'll turn the light on," he said.

She walked as far away from Dick Carr as she could, keeping to the corners of the room.

"It was an accident," she said as she left, but Will did not answer, and his face across the room was in shadows so she could not see the expression.

Her first thought had been to run as though she could simply by sprinting beyond the Senior Shack and down the hill outdistance the events. The desire to run was physical, propelling her body. She had to resist it.

Then over and over in her head, she repeated the word as though its repetition solidified in the process of chemical change to final substance. Dead. The word itself was silent, like the sudden absence in the room had been, minutes ago when Will had hit him.

She thought she was going to be sick. Her mind was anesthetized, spinning off beyond her to predetermine sleep as had happened with ether. Her stomach was upset; she had difficulty breathing.

She didn't know what she was going to do until she got in the car next to Eliza and asked for Eliza to drive her home.

"So you *were* there," Eliza said. "Will thought you might be."

"Yes."

She could not tell Eliza. She could barely speak. The fact of what had happened minutes ago had only a physical expression.

"What about Will?"

"He's staying," she said. "We'll go back."

Natty could not tell her, and some instinct for preservation kept Eliza from asking.

On the drive home Natty was struck by physical things—the way the black trees webbed against the street lights, the yellow line down the center of the road brightly painted since yesterday or else distinguished in the dark, the squares of color pasted on the faces of houses with artificial people wandering in orange light. The fluids of her own body seemed to float out of her in short rushes as though she had been skinned, the material in her bones had gone soft and could, she expected, bend as though she hadn't a skeleton at all—the taste in her mouth was specific but unfamiliar and it occurred to her that not long ago she had been kissing Dick Carr with her mouth open, and the strange taste in her mouth was his saliva. Her mind wandered to the life of saliva—whether there was such a thing as life to it and if there was should she preserve this taste of Dick Carr in her mouth? Or should she get rid of it? Have Eliza stop the car on Newark Street immediately.

And then the taste of Dick Carr took over like the strong sweet scent of noxious gases will do, infusing her body and brain. Things became clear to her as if a button like the button lighting maps of battlefields were pressed just above the temple, and the lines of thought running through her head had names, color and form.

It was not an accident. She had provoked Dick Carr. She had wanted to make love to him for the sense of power it gave her over another life. She wanted to repay him in kind for the power he had had over her life.

It was by chance that Will Barnes had come to the Senior Shack at that moment, by chance that he'd connected in anger with the soft center of Dick Carr's brain, but the circumstances which allow for accidents were Natty's doing.

Natty was sure she would be sick before Eliza stopped the car at Highland Place and she got out. She leaned against a tree waiting for the nausea to pass, hoping the cold air would make a difference.

It was after midnight, but the living room of her parents' house was full of light, and she could see Sam Taylor standing by the fireplace fully dressed.

She wanted to run in the house, up the stairs to her own room, shut the door and climb in bed with the lights out. She wanted her father to come up and lock the windows as he used to do.

Instead she walked up to the front porch and knocked, knowing with unrelieved despair that whatever protection Sam Taylor had given her before could not lock out this dark knowledge of her own capacity to destroy.

It was dark when Sam Taylor woke up in his own bed. He was still in the clothes he had worn that day to the office, but except for a slight headache, he felt released, as though on the first day of recovery from a long illness. At first he did not even remember that Natty was gone. He showered, changed to clean clothes, made his bed, organized the papers on his desk, folded his trousers on a hanger, hung up the rumpled shirt he had worn to work that day and slept in, drew his curtains against the Bates' curiosities, set his watch by the clock in his study and went downstairs.

It was just after midnight and he was hungry.

When he saw Ellen sitting in the living room, reading by the fireplace, he remembered about Natty.

"Has there been word?" he asked.

She put her book across her lap. "She's all right," Ellen said. "She sent us letters." She reached in her skirt pocket and pulled out the three notes which had come that day.

"I didn't wake you," Ellen said.

"I've been sleeping nearly twelve hours."

"At first I didn't know you were here," she said. "You must have come while I took Joe to the hospital."

"Then he's gone?"

"I couldn't stand to have him here any longer. They are going to keep him until he's sober, I suppose," she said. "When I got back from the hospital I heard you snoring," she said. "You'd been drinking."

"I was very drunk."

"I thought so."

"A woman found me and brought me home," he said. "Someone I know. I can't remember who."

"You were that drunk?"

"I was very drunk."

He read the notes from Natty.

"I know about this," he said, tossing the notes down on the table.

"Know what?" Ellen asked.

"I know this about Natty," he said. He couldn't explain to her that a whole section of his life had been locked away for forty years as if, like Natty with her withered leg, he'd had to operate incomplete, knowing that one day his survival would depend on the discovery of missing parts. He understood why he had counted on Natty to replace what he had lost in himself.

But he was just out of danger, in the first hours of recovery, and he couldn't name what he knew to Ellen because he could not name it to himself.

"So," he said. "We wait."

"I guess," she said. "Sam?"

"You want to know about the notes."

"Well." She turned up her book as though she were going to read, not certain what to say to this man from whom she'd been separated for months, not remembering him sufficiently. "Andrew Slaughter called," she said.

He did not start. "I expected that eventually he would," he said.

"Who is he?"

"He's a young man I met with Ed Marlowe on Sunday. I'd been drinking then, too," he said. "I've been trying to reach him all week."

"Yes," Ellen said. "He said it must be important. That you'd called about ten times. He said he couldn't imagine. That he hardly knew you."

"It was important at the time," Sam said. "It's not important any longer."

"You don't want to call him."

"No," Sam said. "I don't know what I'd say to him if I did."

He told Ellen as much as he understood of all that had to do with Andrew Slaughter and his father.

"I've always known that I took in drunks because of my father as though it were an act of penance," he said. "That's why Ed Marlowe and all the others. That's why Joe McCarthy and this mess in our lives which came of having him here."

"I know that."

"Some of it I knew," Sam said. "What I didn't understand was penance."

He told Ellen about Andrew Slaughter, who had not looked like his father but had felt like him. "I fell in love with Andrew Slaughter," Sam said simply. "That hasn't happened to me before," he said, "but drinking like my father used to drink, falling in love with a young man I didn't even know who felt like my father to me, going to Lafayette Park even, I found a part of myself which I'd lost when my father died and knew simply as absence."

And he told her about the death of his father as he had remembered it twelve hours ago dark with alcohol at the bottom of his life.

Ellen Taylor had grown up with a sense that it was easy to die. Her mother had died easily at twenty-seven, giving birth to a stillborn son. Five years later, her father had fallen off a ladder fixing the roof, and though he was only bruised in the fall, an old nail from a board on the ground had punctured his calf and he had died slowly, but easily, of gangrene. By the time Ellen was nineteen everyone she had loved was dead except one grandmother with whom she lived, and Ellen had learned to live at a distance like Moslem women in veils, which is how she appeared to the people who knew her, indistinct as though her face were covered by thin cloth, as though she lived in a narrow space of land between living and dying, to be prepared so when it came she would not have far to travel, even as though living was too chancy to risk face on. When she had married the first time she had selected, in the football player from Wisconsin who could withstand the onslaught of armor-suited bodies mashing his own, the most permanent man available. Those early losses had given her a sense of her own impermanence. When the football player grew fat and subject to the failure of flesh, Ellen Taylor searched for someone less susceptible and found him in Sam Taylor. She was beautiful with a kind of mystery, a protection from years of loss. She struck a man as fragile and could have had anyone in 1936 when she was looking.

Samuel Taylor was ordered and puritanical, with the care that comes of knowing the world is a risky place and full of danger, but a careful man has a chance to prevent reversals. He didn't make false moves. At thirty he seemed more invincible than anyone Ellen had known. When they married she loved him as much as it was possible for her to love anyone. Specifically, she felt safe with him. She believed he could prevent disasters because he saw them coming.

As they grew older, she had separated herself from him for other reasons than losses. Occasionally she was angry for the very reason she had married him. She wanted to find the strength for living in herself. She wished there were some soft part of him where she could intrude and feel necessary to his strength. Sometimes between Victorian romances, she day-dreamed of Sam Taylor terminally ill, but not dying—simply ill enough for constant care. And not getting better either. That, Ellen thought, would give her a sense of permanence.

Now, sitting in the bright living room on Highland Place in the early hours of the morning, Samuel Taylor had given her space to intrude.

She reached out her hand and touched his hand lying on the couch beside her.

"I wish you had told me," she said, deeply touched by this new knowledge of a man she'd known nearly her whole life, "so I could have understood."

"I didn't know myself until today," he replied.

257

Sam knew the moments when a man is susceptible to the truth about himself, when he can use it and understand it and live with it. It was necessary, he believed, to be receptive to these moments at personal cost or one will always live incomplete and vulnerable in more dangerous ways.

Sitting now with Ellen waiting for developments with their daughter, Sam felt a strength that he had never known—as though he could cope with anything. Even his love for Natty.

When Natty knocked on the front door, Sam was building a fire. They had decided to wait up.

Ellen answered the door.

Something in her demeanor forbade them. They stood apart, Sam behind Ellen, Natty at the door, like strangers who discover each other in the same room, each thinking that it belongs to him.

"What's the matter?" Sam asked, sensing trouble immediately.

"I've just come home," she said.

"I see you have," Sam said. "Where have you been, for God's sake?"

"I've been at the Senior Shack," she said. "You know? Behind Friends."

"I remember."

"And then Will Barnes came just a while ago," she said, "and had a fight with Dick Carr. Not a fight exactly," she explained. "It was my fault."

"Is Dick Carr badly hurt?" Sam Taylor rushed ahead, sensing the worst.

"Maybe," she said.

She told them that Will was at the Senior Shack with Dick Carr and that she'd come back to call the police and, she guessed, an ambulance.

"Eliza Barnes is in the car," she said. "I'll go back with her and meet the police at Friends."

"We'll follow you," Sam Taylor said.

"I believe," she said to prepare her parents, "that you're right about Dick Carr's being badly hurt."

"He is hurt to death," she wanted to cry out. "Will and I killed him, and if we go now by car to Canada or beyond we could begin again, just the three of us."

She wished for the hard center of Will Barnes which allowed him to sit with the body of Dick Carr, stone-still and clear-headed, free of the need to run, as though he had known his own capacities and had faced the repercussions of them many times. Natty had understood the baseness in other people, especially children, but never in herself.

Now this new knowledge and an overwhelming fear that unlike Will Barnes, she was not equal to it.

Carter Harold was bad-tempered. He had been waiting for Paulette in the living room at Dick Carr's house since ten o'clock. They were going to get pizza and then from one a.m. to four a.m., it was her duty with Natty at the Senior Shack. Once Mrs. Carr had called from Oklahoma and drawled on and on about Dick being out late and getting to Tulsa by the twenty-fourth at the latest and boys, she'd had three of them . . . daughters must be easier. Carter said they were, as if he knew, and agreed with the way Dick kept the place when the Carrs were gone and stayed out after midnight. He said he would drive Dick to the airport himself on the twenty-fourth to make certain that he got to Tulsa Christmas Eve.

The grandfather clock in the hall struck midnight, clanging and clanging; he wanted to kick the long rectangular glass in the clock's stomach and pull the pendulum out.

He had dressed right after supper, which he had eaten regularly and pleasantly with his parents this week in order to avoid suspicions. He had dressed for hours, passing back and forth in front of the mirror with each new article of clothing he put on until finally, fully dressed, he stood in front of the mirror examining himself for mistakes. He didn't look as well as he had expected. It was difficult to pinpoint the problem. Perhaps he'd looked so well in the bathroom mirror at Dick Carr's because it showed only his head. He moved to the mirror over his dresser, which showed only his head and shoulders. It showed no improvement. There had been a specific change which Carter Harold, wise enough to recognize, was not in the actual image of the face as he saw it, but in his imaginings about it.

First off he had lost interest in the Syndicate. He was by nature interested primarily in the process of things. If matters proceeded in certain carefully planned directions, the conclusion was inevitable. Only the beginnings interested Carter Harold.

Besides, he had to admit to himself, the Syndicate was bigger than he had ever intended it should be. Probably when Sam Taylor was accused of homosexuality in tomorrow's paper or when Natty's notes reached him, whichever came first, and he resigned the FCC as a result of one or both—probably Carter Harold would feel sick. Not out of conscience so much as a lack of control.

He was passionate about strategy. It was the only passion he knew. But he didn't like dealing with people. There were too many variables. Things had not gone as he'd expected them to. He had not, for example, expected to fall in love with Paulette Estinet. What he knew of love was with Eliza Barnes—without this terrible longing he had with Paulette except as it applied to sex, and that was curable.

Now he sat in Dick Carr's living room full of suspicions. He had called Anne Lowry at ten-thirty and she had said no, Paulette was probably still at home, and please not to call because she was in trouble with her father for all of these late nights. He had called her home, disguising his voice and calling himself Dick Carr. They had said to please not call so late in the evening but Paulette was at Sukey's house to spend the night and that was all and please goodbye.

The Reverend Moorehead had been fighting with his wife. Carter could hear her in the background. He said that Sukey was sleeping after so many late nights and he would not wake her and no, Paulette wasn't with her. He didn't know Paulette and who was this. Dick Carr, Carter said again.

Al Cox answered the phone when he called.

Have you seen Paulette, he asked, and quickly went on to say he was simply checking to make sure she got to the Senior Shack on time. Al Cox said no and Carter hung up the phone, disbelieving. He believed Paulette was there with Al Cox, that all along this had been developing behind his back in spite of his plans for occupying Al by making him a spy. Then he thought of Buddy Cox and Mrs. Buddy Cox and knew of course that as long as they were there Paulette was not.

By twelve-thirty Carter Harold had the whole picture in mind. Paulette had arranged to meet Dick Carr at the Senior Shack at ten-thirty or eleven. By then Natty would be asleep. Surely she should be tired enough to sleep. Or else they'd wait there until she did fall asleep. And with Natty sleeping on the wicker couch, they would make love on the floor until one-thirty, when Dick Carr would straighten his pants, put his sweater on, wipe the bright-pink lipstick off his face with Paulette Estinet's assistance and come back to N Street in Georgetown, where he had made plans to meet Carter Harold.

Carter could not stand to wait any longer. If he was right, if that was going on in the Senior Shack while he was waiting docile as a lamb in the Carr living room, he was going to find out for himself. In spite of his decision to stay away from the Senior Shack in case of trouble. In spite of every instinct of good sense which told him he should not chance implicating himself—not with the kidnapping of Natty or with the blank-headed Dick Carr or certainly these unfamiliar feelings overtaking his rational mind.

But he went anyway, drove straight down Wisconsin Avenue and right into the Post Office parking lot.

So, he thought as he went up the hill to the Senior Shack and saw the lights and shadows of candles. They're doing it by candlelight. And so certain was he of what he'd find that he stood looking in the window for some time before his eyes adjusted to the light and he realized that the body of Dick Carr was not lying on anything but the floor. And the person on the couch wasn't Natty but Will Barnes, wide awake and sitting up. He was too absorbed to hear the police cars. Two of them drove up, parking beside his car. They turned on their spotlights, drawing a yellow circle around him. Will Barnes saw the lights. He stood up.

Instinctively Carter Harold ran.

Later, thinking back, he was surprised at his bad judgment and blamed it entirely on the situation with Paulette.

The police caught him easily, running and without weapons, though he suspected they would have gladly used weapons had he resisted. At first he said he was going for a walk and their lights had frightened him, but when they didn't buy his story he decided not to talk at all. Which was the only clear-headed decision he had made that night.

When Filip DeAngelis ran home through Georgetown to 39th Street after he'd seen Blanche the Virgin with Larry Luce, he broke all the trophies in his mother's glass case in the living room. He walked in the front door and the first thing he saw was a framed picture of himself from *Life* magazine leading the choir out of the Washington Cathedral as an acolyte. *Life* had taken it when he was fourteen for a series they were doing on world religions, and Rosa had bought forty copies of *Life* and sent the picture to all of her relations and Antonio's in Tuscany and kept twenty for herself. The one she had framed was next to a crucifix Antonio had brought her from Italy, and Filip grabbed the picture off the wall, broke the glass and tore it in small pieces, dropping it on the floor where he stood. Then he saw the trophies. He knew exactly what he was going to do, but first he checked that Elsa and Johnny were still at Children's Hospital and that Angela wasn't home from Christmas shopping yet. He went downstairs and destroyed the trophies one by one, breaking the bottom plastic bases over his knee, tossing the metal players—football players in pass positions, basketball players in jump-shot positions, baseball players bending with their bats swung back—against the wall so the wall was pockmarked and the players lost an occasional hand or arm or baseball bat in the toss. When the case was empty he went upstairs, pulled down his blinds, pulled out the plug of his electric clock and, fully dressed, climbed into bed.

When Rosa came home from work after midnight because her story on Sam Taylor was due and she had not been able to write it, there was a note for her on the front door.

"Mama, I've gone to bed 'cause I'm *dead* tired. See you in the a.m. I don't know what's with Fil. Everything's piled in the middle of the living room so you can see it. I tried to talk to him but he said ——— you. Love, Angela."

On a pile in the middle of the living-room rug where Angela had put them were the pieces of plastic and gold-dipped arms and legs and bats and small gold plates with ALL AMERICAN FOOTBALL and ALL CITY BASEBALL and CLARK GRIFFITH PLAYER OF THE YEAR and either F.DeA. or Fil DeAngelis or Filippo De-Angelis, 1952 or 1953 or 1954.

Filip was stunned. Like after a tackle when the breath is momentarily gone. That kind of stunned. He did not hurt yet, but he did not expect to recover either. At first he went to sleep. As soon as he crawled into bed he fell asleep. He didn't think of Blanche before he slept, and he didn't dream of her. When he woke up it was to the sound of Rosa in the living room, and he got up immediately, sat down in the chair in his bedroom without turning on the lights, expecting her.

"Nothing is the matter," he would say, rehearsing.

"I got food poisoning from the restaurant and took a rest," he'd go on when she insisted.

"It hasn't anything to do with the girl with cotton-candy hair and breasts," he would say easily. "Every girl has breasts, Mother."

"I have decided," he would say when she had sat down on his bed with plans to stay, "*not* to play athletics any more." And when she railed on about how he expected to go to college then he'd say he didn't expect to go to college at all.

He'd ask her if she would mind leaving because he had things to do.

He heard her come up the wood stairs and stiffened in preparation for the rush of light into his room from the hall when she opened the door without knocking. For the small figure in the archway.

The footsteps stopped at the head of the stairs and waited. Then they turned and walked down the hall to her own room.

"Changing," he thought. "To more comfortable things so we

can talk all night." He put his head against the back of the chair. "Terrific," he thought, "all night with Rosa." He wanted to get back in bed and sleep, because already Blanche was back. He wished he could be angry or wish her dead or maimed or prostituted in the Woodrow Wilson High School locker room. Instead he was intolerably lonely and wanted to sleep.

His mother had taken off her shoes, and it was difficult to hear her bare feet. Concentrating, he did hear them coming down the hall toward his room, but they stopped. He couldn't hear them any longer and presumed that she had gone into Johnny's room. Shortly he heard the low moan of Johnny's waking to prove it.

"Johnny," Rosa said, moving him over in the bed so she could sit down. "I'm sorry," she said, taking his hand. "I didn't mean to be home so late."

He wrapped around her like a kitten, nestling his head on her breast.

"I've been thinking how little we know about each other," she said to him, running her fingers through his hair. "Like you," she whispered. "You could be having dreams. You could live in a world with people I can't imagine."

In his sleep Johnny rolled his head and smiled, clutched Rosa's finger, which he held like a baby.

"I've been thinking about your father on the Communist rolls," she said. "Maybe it was all a story that he told us for protection. And we think we know each other so well."

"So what if I were on the Communist rolls in fact?" Antonio had said to Rosa once in the weeks before he died. "That is not the point."

"It is the point," Rosa had said. "You are either implicated or not."

"These men are intruding on people's lives," he said. "Imagine."

"I thought that you were a principled man," she said to him fiercely.

"I am a principled man, Rosa, and I don't believe that an Irish

Catholic Senator from Wisconsin with bad manners should hold this power over my life."

"So how do you stop him?" she said, crawling into bed beside him.

"Best you can."

"So you would lie," she said. "Even to me."

"Listen, Rosa, we have to live as well as possible. Right?"

She nodded.

"You know that. You're the one always worrying about streetcars and airplanes falling out of the sky for no reason."

"And lying. I worry about lying, too."

"Don't let it keep you up all night," he said, "or you'll be fit for nothing tomorrow." He turned off the light and lay with his back to her, his small hard buttocks like a work shoe in bed between them.

"Antonio," she had whispered to his back. "What can you count on then?"

"Ahh," he mumbled to the wall. "The sun coming up tomorrow and that it will be Tuesday."

"Oh, God," she said.

"What do you count on, Rosa?"

"Myself," she said, "and you."

"That's foolish to count on me," he said to her.

"You're getting bitter with this whole thing, Antonio."

"I'm not bitter," he said. "Just sensible."

"Soon you'll be so sensible that you aren't able to get up in the morning," she said, turning over, pulling the covers up to his chin.

Late in the night when Rosa was nearly sleeping, Antonio pulled her to him and they made love.

"Now," he said after they were finished, "I can go to sleep." He patted her buttocks under her gown. "See how sensible I am."

"Antonio," Rosa asked as they were dressing the next morning. "Were you a Communist or not?"

"I was not," he said, "and it's best you believe me. Otherwise, Rosa *mia, you* will not be able to get up in the morning."

―――――――

Rosa lay down on the covers beside Johnny, cradling his head in her arms.

"Tell me a secret," she whispered. His eyes rolled open.

"Agggg," he said, cooed it really, like a happy infant, but his voice was low and guttural, so the sound that came from his throat was harsh.

"Good." She smiled. "You tell me one," she said, "and I'll tell you one."

Rosa's desk at the *News* was in a room of desks with typewriters where stories were banged out all day long and telephones rang and rang as though there were a state of emergency. After Rosa had returned from taking Sam Taylor to Highland Place, she sat at her desk in the newsroom with her notes from Wisconsin. She couldn't write.

"How much space do you need?" the editor asked her.

She made a small box with her fingers.

"I gave you more that that," he said.

"So far I've written nothing."

"Would you be better off in my office where you can be alone?" he asked, anxious that this story not be lost.

"Maybe." She shrugged.

"It's quiet," he said, "and you're not getting it done here."

"This isn't going to be the story that you want," she warned.

"Any story will have to do," he said. "I've promised a story tomorrow and there's a space."

"I'll do a story to fill the space you have," she said, and after he had left she spread out her notes on Samuel Taylor, with whom she was falling magically in love, as if he were a character in a book about whom she knew so much he had become real to her.

I came to Washington, D.C., in 1934, out of Little Italy in Nesquehonong, Pennsylvania, where my Catholic mother spoke broken English and only in the market. I was young and smart and believed I could do anything.

I married and worked and had children as other women my age from working-class backgrounds did. Looking back, I was very happy, though I complained that there was too little money and the children were ill-behaved.

And then in 1953 my husband died of a heart attack on his way to testify before the Permanent Sub-Committee on Investigations of the Senate Committee on Government Operations chaired by Senator Joseph McCarthy.

"Rosa, Rosa," my mother used to say to me when I was young, "life is a burden for everyone. We must take what we get and not complain."

"No," I said to her. "You can do whatever you want to do if you have will enough."

"You will see," she said ominously.

"Life is a burden," I wrote my mother after Antonio died. But unlike my mother, whose patience comes of another generation of women, I was not willing to be silent about it.

I wanted to ruin Joe McCarthy. An eye for an eye, I thought.

When Joe McCarthy, already ruined, moved into the house of Samuel Taylor I wanted to ruin him as well in retaliation.

How easily we forgive and forget, I thought. Especially our children. For Samuel Taylor's daughter was spending all of her time with my son.

I was glad for an opportunity to go to Wisconsin. I wanted to discover damaging secrets about Sam Taylor because of his association with McCarthy and because of his daughter and my son.

I am not, by nature, ideologically inclined. If I'm honest, it was the latter which moved me to Wisconsin and not McCarthy.

I am also fearful of automobiles. I do not drive myself. I cannot ride in planes without bad dreams. Subconsciously I feel my children are open wounds subject to infections from other children. The only way to protect them is to keep the other children away. Since Antonio died I have considered life in an atomic-bomb shelter the only reasonable solution.

I am a Catholic and go regularly to Mass simply for its daily repetition, as though there is, in fact, a scheme of things.

I went to Wisconsin to eliminate the enemy.

I went to Manawa, Wisconsin, and Grand Chute, where McCarthy's from, and Appleton, which is the largest of the three towns, and met Samuel Taylor's family and people who had known Joe McCarthy when he was a boy.

I did not discover in Wisconsin what I had expected. What I found there in the life of Samuel Taylor was myself.

I remember how I felt when I first got off the bus in Washington,

D.C., at seventeen with that raw hope like the sweet juice of berries when you're small and do not know that in winter the berries disappear. They will have another season and another and another, but never so sweet as the first when we believed that they were permanent.

"Mama," I write to my mother, eighty-one years old and keeping her own house, baking bread for the neighbors next door and Sundays for the Catholic Church. "I don't have time to be bitter," I say. "It tires me out. I must do the work that I can do."

"Like you taught me," I say to her when I see her.

"Bah," she says and snaps my knuckles with her cane when I help her to her feet.

I cannot write Sam Taylor's story except to say that we must have arrived in Washington, D.C., on the same bus.

It was a good trip to Wisconsin and I'm glad I went. I don't feel like living in the bomb shelter any longer. It probably smells bad. We might catch cold.

December 23, 1954. R.DeA.

"Shit, Rosa," the editor said when he saw the story.

"I didn't think you'd like it," she said.

"It's not our kind of story. You know that."

"It's the right number of words," she said.

"You promised another story," he said.

"Maybe so," she replied, "but it's the story I found."

Filip could not stand it any longer. He walked down the hall and stood in the entrance to Johnny's bedroom.

"Well," he said to Rosa, lying on the bed next to Johnny.

"Is that you, Filip?"

"Who were you expecting?" he said. "Alice in Wonderland?"

She sat up. "We'd better go in my room, not to wake Johnny."

"I don't know why we should worry about waking Johnny," he said. "You've been talking in here to him for nearly an hour."

He followed her to her room.

"You didn't come in when you got home," he said. "I expected you to come in."

"I thought you were sleeping," she said. "I didn't want to wake you."

"Don't you have anything to say?"

"I'm sorry, Filip," she said softly.

"About what?" he snapped. "About the trophies?"

"Well," she said, "yes, about the trophies." She got in bed, turned on the light. "But primarily I'm sorry about whatever happened to you."

"It's unlike you, Mama, not to turn me inside out to see exactly what has happened."

She was silent.

"Blanche," he said and then he surprised her by weeping, sitting by the side of the bed and sobbing. From time to time she touched his hand, but she didn't hold him, much as she was inclined to hold him, and she didn't talk.

Filip could not sleep. He watched the shadows of cars on the wall and listened to the trolleys. He tried not to think, but almost by accident he was thinking, replaying the game on Wednesday, watching himself foul out intentionally. For as he saw the game in his head between the actual shadows of cars down 39th Street he knew he had wanted to foul out. To sit on the bench, to watch the game without the expectations of the coaches and the players, the scouts from Harvard, to leave the gymnasium without the string of intruding reporters. To sit out so he did not have to face the chance of failure.

At his father's funeral Filip had not wept.

"He was amazing," friends told Rosa afterward.

"You're so lucky to have him," they told her.

He had walked away dry-eyed from the gravesite, holding Rosa's arm in his own.

He had walked away as though he could by choice walk away from his father's death and deny his absence.

He wept now into the soft cave of his pillow so Rosa would not know.

For a long time Rosa lay awake watching the shadows on the ceiling, listening for Filip, who must have slept.

She felt immensely sad for him, but she was glad that it had

269

happened as well. He would be more careful now. He was safer than he had been.

Just before falling asleep she thought about Samuel Taylor and Ravilla, herself and Filip now, knowing that we have within the limitations of our paralysis the capacity to use other limbs.

Natty was at the Senior Shack when the rescue squad wrapped the body of Dick Carr in a sheet, lifted it on a stretcher and carried it down the hill to the back of the ambulance. She knew when she looked at his face as they rolled the body over that she shouldn't have done it, that it was a picture which would stay in her mind for years, forever.

"Did you look?" Natty asked Will Barnes later.

He nodded. "I had to."

"I know," she said.

She wanted to pay right now for the whole thing, to clear the air—pay in cash with everything she had. But she knew this terrible sense of loss, this dying which was Dick Carr's dying and her own as well, was permanent.

Samuel and Ellen Taylor sat on the opposite side of the Senior Shack. Ellen neatly with her hands folded like a Victorian portrait of a wellborn child, and Sam on the edge of a wicker chair from the Lowrys' summer home in Mississippi, holding his felt hat in his hands, rolling it through his fingers until it burned. He looked small to Natty. On the floor beside them Eliza Barnes was crying.

The police disagreed on what should be done with Will. Will did not intervene. From time to time he looked at his injured knuckle, which was swollen considerably, and one policeman asked if that had happened when he hit Dick Carr.

"It happened when I hit a cement pillar," Will said evenly.

The policemen exchanged glances.

"Hot-tempered," the one said to the other, who was taking notes. He did not write it down.

———

Will's explanation of events was simple.

"I came up here looking for Natty Taylor, who had run away from home, and saw Natty on the couch and Dick on top of her," he said. "I ran in the shack and hit him," he said. "Once."

"Once was enough," the one policeman said.

They asked Natty why she had run away.

"Because of my father," she said automatically and then confused in her own mind. "Senator McCarthy was living in our house."

The young policeman sitting next to her looked up.

"Was it specific why you ran away?" he asked. "What did your father do?"

"Nothing," she said, irritated because her reasons, lost in the events of these last few hours, were of a dimension she did not understand herself. "I was responsible for too much," she said.

"Responsible for what?"

"Oh, I don't know," she said, moving to the back of the wicker couch as far away as possible from the policeman with his notebook, drawing up her legs. "For my father," she said, "I had to be everything."

Since Natty was a child, she had wanted to make mistakes, dozens of small ones to maintain a sense of balance and require that Sam Taylor make adjustments.

The policeman taking notes looked over at his colleague and shook his head.

"Was that your boy friend?" he asked, indicating the door through which Dick Carr had recently been carried.

"No," she said.

"Is he?" He indicated Will Barnes. Natty didn't answer.

"Easy now. Easy," the policeman said to Eliza, who was crying.

"We'll go get Mrs. Barnes," Sam Taylor said and took Eliza by the shoulders. "Let's go and get your mother. It will be easier for her if she finds out through us."

"I'm taking them to the Eighth Precinct," the policeman with the notebook said. "You can meet us there."

"I still don't know why you hit the other young man unless it was in self-defense," the policeman said to Will as they were walking out to the car.

"It was for me," Natty said quickly.

"Oh," the policeman said.

"Jealousy?" the young policeman said quietly to his colleague. "Now we're making some sense of things."

"No," she said. "He thought Dick was hurting me."

Will and Natty were taken to the Eighth Precinct in one patrol car, which was followed by a second patrol car with Carter Harold in the back.

"It's like a dream," Natty whispered as they drove down Wisconsin Avenue. Will Barnes put his hand on top of hers. It was not like a dream to him. The things that happened in his dreams were making love to Natty Taylor behind the barn. His head was clear. He expected that he would be sent away. He was eighteen and he had killed a man. Without great difficulty a case could be made that he had killed a man in cold blood. He wondered as the patrol car rode through Georgetown if this was how it felt to kill the enemy in war. He was horrified that he had done it, but at a distance, as though he were watching it on a film. He was amazed that it had been done so easily. Except for Nell, he did not feel remorse. In fact, he felt great relief. There had been times today when his anger was great enough to injure people who were innocent of blame. And Dick Carr was not that.

Carter Harold called his parents and told his mother he had been detained and would be home very late.

"We want your parents here," the policeman said.

"I am eighteen," he said, thinking of his parents and their faith in him. "My father has a heart condition," he lied. "It could be dangerous to wake him in the middle of the night for this."

They waited for Nell Barnes to come with Eliza and Sam Taylor. No one talked. Natty sat on a hard wood bench next to her mother. Will stood, leaning against the counter which separated them from the desks of the Eighth Precinct police.

Once Carter Harold, looking at the mug shots of criminals on the bulletin board, said, "I wonder how my father would feel to see me here," but no one in the room responded.

Natty could not stand the silence any longer.

"It was my fault," she whispered to her mother.

Her mother put her fingers to her lips and did not look at Natty.

When Natty was small she had spent a summer at a cousin's house on a lake in New Hampshire. She had just learned to walk after the sledding accident and had been told it would be good for her to learn to swim. So she spent hours on the lake in front of the cottage, but did not learn to swim.

It was a large lake, shallow around the shore with a gradual decline for many yards and then a sudden sharp drop. If Natty looked down, it was not difficult to determine when the drop was coming, because there was a definite line where the water turned blue-black. But she didn't like to look down. She liked instead to walk along the sandy bottom feeling the cool water move up her legs and torso, up her chest as she tilted her head toward the sun—then drop and with a wild flutter of arms and legs, exhilarated by danger, she'd make it back where she could touch the bottom.

"You could drown," her cousin said.

"No." She shook her head. "I couldn't."

"You're so bull-headed, Natty," the cousin said. "I wish you'd learn to swim so I don't have to watch you all the time."

"You don't have to watch me," Natty said. "I'm careful."

The cousin shrugged and gave up watching Natty all the time.

Of course she almost drowned. One Sunday morning, walking out in the lake for the tenth or fifteenth time that morning, bored with it by now and thinking of other things besides the quick thrill of danger, she reacted late and panicked. Beating in the water with her legs and arms, she seemed to move farther into the blue-black and breathe like snapping bellows.

Her cousin sent the boy next door to pull her in.

"I want to go home," Natty said that night at supper.

"You can't," the cousin said. "Your parents sent you here to spend a month."

"I am going home tomorrow morning," she said.

"You can't go home until you learn to swim," the cousin said, not warmly.

"You haven't even tried to teach me," Natty said belligerently.

"Teach yourself," the cousin said. "There is only one job you have, and that's to take care of your own self. If you do that very well, then you will be happy."

"I am happy," Natty said. "I'm just not happy here. I want to go home."

"Then learn to swim," the cousin said.

She was a hard woman.

Lately Natty had felt as she had that morning at the lake when the bottom gave and her accustomed defense failed her. Now that sense she had of being pulled to shore by the neighborhood boy next door. She wanted to go home.

"How long do you think we'll be here?" she whispered to her mother.

Again her mother shook her head and put her fingers to her lips.

Eliza told everything she knew about the Syndicate, which was not everything, because she wasn't involved and had only overheard a few things while she had been at Dick Carr's. Everything would never be known, because Dick Carr was dead and Carter Harold didn't talk at all or look at Eliza while she spoke. But what Eliza knew was enough for implications.

From time to time the policeman taking notes turned to Carter Harold. "Is that true?" he'd ask.

"I don't know," Carter would reply, and finally he said he wouldn't talk at all, that if he had a statement to make, it would be through his lawyer.

———

Will Barnes called Senator Carr in Oklahoma.

"We'll notify the Senator," the police said.

"No," Will said. "I will."

He sat in the telephone booth for a long time after he had called. There was a young policeman posted in the corner of the room on watch.

"You think I'd bolt?" Will asked, walking back to the main office.

"Some do," the officer said.

"I never would," Will replied.

Will Barnes was released to his mother at five a.m. Samuel Taylor posted bond for him.

Eliza lay in the back seat weeping quietly, curled in the corner like a young animal.

"How come you didn't say all this before, Lizey?" Will asked her once.

She couldn't answer. So he answered it for himself.

"Carter Harold," he said. "It was because of him."

Will drove. From time to time he looked at his mother's face for signs.

"Do you feel okay?" he asked her.

"I'm fine," she said. "I carry oxygen and nitroglycerin," she said. "I'll be all right."

She looked young to him in the early dawn and beautiful and strong.

"I'm sorry."

"I know, Will," she said. "Some people belong in the country with animals instead of human beings. We understand thunderstorms and predatory animals and self-defense. We can watch a groundhog and know he'll eat a rat for sustenance and steal our vegetables, so we fence our gardens in and are grateful for his habits with rats. It makes sense," she said. "All you need is eyes."

"Natty took the blame herself," Will said.

"We all should," Nell said quietly. And they drove through the night, lulled by the soft weeping of Eliza, like bandits in league, stealing off to their hideaway with their own lives.

It was dawn when Samuel Taylor and his family walked up the front steps of the house on Highland Place. The Washington *Post* was already delivered, and he put it under his arm and went inside.

In the kitchen Ellen Taylor made breakfast. Natty took a shower and came down in a robe.

Sam Taylor read the front page of the paper without speaking, turned to the middle of the first section and put it in the center of the table while he ate.

The center front picture on the first page showed Samuel Taylor with his arm over the shoulder of a man he remembered, not yesterday because yesterday he had had too much to drink, but from the day before. Although the man's face was not to the camera—could be construed in fact to be nestled in the neck of Samuel Taylor—he had a muffler around his neck which hung down his back to his waist.

The caption under the pictures said: SAMUEL TAYLOR, CHAIRMAN OF THE FCC. There was no story, simply a short note under the picture which read, "Samuel Taylor was found inebriated Wednesday afternoon at Lafayette Park with the young man pictured here, who did not give his name. Mr. Taylor has recently been under pressure for his alleged association with Senator Joseph McCarthy." The note at the bottom indicated more on page A5. On page A5 was another picture of Sam Taylor struggling to get up from the ground. The man with the red muffler had both arms around him possibly in an effort to lift him up. The young man was described as a regular at Lafayette Park. The second picture on A5 showed Sam Taylor standing off balance with his arm raised against an unknown figure to the left. There was no comment under that except his name.

"I don't remember any of this," Sam later said to Ellen, "but obviously it happened."

Natty read the paper and pushed her plate away.

"Eat," Sam said. "You've been up all night and will be sick."

"I can't," she replied, crying.

"You have to," he said crossly, not wanting the responsibility for tears, and pushed her plate back in front of her.

"I'm too tired," she said. "Is the story true?"

"What you see there has to be true because there are pictures," he said.

"I know that."

"The other is not true," Sam Taylor said. "But I was drunk and I suppose I was subconsciously at Lafayette Park for something." He cleared his plate. "It's difficult to explain," he said, "but it has to do with my father."

So he explained to Natty about the last few days as he understood it.

"I expect," he said to Ellen after Natty had left the room, "I'll be asked to resign as a result of this."

"Why don't you call the President and explain?"

"There isn't anything to explain to the President."

"And leave it up to him?"

"I won't leave my decision up to him," he said. "That's my own to make, but it doesn't necessarily mean that my decision will be the final one."

At nine Sam spoke with the President and made plans to leave immediately and meet with him at the Oval Office.

The press was in front of his house on Highland Place. One reporter was sitting on the hood of his car.

"Excuse me," Sam said getting in.

"Mr. Taylor," the reporter said. "Do you have a statement?"

"No," Sam said. "I haven't got a statement."

"I understand your daughter's back," he said.

"Yes, she is."

"Senator Carr's son was killed last night and she was there," he said. "Do you have a statement about that?"

"I don't have a statement about anything just now," Sam said.

―――――

277

When Samuel Taylor walked into the White House to meet the President he felt as he had felt when he was a boy and knew with certainty that with a running start he could jump Cobb's Creek without getting his feet wet.

In the morning Ellen Taylor organized her room, looking out the window from time to time to see the street filled with reporters, answering the telephone calls from Ed Marlowe, who would be over immediately, he said, thick with drink, but she said no, that was very kind, but no, and Jean McCarthy, who thanked Ellen for everything and said things were going very well and the Senator should be home by Christmas, and Natty's friends, who had heard about Dick Carr although the story wasn't in the paper yet.

Mostly she cleaned and rearranged the room the way you do after someone has died, knowing however much the room is fresh and altered, the ghost will still be there but the *sense* of dying can be gotten rid of. She put away her books so the endless gothic covers of pink-frocked maidens running in terror from dark houses did not clutter up the room.

She took a long time dressing. When Sam came home from the White House, she wanted to look beautiful. She wanted to take the place in his life which required romance and which she had forfeited last summer. She wanted him to dream about her, as though his dreams of her gave her new vitality.

Tonight, she thought, she would ask him to sleep in her room.

In the study Natty practiced the cello. At first she couldn't get the face of Dick Carr out of her head, and then Filip DeAngelis and Will and the last few days spinning around and around. But gradually as she played, concentrating on the process of playing first, the sound of the music took over.

Filip called at noon, and Natty answered. He called to say it was terrible what had happened.

"Will Barnes hit him?" he asked. "That's what I heard."

"Once," Natty said. "Just once," as though that lessened his death.

"Was it an accident?"

"Not exactly," she said. "You don't hit someone by accident," she said. "The place he hit him was accidental."

"You told me once that Will Barnes could do anything."

"It was my fault, too," Natty said.

"How come?"

"It's hard to say," she said.

"Will he go to prison?"

"My father says no," Natty said. "It's a complicated story. There are these other things—there was a whole group who got together to force my father to resign from the FCC."

"My mother was called this morning to do a story about it," Filip said. "The group was called the Syndicate, and Dick Carr was in it."

"Nothing will happen to them, my father says. It will just be embarrassing to be in the paper."

"I saw the awful thing about your father in the paper this morning."

"It's not true."

"I know," Filip said. "Mother told me."

"Well," she said, at a loss for what to say as though it had been years instead of days since they had been together. "I guess I'll see you sometime."

"I'm really sorry, Nat."

"That's okay."

She hung up. She didn't want him to be sorry about things. She wanted him to run over in his football uniform and level the reporters gathered like city rats outside the library window. Or else go away. Move to Florence or Minneapolis. Become a priest. Sometime she could see him without disappointment, but not yet. She wondered if he was disappointed in her as well. He had a right to be.

"What are you so dressed up for?" Natty asked her mother when she came in with curled hair and a new dress.

"I'm not really," she said. "It's just that I've never worn this dress, but I've had it."

"It isn't just your dress. Are we inviting the group outside for dinner?"

"We will have to make a statement when Daddy gets home," Ellen said. "That's what they're waiting for."

"It's not true what the paper said. Why should he have to resign?"

"He was drinking. That much is true." She sat down on the chair.

Watching her, Natty wondered at the courage of women whose daily lives are measured in details which would seem by their limitations to prevent large lives and paradoxically made the lives of others possible. She wouldn't be that kind of woman. Like her father she wanted a leading role. But she needed her mother, and she'd never considered that since she was small.

"I know he was drinking," Natty said, "but he wouldn't have to resign for drinking, and the rest they insinuated in the paper isn't true."

"We're impatient and act too often on what seems to be true without waiting to find out whether or not it is," she said.

Samuel Taylor came home shortly after noon, and Natty followed him to the library with Ellen as though it had been prearranged.

The members of the Syndicate had gathered with their parents in a large room of the Eighth Precinct. Choo Choo was not there. Her mother said it wasn't possible for Choo Choo to come but she would come herself. Paulette Estinet was there without her parents.

"They would be confused because of their English," she said.

"It's true they'd be confused," Rosa told Filip later, "but not because of their English, which is as good as mine."

Rosa had come in late.

"Do you know what happened?" Rosa asked the policeman who had been taking notes.

He shook his head, put up his palms. "It's very hard to say."

"Who started it?" Al Cox asked. "I can't remember. Carter called to ask me to join."

"He asked me as well," Anne Lowry said. "Remember?" She turned to Carter. "You asked me several weeks ago."

"In fact, Dick Carr came to me about the situation," Carter said.

"What situation?" Rosa asked.

"The situation with Senator McCarthy and Sam Taylor," Anne Lowry said.

"I don't understand your motive," Rosa said.

The room had folding chairs, and the children sat with their parents. There was an unconscious association by blood, as though the parents were members of the Syndicate as well. Anne Lowry was next to the Senator from Mississippi. Mrs. Lowry had bronchitis. Carter Harold with his parents on either side. Mrs. Cox was there, and John Epps, who had been drinking and slept from time to time. Sukey's father was with her, in collar this morning, although usually he dressed in regular clothes.

"I don't know," Paulette said, her accent particularly thick. "Usually I don't believe in causes, but Carter persuaded me this was important. Right?" She smiled at Carter. It was not a habit of hers to smile. "Undermining. I think that's the word that Carter used. Natty was undermining the principles of Friends School because of herself, and then this terrible thing of the criminal Joe McCarthy living at her house."

"We felt a responsibility," Sukey said.

"To do what?" Rosa asked.

"To make Natty realize what she was doing," Carter said.

"There was no ultimate plan," Al Cox said. "We simply wanted to make her aware of what she was doing."

They said that the cat had been Dick Carr's idea. He had found the cat on the street and nailed it on the door for a joke really.

"You know how kids are," Al Cox said. "It wasn't anything." They insisted that the accident at Carter Harold's farm was just that.

"I saw it," Anne Lowry insisted. "And it was entirely accidental." And by chance Al Cox had seen Sam Taylor downtown drunk and then at Lafayette Park, which was how Natty's kidnapping came about. The kidnapping was Natty's own idea and seemed at the time a graceful way to protect Sam Taylor.

"Obviously," Carter Harold said, "we haven't been wise about this, but our intentions were good."

They all agreed that the death of Dick Carr was terrible, but as accidental as Natty's fall and had nothing to do with the Syndicate. They defended themselves uniformly, but stunned like children who are awakened in the midst of a house fire and do not know what has happened or if they will die in it.

"Will Barnes has a temper," Carter said.

"And he's got a thing for Natty," Al Cox added.

"Dick Carr called the *News* about Sam Taylor," Carter interrupted out of turn. "I would have discouraged him if I had known, but Dick felt strongly about homosexuals."

"He hated them," Al Cox added.

Then Rosa asked the parents what they thought.

"I think it's a terrible business," Senator Lowry said, familiar lines, "but then the raising of children is a terrible business."

"Certainly it was innocent enough," Mrs. Harold said, "but such accidents."

"Why did you do it?" Reverend Moorehead asked Sukey quietly.

"I thought it was right," Sukey said. "I thought I should." She was beginning to cry. "I thought it was something you would want me to do."

"We all did," Carter said.

"That I would want you to do?" he asked, astonished.

"It seemed brave," Sukey said and had to leave the room because she didn't want to cry in public.

"We believed that Natty was a negative influence in the school," Anne Lowry said. "All along it seemed we were doing the right thing."

"It happened so quickly, the bad things," Paulette said. "They just rolled over us."

"I suppose a lot of it had to do with Dick Carr," Carter said.

"Dick Carr isn't here to speak for himself," Choo Choo's mother said.

"We're just trying to give the whole picture," Carter said. "We have not been sensible."

"You've been crazy," Choo Choo's mother said. "You're children!"

"They believed in what they were doing," Senator Lowry said.

"So did Joe McCarthy, I presume," she said. "I do not see much difference in what Senator McCarthy was doing in a large way and what all of you have done to Natty Taylor and her father."

"The real tragedy of this group has been the death of Dick Carr, and that was an accident," Mr. Harold said.

"That may be true, and Will Barnes is an intemperate boy."

"It's not that simple," Choo Choo's mother said. "It's the conditions that allow for accidents."

"These are children," Mrs. Harold said. "We cannot expect them to understand the possibilities."

"So were we children," Choo Choo's mother said, "and we owe them that understanding."

The chief of police broke up the conference at noon and asked Rosa to leave so they could continue questioning in the afternoon.

"You see . . ." Choo Choo's mother grabbed Rosa by the arm before she left. "We can't be too careful. Poor Choo Choo," she said of the child who painted lavender hearts on her cheeks. "She misunderstood."

The press was alerted that Samuel Taylor would make a statement at five P.M. It was raining hard by then, not cold but a penetrating damp, and newsmen stood in clusters under large umbrellas talking among themselves, primarily about their expectations that Samuel Taylor would resign from the FCC.

At five o'clock exactly, Samuel Taylor came out on the front porch of his house on Highland Place to make a public state-ment to the press, which included all three daily newspapers. The television cameras from NBC moved across the lawn filming tape which would be back in the studio in time for the six-o'clock news.

"The Taylor family," one reporter wrote, "were self-contained and dignified throughout." Every newspaper report remarked on their strength, and one newspaper reporter said, "There was a kind of nobility about Sam Taylor and his family."

"I will speak of the events which led to the situation this evening as best I can. Some of course are private and of interest and value only to me. I will not mention these.

"Last week I invited Joe McCarthy to stay with us while his wife was out of town because he had not been well. Concurrently a group of children at my daughter's school decided for reasons which perhaps will always be unclear to force my resignation as chairman of the FCC by persecuting my daughter. Which they did. My daughter was not entirely aware of this nor was I.

"We were both aware of forces working in ways against us—some of which were forces of our own making, of course. I began to drink heavily and on two occasions went to Lafayette Park, where I met and spoke with a young man. I was very drunk and arrested for it, as was certainly obvious in this morn-ing's stories in the *Post*, but I did not in my conscious memory make advances or arrangements with anyone I met in Lafayette Park.

"I am not homosexual but whether I am or not is not the business of the press or the public.

"A man is responsible for doing his work honestly and well and that is all. The rest is his business.

"I have spoken with the President, who has not asked me to resign.

"And therefore I will not. I have done my job responsibly, and that is that."

"What will happen if public opinion is strong enough against what's happened with you?" one reporter asked.

"Then I'll be fired," Sam said.

"But you won't resign."

"No, I won't."

"Can you comment on your daughter's involvement in the death of Dick Carr? Why was she there?"

"My only comment on the death of Dick Carr is to extend my deepest sympathy to his family. I can imagine nothing as terrible as losing a child."

It was dark, darker with the steady rain and the press, many of whom had waited all day, were anxious to go back to their offices and write the story, which had less drama than they had hoped it would.

Ellen asked Sam about going home before she went upstairs. "What for?"

"Just after Christmas for a few days. Christmas is more like Christmas in Wisconsin," she said.

"I suppose it is."

"Sam." She stopped at the landing. "Will you be fired?"

"I don't know," he said, "and it doesn't matter greatly one way or another."

In the kitchen Natty was making supper. Sam Taylor sat down in the darkened living room and listened to her work.

At her desk in the living room of her own home, Rosa finished the article on the Syndicate. Upstairs she heard Fil and Angela talking in Johnny's room and felt the momentary calm of mothers whose grown children are home and safe. Outside the rain was steady and made her drowsy with its repetition.

The story was longer than she had expected it to be, because the actual facts of what had happened in the last few days were lost with the death of Dick Carr, and even, she suspected, if he had not died, the real story would never be known even to those who had made it. But the circumstances were obvious and dangerous. In conclusion, Rosa made her own assessment with the understanding that her children could have been in the Syndicate or Natty Taylor or children anywhere who seek their own identity outside themselves.

"These are children of superlatives," she wrote. "They live in the *richest* land with the *most* opportunity, the *greatest* degree of individual freedom, and their lives are full of enormous spaces such as the early settlers found moving west and claimed by 'squatter's rights'—theirs as long as it didn't infringe on the land of another man, but that's a difficult claim to make, for who's to say when one life infringes on the life of another."

She thought of Filip in his blue-and-white uniform running down the field to the cheers, to the crazy adoration of crowds who at this particular moment in history had chosen him— because he ran fast, because he was good with balls. Like Filip, these children had misunderstood their inheritance. It struck her that one of the dangers of a rich land is carelessness because the wealth promises a permanence which is ultimately false.

She finished the article and put it with her things to take downtown first thing. The mail was on the radiator in the hall, and she sorted through the bills, piling them up face down and unopened on the other side. Just before she went upstairs Samuel Taylor called her. He was formal and distant, but he had called to thank her, he said. He had just determined that she was the familiar woman who had rescued him in Lafayette Park. She suspected that even in his drunkenness that morning he knew they had shared in an unspoken language their common knowledge of failures to children.

Upstairs Rosa kissed her children goodnight and lay in bed eased by the sound of their voices in the next room.

Natty and Sam Taylor talked late into the night, spinning out the last days in incidentals to be rid of their constrictions. He told her about the farmhouse in Manawa, how it had looked when he was young, what the fields were like in spring. He told her in some detail about the care of young calves as though it were a subject of interest to them both. He imitated Adelaide squawking about the germs and bad manners and the bathroom floors until Natty laughed. He told her about Mazie Gordon in Madison, who had poisoned eight husbands, and how bad he had felt as the crime reporter who covered her trial that Mazie had to die for it.

Nothing will happen to the Syndicate, he said when Natty brought it up, because nothing can be proved. And Will Barnes should be as free as you can be with the responsibility for another life.

"I have that responsibility, too," Natty said.

"That's what I learned about myself when I understood my father's death," he said. "We have to know our own failures or we're susceptible to everything, like children who haven't got natural immunities to disease."

He changed the subject to Christmas in Wisconsin and how he'd like to see Ravilla with her donkey in the living room and summer dresses in the middle of winter, forgetting to turn up the furnace because she had no sense of hot and cold.

"We'll stay at Mother's," he said. "It will drive her crazy to have me in the house."

They fixed a kitchen chair which had been broken for months, getting down on the floor together, nailing it and gluing it as though it were perfectly normal to repair furniture in the middle of the night.

"Aren't you ever going to bed?" Natty asked.

"When I get tired," Sam Taylor replied.

"And you're not tired yet?" she said. "I can hardly move."

Sam Taylor was not tired any longer. He had recovered in the sense that a man can recover lost parts, or from old illnesses, function makeshift but extremely well as long as he has the energy which Sam Taylor had now.

He made a chocolate milkshake and sliced mushrooms into hot butter spitting on the stove.

"I haven't eaten for days," he explained. Then he sat down at the kitchen table and with some care opened the morning paper, cutting out the pictures taken of him the day before.

"Why?" Natty asked.

"As warnings," he said.

Natty refused the mushrooms and coffee and milkshake, propped her head up against the back of a chair, determined to outlast him.

He set the table for himself with a linen napkin, lit a candle in the center as though it were a celebration.

"So, Nat," he said to her, leaning over the table toward her. "Tell me the whole story, beginning to end."

"There isn't a story," she said.

"Then go to bed before you fall over."

She sat across from him, distant as undiscovered relations, resisting his hold on her, which was forceful as a current pull to shore, and he sensed that she wanted to be his daughter and to be free of him altogether. Both. She treaded against her inclinations. But she sat there. He was near enough to reach out and touch her, hold her as he had when she was a child and her night cries gave unnatural rhythm to his sleep. He had a sense that this moment between them, reverberating like cello strings drawn taut to breaking, was permanent.

"I felt I owed you everything," Natty said contentiously.

Sam Taylor was thoughtful. He had expected this and asked for it. He had heard her tell a strange policeman in front of foreigners the same thing.

"You owe yourself to live the best you can," he said. "And I owe that to you because you are my daughter. We simply can't act as if we're going to die, even though we are." He ran his finger across her closed fist. "That kind of illusion is important as long as you know it for what it is. Now go to bed."

He finished his late supper, checked the back window for the Bates, who had gone to bed in spite of their curiosities, unless, of course, they were standing in the darkness of their bathroom watching him move about his bright kitchen, waiting for accidents. He folded the pictures from the paper together and put them in the back of Ellen's recipe box with the intention of moving them at a later date to more appropriate quarters, but he was struck simultaneously with a picture of Natty's daughter at seventeen finding while she searched for old-fashioned recipes her grandfather's pictures filed irreverently under pastries or casseroles.

When he looked over at his daughter, who had been resting her chin in fists stacked on top of each other, she was asleep. He picked her up in his arms and carried her up the back stairs to bed, laying her there, covering her with a quilt. And just before he left the room, he checked as he always had that the windows beside her desk and over her bed were closed and locked.

CHRISTMAS EVE
1954

The television cameras from NBC were in place in the West
Nave on the balconies overlooking the Great Choir of the Washington Cathedral. It was a medieval gothic cathedral, built, still
in the process of being built, with hand-carved gargoyles around
the flying buttresses, copied from the faces of living men to fight
off the unlikely demons of a new century which did not require
cathedrals, set at the highest point of the city visible from the
Potomac.

"Ready?" the chief crewman from NBC said to the verger in
charge. The verger nodded, and somewhere up in the tower the
bells began, the Washington Cathedral boys' choir lined up at
the North Transept, followed by the men's choir and the dean,
the canons of the cathedral, the bishop of Washington, and on
the organ, the ancient birth was announced to the company of
trumpets.

On the first stage of the Great Choir, Natty Taylor and the
other musicians sat just to the left of the procession. She did not

watch as the procession with Filip DeAngelis among the acolytes filed by.

At Twin Oaks Farm, Nell Barnes turned on the television as the choir finished the opening hymn and sat down between her children to watch.

The television was on in Senator Joseph McCarthy's hospital room at Doctor's as well for the young nurse who watched with the volume turned low not to wake the sleeping senator.

Samuel Taylor came in late, just after Natty had begun to play, and to him, standing at the back of the cathedral, she was a familiar child set against the grand proportions of stone, whose face distilled in shadows was Ellen's face and the face of his father, of Ravilla Taylor and his own. The music she played was simple, even beautiful, not perfect certainly, diminished by the space it had to fill. But it was a beginning which seemed to Samuel Taylor, as he slid into the chair next to Ellen, appropriate.

And outside the cathedral the winter air was silent without birds, dark above the federal city. On the top of the gothic tower, visible from everywhere, predictable as stars, a single red light defied the blackness in a warning to airplanes.